The Crystal Palace Chronicles

GRAHAM WHITLOCK

Star of Nimrod

First edition.
ISBN-978-1-7399804-0-5

Cover design by Florian Mefisheye Garbay
Illustration © 2021, Florian Garbay
www.grahamwhitlock.com

For my family.

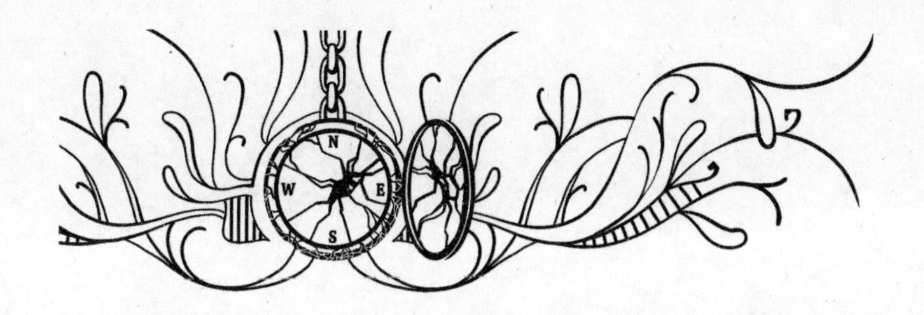

CONTENTS

'It is my earnest wish and hope
That this wonderful structure
And the treasures of art and knowledge
Which it contains
May long continue to delight and amuse
The minds of all classes of my people.'

Queen Victoria, June 10, 1854 at the opening of the new Crystal Palace on Norwood Heights

'As though 'twere by a Wizard's rod
A blazing arch of lucid glass
Leaps like a fountain from the grass
To meet the sun.'

W M Thackeray, author

THE END. 30 NOVEMBER 1936

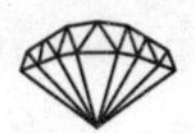

Flames erupt from the Crystal Palace like a thousand Bonfire Nights rolled into one, drawing London in to see the giant pleasure dome's final breath-taking spectacle.

Crowds block roads winding up to the city's highest point where the Crystal Palace has looked out for eight decades. A glittering glass people's palace displaying dinosaurs, recreating Ancient Egypt, Rome, Assyria, exhibiting wonders of science and engineering, hosting concerts, festivals, fireworks, and the first FA Cup finals. The Crystal Palace witnessed the world's earliest flying machines; now their aeroplane offspring circle overhead like vultures, carrying newspaper photographers capturing the final hours of the Eighth Wonder of the World.

Fireballs fall for miles around. London hasn't seen such a blaze since The Great Fire in 1666 and won't see fire on this scale for another four years until the outbreak of World War Two and the Blitz. Local kids get woken from their beds by their parents and gawk.

Except one.

This child stands in silence, on the surface appearing no older than the other kids but without parents to pass a hastily prepared sandwich. This child is alone, hands in pockets, gripping a hidden box of used matches.

The inferno's heat reignites the pain of scars carved across the Alone Child's face, scars which begin to burn like rivers of fire.

A nearby bunch of kids squeal with excitement. A freckle-faced girl cries, "Will they save it?" pointing at a fireman fighting the flames, his hose no more likely to quench the blaze than a water pistol squirting a crematorium furnace.

"They *won't* save it," snorts a swaggering lad. "*My* dad says the owners started the fire cos it costs too much to keep the place going."

The Alone Child squeezes the box of matches and shoots the lad a look of contempt with eyes that cry, YOU KNOW NOTHING.

The swaggering lad would ordinarily punch any face daring to look at him like this. But his swagger fails him, and he shivers under the Alone Child's gaze despite the heat from the flames.

"Come on," the lad mutters quickly to the other kids, "we can get a better view over there." He pushes through the crowd, avoiding those eyes.

The Alone Child is used to this.

The Alone Child's eyes hold secrets, the kind you don't wish to know if you want to sleep at night, secrets melting with iron and glass. A tiny smile flickers; it's not pleasure, such a thing hasn't lit the Alone Child's lips for five decades. It's satisfaction at a task finally complete and anticipation of rest that might follow.

Let me sleep, spirits of the ancient woods. Let me sleep.

Spectators are silenced by a great groan as the palace's enormous iron ribs buckle like a wounded giant in its death throes. Waterfalls of molten glass from a thousand panes gush down terrace steps like lava.

"Make way!" shouts a policeman holding back the heaving throng so a gentleman can pass.

An onlooker whispers, "That's Winston Churchill."

Like everyone else, Churchill's gaze is fixed upwards, his plans for the evening set aside to watch history in the making, or rather ending, as a masterpiece of Victorian ingenuity disappears forever. The Alone Child watches a tear fall down the future prime minister's face.

"This is the end of an age," declares Churchill.

I hope so, thinks the Alone Child.

I hope so.

PRESENT DAY
CHAPTER 1

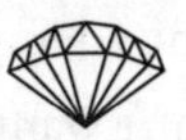

"Get down!" whispers Joe as his little sister pokes her head through the bush.

"Don't be such a big wuss, they're not following. Just as well." Lauren juts her chin and wields her skateboard, Unicorn of Death.

Joe blows his floppy fringe out of his eyes, one electric blue the other emerald green. He risks a peek from their hiding place; a poodle being walked by a man with matching hair, a gang of mums pushing buggies, a fox staring at him with disdain, the usual afternoon array of park life.

"Wait," he orders.

Lauren ignores him as usual, bouncing out of the bush with half of it stuck in her scraggle of untamed hair. Joe grabs Skull Rider, his own prized Supreme Skull Pile skateboard and steps onto the sun-baked path. Coast clear, his heart still pounds against the wall of his chest.

Lauren says, "Let's go back to the skate park."

"Go back?! Thanks to you, I won't be going back for the whole summer holiday unless I want my board shoved up my butt."

Lauren licks her braces. "They spat and laughed at *me*."

"*You* laughed at *them* first when they fell! That's why they spat at you."

"It was funny. Sorry."

"No, you're not."

"No, I'm not."

"You *will* be when I take you back to Dad and tell him what you called them."

Her face crumples. Who wants to be stuck in the restaurant on the hottest day of the hottest summer ever?

"Least I stick up for myself, you're just a big ...." Her sassy response falters. Lauren's eyes widen.

Joe spins. Two big lads thunder towards them on skateboards, their scowls suggesting they don't want advice on the finer points of a dragon flip.

"Go!" Joe hurls his skateboard along the path, leaping on board.

Lauren does likewise, both pumping hard to gain speed. Joe considers overtaking Lauren; his sister is a gold medal winning nightmare, but he can't abandon her.

Instead he cries, "Faster!"

They bomb along the path spanning the lower side of Crystal Palace Park, racing past the leaning tree, navigating little kids heading to the playground, past the tired concrete of the former National Sports Centre in the middle of the park.

Their pursuers show no sign of letting up. Joe and Lauren curve through winding tree-lined paths around the boating lake. Wheels clatter across the wooden bridge. Here in the far corner of the park lies Dinosaur Island, home to giant grey models built only thirty years after the very first dinosaur fossils were discovered. Joe's days of begging to see these hulking beasts had long gone, although now he wishes he could Dolphin-flip over to the island and into the hollow Iguanodon where its creator Benjamin Waterhouse Hawkins hosted a New Year dinner upon their completion in 1854.

Lauren loses speed. Crystal Palace Park is a giant back garden for Joe, but their pursuers have them in their sights. There's no chance of ducking into any of its nooks, crannies and corners. Nor will they make it up to the Triangle to find refuge in Paradise. The bullies might not beat up an eleven-year-old, at least until she opens her big trap and then frankly, Joe wouldn't blame them. The likely outcome is Joe beaten up on her behalf and never being able to return to the skate park. He curses his sister, his summer, his life.

"They're catching up," Lauren pants.

Think quick.

"This way." Joe's skateboard switches up the left-hand fork towards Capel Manor Farm. He hopes they'll lose the lads among crowds of kids 'wowing' at the massiveness of a real pig or 'ewing' at the tarantula in the insect house or 'awing' at the meercats.

Capel Manor Farm is built on two levels of enclosures and classrooms where volunteers and college students learn animal care. Joe leads Lauren to the pony enclosure. They crouch behind a fern filled planter. He spies the lads circling in the centre of the courtyard deciding which way to go. Finally, they head for the insect house, one taking the entrance, the other moving to the exit in a pincer movement to trap their pray.

"Yes!" Joe fists the air. His first bit of good luck in forever. It'll give them time to double back to the gate, out of the farm and up to the Triangle.

Lauren, meanwhile, is nuzzling the nose of a shaggy Shetland. Joe drags her up. She yanks herself free.

"Lauren, stop being an idiot and come on."

"You're being an idiot, idiot."

Just as they reach the middle of the courtyard, one of the lads steps out of the insect house.

His eyes lock on Joe.

They're equal distance from the gate, but an exiting family blocks Joe's escape.

The second lad joins his mate, grinning.

It's a Mexican stand-off across the courtyard. Each side waits for the other to make the first move.

Joe's eyes dart to the top level of the farm.

Sweeping an animal pen is a girl in a green sweatshirt worn by farm volunteers.

A possibility pings into his head.

Joe grabs Lauren's hand and slowly walks away from the gate towards the ramp leading to the upper level of the farm.

The lads mirror each other, wielding their skateboards as weapons.

"Joe, why we going up there? We'll be trapped."

"Trust me. Running on the count of three. One, T—"

"Three!" Lauren bolts up the ramp, her despairing brother hot on her heels, the lads in pursuit.

At the top of the ramp, Joe and Lauren speed past chickens and bunnies. They reach a single-storey barn with a sign reading 'Obama the Llama.' He's nowhere to be seen but a girl a little older than Joe sweeps the enclosure and belts out Ariana Grande's "God is a Woman."

"Aaliyah!" the siblings cry in unison.

The girl stops sweeping, her surprise morphing into curious concern.

"You've gotta help us!"

The lads find the enclosure empty but the gate open. Obama the Llama's sign says, 'Strictly no entry, Capel Manor personnel only.' But where else could their quarry have gone? From the hut comes the unmistakeable giggle of a big mouthed little girl who needs to be taught a lesson ....

The lads slowly enter the hut, eyes adjusting to the darkness, to find themselves face-to-face with a six-foot Llama.

With a supercilious snort Obama the Llama shows his displeasure at their intrusion by spitting a shower of thick phlegm. As an encore, he pulls back his ears and lets out a blood-curdling 'MWAA!" The lads fall over each other trying to escape.

Joe, Lauren, Aaliyah and Obama the Llama emerge to watch them run down the ramp, cross the courtyard and flee the farm, soaked in spit.

Aaliyah Duke pats Obama the Llama and gives him a biscuit. He grunts his gratitude.

"That was three stomachs worth of spit."

"That was AWESOME!" cries Lauren. "Cuz, you're the best!"

"Well, little cuz, who am I to fly in the face of popular opinion?"

The Dukes are family to Joe and Lauren in all but blood, with Aaliyah's parents 'Uncle' Tyrell and 'Aunty' Salma running Paradise with Dad. Lauren idolises their 'cuz.' This only increases Joe's desire to kick away the pedestal everyone puts Aaliyah on.

"Joe, what stupidness did you get into now?" Aaliyah's only eleven months older but acts like this gives her the right to boss Joe about.

"It wasn't my fault!" Joe hears the whine in his voice and hates himself. "It was *her*."

"'*It was her,*'" mimics Lauren.

"You're so immature." Joe shoves his sister.

"Says the boy shoving an eleven-year-old," counters Aaliyah, stepping between the siblings.

"Fine, *you* look after her."

"Um, no, news flash, some of us are doing something constructive with our summer holiday."

"Oh, right, sweeping up Llama crap is really truly constructive."

Obama the Llama joins Aaliyah in a scornful snort.

"*Constructive* is learning how to care for animals so I can become a vet helping endangered species around the world. *Unconstructive* is you, acting out at everyone like a moody teenage cliché just because your best friend moves away."

Aaliyah's superiority complex is infuriating enough, but dismissing Zahid moving away forever with a 'just because' ignites Joe's rage.

"You don't know nothing!"

"I know I don't have time for this stupidness."

"Please can I stay with you?" pipes up Lauren. "I don't mind Llama poo."

"Sorry, little cuz, when you turn fourteen, you can volunteer here, unquestionably."

Lauren's downcast face brightens, but not even a comedy sneeze from Obama the Llama can calm Joe. Grabbing his skateboard, he storms out of the farm and into the park, not bothering to check if his sister is following. But with his luck, she will be.

Joe's too busy conjuring up put-downs he wishes he'd used on Aaliyah. He doesn't notice eyes watching him from a dark brambly dell the sun will never reach.

The eyes of the Alone Child.

Chapter 2

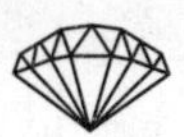

Lauren's skateboard wheels trundle behind Joe as he steams up the path to the top of Crystal Palace Park. She'd best keep a safe distance. Soon they'd reach the Triangle and she'll be Dad's problem, not Joe's.

They skate by the train station with its majestic brick arches and staircases, which used to bring millions of visitors to the old palace.

The palace once dominated the top of the grounds, replaced over time with trees and brambles. The one new structure is the transmitter antenna thrusting into the sky like South London's Eiffel Tower broadcasting television across the capital. The only evidence the palace ever existed are the long, wide Upper and Italian terraces. They run the width of the park, each level lined with crumbling stone arches and a scattering of urns, broken statues, and stone sphinxes like fading phantoms from the past.

In happier times, on family picnics, Joe concocted elaborate games here with Lauren, Aaliyah and her twin brothers imagining they'd discovered an ancient lost city. Fading phantoms from Joe's past.

Joe spies a dozen people crossing the Italian terrace towards imposing steps. Once upon a time, these steps rose to the palace's central Grand Transept; now they lead nowhere. The group assemble around a lady lolloping along carrying a walking stick and an open umbrella decorated with Elvis Presley's.

"Nan!" cries Lauren.

Joe's face also lights up, an effect Ivy Cook has on anyone she meets, unless it's an officious council officer or a dodgy developer planning anything that might damage her neighbourhood's heritage.

The siblings cross the terrace to the Grand Transept steps which serve as Ivy's stage. The tour group gather around this ball of energy, her sparkling eyes magnified by inch-thick glasses. Joe can recite Nan's talks off by heart. Although his fascination with their area's history is history, he still enjoys watching her do what she loves best, performing to a captive audience.

"Right you lot. Look around!" She waves her cane towards the bottom of the park where rolling suburbs rise into a horizon of Surrey and Kent hills. "Cast your minds back one hundred and seventy years. Here on the Norwood Ridge, high above the smog of the old city of London, you'd be standing in the ancient Great North Wood. Where dangerous Faeries dance cursing those who crossed 'em. Where rogues and robbers hid.

"Where the celebrated Queen of the Gypsies told fortunes to folk like the wife of Samuel Pepys, so his diary tells us.

"Around us stood mighty magical Ancient Oaks untouched for an age. Wilderness dotted with farms and the tiny villages of Penge and Sydenham. Until ..."

Her voice lowers. The group lean in. Joe gives her a small wave while Lauren shuffles herself to the front signifying proudly, 'That's *my* Nan.' Ivy gives both grandchildren a big wink.

"Until ... the 1851 Great Exhibition in Hyde Park. Organised by Prince Albert, Queen Victoria's other half. A big blockbuster exhibition of culture and industry from around the world. It ran for six months. But afterwards, nobody could agree what to do with the enormous glass and iron Crystal Palace built to house the exhibition. MPs rowed in Parliament shouting 'pull it down,' until the genius who designed it, a fella named Joseph Paxton, who used to be a gardener, which explains why it looked like a colossal greenhouse . . . Paxton comes up with the plan to move it. Here. To Sydenham Place, piece by piece and rebuild it.

"The ancient woods got cleared away and in their place rose a towering palace even bigger than the original. The Grand Transept in the middle where these steps led used to be tall enough to fit Nelson's Column inside, and the palace had enough space to fit twenty-six football pitches. So, what, I hear you cry, did they fill that with?"

Although she pauses, Nan never waits for an answer.

"I'll tell you! It wasn't none of the artefacts displayed in the Great Exhibition, all that stuff looted from around the world ended up in the new museums funded by profits from the Exhibition.

"No, this *new* Crystal Palace was a 'People's Palace.' Filled with courts, each one recreating great civilisations of the past. The palace and the grounds became the world's first theme park, offering education, entertainment, even a rollercoaster. Imagine Disneyland but instead of *Pirates of the Caribbean* and Mickey's castle, they built from scratch the inside of a Roman villa from Pompeii, built a replica of an ancient Egyptian tomb complete with statues of Rameses made out of plaster cast, and the Nineveh Court bringing back to life palaces of the kings of Assyria lost to the desert. Remember, this was before TV so you and me would have no idea what the past looked like.

"1854, Queen Victoria declares the new palace open! Over two million visitors every year flock to promenade around the pleasure gardens which boast fountains with jets higher than Versailles and a great maze where you can still get lost today.

"Overnight this area changed. Navvies who constructed the palace settled in Norwood New Town which had a wall built around it to keep these ne'er-do-wells away from 'polite society.' Grand villas are built by industrialists yearning for power; pioneers of science came searching for hidden truths; bored socialites came seeking fresh air, amusement and mischief. The new Crystal Palace changes life here forever.

"And now as a special tour bonus, take a good look at my gorgeous grandkids here, and you'll see before you descendants of one of them that built the palace!"

Eyes stare at Joe as if he belongs in the Crystal Palace Museum. He flushes red, whereas Lauren laps up the attention as if she built the old palace herself.

Nan cackles at Joe's embarrassment.

"Come on, be proud of your past, tell 'em about it!"

Lauren shoots her hand in the air.

"I'll tell! Our granddad never talked to Nan about his past ..."

Joe rolls his eyes. *Probably couldn't get a word in ...*

"When my brother—him—did family trees at school, Nan helped research, but there was no trace of granddad's family. It was a *mystery!* But she *did* find a photo showing a big ceremony laying the palace's first pillar and *in that photo* was a man we think is *my great-great-grandad!"*

Joe silently seethes. *He'd* been the one examining that fading black-and-white photo of men in Sunday suits carrying spades. *He'd* spotted a young face among them, a face looking a dead ringer for dad (and these days like Joe too).

"That's my girl!" Nan twirls her walking stick at a beaming Lauren. "You lot wanna see that photo from 1852? I've got it on my phone. Obviously not *taken* on my phone! Hand it round, careful, don't drop it, then go up these steps, we'll move to the spot the fire started in 1936 bringing the palace to its burning end."

Ivy points her stick up the steps, opening up her arm to give Lauren a big hug.

"Hello Little Bum Face and Big Bum Face, what brings you pair to one of my tours? Especially you, Joe. I know you *lurve* local history."

Joe groans at her sarcastic wink; at the start of the holidays Nan suggested he help out at the Crystal Palace Museum. He mistakenly described history as 'boring,' a mistake because Nan never ever forgets, making her an ideal local historian, but also meaning Joe faces a lifetime of sly digs.

"Come on, don't be a silly sausage." She gives Joe's cheek a tweak, squeezing out a small smile.

"Can I stay with you, Nan?" Lauren shoots her brother a look. "I LOVE hearing all about old history stuff."

Joe bites his lip, not wanting to lose the opportunity to lose Lauren.

"A pleasure to have you."

"Can I play on your phone too?"

"You'll never beat my Candy Crush score."

"Watch me!"

"Atta girl, gotta love your fighting spirit!"

Lauren skips off to retrieve the phone from the tour guests. Nan's smile slips into unusual seriousness.

"How'd your dad get on at the hospital? He's not returning my calls."

"Hospital?"

"His appointment yesterday."

"Oh, yeah, umm, okay I think."

"You mean you never asked."

"Nooo ..." Joe grinds the gravel under his trainer. "I mean ... no."

Nan sucks in her cheeks and shakes her head.

"Like father, like son, like granddad, closed up like clams the lot of you. It's not just dicky tickers running in the family." She rolls her frowning eyes skyward as if seeing the old palace's shadow. "Right. My audience awaits. You joining us?"

Joe hesitates. "Nah, got stuff to do."

"On your own?"

"So what?"

"So how about calling up some of your old mates?"

Joe stares at the ground so his floppy fringe hides his glower.

Nan takes a deep breath. "Listen, I know you're still gutted you're not visiting Australia—"

"No, I'm not. It was never gonna happen. Mum doesn't wanna see us."

"Your mum's a selfish cow and if she was here I'd wring her bloomin' neck like I should'a done years ago. But listen to an old girl. Don't push everyone away. Life's too short to live it alone, kiddo."

Joe taps his fingers on Skull Rider waiting for the lecture to end.

Nan sighs and waves her stick at Lauren. "Come on, Little Bum Face." She opens her Elvis umbrella over Lauren to shade them both from the sun. Lauren wraps her arm around her waist. Joe watches them climb the steps, relieved to be free of lectures and rid of his sister.

Yet feeling no happier to be alone.

"Hey, Sphinxy!" Joe greets the stone sphinx where he comes to practice parkour, seeing free jumping as skateboarding without wheels.

The sphinxes sit silently guarding steps once leading to the North Transept of the old palace. Now the steps end at a long high wire fence, on the other side the transmitter tower and further along a tangle of briars. Joe feels kinship with the sphinxes and their four siblings at the south steps, they'd been restored to their original terracotta red after a campaign involving (as ever) his Nan.

"Here's a riddle for you, Sphinxy."

Joe clambers onto its lion's back. The sphinx's eyes gaze out across the park in stony silence.

"What can you hold in your right hand, but not in your left? Come on, you're the mythical beast of riddles. Fine, I'll tell you. Your left hand. *Your left hand!* Geddit?"

Joe checks WhatsApp. Still nothing from Zahid. Fair enough. Probably hanging out with new friends. Probably perfected his dragon flip and showing it off right now. Which is fine. Just fine.

Joe pats the sphinx's human head for luck, takes a breath and leaps through the air, landing neatly feet together on the stone slab behind the statue.

"And for my next trick ..."

Joe climbs back onto the sphinx's head for a double jump, the kind of move Zahid used to capture on his phone so they could watch back and critique their technique.

Oh great …

On the steps, next to the sphinx, stand his friends from the skate park, their hair still styled with Llama spit, grinning triumphantly. Joe groans. Perched on top of the sphinx he could kick them off should they climb up to grab his legs, or Joe could execute a leap down and make a run for it on Skull Rider ….

Skull Rider!

He'd left it leaning at the base of the sphinx. Now the lads have it.

"Ah, come on, don't mess with another man's ride ..." But the pair march his prized possession along the wire fence. "Listen, you want money, I'll give you money, I've got almost a tenner."

Joe watches helplessly from his perch. With a hefty fling, they send his skateboard sailing over the fence, disappearing into the transmitter tower compound.

The lads laugh. "We ever see you at the skatepark again, next time it's you we throw over, in a body bag."

"And your sister."

Don't worry. I'm putting her in a body bag first.

Skull Rider must've landed among the power substations at the base of the transmitter tower. Joe doesn't fancy taking his chances with the barbed wire at the top of the perimeter fence. There has to be another way in.

Yes!

There's a tear in the fence near the top of a concrete staircase rising alongside the base. If Joe can get to it, he can get in. Problem is, clawing right up against the fence is a wall of brambles. Joe's only choice is to work his way deep into the undergrowth and find a path to the hole.

Joe pushes into bushes. Thorns tear at skin like he's a fairy-tale prince battling through enchanted briars. The ground is littered with broken bottles and rubbish blown in from the park, debris slowly submerging into the earth to join the foundations of the old palace that lie beneath. Over the years, Joe had explored most of the park playing hide-and-seek. But he's never ventured here.

Using the transmitter antenna towering above to judge his location Joe finally guesses he's level with his target. But there's no clear route to the fence, at least not standing upright. Joe drops to his knees and crawls, quickly gathering a fine collection of stinging nettle stings.

Silence surrounds.

No sound of traffic.

No leaves rustling.

No birdsong.

Just a growing sense Joe's not alone …

Yes!

The hole in the fence lays ahead.

Joe yelps. Something sharp digs deep inside his palm. Red blood oozes out. A drop falls onto the offending object. Expecting a broken bottle buried in the soil, Joe finds instead a round metal object.

A compass.

Joe digs it out, carefully brushing aside dirt with his T-shirt to avoid further cuts from the shattered glass face. It isn't like the plastic compasses Joe uses in Scouts. This is old, made of metal, possibly silver. Joe holds it up close. His blood has sunk between the shattered fragments, colouring it like a stained-glass window, but he can still make out elaborate engravings showing N for North, E for East, S for South and W for West. In between these four points, a tiny ornate arrow flutters from side to side as the compass tilts. On the back are engraved three letters—HSM. Maybe someone dropped it orienteering through the undergrowth?

But now it's mine.

Joe jumps at the sudden sound of crows cackling around the trees.

Get a grip.

He pops the compass into his shorts pocket, gives his bleeding palm a suck and crawls forward to rescue his beloved.

Squeezing through the fence, running down the concrete stairs, ducking CCTV cameras, Joe's joy at finding Skull Rider vanishes. The front wheel axle has snapped, probably bouncing off concrete. Not the kind of easy fix Joe can attempt, and Dad is about as much use when it comes to DIY as he is at saying 'no' to Lauren. This means taking it to Brixton's Baddest Skate Shop but a new Bones Deep Dye VI Street Tech wheel would set Joe back forty pounds he doesn't possess, having blown his savings on Dad's upcoming fortieth birthday present, tickets to see The Specials at Brixton Academy. Even if he saves every penny of his pocket money he'll be waiting the whole summer before riding again.

Joe spots blood smears under his skateboard from the oozing cut on his palm, reminding him of his buried treasure. Joe feels for the shattered compass, lips forming a thin smile as an idea comes together, one that might just get him back on his wheels.

The Alone Child smiles too.

It begins again.

Chapter 3

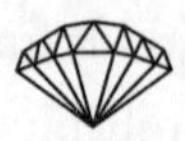

Forced on foot Joe carries his busted skateboard along Crystal Palace Parade. His mission; get money to get it fixed.

He trudges past the bus station to the edge of the Triangle shaped by three streets—Church Road, Westow Street, and Westow Hill. Grand Victorian boozers stand on three corners and narrow pavements bustle with independent cafes and restaurants catering every cuisine. Forever-changing assortments of home furnishing stores sit alongside old vintage shops packed with second-hand treasures. Boarded-up shop fronts prove Dad's mantra, trading on the Triangle is tough.

The Triangle reminds Joe of an old Wild West town, a boomtown whose jumble of faded Victorian facades with swinging shop signs were thrown up to meet the gold rush of visitors to the palace, before falling into a ghost town of tumbleweeds when it burned down, only now slowly emerging into an area 'on the up' as Dad says to convince himself their restaurant has a future.

Joe never bores of gazing down the side streets off Westow Hill which plummet steeply to reveal views across the whole London skyline. He lingers at the top of Gipsy Hill. The Shard, St Pauls, Big Ben glitter in the sun. Nan reckons generations of his family must've stood here. But Joe swears he'll be the one to escape down there where the real excitement is.

Joe wanders along Westow Street and cuts down a dead-end lane on a sharp slope. Tucked behind Sainsburys delivery car park is Haynes Lane Indoor Market, a horseshoe courtyard of ramshackle buildings.

Joe takes the shattered compass from his pocket. It's busted but his discovery doesn't look any worse than the other weird vintage odds and ends sold by indoor market traders in their little booths. A narrow alley leads to the upper floor of the market, crumbling brick work strung with fairy lights, lined with bright plastic flowers and crates of second-hand books. It always struck Joe how stall holders rely on the honesty of bargain hunters because anyone can walk into the alley and help themselves. Not that this stuff's worth nicking. Plus, there's something about the alley. A feeling of being watched ...

Joe jumps.

A robin red-breast dances around crates of china teapots, examining Joe with deep curiosity. Joe lets out a nervous laugh of relief.

"What you looking at?"

The robin chirps a reply which sounds uncannily like; *You, Joe Cook.*

The upper floor of Haynes Lane Indoor Market is a barn divided into booths creating an Aladdin's cave of collectables; rows of military uniforms and feathered ladies' hats; cabinets of toys from childhoods past ranging from Peppa Pig to original *Star Wars* figures; furniture to give your place a '70s makeover. *Why do grown-ups want to live in the past?* Growing up Joe had mooched here through old boxes of comics for editions of *Fantastic Four* while Dad spent what spare time he had from the restaurant searching out old vinyl Two-Tone special editions by bands like The Selecter.

In the corner a vinyl record hisses from the trumpet of an old gramophone and a singer croons above a crackling orchestra.

"For I'm Dancing with tears in my eyes

Coz the girl in my arms isn't you ..."

A tiny man whistles and sways in his booth to the music. Beneath his oversized woolly hat flows thick, greying, curly hair and a beard that makes him look like he plans a future career as Father Christmas. Robin Wood is almost as familiar a sight around the triangle as the transmitter antenna, passing the time of day with traders dragging his trolley bag of uncovered curiosities between the market and his home, a caravan on

Crystal Palace Caravan and Campsite on the edge of the park.

As he grooves, Robin Wood peers over his sellotaped glasses, delicately squeezing toothpaste onto a silver brooch before rubbing it off with a lint cloth, leaving the metal gleaming in the gloom.

"Anything I can help you with, young sir?" he asks without taking his eyes off the brooch.

"Um, yeah, maybe." Joe steps forward holding out his hand to show the shattered compass. He waits for Robin Wood to look up. Seconds pass. "It's right here. Bit broken but looks pretty old so might be worth something?"

"How much?" asks Robin Wood, still looking down as he twirls his nose hair in time to the music.

Joe scrunches his face. "Umm, well, dunno. Say forty quid?"

Robin Wood chuckles. He holds the cleaned brooch aloft. Silver catches a shaft of sunlight shining from a hole in the roof, bouncing into Joe's eyes. Joe squints. When his vision adjusts, Robin Wood is stood in his face, eyes bright.

"How much is she worth to *you*?"

Joe steps back to regain some personal space.

"Er, thirty?" offers Joe before realising he's haggling in the wrong direction.

Robin Wood draws in a long breath, exhaling with a head wobble. "Her value is a good deal greater."

Joe mirrors his smile, mind conjuring up a brand-new Death OG Skateboard. This image falters when he realises Robin Wood hasn't even looked at the shattered compass yet to gauge its value. "How great? I mean how much?"

"That, young sir, is for you to discover."

Robin Wood lifts a wooden amulet worn around his neck, ornately carved into the shape of an oak tree. He kisses it gently and says to it softly, "We stand on ancient boundaries between places, between possibilities, between the world of mortals and the world of magic. All we need to unlock them is the key."

"Oo-kay then." Joe nods, deciding Robin Wood must've been smoking his toothpaste. He's about to put it back in his pocket when Robin Wood shoots out his paw and wraps it tightly around his hand.

"Keep her mystical powers close."

Joe yanks his arm away. Robin Wood doesn't resist.

"Sure," Joe says, backing away towards the exit. "Will do. Or I might just try eBay."

Squeezed in between the barbers and the post office, Paradise Bar and Restaurant is long and lively, a line of wooden tables-for-two on one side and on the other extended tables for celebrations wanting a touch of Trinidad and Tobago carnival.

A bright underwater mural covers one wall, painted eight years ago when the restaurant opened. It's the only contribution made by Joe's mum before she moved to Australia to run a donkey sanctuary, caring more for four-legged animals than her two-legged children according to Dad.

The deformed reef shark was Joe's handiwork. Dad point blank refuses Joe's pleas to paint over it, insisting it's his favourite feature (until Lauren cried and Dad changed to joint-favourite alongside the star fish she'd literally painted with her three-year-old hands).

Laughter erupts from a long table with a helium balloon shaped in a number eighteen; lots of customers equals a happy Dad who might just pay to repair Joe's skateboard wheel.

Aunty Salma's flowing robes and big homemade jewellery gracefully swoop around tables, whipping up the atmosphere with breezy style as she calls out the names of dishes. She knows exactly who ordered what but takes pleasure seeing customers eagerly waving hands in anticipation of fried dough balls with salt fish or mac-and-cheese.

At the end of the restaurant, through the open hatch, Uncle Tyrell dances around the kitchen like an octopus singing Calypso classics by

The Mighty Sparrow and somehow never getting a stain on his crisp white shirt and apron.

On backing vocals, behind the bamboo bar, sings Simon Cook, a.k.a Dad in his trademark lairy shirt, his rusty coloured hair frosted blonde at the tips. In charge of the bar and books thanks to his BTEC in business catering, Joe's dad leisurely shakes a cocktail mixer in time to the beat before pouring the contents into a line of glasses on the bar and throwing a cocktail umbrella and straw into each with practiced precision.

Uncle Tyrell and Dad have been thick as thieves since secondary school when they began dreaming of opening a restaurant serving Tyrell's mum's classic Trinidadian recipes. She'd lived long enough to see the two scallywags open Paradise and still looks down on them from a large photo behind the bar.

On stools at the bar, swinging their legs sits Salma and Tyrell's twins, Brendon and Kendon, blowing bubbles in their milkshakes and scanning the place for mischief. Joe counts himself lucky he hasn't been stuck babysitting that pair of mini tornadoes, although their sister Aaliyah has a freakish ability to control them. Not that she ever gets lumbered babysitting these days. Too busy 'saving the world.'

"Hola!" Dad shouts over the noise. "Here, grab some of these milkshakes, will you?"

Joe grins back, relieved he's not in trouble for dumping Lauren. The bustling business has put Dad in a good mood so, keen to convert this into hard cash for his skateboard wheel, Joe willingly takes two of Paradise's legendary milkshakes to the long table.

"Hey, Joe!" calls a lad sat at the end.

It takes a moment before Joe recognizes his old Rockmount primary school mate.

"Lenny!" They'd not bumped into each other for years. Now Lenny looks like someone stuck a pump in his ear to inflate his shoulders and chest until he resembles one of the superhero costumes with fake padded muscles they'd dressed up in years ago. "How you doing?"

"Better when you pass my milkshake."

"What happened to your voice?!"

Lenny's squeaky pitch has been swapped with a deep bass.

"What can I say? I'm a man!" he declares with a comedy growl. "You'll get there one day, my boy."

"Yeah, yeah. When I do, you know I'm marrying your sister."

Joe grins down the table to the smiling birthday girl, Crystal, a smile he always admires when she works behind the counter at La Bruschetta cafe on Fridays between 4:15 p.m. and closing ....

"Ha! I knew you losers really came round to see her not me."

"We didn't come round for you *or* your sister. We came round for your Nintendo Switch."

"Ha, still funny."

"Still always."

"How's Zahid? You two still tight?"

Joe shrugs. "Yeah, but his parents moved away to live near his grandparents."

"In Bangladesh?"

"Birmingham. Where his dad's parents live." But might as well be Bangladesh.

Lenny gives his milkshake a sympathetic slurp.

Nan's words return, urging Joe to stop moping and hook up with his old mates. He takes a moment to pitch his voice—doesn't want to sound desperate.

"Would be good for you and me to catch up, you know, over the holidays or something . . . ." Joe's eyes glance around in case they make him look like a beggar. Finally Lenny replies;

"Yeah, definitely."

"Yeah?" Joe's mind flashes an itinerary of gaming and box sets and being near Crystal.

"But . . ."

Course. Had to be a big, hairy 'but'…

"… from Monday I'm signed up for sports programme for four weeks."

"Sure, no worries." Joe does his best to nod casually. Okay, one last shot. "Maybe we can hang out at the weekend?"

"Yeah, maybe."

Right. 'Maybe' equals 'Don't call us, we'll call you.' Fair enough, probably seeing his new mates from secondary school, why would he want to waste time dragging up the past with Joe?

"Why don't you sign up too? It's at the Sports Centre in Crystal Palace Park and you get to do all sorts, football, basketball, tennis."

Joe nods even though team sports have never been his thing, preferring the solo challenge of the skateboard.

"Plus, my mum says it's not too expensive."

"Yeah?" says Joe coming round to the idea. "Yeah, sounds good!"

As Joe glances up the table, he catches the attention of the birthday girl. Crystal gives him a bright smile and raises her now-legal-to-drink cocktail. Joe feels his face flush but manages to mouth 'Happy Birthday,' giving Lenny a cheeky wink. Lenny's eyes roll.

"You've got good taste," says a honey-coated voice in Joe's ear and he grins up at Aunty Salma. Suddenly the twins, Brendon and Kendon, appear at her elbow.

"Joey is in lur-uve," says Brendon.

"LU-V-ER!" chimes in Kendon, each of them smooching the air like snogging camels.

Joe surreptitiously flicks a middle finger at both.

"Boys …" Salma peers down with a warning eyebrow raised.

Joe reels in his fingers. The twins swagger off still smooching the air.

She ruffles Joe's hair and cries, "I've still got one more portion of coconut sugar cake, no-one want it?" pretending not to notice Lenny's wide-eyed cousin vibrating on her seat waving for the luscious dessert.

"Me! Me!"

"Ah, me me what ...?"

"Me PLEASE!" says the kid who is fit to burst but remembers Aunty Salma's house rule—manners at all times at the table.

Joe's eyes are drawn to a figure across the road.

The Alone Child stands there.

Hood drawn up despite the heat.

Staring through the window of Paradise.

Goosebumps climb Joe's neck.

"Joe, where's your sister?" asks Dad as he delivers a cocktail to the party, looking around as if expecting Lauren to emerge from under one of the tables.

Joe looks at Dad and gulps.

When he glances back outside, the Alone Child has vanished.

"Er, didn't Nan text you?"

"Text me what?"

"Lauren's with Nan."

"Since when?"

"Since earlier."

"But she's supposed to be with you."

"And she was but now she's not. She's with Nan."

"Okay, fine." He slouches back to the bar. Joe follows, sliding onto a bar stool. His eyes narrow when he spots the twins with their foreheads together, plotting, and quickly checks his stool to make sure they haven't left a ball of bubble gum for him to sit on.

"Dad, you never said Lenny and his family were booked in."

"Oh, sorry, got a lot going on."

"Oh. Yeah. How'd it go at the hospital?"

"All good, they'll get in touch if there's anything to worry about. Nurse said there's never been a thirty-nine-and-three-quarters-year-old so fit in every sense!" He strikes a pouting catwalk pose provoking an eye-roll from Joe.

"You say so. Dad?"

"Yep?"

"Can I go to the holiday sports club with Lenny?"

Dad's cheeks flush. "Lenny's mum was telling me about it."

"So, I can go?"

Dad's head wobbles in an all-too familiar way, unwilling to shake yet unable to nod.

"Thing is, it's quite a bit of money."

"But you've done well today."

"Today, yep, and if Tuesday to Thursday was as busy ... maybe, but ..." He turns to pour rum into the cocktail shaker.

Joe glances back at Lenny laughing along with his family. Any excitement he'd felt at the prospect of hanging out with his old mate evaporates into resentment. He's on his own. Again. Fine. Dad would have to pay for his skateboard.

"Fine. Can I have forty pounds?"

"Forty quid?"

"My skateboard's busted."

"You should take better care of it."

"It wasn't my fault."

Dad resists replying '*it never is*' but his rolling eyes say it all.

"Fine, don't believe me."

"What do you do with your pocket money?"

Joe resists the temptation to retort, '*Used it on your fortieth birthday present if you must know.*'

"Probably blowing it on video game extras."

"Not true."

"You say so."

Joe steams. Can he get a refund on Dad's concert tickets ...?

"Listen, tell you what? How about you help out here for the rest of the day and next week and we'll see what we can sort?"

"That's forced labour."

"That's earning a living."

"Other kids just get pocket money, period, they don't have to work for it."

Dad rubs his temples. "It is what it is."

"Yeah, but," Joe's on a roll, "how comes Aaliyah never has to help out anymore?"

"Well, she's volunteering at the farm. She's studying."

"I've got studies."

"Fortnite is not a GCSE option last time I checked." Dad chuckles but his joke does nothing to dampen Joe's rising sense of injustice.

"And Lauren, she never does half the stuff around here you used to make me do when I was her age."

Dad slams the shaker onto the counter. "Joe, you always *wanted* to help out. You loved it, laying tables, organising napkins, nobody forced you to do that stuff so don't re-write history to suit your sulky teenage pity party."

"Pity party?" Joe splutters.

"Hey, you two know I won't have bad words in my front of house," cautions Aunty Salma.

She places a soothing hand on Joe's shoulder, helping him regulate his rising emotions. Joe glares down at the bar. Dad ducks down into his eye line with a conciliatory smile.

"Hey, Joe, how about I rustle you and me up a sweet lime mango milkshake to share?"

"Make that two!" shouts Uncle Tyrell from the kitchen. "It's almost as hot in here as my wife the day we met at Carnival."

"Ha!" Aunty Salma gives a twirl. "I might just need to dust down that sequined bathing suit and give everyone a treat."

"Eghhhh, Muuuuum," chorus the twins, and even Joe cracks a small smile.

She picks up a pile of linen napkins. Joe notices the twins shaking like bottles of lemonade about to explode as their mum unfolds the top napkin to reveal ...

A huge spider.

Salma lets out a scream and next it's raining napkins. The twins slap each other in hysterics and Tyrell holds his sides as Salma performs a jig to avoid the eight-legged discovery, realising too late it's only rubber. Joe, Dad, and the customers are already laughing, which doubles when Salma grabs a napkin and chases the twins out back with a lethal flick at their legs.

Joe's laughter fades. Emptiness creeps back. It cuts even deeper knowing Dad's right; Paradise had been his life and he hates feeling like an outsider looking in on a world he once loved. But now he longs for something more to make these feelings go away, scratch the itch he has inside to escape.

But with no skateboard, no money, and no mates? There's no chance.

Chapter 4

Strange shaped clouds tumble across a deep blue and purple sky, like a heavyweight champion had gone twelve rounds with the heavens.

"Hey Sphinxy." Joe pats its lion's chest. "Got a riddle for me?"

The sphinx's eyes gaze out across an empty park.

"No? Try this." Joe clambers onto its back. "What flies when it's born, lies when it's alive, and runs when it's dead?"

"That's easy," replies the sphinx.

Joe half-falls, half-leaps off the talking statue, landing with a thump on the grass. He stares up at the stone face, now silent as it had ever been. Pushing himself onto his elbows, he splutters, "Did ... did you ...?"

"Say it's easy? Yes." The sphinx's long, proud Egyptian beard bobs up and down as it speaks in a voice reminding Joe of Mr Baruti, his science teacher, a voice like melting chocolate.

"Wow!"

"Snow," corrects the sphinx.

"What?"

"Snow," irritated having to keep repeating itself. "What flies when it's born, a snowflake, what lies when it's alive, snow, and what runs when it's dead—or melted, SNOW."

The sphinx smiles smugly.

Joe reaches out, tempted to touch the statue but, safety first, keeps his distance.

"I ... must be dreaming."

"You talk at me all the time. Am I dreaming when you do?"

"I'm supposed to talk. I'm human."

"I'm supposed to tell riddles, I'm a sphinx, but do I moan when you

bore me with your Key Stage One efforts?"

"Um, well, no, but ..."

"Then listen now. I have a riddle for you."

The sphinx milks the moment with a long dramatic pause.

"Follow in their footsteps.

"Pause here a while.

"Listen to the echoes

"Past, present, future."

Joe frowns. "Er, aren't riddles supposed to be, well, questions? Like your Greek sphinx cousin asked Oedipus? Question. 'What walks on four legs in the morning, two in the afternoon and three at night.' Answer. 'Man', cos he crawls on all fours as a baby, walks upright as an adult and with a cane when he's old.' Question and answer, you know?"

"Of course I know. I'm a sphinx. Knowing is what we do. MY question is what will YOU do when faced with the past, present and future?"

What kind of question ...

Suddenly Joe's pocket feels hot.

He pulls out the shattered compass, its silver case warm to touch.

The arrow spins. Faster and faster.

Clouds above switch direction, blown backwards by a howling wind. Joe's eyes weep. He throws up his arms to protect his face. They're yanked away by the wind. He cries out, voice lost in the gale ....

Joe leaps from his sweat-soaked bed, gasping for air but finding none on this still hot night. The streetlamp shines through his open window, cutting through bedroom shadows.

Settling back on his bed (which takes up most of his room) Joe gazes up at the swirling Victorian plaster ceiling cut off abruptly by a thin partition wall between his room and Lauren's. Their two-bedroom flat occupies the top corner of a Gothic villa carved up in the 1980s by developers into as many units as possible making the ceilings taller than the rooms are wide.

Joe makes his way to the narrow kitchen, filling his glass with water too tepid to quench his dry mouth.

He listens for Dad's snores from his sofa bed in the living room, but instead catches murmurs.

"... if there's anything, I'll tell you okay ...?"

Joe lingers in the hallway, ears strained, like Dad's voice:

"Yeah, yeah, no male Cook ever made it past forty, thanks Mum, but I'm fine, honest, nothing a decent night's kip won't sort .... Sure, Lauren will love that, can't see Joe wanting to go though, miserable little sod .... Great, and next time you think about ringing at midnight, you can always send a text. Love ya. 'Night."

Returning to his room, Joe wonders what Nan has planned for Lauren; whatever it is Dad's probably right. Joe won't want to go. Still, nice to be asked.

Joe's drawn to his bedroom window. The silence in the street below broken by a car speeding past into the night. An owl hoots in nearby Stambourne Woods.

Joe blinks.

Below, in the shadow of a great elm tree between the drive and the pavement, stands a small hooded figure. The shadow of a child. Alone. Staring up at him.

Joe rubs his eyes.

The Alone Child steps back, disappearing into darkness.

He shivers in spite of the heat.

Joe closes the window, careful to leave just enough of a crack to let in air ...

But nothing else.

Joe's head rests on his scrunched up Scout polo shirt. It's too blisteringly hot to wear uniform so while the leaders aren't around Joe sports one of his eight skull T-shirts. He yawns, fanning himself with the clipboard; it will be ages before any Cubs find the first three clues leading them into Crystal Palace Park maze. Longer still until they navigate its twists and dead ends and reach the centre where Joe waits to tick off their names, earning them their Treasure Hunt badge and contributing towards Joe's Scout Leadership badge. Dad had 'volunteered' Joe to help out even though he'd wanted to drop Scouts for ages. Dad insists it's good for him. Like he'd know.

In the centre of the maze stands a circle of six silver birch trees. Between them are stone benches where Joe splays alongside his broken skateboard, gaffer tape hanging uselessly from the wheel. He'd hoped the tape might hold the wheel in place so he could practice tricks whilst waiting for the Cubs, but one flip and the tape ripped.

To break the boredom, Joe decides to do something constructive; put yesterday's discovery on eBay. He pulls the shattered compass out of his shorts pocket. The metal case gleams since cleaning it using Robin Wood's toothpaste trick. Dark traces of Joe's dried blood remain stuck between the glass cracks, but whoever buys it will have to replace the glass anyhow. Fishing out his mobile to take a photo, Joe realises he holds in his hands two bits of ground-breaking tech from different ages.

As he takes the photo, WhatsApp pings.

Zahid!

The message reveals a photo of Zahid striking a ludicrous pose in his dayglow orange shorts next to a giant waterslide.

The message reads, '@Waterpark! Awesome slides! You'd love it!'

Yeah. I would. Thanks for asking what I'm up to. A big fat nothing.

Just to add to his woes, Joe's phone is nearly dead, the curse of having a hand-me-down handset previously Candy-Crushed to near-death by Nan.

"Hey!" shouts a familiar voice.

Down the hedge-lined corridor from the centre of the maze to the exit gate stands Brendon and Kendon Duke in their green Cubs sweaters smothered with badges (the Duke family are nothing if not over-achievers).

"Let us through," Brendon shouts, starting to open the exit gate and sneak to the middle of the maze.

"Hey, no way. No shortcuts."

Joe's too far away to hear the names the twins call him as they disappear to tackle one of the largest mazes in the country. Planted for the palace pleasure gardens, in wintertime it's easy to cheat and sneak through gaps in the hedges. Now the thick foliage walls are impenetrable.

Beneath Joe's feet the dark and light grey paving stones recreate a circular map of the maze. Encircling the map is a ring inscribed with words. Joe cocks his head to one side, walking around the circle, reading under his breath.

"Follow—in—their—footsteps ...."

Where had he heard that before?

"Pause—here—a—while ...."

Racking his brain ...

"Listen—to—the—echoes ...."

Definitely recently.

"Past, present, future."

Joe freezes.

His dream floods back.

His heart pumps in his chest.

Get a grip. Must've read these words before, going around the maze, the phrase subconsciously waiting to pop into a weird dream on a hot night.

"Joe!"

Snapping back to the present, he stands on tiptoes. Who's calling his name? A dozen hedges away two pairs of hands jump in and out of view.

"Help us!" cry Kendon and Brendon.

"No!" Why should he when all they give him is grief?

"*Joe! Help us,*" cries another voice.

A child's voice.

Joe shivers despite the heat.

This voice belongs to neither twin. Maybe one of the other pairs of Cubs had reached the maze?

Kids of today. Don't they realise this exercise is about finding their own paths?

Then again, Joe's job is to keep an eye out, make sure they're okay. The stone bench gives him just enough height over the towering hedges. He glimpses a sun hat belonging to a man with his wife and their kid in a buggy.

"Joe! Help us!"

Definitely the twins.

"Joe! Help us," cries the other voice. Now behind him. Joe spins around.

"Who is that?"

Silence.

"Help yourself then, that's the whole point," Joe says.

"Joe! Help us!" cry the twins.

"Joe! Help us," echoes the voice.

Okay. Great. The twins are in full wind-up mode, clearly enlisting another Cub to shout out. Bet they're trying to get him to enter the maze and end up lost. Fat chance. Joe cracked the maze long ago: keep to the right you'll eventually work your way to the centre.

"Joe! Help us," cries the voice.

Joe shivers in the sunlight.

It would be just his luck if one of the Cubs twisted an ankle or had an asthma attack on his watch.

"Fine," he mutters, jumping down from the bench and grabbing his skateboard. No way is he leaving Skull Rider for the twins to swipe and use in their latest wind up. He turns into the maze, working his way around in reverse. The voice came from the back of the maze, approximately north east.

A left, a right, keeping the hedge on the right-hand side, until ...

Dead-end.

It had been a few years since Joe had navigated the maze. Bound to be a bit rusty.

He doubles back. The hedge divides into two directions. Remembering the rule, Joe keeps right.

It hits him. He stops in his tracks.

Keeping to the right is how you get from the start of the maze to the centre, whereas he'd started from the centre to work his way to the start. He should've been keeping to the *left*. How could he be so stupid? He considers working his way back to the centre and starting again but dismisses the idea with a snort—if his ten-year-old self had beaten the maze, it would be no challenge for him now.

The shattered compass remains in his palm. Surprisingly the arrow moves when he moves and points north as a compass should.

"Still works." Joe notes this for the eBay listing. The compass confirms which direction is north-east. Opting for the left fork, Joe follows a long semi-circular path around the maze's circumference.

A breeze begins blowing. Fast moving pink clouds dot the sky. The path ends with … a dead end.

Damn it!

Joe stomps back on himself. The shattered compass arrow slowly spins round and around.

"Great," he mutters, adjusting the eBay listing in his head: *works when it wants to, just not when it's needed.*

Swollen clouds circle above as if someone is rewinding the sky, adjusting the colour to deep purples and blues. Joe finds a green dead end in front of his face. Yet he'd walked here moments ago ....

"Must've missed a turning while looking at this poxy compass." Joe pivots back on himself, again, the breeze now blowing hard on his face, until ... another wall of hedge blocks his path.

How is this possible? There's no way out.

Joe strides back on himself, again, ordering himself to ignore the compass and the crazy clouds above and focus on a way out. The breeze changes direction; the maze must create some sort of circular wind tunnel. He halts at a gap on his right which he swears wasn't there before. A robin hops around in the gap as if inviting Joe in, feathers billowing in the wind.

"So, this must be my way out," Joe tells the bird, although logically it also had to have been his way in, but he honestly doesn't remember entering this double-dead-end pathway from the middle.

The shattered compass spins like crazy.

Joe quickens into a jog, catching sight of the couple with their buggy through a turning further on, feeling stupid at feeling so relieved to see someone else.

Only ...

The couple are walking backwards. Must be easier to drag the buggy in reverse over the gravel pathways. But why is the mum walking backwards too if she isn't pulling the buggy? By the time Joe reaches the bend, the odd couple are nowhere to be seen.

The pathway curls. Through a gap in the hedge, he glimpses Brendon and Kendon, both also walking backwards.

"What are you two up to?" But they're gone. In the words of their big sister, Aaliyah, up to stupidness. But how had the twins convinced that couple to copy their stupidness?

A fork lays ahead in the maze.

Which way to turn?

"Joe! Help us!" cry the twins from the direction of the right-hand turn.

"*Joe! Help us,*" echoes the child's voice beyond the left-hand turn.

Joe's legs yearn to turn right and find the twins, find comfort in the known, even if it is annoying and monotonous.

Yet there's something familiar about the unknown voice ... as if the caller needs him ... really truly needs him ....

The wind rises in great gusts. The hedgerow shakes. The spinning compass arrow is a blur.

Clutching his skateboard, Joe takes the left-hand turn, changing his life forever.

Chapter 5

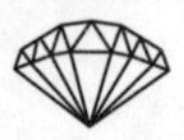

Left through the maze, a right, another right, Joe turns a blind corner and walks straight into a couple.

"Are you alright?" the man asks.

"Sorry!" replies Joe, grateful to finally make human contact with people who aren't weirdly walking backwards.

Although this couple are dressed weirdly.

The man wears a long double-breasted coat down to his knees, pin-striped trousers and top hat, sporting sideburns and a moustache that would be the envy of any Crystal Palace hipster. Yet his elegant style pales next to his partner. She wears a bottle green dress bunched up high at the rear, so long she has to hold it up to stop it dragging on the ground. In her other hand, a parasol provides shelter against the hot sun, held over her tiny top hat adorned with purple feathers.

The couple look Joe up and down with curiosity. She says, "You look like you've seen a ghost."

"I'm fine, thanks." Joe squeezes past, adding, "Great costumes."

Must be dressed up for a new immersive performance planned by the Crystal Palace Festival, like their Labyrinth of Lost Stories.

Finally.

The outer pathway of the maze.

Joe hasn't found the owner of the child's voice crying for help, but now all he wants is to be free from hedges and back into familiar surroundings. Ahead stands the iron entrance gate where the circle of trees surrounding the maze ends revealing views into the park. Joe quickens his pace, steps through the gate and stops dead in his tracks.

Joe blinks.

Blinks again.

Rubs his eyes but the view of the park remains unchanged.

Only ... it *has* changed.

Gone is the transmitter tower pointing into the heavens. In its place is an eighty-five-metre water tower. Its twin tower stands in the distance on the other side of the park.

The ruined arches of the Italian terrace are restored and lined with lush lawns and magnificent flower beds.

The brambles, trees and bushes along the upper terrace have disappeared.

Rising in their place is the Crystal Palace.

Joe's jaw drops open. He's too gobsmacked to shut it.

The summer sky gives the palace a blue shimmer as the glass glitters in the sunshine. It's spectacularly huge. The towering arched halls of the South Transept and North Transept rise up at each end of the nave, yet both are dwarfed by the Grand Transept in the centre of the palace.

Not only has the view transformed.

So have the people.

Promenading couples with top hats and bonnets replace joggers and dog walkers. Families and friends still enjoy picnics, but instead of bikini tops and summer shorts, they wear suits and flouncy bustled dresses. The single cyclist Joe spots rides a Penny Farthing bike with a tiny back wheel and an enormous front wheel.

Joe's head spins.

Has he walked into a film set?

Perhaps the Crystal Palace Festival went overboard with a re-enactment of the old palace?

Maybe Brendon and Kendon's practical jokes have gone supernova?

Joe never believed people really pinch themselves yet squeezes the skin on his arm so hard he yells out loud.

But before him remains Victorian Crystal Palace.

The maze! This must have something to do with that baffling wind-blowing reversing weirdness. Would retracing his steps lead him back to reality?

But, if this *is* real …

If he'd really travelled back in time through the maze, did he want to get back without first exploring?

At least for a bit ...

Otherwise Nan would kill him. Imagine the stories he could tell *her* for a change.

Joe pulls out his mobile but hopes of snapping the palace vanish. The screen is dead.

A lad wearing a bowler hat and a threadbare blue suit made for someone not quite as chunky sits on the grass. Nose in a book, his wooden crutch laying at his side reminds Joe of a teenage Tiny Tim. Joe approaches, opens his mouth, promptly shuts it again.

Where to start? What to ask?

The boy senses his presence, squinting up with droopy eyes.

"May I assist you in any way?" he asks with a lofty air.

Joe looks stupid for a bit longer before blurting, "What's the date?"

"Twenty-seventh of July. Twelve days until my splint comes off according to the bone setter," he adds as if Joe had been asking, giving his left leg a tap. "Dr Doyle agrees, and he plays cricket with Father."

Twenty-seventh of July—so the day and month is the same. But ...

"What year is it?"

The lad cocks his head to one side as if deciding whether Joe is stupid or mocking him or both.

"Hmm, well, let's see now. When I started reading *Twenty Thousand Leagues Under the Sea*," he waves his book, "it was 1888, but frankly it's so splendid I might have missed a year."

"1888 ..."

"Are you quite alright? You look like you could do with a sit down."

Joe plonks on the grass next to the lad, mind racing.

1888!

The lad beams at the unexpected company.

"Have you read *Twenty Thousand Leagues Under the Sea*? It's by Jules Verne."

Joe shakes his head distractedly. "No, but I've seen the film."

"Ahhhh," the lad exclaims, nodding knowingly at first but frowning. "What is a 'film?'"

"A film, you know ..." Joe begins before realising he won't know. Films haven't even been invented yet. "Umm, it's like a story you can, er, watch ...."

"Like a play?" suggests the lad eager to help.

"Yes! That's it, like a play."

"But *not* a play ..."

"No, it's pretty much like a play; let's go with play." Joe's visit to the past will require him to tread carefully. The pair sit side by side. Joe can't take his eyes off the palace.

"Let me guess. You're not from around here, are you?"

"No, well yes and no ..."

"Let me guess. You're French!"

"Umm, no."

"Ah."

"Why?"

"Your dress. It's rather peculiar. Why do your shorts have so many pockets?"

"To keep things in," says Joe weakly, giving his thigh pocket a pat. There's something metal inside.

He pulls out the shattered compass, stares at it.

Whatever's happened, however he's ended up in 1888, it has something to do with this compass. Robin Wood's words return … mystical powers and gateways between worlds …

"Is it your first time?"

"What?"

"Visiting the Crystal Palace?"

"Yeah. Well, the first time I've actually seen the palace."

"Guessed as much by the way you look at it." The boy puffs up his chest at his powers of deduction. "You can even see it from Bromley village, which is about the only decent thing you can say about that morbid little place. Father is trying to run a shop there selling china and sporting goods when he's not playing professional cricket which fortunately frequently brings us here, to the palace. He's playing a match today, behind us at the cricket ground, against London County, against none other than W. G. Grace!"

The lad waits for Joe's impressed reaction.

Joe scratches the back of his head.

"The big guy with the big, long beard?" Joe remembers the front of one of Uncle Tyrell's cricket books; *'Let me tell you,'* Tyrell had said, *'this man was a giant on and off the field, the best all-rounder of all time, single handedly invented modern batsmanship.'*"

"Correct!" Bertie flicks the pages of his book. "I'm not watching the game because I don't much care for sports. On account of my lung condition. Besides, I've got to the chapter where the giant octopus attacks Captain Nemo's *Nautilus*. How did they achieve that effect on stage?"

"Umm, lots of dry ice?"

"Dry ice." He nods sagely.

"I'll leave you to find out what happens next," says Joe rising with a genuine smile.

His companion's disappointed round face brightens as a thought hits. "Tell you what, as it's your first visit, you'll need a guide and I know just the right person." He adjusts his bow tie. "Me!"

He doesn't want to hurt the lad's feelings, but if Joe talks much longer he's bound to put his foot in it.

"S'okay. You look like you need to rest your leg."

"Oh, on the contrary. Dr Doyle told me I must exercise my muscles."

"Honestly, there's no need—"

"No problem whatsoever." He places his crutch under his arm to push himself up.

Joe's instinct to help kicks in, reaching to hold the lad's arm.

"I can do it myself." He totters but his resolute tone makes Joe step back. With a grunt, he hauls himself to his feet and thrusts out his hand.

"Herbert George Wells," he announces. "But my friends call me Bertie."

Joe shakes his hand. "Joseph Cook. My mates call me Joe."

"Well then, Joe, let's show you the Eighth Wonder of the World!"

CHAPTER 6

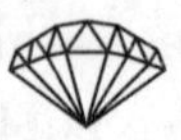

The closer they get to the Crystal Palace, the more Joe marvels at its scale.

Fountains shoot jets of water high into the blue sky. A group of ladies stand near the edge of one of the fountain's great pools. Bertie nudges Joe.

"Wait until the wind blows!"

Right on cue, a gust catches drops of the water jet. A mist of spray showers the ladies. Joe and Bertie crease up as some ladies squeal in delight, others in dismay, all rushing out of the waters reach quickly as their enormous dresses will allow. Spray sprinkles Joe's face. If this is a dream, it doesn't wake him up. But the welcome water cools him under the hot sun.

"Now Joe, although we're nearer the North Transept, to truly appreciate the palace, you must enter in the middle. Through the Grand Transept."

They pass through spectacular gardens, approaching the great staircase where Nan had stood with her tour group; as vividly as she'd conjured up the palace, nothing compares to the real thing.

The Grand Transept rises up and fans at the top like a lily leaf, the design inspired by giant water lilies grown by their architect Joseph Paxton when he'd been head gardener at Chatsworth House creating the most renowned garden in the country.

The terrace running the length of the palace is packed with people strolling in their best clothes. Halfway up the Grand Transept, ladies and gentlemen dine on a balcony shaded by a yellow canopy enjoying the view and enjoying being viewed.

A pair of sphinxes stand guard on either side of the great staircase. Joe would hardly be surprised if they turn and ask how he's enjoying these 'echoes of the past,' and perform a floss to welcome him in.

"How long are you here for?" Bertie's eagerness reminds Joe how he'd sounded asking Lenny if they could hang out.

Joe looks around longingly. "Guess I have to get home soon."

"Ah, of course." Bertie gives the step a jaunty tap with his crutch. "Understood. A whistle stop tour it is."

They step through a long row of doors into the palace.

Inside is even more impressive. A vast cathedral of glass and iron, its vaulted, barrelled ceiling stretches north and south as far as the eye can see. Whereas cathedrals Joe had visited were places of silence and whispering, the Crystal Palace resounds with noise and life; crowds chattering and laughing; multi-coloured birds fly overhead, singing as if auditioning for one of the palace's famed concerts.

The warm air smells like a tropical rainforest thanks to green towering palm trees and lush vines hanging from the palace's blue painted iron framework and red balconies. He'd looked at many black and white photos at the Crystal Palace Museum, but seeing the palace in all its glory, Joe is struck by its colour.

Visitors pack the wide concourse which runs from one end of the palace to the other, lined with gleaming white statues recast from antiquity depicting heroes and gods, urns of flowers from around the world and fountains and pools where giant lily pads float.

On either side of the concourse stand the twelve Courts, each one expertly recreating an era such as Ancient Rome, Greece and Egypt. Above the Courts running the length of the palace are three levels of balconies hosting exhibitions, stalls and showrooms.

"That," says Bertie, pointing above a rising semi-circle of seats the width of the Grand Transept, "is the Handel Organ, largest in the world."

The organ's pipes rise up almost the full height of the palace.

Joe cranes his neck back. A high wire runs across the top of the Transept where the roof curves. Three men, tiny at this distance, are on a platform pulling on the wire, one turning a crank whilst another tests how taut the wire becomes.

"What are they— Ow!"

With his eyes fixed in the air Joe barges into a small girl in a pink dress. He lurches to save her, but she sprawls onto the wooden floor.

"Oh ... sorry." Joe reaches down to help up the girl who he guesses is no older than seven.

She shoves his arm away with a snarl that, with her blonde curled ringlets, makes her resemble a lion. She spits words at Joe in French— his language options are Spanish and German, but he can still work out he's getting cussed.

"I can help translate!" offers Bertie, arm in the air. "She says 'of all the stinking English moron's she's met, you are by far the biggest.'" Bertie grins a little too enthusiastically for Joe's liking. "Rather vulgar for a little girl, isn't she?"

She fixes Bertie with a scowl.

"Make zat ze *second* biggest moron."

"Oh, you speak English." Bertie's round cheeks blush. "There's no need for name-calling."

A dainty neat man with the grace of a dancer appears and helps up the girl, wearing a rich velvet suit and an amused expression.

"Mon cheri," he chides, adjusting her dress. "Forgive my daughter, little gentlemen."

"It's my fault. I was looking up there." Joe points up at the wire across the transept. Bertie frantically taps Joe's arm like he's sending Morse code.

"Oh yes! They're preparing for the Great Blondin to perform."

"Blondin?!"

The French daredevil had been a hero of Joe's since learning about his amazing feats from a guided tour at the Crystal Palace Museum organised by Nan who'd dragged him along knowing his love of parkour. "He was the greatest acrobat in the world."

"*Was?*" The Frenchman arches an eyebrow. "Has another surpassed his skill?"

"Er, no, I mean he *is* the greatest. He crossed Niagara Falls on a tight rope and stopped in the middle to fry an egg."

"Oo, yes, I read all about that," Bertie exclaims.

"I recall it was an omelette." The Frenchman smooths his neat goatee beard. "But what's a cracked egg between friends?"

His daughter shakes her head muttering, "Sacre bleu."

"He performed here at the Crystal Palace," continues Joe waving around them, "crossing the Grand Transept on stilts!"

"Pardon, correction again, mon ami. He has not done so." The Frenchman's eyes twinkle. "Yet."

"Oh, yeah, right." Joe kicks himself again.

"Papa, tell them!" growls the girl.

"Nevertheless, he *will* do so," the Frenchman says kindly.

"On Friday," adds Bertie. "Will you be going?"

The Frenchman laughs. "I could not possibly miss it."

Joe's shoulders sag. "I won't be."

"We could go together, old chap! You and I, there may still be tickets available."

"I wish I could. I'd love to meet him."

The Frenchman places his hands on Joe and Bertie's shoulders. "That *could* be arranged ...."

The curly haired girl slaps her hand against her forehead and cries "Zis is him, you English morons! Papa *is* Blondin!"

The Frenchman takes a small bow.

Joe steps back to take in his hero. "Blondin! I mean, Mr Blondin. Or, I guess, Monsieur Blondin ..."

"You may call me Chevalier."

Bertie thrusts out his hand. "It is truly an honour, Mr Chevalier, sir. Herbert George Wells, but my friends call me Bertie."

"It would be my honour to be counted among them, Bertie. I hope you have not injured yourself emulating some of my tricks?" he asks, tapping Bertie's crutch.

"Oh no, balance and Bertie have never been bedfellows, but I very much admire your showmanship."

"Balance is all in the mind." Blondin taps his forehead. "If you believe, you will achieve."

"Papa, can we goooo? You promised ice cream."

"Forgive Iris. It is tiresome to have your papa's attention stolen away."

Joe nods, knowing what it's like to have your dad preoccupied all the time. "Hold on." He studies Iris, remembering more details from the talk. "You perform with your dad, up on the high wire, scattering rose petals on the crowd below!"

Iris's scowl softens. She says with a shrug of insouciance, "Daredevilry is in our blood. Papa performed at my age and was called 'La Petit Wonder.'"

Blondin strokes her cheek proudly. "Now there is a new Little Wonder."

Joe realises this is a once-in-a-lifetime opportunity to get the autograph of his hero and a souvenir of his visit to the past.

"Excuse me, but would it be okay if—"

Suddenly they're interrupted by a bustling man in a top hat and white bushy whiskers—George Grove, the Secretary of the Crystal Palace Company and the man responsible for its operation.

"Ah, Monsieur Blondin, wonderful, marvellous."

"Mr Grove," replies Blondin with a bow. "How may I be of service?"

"We have a royal visitor in our midst!"

"Oh?" Blondin's face lights up. "Is it the Prince of Wales? Perhaps he regrets turning down my offer to carry him on my back across Niagara Falls."

"Ha ha! Marvellous. No. It is not His Highness, though he is a regular visitor of ours. It is His Majesty the Shah of Persia!"

The Shah of Persia; Joe remembers how dignitaries from around the world were just as eager as everyone else to visit the palace.

Blondin claps his hands together.

"Ah yes, I believe he is attending my performance on Friday."

"Wonderful. Yes. We are building a royal enclosure especially for the occasion. But he is paying us an unexpected visit at this very moment to inspect the reconstruction of the Nineveh Court and I'm certain he would enjoy meeting you."

Iris's face darkens as she growls "Ice cream, Papaaa ..."

But Blondin gives her scowling cheek an apologetic stroke.

"I cannot let down a fan. Au revoir my friends." And before Joe can utter, *Can this fan have your autograph first*, Blondin leads Iris after Mr Grove in the direction of the North Transept.

"Cripes! I cannot believe I just shook the hand of The Great Blondin!" Bertie stares at his own hand as if Blondin's skills might be contagious and enable him to traverse the Transept.

Joe drags his fingers through his floppy fringe. "I can't believe I didn't get his autograph." He catches Bertie's eye. "I mean his signature."

"I *do* know what an autograph is."

"Oh, right, you have those."

"Yes, and so shall you!"

Before Joe has a chance to open his mouth Bertie hobbles off through the crowds after Blondin.

"Come along, Joe! Seize the day!"

Chapter 7

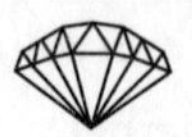

To reach the North Transept, Joe and Bertie pass the colonnades of the Greek Court, the red Moorish glory of the Alhambra Palace Court of Lions, and the Egyptian Court guarded by a giant statue of Rameses the Great. Joe wishes he had time to explore, but Bertie moves surprisingly swiftly on his crutch, weaving in and out of the crowds on their mission to get Blondin's autograph.

"Hold up," shouts Joe spotting a line of posters on a notice board:

BLONDIN OF NIAGARA CELEBRITY WILL MAKE HIS FIRST ASCENT IN ENGLAND IN THE CRYSTAL PALACE. ADMISSION—ONE SHILLING.

Joe carefully peels off a poster.

"An autographed poster," beams Bertie. "Stupendous plan."

"I'll get one for you." Joe begins to peel the next poster.

"Oye!" cries a young voice behind them. "I just put 'em up!"

Their busted faces turn to find a boy probably their own age, but shorter, leaning on a broom. He wears a grubby blue collarless shirt and braces hold his trousers up. Beside him is a bucket of posters. Joe says,

"Sorry, we just wanted Blondin to sign a poster for us."

The boy shifts his cap which has the lip turned up, emulating his smirk.

"Okey-dokey. As it happens, I've got a fresh one right here, if you fancy." He shakes his bucket, glancing around conspiratorially.

"Why that's decent of you, old chap." Bertie goes to take one of the rolled-up posters from the bucket, but he pulls it away.

"Hold up, hold up. Decent's got nothing to do with it. What's it worth?"

"I've got no money." Even if Joe did, it wouldn't be legal tender in 1888.

"Those posters don't belong to you," says Bertie crossly.

"And they won't belong to you neither if you don't cough up," replies the lad, striking blue eyes sparkling.

"Fine, here, I have a farthing. Will that suffice?"

"Suffice it will, young sir." The lad hands over a poster. "Pleasure doing business with you."

"Humph. Come along Joe, this way."

They reach the nave of the North Transept and the final court in the palace—the Nineveh Court.

The area is barred from the public by rope. Beyond, craftsman busy themselves with tools and pots of paint. Some stand on wooden planks resting halfway up stepladders so they can chisel final details of snarling lion's teeth in a scene showing the kings of Assyria riding chariots on a lion hunt.

Flanking the entrance to the Court, two human-headed, colossal winged bulls stand as guardians protecting the temple recreated inside. The hairs on the back of Joe's neck inexplicably rise alerting him to some unseen danger.

At the feet of the colossal winged bulls, a group of dignitaries gather to meet the shah. Among them is Blondin, his daughter Iris sulking at his side dreaming of ice cream.

"There he is!" points Bertie.

"On the wrong side of that rope," notes Joe, trying to shake off his strange feeling. "Come on, let's get as close as we can. What's with all the building work?"

"A fire destroyed this end of the palace so they're restoring it."

Joe racks his brain. The great fire that destroyed the Crystal Palace didn't happen until 1936, another forty-eight years from now. Nan's tours mention various other fires breaking out over the years before the Big One hit. The palace may be built from glass and iron, but the wooden floors running its length were a tinderbox just waiting for a careless brazier to ignite.

"Mind your back," warns a workman.

Joe and Bertie step aside to let him past carrying a large lion-skin rug, the lion's face seeming to leer at Joe as it passes.

"Take the lion to the inner chamber and lay it in front of the altar," booms Owen Jones, the designer of much of the Crystal Palace's interiors. He's a big bear of a man with a black beard and a melodious Welsh voice.

"Very good, Mr Jones," the workman replies, joining the hive of activity beyond the rope.

"Maybe we can get Blondin's attention." Bertie waves his crutch in the air.

But the only member of the party looking their way is Mr Grove, and he's searching over their heads for their royal guest as a maintenance worker approaches.

"Mr Grove, sir — "

"Not now, Mr Wilson."

"But the clock, Dent's clock. It stopped dead, sir. An hour ago."

High in the roof at the end of the Nave the clock's great face looks down on the crowds. The gigantic dial, twice the diameter of Big Ben, is silent. Its hands still.

"Well chop chop, see to its repair, Mr Wilson, everything must be in full working order for our royal visitor. Oh!"

Suddenly, Mr Grove nudges Owen Jones, sending a ripple of nudges through the group.

An entourage approaches, impressive as anything in the palace; six guards in full Persian military regalia with bejewelled swords at their sides. In their midst is the Shah of Persia. His tall hat is decorated with an ostrich feather. Pinned to his breast, a dazzling blue jewel catches the light like a teardrop from the Crystal Palace. A small crowd of onlookers follow, excited to have a royal visit thrown into the price of their ticket.

Mr Grove pulls aside the rope and bows deeply.

"Your Majesty, a marvellous splendid honour to welcome you to the Crystal Palace."

"Forgive me," the shah replies, "I am not scheduled to visit until tomorrow, but I could not wait. I so want to see your replica of my nation's city of Nineveh."

"Marvellous. And may I introduce you to the architect of the work, Mr Owen Jones, who has devoted himself to the study of Assyrian architecture and spared no pains to recreate every fragment of ornament and detail."

"An honour, Your Majesty."

"The honour is mine." The shah surveys the Court with wonder. "Our ancient city was destroyed by an army of Babylonians six hundred years before Christ. However, were it to rise again from the desert sands it would surely look exactly like the replica you have painstakingly created. And I speak as an enthusiastic painter myself."

Owen Jones beams. "You do me a great kindness. We have done our best to capture the spirit of the ancient Assyrians."

As they talk, Joe lingers near the elbow of Mr Grove, trying to catch Blondin's eye whilst avoiding the hard stare of the nearest Royal Guard who evidently dislikes urchins near the royal personage. Finally, Iris's downcast eyes glance up. She pokes her tongue out at Joe. He responds in kind and is glad when she actually cracks a smile and skips over to the rope.

"Moronic boys. Can I help you?"

Joe can't help laughing at her blatant rudeness.

"Yeah, actually. Any chance you can get us your papa's autograph?" Her scowl returns so Joe quickly adds, "And yours too, the new 'Little Wonder.'"

Iris twirls a ringlet. "If you insist."

"Anyone got a pen?"

Bertie fetches a fountain pen from his satchel and hands it to Iris along with his poster. "Here we are."

"What are you moronic boys called?"

"I'm Joe. This is Bertie."

"Joe, turn around."

Ordinarily Joe wouldn't let himself get bossed around by someone half his age but he lets her lean on his back and sign the posters.

Mr Grove waves over Joe's head at a gentleman approaching.

"Marvellous. Here's Sir Henry Majoure who is on our board of directors for the Crystal Palace Company."

Sir Henry wears his power like a second skin. He walks with an ivory tipped cane carved into the head of a bird of prey, emulating his own hawkish features. His overcoat has a fur collar despite the heat, as if he feels some unknown cold.

The Shah turns to greet the new arrival.

"Sir Henry, thank you for your personal invitation to visit the Crystal Palace. I understand you generously funded the restoration work after the terrible fire."

Sir Henry bats away the compliment with a gloved hand and replies in a voice of pure silk;

"What is wealth if not to resurrect the magical wonders of the past?"

"A worthy sentiment," agrees the shah as Sir Henry's eagle eyes fix on his jewelled brooch.

"I believe you wear one such magical wonder. The Star of Nimrod."

The shah's fingers caress the jewel. "You know your sacred stones."

"I dabble in mystical objects. A harmless pastime."

"One of the treasures of Nineveh," declares Owen Jones, "belonging to Nimrod, first king of Assyria and founder of Nineveh."

But the shah's attention moves behind Owen Jones.

"I believe I see another star, one in human form. The Great Blondin himself!"

The small Frenchman skips forward, spotting Joe and Bertie and giving them a wink.

The shah claps his hands with delight.

"I felt like a child again when I heard my visit to England would coincide with a performance from the Great Blondin. And is this lady your daughter?"

"Yes. May I introduce ma fille cherie, le Petit Wonder."

Iris gives the shah a curtsy before handing her papa the pen and posters to sign, gesturing Joe and Bertie with her thumb. Blondin happily obliges, signing the first poster as the shah addresses Iris.

"I hear you quite literally follow in your father's footsteps on the tightrope."

Iris sticks out her chin. "I fear nothing."

The shah applauds, but Sir Henry Majoure says to Iris in an icy tone, "Sadly, *I* fear you won't be performing at the Crystal Palace, young lady."

"Says who?" snaps Iris.

Mr Grove interjects with diplomacy, "Sir Henry, with respect you did express reservations about hosting Mr Blondin's performance. However, the rest of the board of director's agreed it would be most thrilling. And lucrative."

"If the Crystal Palace, a place of enlightenment, is to host circus acts so be it. But a father risking his daughter for thrills is a reckless and aimless endangerment of life."

Blondin lowers the pen before he can sign the second poster, placing a protective hand on his daughter's shoulder.

"Your concern for my daughter is appreciated, sir, but misplaced."

"What you are permitted to do in Paris or America is not permitted in England. As a devoted father myself, I would never endanger my daughter."

"I am not endangered. I am Le Petit Wonder!"

Before he can stop himself, Joe finds his mouth leaping to their defence. "They're safe, honestly. Blondin never gets hurt, ever. He's the best."

Everyone stares at Joe, Blondin and Iris with surprise, Bertie with admiration.

Sir Henry Majoure stares at Joe with pupils dark as night. Joe drags his eyes away. Sir Henry's lips curl.

"Mr Blondin may never have been injured. However, two of his workers in Dublin were not so fortunate when his rope broke, and the scaffold collapsed. They fell to their deaths."

Blondin's face darkens. Joe thinks hard, remembering there *had* been an accident in Dublin.

"Zat was not Papa's fault," declares Iris with angry tears welling up.

"The magistrate found the fault lay with the rope manufacturer," adds Mr Grove. "Mr Blondin was blameless."

Sir Henry sniffs. "Be that as it may, there have been letters to the newspapers demanding this girl does not perform."

From Sir Henry's tone, Joe's certain he's behind the letters, the man is clearly used to getting his own way no matter what.

"I have received word from my personal friend, the home secretary." Sir Henry smirks. "Her Majesty's government will not allow the child to perform."

"Ah." Mr Grove turns to Blondin. "I fear that puts a different perspective on things."

"But Papa ..." Iris's words falter as Blondin gives her a sad smile.

"Mon cheri ..."

Iris's floodgates almost open but defiant to the last, she isn't going to cry in front of others. Iris storms off. Blondin follows, quickly handing Bertie the posters as he passes.

As Iris pushes past Joe, he finds himself backing into Sir Henry.

Sir Henry glares daggers and shoves Joe with his ivory cane.

Joe stumbles.

His skateboard clatters to the wooden floor.

Clenched fists open. The compass Joe's gripped since arriving in the past falls and rolls away.

Joe drops down to grab it.

Reaches out.

The shoe of a passer-by kicks the compass.

It skids across the floor, lost among crowds of feet.

Joe's stomach flips.

No compass, no way of getting home.

Bertie calls his name, but Joe has no time to answer. Crouching low, he rushes into the crowd, searching left and right at patent leather shoes and the hems of bustling dresses. The wooden floors are designed with gaps between floorboards. If the compass falls between them ...

There it is!

Joe dashes forward.

He pushes people aside, ignoring indignant complaints.

He gets to the compass, but …

A lady passes over it.

Her dress sweeps up the compass.

It disappears under the hem.

Heart in his mouth, Joe runs after her, not taking his eyes off the floor in case the compass comes loose.

The lady pauses to admire the siren's fountain where multi-coloured birds merrily sing in an olive tree.

Nobody takes any notice of Joe.

He gets as close as he can behind her.

Drops down pretending to tie his shoelace.

Instead, he gently lifts the pleated hemline of her dress to peer underneath.

"You can get arrested for that, sneaking a peek at a lady's ankle."

Joe drops the dress and jumps up, finding himself face to face with the boy who'd sold them Blondin's poster.

"I wasn't!"

"You say so. Ankle peeper." The boy's mocking blue eyes stand out against his tanned skin.

"I don't care about ladies' ankles," Joe insists as the lady moves away.

Revealing the compass.

It teeters on the edge of a gap in the floorboards.

Joe lunges.

Just as his fingers are about to wrap around the compass …

It tilts ….

Falls …

And disappears beneath the palace.

With it any hope of Joe getting back home.

CHAPTER 8

Joe peers through the narrow gap in the floorboards, hoping in vain for a glimmer of the compass. All he sees is darkness in the pit of the palace. A queasy feeling spreads.

He'll never laugh at Dad's lairy shirts again. Never hear Lauren 'blah blah blah' him or Aaliyah karaoke or Nan tell a ghost story or the twins burp the national anthem or get a feast from Uncle Tyrell or a snuggle from Auntie Salma—

"Joe!"

The familiar voice seems far, far away. Bertie hobbles over, carrying Joe's skateboard as fast as his crutch will allow, face full of concern.

"Why did you run away from me?" He waves the posters. "Blondin signed my poster, but not yours I'm afraid. Why exactly are you on the floor ...?"

"I've lost it," Joe mumbles.

"You've lost it?" Bertie repeats slowly. "Lost what exactly?" Bertie's tone suggests it might be his mind.

Joe points a shaking finger at the floorboards. "My compass."

"What? Oh no, that's totally terrible news. I have a compass, it belonged to Great Uncle Sidney. You're welcome to it if you like."

Bertie's heartfelt offer sends a throb of comfort through Joe's despair. He smiles weakly. "It's not the same."

"No, of course not, silly of me. Well, perhaps we can ..." Bertie's eyes cast around for inspiration before lighting up with a cunning plan. "We can borrow a fishing rod from Father's shop, attach a magnet to the end and we can dangle it through the gap until it picks up the compass!"

Joe rises on legs of lead. "It'll never work."

"Perhaps, but you never know until you try, do you?"

Ludicrous as Bertie's idea sounds it may be Joe's only option, even though his track record seizing a prize from a claw-grabbing amusement arcade game was abysmal. This time he'd be trying it blind.

"There's probably loads of lost things down there."

"No, there ain't, Ankle Peeper."

The blue-eyed lad leans on his broom.

"What do you mean?" asks Joe, ignoring the ankle-peeping taunt.

"I mean everything falling under the floors gets cleared up by the master sweeps whose number includes none other than yours truly."

He hooks his thumb into his braces.

"You mean you can get down there? You can get my compass?"

"It's worth a lot then, is it? This compass of yours?"

Joe hesitates, seeing visions of the lad going down there and getting it for himself or demanding an extortionate payment to help.

"I told you I don't have any money."

"I gave you my farthing." Bertie scowls.

The lad takes an indignant step back. "I didn't ask for no money, did I?"

"No, sorry." Joe's desperate not to offend his chance of getting back the compass.

"I was only offering to help, that's all." The lad starts turning away.

"Wait, please." Joe grabs his shoulder. The lad gives Joe's hand a hard stare. Joe quickly removes it. "Please help me."

"You must need that compass pret-ty bad."

"Like you wouldn't believe."

"Okey-dokey." He turns and walks off towards the back of the North Transept.

Joe and Bertie chase after, Bertie hissing to Joe, "I don't trust him."

"What choice have I got?"

"There's always the fishing rod and magnet."

The lad stops at a spiral staircase leading up to the gallery levels. The staircase also leads down beneath the palace, a chain pulled across the top step with a sign saying, 'Private.' The lad pulls across the chain and passes onto the staircase. Before Joe can follow, he clips the chain back and says with a cocky wink. "Staff only."

"I'm coming with you." Before the lad has a chance to get all offended again Joe adds, "Four eyes are better than two."

"S'pose."

"And six eyes are better still," declares Bertie, but the lad points at his crutch.

"You can't be clambering down there, believe me."

Bertie scowls as if believing him was the last thing he'd do. Joe pats his arm.

"We won't be long. And listen, I need your help up here to show us exactly where my compass fell. We'll shout up when we think we're in the right area. You call down and your voice will help guide us."

Bertie's eyes brighten. "Ooo! I've a better plan! I'll find some string, or perhaps a long stick, dangle it through the gap in the floorboards and show you where the compass fell!"

"Great plan."

"I know!" Bertie leans in and whispers, "Be careful down there. I'll be right up here if you need me."

"Thanks. I know you've got my back."

"Got your back," says Bertie, enjoying the phrase before glancing down at the floorboards. "You *are* coming back, aren't you?"

"Damn right, 'cos you're looking after this." Joe hands him his skateboard.

Bertie grins from ear to ear.

"An honour! And when you return, *with* the compass," he adds firmly, "we'll find Blondin and get your autograph."

Despite the turmoil inside, Joe can't help smiling at the optimism of his new friend, sincerely hoping his prediction is right.

Chapter 9

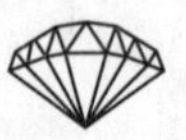

Joe's trainers clump down the iron, spiral staircase following the lad into the depths of the palace. Is this how the compass ends up lost in the first place? Dropped into the belly of the palace where it stays until everything burns down on top of it fifty years from now, only to be discovered eighty years on by Joe?

If so, I'm well and truly stuck in the past.

The staircase stops in a wide corridor running off in the distance in both directions. Huge pipes, like the palace's intestines, are bolted to the walls and ceiling. Bustling in and out of countless doors through pools of light from oil lamps are scullery maids, cooks, kitchen porters, master carpenters. They remind Joe of the hard work of swan's feet feverishly paddling underwater so the swan can glide gracefully above.

"Welcome to my office!" The lad waves his arms around. "Paxton's tunnel. Goes the whole length of the palace. All the nuts and bolts keeping the place together are down here: nine furnaces, fourteen kitchens for the twelve restaurants, fifteen sculleries to wash the quarter of a million plates we've got, plus all the storerooms with food to feed the thousands." The proud way the lad reels off his knowledge reminds Joe of Nan.

A side door opens. Two men in sooty overalls emerge carrying sacks. One has a weather-beaten face grimed with smoke. His menacing red-rimmed eyes fix on Joe.

"New recruit?" he growls.

The lad scratches his chin. "We'll see if he'll cut the mustard and join the master sweeps."

"If not, I'll find a use for him." The man steps threateningly towards

Joe, holding out his sack and giving it a slow hard shake. Joe gulps, unsure whether he plans for Joe to carry the sack or end up inside it. The man breaks into a gravelly chuckle.

"This one needs to lighten up if he's gonna survive down here."

The lad laughs along. "Don't worry, Mr Grimes. I'll break him in."

Hauling the sack over his shoulder Mr Grimes turns down the corridor. "Give your Aunty Doll my best."

"Will do, Mr Grimes."

Joe gives the lad a dirty look. He doesn't appreciate being the butt of everyone's joke. This does the trick, the lad switching his mocking sneer to a friendly grin.

"You got a name?"

"Joe." He tries not to sound too sulky.

"Elias. Pleasure to meet you, Joe. So, Joe. You dropped your compass by the Fountain of Sirens, right?"

"I didn't drop it. It was knocked out of my hand. But yeah, it fell just next to the fountain."

"Knocked, dropped, whatever. So, come on, Joe, let's go!"

Off they set down Paxton's Tunnel.

A few hundred paces in, Elias stops at a metal ladder fixed to the wall leading to a wooden hatch two metres up. Elias scampers up the ladder holding onto his broom, opens the hatch and climbs inside. Joe wonders whether to follow. Elias's head pops back through the hatch.

"You coming or what?"

"I'm coming. I'm coming."

The hatch leads into a long low expanse of space just high enough for Joe to stand up with his head bent. Elias is short enough to manage upright. They're directly underneath the palace floorboards. Chattering voices reverberate from above. Shafts of light shine through regular gaps in the floorboards whilst every fifteen paces iron grates enable glimpses of feet walking to and fro. Specks of dust dance from above find their way to Joe's nose. He gives a loud sneeze.

"Oy!" cries Elias. "You saying down here's dirty? You saying us master sweeps, ain't doing our job?"

"No." Joe's actually surprised how free it is from dust and debris.

"I'm pulling your leg. Lighten up a bit."

"I will when I have my compass back."

"Y'know your problem?"

"Yep, I've lost my compass."

"Stop fretting, have a bit of faith."

Before he can tell Elias where to stick his faith, and his broom, Joe cracks his head on a crossbeam.

"Oh yeah, and mind yer head!" Elias giggles, scampering off.

Joe follows, rubbing his head and cursing under his breath.

The under-floor is supported by thick red brick walls dividing the space into lanes running the length of the palace. The air is surprisingly cool, a gentle breeze blowing against Joe's hot cheeks. They come to an arch in the brick wall, nipping through to the next lane. Elias bangs a metal pipe with his broom.

"They feed water from the North Water Tower to your fountain, so it's easy to find the right spot. We find all sorts down here."

"I'm not surprised with all these gaps in the floorboards," replies Joe ruefully.

"Palace couldn't run without them gaps."

"How do you mean?"

"They keep the whole place cool. Let's face it, it's a giant greenhouse. But air flows under the floor, up between the gaps, getting drawn up by warm air pressure from the louvres."

"The what?"

"Louvres, vents up in the roof of the palace opened up to let the stale air escape, drawing up cool air from down here. Without it, we wouldn't only have the temples of Ancient Egypt, we'd have the weather too."

"Right." Joe's impressed at Elias's technical knowledge of the Crystal

Palace's pioneering air conditioning.

"What I don't know about the Crystal Palace could be scribbled on me fingernail. Soon I'll be too big to work the under-floor," says Elias, stretching his neck anticipating a growth spurt at any moment. "Then I'll join the Navvie crew repairing the iron frame, replacing the glass, keeping it ship shape, just like my dad did."

"What's does he do now? Your dad?"

"Not a lot. He's dead."

Joe stops at this blunt revelation, but Elias doesn't drop his pace.

"Sorry," Joe offers, catching him up.

"Why? Did you cause the storm that blew him off the roof?"

Elias manages a grin but can't hide the sadness in his bright blue eyes. "My old man was a Navvie. Comes from Navigators, they dug the canals and railways all over England. He was a Cornishman, from Truro, came here like thousands to build the Eighth Wonder of the World." Elias looks around with pride at the monument to his father's endeavour. "In fact, he helped lay the palace's foundation pillar in a big grand ceremony with Paxton himself."

"I've seen a photo of that!" Joe's mind goes straight to the fading black and white picture Nan had shown off to her tour group. "In fact, my …" Joe halts; he can't reveal *his* Great-Great-Grandad had been there too.

"What?"

"Er, my nan. She'd love to meet you. She loves this place."

"Sounds my kinda lady. With the palace built, my old man lost his roaming bug and settled down, joining the crew what keep her in all her glory. And one day, soon, I will too. The hoity-toity folk have their posh palaces. But this is *our* palace. For the people."

Elias thumbs his braces proudly as voices carry from above.

"*What would your brother do if he found out?*"

"*Damn him, Christabel. I love you!*"

Elias nudges Joe.

"You would not believe some of the stuff we overhear down here!"

"I bet."

As they resume their journey, Joe tunes his ears to snippets of conversation above.

"Don't blame me Stanley, you had the map..."

...

"Mother, I'm huuuungry..."

...

"Look! A hippopotamus!"

...

"There's the diamond on the shah's brooch."

The last sentence prompts Joe to pause, neck craning so his ears are closer to the floorboards.

"*Impressive,*" replies a man with an American accent. *"I hear he never takes it off, only at night when it's protected by his elite guard."*

An oily nasal South London voice replies, "*So, you're saying it can't be done?*"

"Don't recall saying that. Anything can be taken, for a price."

"Money is no problem."

"Really? I hear money is *a problem these days for your employer."*

"You hear wrong."

"Excellent. Not that I'm doing it for the money. That is, not just the money. Life's dull without a challenge."

Joe tries peering up through the gap in the floorboards to see their faces but can only make out a pair of black riding boots.

Elias cuts back with a questioning look. Joe puts his fingers to his lips, pointing upwards as the American says, "*I have an idea.*"

"Care to share?"

"No. Let's just say when the shah is looking up, we'll make the switch right under his nose."

"The guards?"

"Won't see a thing."

Elias rests his broom against the wall. The twigs disturb fresh dust. Particles float through the air.

Straight up Joe's nostrils.

Before he can catch the sneeze it erupts. Echoing like a gunshot.

Joe curses himself under his breath, peering up in case the men heard.

Their voices fall silent.

Riding boots disappear from view.

They've gone.

Joe and Elias heave a sigh of relief.

Suddenly an angry eye appears in the gap in the floorboards.

Staring right at them.

In his panic, Joe straightens, banging his head on the struts. He yelps.

Elias grabs Joe's collar and drags him away from the angry eye to the next archway, pausing to catch their breath.

"He saw us!" Joe hisses.

"So what?"

"So what? Did you hear what they were saying?"

"Something about the shah and switching—"

"Exactly! They're planning to steal a diamond from the Shah of Persia." Back along the lane, where they were eavesdropping, Joe half expects to see the plotting thieves chasing them.

"I told you, you worry too much." Elias pats Joe on the back. "They can't get down here."

Joe nods, now glad for their long winding journey underneath the palace. "Come on, let's get my compass and get out of here."

Above their heads the palace band strike up their lunchtime concert. Over the music Joe catches the sharp clanging sound of metal on metal.

"You hear that?"

"Ha! Someone needs to tune their triangle!"

But Joe's eyes narrow, looking back to where they heard the men plotting. "Someone's forcing open a grate in the floor."

"Nah, they wouldn't ..."

CRASH!

A grate clatters down into the under-floor.

A pair of black riding boots drop down after.

Joe and Elias turn to each other and simultaneously cry, "RUN!"

Chapter 10

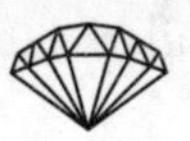

"RUN!"

To escape the thieves, Joe and Elias dive through the arch into the next lane of the palace under-floor.

Ahead lies the sunken stone basin of the Fountain of Sirens. A stick dangles down between the gap in the floorboards waggling backwards and forwards.

"Bertie! He's showing us where the compass fell."

Sure enough, a shaft of light shines through the floorboards catching the compass.

"There's no time to get it," cries Elias running in the other direction as riding boots thunder towards them.

Going for the compass risks getting caught.

But if he doesn't grab it now, Joe risks getting stuck in the past forever.

The black booted man appears in the archway. He carries a jemmy in one hand and a riding whip in the other, wearing a smile that sends shivers through Joe. Instinctively, Joe grabs Bertie's stick poking through the floorboards in the vain hope it will offer protection.

"Hello?" cries Bertie from above. "Is that you down there, Joe?"

With no time to reply Joe dashes to grab the compass. Just as his fingers reach out ...

CRACK.

Smiler's whip sends the compass spinning into the air, landing out of Joe's reach. Smiler makes no move, watching Joe with the deadly grinning curiosity of a cat with its paws on the tail of a helpless mouse.

If Joe runs for the compass, Smiler will whip it away again and undoubtedly catch him.

The compass is safe where it is—unlike me if I don't leg it.

Smiler cries after the fleeing Joe, "You can't run, boy."

Elias is nowhere to be seen. Without his guide, Joe's lost in the under-floor at the mercy of Smiler. Suddenly a voice cries, "What you dawdling for?"

Elias waits through another archway, holding open an escape hatch. "This way, up through the School of Music."

Joe didn't know the Crystal Palace had a School of Music, but this isn't the time for a Q&A with his guide. He dives after Elias, slamming the hatch shut.

Another spiral staircase leads to a landing. Elias tries the door. "Locked."

Boots stomp on stairs below.

The pair run up another level.

Try the next door.

It opens.

They stumble into a dark rehearsal room.

Heavy curtains are drawn but the room resounds with music played by a girl sat at a grand piano. She has her back to them and doesn't seem to notice their intrusion, not dropping a note.

Elias runs towards the double doors. Joe grabs his arm, pointing at the curtains, the perfect hiding place. Elias frowns but follows Joe, both ducking behind, holding their breath, listening.

The girl continues playing piano.

The door slams open.

Footsteps hit the parquet floor.

Joe prays Smiler and his accomplice will cross the room and exit through the double doors.

Instead the piano stops.

Silence.

Joe's heart beats so loudly he's sure they'll hear beyond the curtain.

Finally, the girl asks in a self-assured voice, "Can I help you?"

An American voice politely replies, "Excuse us, little lady, did you happen to see two young fellas run through here?"

Before the girl can speak, Smiler snorts dismissively, "Course she didn't *see*, she's bloody blind."

That's why she hadn't bothered opening the curtains.

"Come on, the little rats must've scurried this way," snarls Smiler.

"Apologies for the intrusion," offers the American, "and his manners."

Footsteps hurry. The double doors swing shut.

Elias gives Joe a wink, gesturing to hide for a few seconds more, just to be certain, when the girl says, "You can come out now."

Neither Joe nor Elias make a move.

"I know you're behind the curtain. I might have told those men had they been a little politer."

Joe steps out. The girl now sits facing them on the piano stool. Her eyes are hidden behind round sunglasses black as her eyebrows, which together make her pale skin seem ghostly white.

"How did you know we're here if you can't see us?" asks Joe.

"I can smell you both," she replies in a tone suggesting this isn't a compliment.

"Hey!" snaps Elias, stepping out too. "What you implying? I had a bath last Wednesday."

"Really? Smells more like last Monday but I'll take your word for it."

Elias's mouth drops with indignation. Joe enjoys Elias being on the receiving end of a roasting.

"And you," she continues, tilting her head towards Joe and twitching her nose. "You smell like my Great Aunt Maude. Fragranced and creamed."

Joe's grin falters at having his odour compared to an old lady, but figures his soap, shampoo, and Lynx body spray must smell pretty unusual a hundred and thirty years ago.

"Thanks for covering for us, I mean helping us," Joe adds in case 'covering' isn't a familiar phrase.

"Any particular reason they're chasing you?"

"Good question, Joe. What was all that?"

"Didn't you hear?" Joe whispers. "They're planning to steal a diamond from the Shah of Persia."

"Steal a diamond?" The girl jumps up excitedly. "I'm blind by the way, not deaf. We should go to the police."

"Oy, since when did *you* join our 'we'?"

"Since I became a witness," she replies sharply, prompting Elias to retort, "A witness *sees* something, you didn't, not being funny."

"Correct," she replies with defiance. "But I could pick out their voices from a thousand people, not being funny."

Elias whistles, impressed. "And you got a look at them, didn't you?"

Joe throws his hands in the air; no way can he get caught up with foiling a diamond heist. "One of them, but listen, I just need to get my compass and get home."

The girl's eyebrows knit together. "You need a compass to get home? Curious. Where exactly do you live?"

Elias raises a brow. "Yeah, good question. Where *are* you from?"

Joe ignores the question. "We need to get back down there."

"Your compass is going nowhere."

Nor am I without it. But before Joe can argue, the double doors burst open.

Joe and Elias jump, fearing the men have returned. They relax as a slender boy enters the rehearsal room. He carries a violin case and wears a wide-brimmed felt boater over his soft Afro waves. Giving Joe and Elias a quizzical look, he says drily, "Umm, Winnie, are we now playing in a quartet?"

"Good question, Sam. Do you two happen to play an instrument?"

"I'm pretty mean on the spoons," Elias boasts, thumbing his braces.

"Sam, a spoon solo would certainly make your next composition quite unique."

Sam's elegant fingers stroke his chin. He may be actually considering the idea, but Joe has bigger things to worry about and asks, "Did you see two men out there?"

Sam's wide eyes blink rapidly. "Ohhhhh, so you two must be the boys they're looking for. A downbeat man with a very creepy smile is offering a guinea for your whereabouts."

"A guinea?" Winnie exclaims. "If I'd known, I'd have given you up."

Elias whistles. "For a guinea I might give myself up." He catches Joe's serious expression. "Come on, you and me best get outta the palace 'til the coast's clear."

"But my compass—"

"Will still be there later when the palace closes. That's when my master sweeps clear up. They'll help us find it. Or you can chance your luck on your own."

Joe is sorely tempted. But, knowing his luck, reluctantly concludes he's more chance of success with help.

"Don't worry, I know how to get us out of the palace with no chance of bumping into our unwanted friends."

"Fine."

"Pleasure's all mine."

"Sorry, thanks."

"Okey-dokey, we'll leave you to your rehearsal. Maybe we'll see each other again ...." As the words come out Elias remembers Winnie can't see. "I mean, that is to say ..."

Winnie cracks her knuckles. "Take your foot out of your mouth. You'll need it for your getaway. And next time we *see* each other, we'll have to hear your spoons."

"Mmmm," murmurs Sam. "A rhapsody on spoons ...."

Elias grins. "I'll make sure I bring 'em."

They laugh. Except Joe. Joe rubs his temples, hard. It's a matter of time before Dad wonders where he's got to. He just needs to keep his head down, get back the compass, and get home. What could possibly go wrong?

Chapter 11

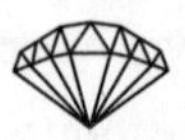

Elias leads Joe through a myriad of storerooms and corridors, finally emerging onto Crystal Palace Parade, which clatters with horse drawn carriages collecting wealthier visitors.

Joe scans the faces of passing people searching for Smiler when a thought hits him. "Bertie! I bet he's still there."

He pictures his companion loyally waving another stick in vain, remembering he still has Skull Rider, although skateboards are now very much at the bottom of his priority list.

"You wanna go back, that's your business. Me, I'm not getting nabbed nor am I missing teatime. Aunty Doll can spare a morsel if you fancy?" Elias holds up a cloth bag of left-over cuts of meat and cheese collected from one of the kitchens on their journey through the palace.

Despite Joe's guilt at abandoning Bertie, there's no guarantee he'll still be there. He has to stick with Elias to stand any chance of retrieving his compass.

"Cheers, I'm starving."

"We can share a nibble now I suppose." Elias fetches out a crust of bread.

The bus station still stands on the corner of the parade, horse-drawn double-deckers and trams heading up and down Anerley Hill. The Triangle bustles, traders spilling their goods onto the street to tempt palace clientele who stroll beneath awnings that hang over shop fronts. Towards London, the only familiar landmark is the dome of St Pauls Cathedral dominating the skyline (although the Crystal Palace is three times bigger). Misty smog hangs over the city, plumes of smoke rising from factory chimneys. No wonder people were drawn to the heights of Upper Norwood by the poster laying claim to be 'The Fresh Air Suburb,' a poster which in Joe's time became de rigueur for locals wanting a taste of history on their toilet walls.

Elias licks his lips of breadcrumbs. "Ain't you got nowhere to be?"

Yeah, a hundred and thirty years in the future.

"I can't go anywhere until I get that compass back."

"Ah." Elias nods knowingly. "My Aunty Doll's the same if I lose anything. 'Don't come home 'til you found it!' she says. S'why I never let my broom out of my sight. One time I lost it, she made me a new one and used my backside to check it was strong enough."

"For real?" If Brendon and Kendon got thrashed whenever they lose something they'd never be able to sit down.

"She's the best, but Aunty Doll don't take no nonsense from no-one."

Joe notes to be on best behaviour.

At the corner of the Triangle, the cobbled street ends and the road turns to baked hard mud. Orchards sweep down to Gipsy Hill Train Station and Central Hill is lined with pastures.

It feels like the countryside; Joe realises it basically *is* the countryside. Cattle graze in fields divided by hedgerows. The smell of grass and honeysuckle fuses with the occasional waft of manure. There's even a horse-drawn plough in the distance. However, rows of brand new red brick chimneys pepper the greenery, signs of the spreading suburbs to come.

Descending Central Hill are a cluster of terraced houses on the left surrounded by a wall two-metres tall. The wall and houses stop near the edge of the River Effra running through the dale below, little more than a stream at this point on its journey towards the Thames.

"There it is." Elias points at the walled streets. "Norwood New Town."

"Norwood New Town?" Joe searches his brain for Nan's words:

'Navvies who constructed the palace moved to Norwood New Town which had a wall built around it to keep these ne'er-do-wells away from polite society.'

Dozens of younger kids leave a large red brick building next to the Effra. Boys wear a white hankie hanging out of their pockets while the girls have theirs pinned to their dresses. This jogs Joe's memory of his thematic term at primary school. "Rockmount! My old school!"

"Your *old school*?" Elias stops. "How's that?"

"Er, how's what?" mumbles Joe, mind racing for ways out of his mistake.

"Well, first off, that school's got no name and it's not old. Been there four years. And I went to it for two of those years and never saw *you*."

"Sure, I mean, when I said 'Rockmount, my old school,' I meant to say it *reminds* me of my old school. Called Rockmount."

"Okey-dokey," says Elias slowly, seeming satisfied enough for Joe to breathe again.

"How come you only went for two years?" Joe's keen to get Elias to do the talking. Elias doesn't disappoint, exploding into a rant.

"When the powers-that-be in their wisdom made kids go to school, I *had* to go even though Aunty Doll taught me how to read and write just fine. Just as well it was only 'til I was ten cos it cost her a tu'pence and she has her own little horrors to pay for. I say they should be paying *us* to go."

Joe watches his primary school predecessors play some kind of chase game. One ends up captured and surrounded by the opposing team. His team chant, "Release! Release!"

The kid tries bursting through the circle of captors but they knock him back with kicks. Joe stares in fascination at the brutality of the booting until the captured kid finally bursts through, running to his cheering team mates to show off his bloodied nose.

"Kids," says Elias with the eye roll of one far older and wiser.

Everyone they pass waves at Elias who leads Joe through the gap in the wall into Norwood New Town.

Having studied the Industrial Revolution at Kingsdale and read about Victorian ghettos, Joe expects a scene from Oliver Twist. Plus, Nan spoke of the place's bad reputation —as far as the police were concerned what goes on in New Town can go on so long as it stays there.

However, while a definite sewer smell lingers, the tumbledown, tightly packed, terraced houses sloping south are alive with women stringing washing, old men on steps passing the time of day, and small children playing hopscotch and leapfrog. Their tough faces break into warm smiles as Elias passes and he calls to each by name. As a rule Joe shuns 'popular kids,' but finds himself with a bounce in his step walking at Elias's side.

"I live down Big Eagle." Elias points down a road plunging sharply a hundred metres.

Three brawny men stand chatting over a beer under a pub sign painted with an eagle. One asks, "Elias, you mended your racing machine yet, lad?"

"Finished her last night, she's ready for her maiden voyage!"

The man raises his tankard. "Can't wait to see that."

"Racing machine?" asks Joe, intrigued.

Elias thumbs his braces. "No-one can do the Big Eagle Run faster than the *Queen Marsh*. Fancy a peek before Aunty Doll gets home?"

The *Queen Marsh* turns out to be a go-cart created by Elias from planks of wood and a beaten old pram chassis. Joe helps Elias fetch it from a tiny yard at the back of the terraced house shared with his cousins.

"There's Mabel and Ginnie and Sidney and Frank and Ethel and Maud and Fred and Arthur. And Jim."

"You *all* live in this house?" asks Joe as they squeeze the cart through the narrow corridor.

"Nah. Oh, lower your end! We all live downstairs. Upstairs you've got the Dunnicliffe's, and there's fifteen of them! Gets a bit friendly but could be worse. You?"

"It's just my sister, Lauren, and my dad."

"What, only three of you, in one room?"

"Actually, we've got three rooms, four with the kitchen." In his own time, he'd felt embarrassed living in a small flat where Dad sleeps in the living room. Now he's embarrassed at how luxurious his living arrangements seem compared to Elias, who pulls a mocking face.

"Ooo, I didn't know I was in the company of a gentleman!"

Joe flushes and does his best to laugh along.

"What about your ma?" asks Elias as they manoeuvre through the front door.

"She left us."

"Mine too. Tuberculosis. Yours?"

"Umm, no, she's not dead, she left us. Moved to Australia."

Elias nearly drops the cart. "Transported? What was her crime?"

"No, she wasn't a convict. She chose to go."

Confusion screws Elias's face. "She abandoned you?"

"Yep." Joe lets the cart drop onto the street with a bang. "Sorry. And sorry about your mum."

Elias tenderly caresses the cart. "Yeah, well I still got me Aunty Ivy and cousins. And least you got your dad and sister."

Only if I get back that compass.

By the time they get the go-cart to the top of Eagle Hill, word spread; Elias is attempting Big Eagle Run. A gaggle of younger kids gather expectantly. More punters come out of the pub to watch. Elias laps up the attention like a Formula One racing driver on his winner's podium.

"Roll up! Roll up and witness the maiden voyage of the *Queen Marsh* on Big Eagle Run!"

Joe stares down the treacherously steep hill. "So, you never tried this before?"

"Course I have." Elias gives Joe's back a reassuring pat. "When it snows, we go down all the time on our sledges."

It would be amazing to bomb down a snowy Big Eagle. However, today the road is hard-packed lumpy mud. Joe has prickles of concern for his new friend's safety. "But you've never been down here on the *Queen Marsh?*"

"Sort of, before I made modifications." Elias gives the nailed wooden extension a proud pat.

"Yeah," pipes up a skinny girl among the eager onlookers, "and he crashed halfway at Eagle Turn!"

Laughter ripples among the kids which Elias dismisses with a superior smile.

"You reckon Robert Stephenson mastered *The Rocket* on his first try out? 'Course not," he continues, happy to answer his own question as the kids quit their tittering and solemnly shake their heads. "Besides, I've deduced last time I never had sufficient ballast at the back to keep her straight on course. Whereas now I've got me a co-pilot."

Elias places his arm around Joe.

Joe freezes. "Hold up ... You expect me, to go down there, with you, on that?!"

Elias's smile broadens into a beam. "What a tiptop idea!"

"Hold on a second—"

"We don't have a second to lose." Elias clambers into the pram, just about squeezing in. "You stand on the steering platform at the back." He gestures the plank of wood bound by rope to the rear of the pram chassis. "And when we hit Eagle Turn, we both lean right."

Elias points down at a road cutting across Big Eagle Hill where the hill sidesteps to the right to continue down Little Eagle.

The theory sounds fine, but the practice conjures images of the *Queen Marsh* hitting a bump in the hard-packed mud and catapulting them down the rest of the hill.

"I'll be your co-pilot," volunteers the skinny girl, obviously seeing the dread in Joe's eyes.

"Eat your dumplings and come back in two years. Besides, Joe here ain't gonna back out on me, are you?"

Joe isn't sure he can technically back out of something he's never agreed to in the first place. But the eyes of the ever-growing crowd are on him. As are Elias's sparkling blues—Elias, who had gone out of his way to help him, even putting himself in life-threatening danger (not that this impending danger seems any less life-threatening right now).

So with a sigh and a prayer, Joe steps onto the back plank. "Here goes nothing."

"Okey-dokey! Push us off, compadre."

Joe pushes with his right foot as he would his skateboard, but their combined weight has sunk the *Queen Marsh* a few centimetres into the mud. Joe steps off the plank to push. It still doesn't budge.

The skinny girl cries, "We'll help!"

Dozens of small hands clasp the contraption and shove. The *Queen Marsh* lurches forward to a great cheer.

"Yippeee!" cries Elias.

"Whooo!" yells Joe.

There's no slow gradual build of speed. The kids try running alongside but are soon left behind.

Joe's teeth and bones bounce as he clings on to the handle of the pram, more alive than he's felt in a long time, using all his parkour and boarding skills to keep balance.

They hurtle down Big Eagle towards Eagle Turn.

Only ...

They're aimed too far over to the left. Instead of crossing the path and continuing their bullet run down Little Eagle, they're set to smash right into the corner house.

"Lean right!" Elias yells.

"I'm leaning, I'm leaning."

But the pram wheels show no sign of turning off their collision course.

Just then, two women appear on the path at the bottom of Big Eagle. The older is a tall, grand lady with a feathered hat while her companion is small and wiry, wearing a dusty apron. Both are deep in conversation, unaware they're walking into the path of a runaway death trap.

"Aunty Doll!" Elias shouts. "Look out!"

The smaller woman turns, irritated at the interruption but scolding will have to wait; her eyes bulge seeing them coming straight at her.

"Lean! Lean!" Joe shouts.

Elias leans so far over he might tumble out. For a split second, Joe considers jumping off, but he'd be leaving Elias doomed to knock the women over like ten pins in a bowling alley before smashing to smithereens against the corner house. So with one last effort, he throws his weight right, leaning so far over the skin of his face feels it will be sheared off on the dry mud.

At the final second, the *Queen Marsh* steers over. They fly past the open-mouthed women, missing the corner house by millimetres.

"Wohooo!" yell Elias and Joe.

They hurtle down Little Eagle towards the gap in the wall running along the bottom of New Town.

Elias grins back. "Steady as she goes!"

The nearer they get to the gap, the narrower it seems.

"Stay on target," Joe cries, hoping no straggling Rockmount pupil steps through the gap.

Joe grips tight.

They zoom out of New Town into wide shrubland.

The slope subsides into a gentle incline but they're still speeding towards the River Effra.

"How do we stop?"

"Aim for the bridge."

In Joe's view 'bridge' is pushing it to describe three planks of wood over the Effra.

"We won't make it over."

"We will!"

"We won't!"

"We will!"

But they don't.

As the *Queen Marsh* hits the planks of wood, the left wheels veer into mid-air, sending them plunging into the river. Fortunately, the Effra is barely waist deep, enough to cushion their fall as they tumble out and sit next to the upturned *Queen Marsh*, its wheels spinning as they laugh and laugh.

On their victory climb up Big Eagle, the soaked heroes are flanked by kids regaling their triumph. Elias enlists them to carry the battered *Queen Marsh*, which they readily do with all the ceremony of carrying Queen Victoria.

However, the jubilation is cut short. Aunty Doll taps her foot on the step of her house with the other lady they'd almost mown down. Judging by her glare a thrashing seems the least of Aunty Doll's punishment plans. Joe hopes to blend in with the other kids eagerly awaiting the next instalment of the afternoon entertainment. Which looks set to be Elias's execution.

"Elias, you daft apeth. You might have a death wish but that don't give you the right to take me and Miss Marsh along for the ride. And what did I tell you about using that perambulator for your shenanigans? I promised it Mrs Chorley for baby Genevieve."

"Sorry, Aunty Doll." For the first time since Joe met Elias his cocky demeanour disappears, swapped with a sheepish examination of his worn shoes. However, he can't stop himself adding, "But I was the one what found it."

Before Aunty Doll can sharpen her tongue for a reply, Catherine Marsh says in a warm majestic voice, "I was intrigued by the name of your riding machine. These youngsters called it the *Queen Marsh*, and I wondered if she were a relation of mine?"

"Well, I meant no disrespect, Miss Marsh," says Elias with exaggerated solemnity, hand on his heart. "It was so named in your honour, what with the way you look out for us and our neighbours, which makes you the queen of New Town."

"Why, you cheeky little blighter ..." Aunty Doll begins, but Miss Marsh chuckles and puts on a Sunday sermon voice.

"It has been my privilege to count as friends the most noble of Britain's sons who laboured with strength and skill to rear the colossal Palace. Yet now," she says with a sparkle in her eyes, "to be the namesake of so ingenious an invention, that privilege has become an honour!"

Elias bows deeply. "The privilege and honour is all mine, Your Majesty."

She lets out a hearty laugh as Joe's memory bank identifies Catherine Marsh as Nan's historical heroine, a fearless social campaigner.

Aunty Doll tuts. "Elias, your silver tongue will be the death of you. If I don't get there first."

Elias gives Joe a sideways wink. Aunty Doll follows her nephew's gaze, locking Joe with a look so hot he feels his hair dry.

"As for you. Yes you! Get here."

She points to the spot right in front of her. Reluctant to move within striking distance, Joe decides disobedience is more dangerous. She demands, "What you got to say for yourself?"

"This here is Joe. None of it was his fault."

"I'm aware you need no encouragement when it comes to doing stupid things, Elias."

"But I *am* sorry," Joe adds hoping this might help. Aunty Doll nods her approval.

"Can Joe stay for tea?" asks Elias brightly.

"He not got someone to feed him?"

Her words send a rush of sadness through Joe as he realises he doesn't. Aunty Doll picks up on this and with a roll of her eyes says in a softer tone, "What's one more mouth to feed, eh?"

"You're the best! And did you see the veritable feast I left in the parlour? Cuts of the palace's finest cheese and bacon." Elias nudges Joe. "And after tea you and me will go back to the palace and get you your compass."

"Thanks." Joe smiles. "You're a life saver."

Chapter 12

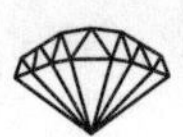

The sun disappears over the horizon sending long shadows across the fields of Norwood. Joe and Elias stroll up Central Hill towards the Triangle. They aren't alone; dozens of New Towners and others from the villages of Lower Norwood, Streatham and beyond make their way up hill to the palace grounds, off to see the legendary Brock's Fireworks, speculating excitedly about delights Mr Brock has in store this week.

A plume of smoke rises from a steam train crossing the fields below. As it pulls into Gipsy Hill Station, it passes a copse where the flames of a bonfire dance against the twilight. Music carries on the breeze.

"Down there's Gipsy House," Elias explains. "Royal residence of our most famous celebrity."

"Royal?"

Elias announces with great reverence, "Home to Margaret Finch, Queen of the Gypsies."

A name Joe recognises, her presence remembered in local road names like Gipsy Hill, Gipsy Road and Romany Road. Although the current Queen must be the original Margaret Finch's great-granddaughter otherwise she'd be two hundred years old …

"Long before the Crystal Palace drew in the crowds, folk came from miles around so she can tell 'em their destiny."

What would she say about my future?

Joe's drawn towards the flickering flames …. But he can't be swayed from his mission; get back the compass, watch the fireworks, then as people leave the grounds, make his way to the Maze and return home. Hopefully back to exactly the same date and time so Dad won't fret.

Much as Joe is beginning to enjoy this strange world and the company of his new friend he can't risk staying much longer.

However, his plans evaporate into the night like bonfire smoke when they reach the underbelly of the palace …

"Okey-dokey, the compass has gotta be *somewhere* down here."

Elias's optimism fails to inspire hope in Joe. What hope is there after an hour scouring the spot Joe last saw the compass? In spite of help from the ten-strong master sweep team enlisted by Elias to check all the nooks and crannies, Joe's ticket back to the future had disappeared.

Brain on fire, panic rising, Joe's desperation gets the better of him. Eying the master sweeps, he hisses to Elias, "One of them must've taken it."

Elias's face hardens.

"Elias, no offence, but if they did, I don't mind, so long as I get it back. You don't understand how important it is."

"Oh, I understand alright. Just coz we're not all 'la-de-da,' you reckon we're thieves."

"No, not you. But I don't know *them* and—"

"I've vouched for you. They'd never cross their own. Ever."

Joe bites his lip. He believes him, he'd seen the way the master sweeps admire Elias, taking on his mission to "find my new friend's family heirloom" with the enthusiasm of winning contestants on *The Crystal Maze*.

Joe slumps to the floor, deliberately banging the back of his head against the brickwork.

Elias sits beside him.

"Sorry," Joe offers, feeling his tear ducts start to fill.

"S'alright. I get it. Aunty Doll would skin me alive if my family ever had itself an heirloom to lose. You'll get grief, sure, but your old man will forgive you eventually. Far as I'm concerned, it's *people* what's important, not things."

Joe agrees a hundred percent, but can't tell Elias that without the compass he'll never see his people again. "I should never have come to the palace. Should've just gone straight home. I'm so stupid."

"Yeah, maybe, but you wouldn't have met me." Elias gives Joe a playful nudge.

But Joe's in no mood for comfort or jokes. If only he hadn't overheard those two men plotting to steal the diamond. If only he hadn't sneezed, and Smiler given chase and ...

Joe jerks like he's been electrocuted.

"What?"

"Smiler and that American who chased us. They're thieves, right? Smiler saw me trying to get the compass and whipped it out of reach. I bet he came back after he lost us and took it. Maybe he thinks it might lead him to me."

"Can it? It ain't got your name or address engraved on it or nothing, cos that's one fella you don't want knocking on your door."

Joe hesitates. He doesn't like lying to his new friend but can't tell him the compass in truth isn't an old family heirloom, but the key to a gateway across time—not that Elias would ever believe him. The only engraving on the compass are the initials 'HSM' which must spell the name of the original owner.

"There's nothing on it to lead him to me," Joe says truthfully.

BOOMA!

Explosions echo throughout the under-floor making Joe jump.

"That's just the maroon rockets sounding to clear the grounds for the fireworks to begin," reassures Elias as Dick, one of the master sweeps, approaches.

"Really sorry, we looked and looked again, no sign."

"Thanks for trying," Joe says quietly, ashamed of his past suspicions.

"No worries, any friend of Elias is a friend of ours."

Elias jumps to his feet. "Come on, we'll work out what to do. But for now, I'll take you to watch the fireworks from the best spot in the palace, where not even Queen Victoria herself gets to go."

Joe runs his hands through his hair and follows, but his thoughts are already wondering how on Earth he'll track down Smiler and get the compass back.

Elias leads Joe from the under-floor into a palace eerily empty of people. The only others inside are standing beneath Dent's giant clock where Mr Wilson, responsible for the winding and tending of the timepiece, scratches his head alongside six other baffled horologists brought in to solve the mystery of the stopped clock.

Crowds pack the terraces outside, but they don't try and squeeze in among them. Instead, Elias takes Joe up an iron spiral staircase rising to the roof of the Grand Transept. They climb up past the towering pipes of the Great Organ, past rigging for Blondin's forthcoming performance. Joe can't help thinking of the accident Sir Henry Majoure had referred to in Dublin. If something similar happened here, there's no way anyone would survive the plummet to the palace floor far below.

Elias beckons as they reach the top of the spiral staircase. "This way."

One of the rectangular iron window frames is hinged. Elias flicks a latch, swings it open, and leads Joe onto the palace roof.

The Grand Transept rises beside them in a curved barrel. Filling the night sky to their right are thousands of new multi-coloured stars flickering for a few seconds, greeted with 'ooh's' and 'aah's' from crowds below. In contrast, London on the left lies in shadows—with no orange light pollution darkness rules the night and a trillion stars seeming close enough to touch shine with a brightness Joe has never seen in his own time.

"Follow me," Elias instructs, making his way to the back of the palace to watch the fireworks. "The glass should take your weight unless you jump on it, but best keep your feet on the iron frame."

Joe grew up attending Bonfire Night displays set off over the palace terraces. Amazing as they always were, they're a box of sparklers compared to Brock's magnificent display which prove a striking distraction for Joe's turmoil.

A sequence of red, white, and blue rockets spiral, erupting into showering umbrellas of shimmering light. An enormous frame erected between the central fountains flashes into life, depicting two colossal winged bulls like the pair guarding the rebuilt Nineveh Court. Between the bulls, a portrait in fireworks lights up wearing a distinctive diamond broach.

"That's the Shah of Persia!" Joe exclaims, wondering how on Earth Brock paints with fireworks.

"Yeah, Brock always makes his displays in tribute to visiting guests of honour. The shah will be watching from the Grand Salon Restaurant balcony just down there."

Elias points to the balcony below running the width of the Grand Transept. VIPs with top hats and outrageous feathered bonnets surround the shah.

"They reckon they've got the best view, but that, my friend, belongs to me and you!"

"And moi," adds a small voice.

Startled, Joe and Elias grab onto each other to stop themselves falling off the roof. Just below them, on a narrow ledge, her feet dangling in the air, sits Iris Blondin.

"How the ...?" splutters Elias. "Who the ...? What the hell are you doing?"

Iris shrugs. "Watching ze fireworks." She turns to Joe with a roll of her eyes. "Congratulations, you found a friend even more moronic zen you and your other moron friend."

Unable not to laugh, Joe's amusement doubles as Elias's mouth opens and closes like a fish while he struggles to compute the insolence of a kid half his age. Finally he blurts,

"Hey, you shouldn't be up here, it's dangerous!"

Iris snorts. "You English are always about ze dangerous zis and ze dangerous zat, but *you* are up here."

"Yeah, well I work here, I know the palace like the back of my hand, and you're—"

"Don't say it," whispers Joe before Elias suggests she's 'just a little kid.'

"You know her?"

"This is Iris *Blondin*."

Elias whistles, a mix of sudden understanding and amazement. "Blondin's daughter?"

"Yes, yes, yes," says Iris wobbling her head irritably.

Elias turns to Joe with new admiration. "You telling me you know Blondin?!"

Joe shrugs modestly. "Yeah, well, we've met. And Iris here ..."

Her ledge lies empty.

For a split second, Joe fears she's fallen before noticing Iris has clambered off to sit several metres away.

"What's her problem?" demands Elias. "Apart from being bloody rude."

"Give her a break. She's hacked off they won't let her perform with her dad. Come on."

Joe and Elias carefully make their way along the ledge created by one of the Grand Transepts iron girders to join Iris. They sit down next to her, all three dangling their legs in the night air. Iris sighs but doesn't object to the company and they watch a firework fountain whoosh into the sky.

"Must be the bee's knees, Blondin as your old man," says Elias.

"Oh yes," she replies with heavy sarcasm. "People come from all over in ze hope of seeing Papa fall splat onto ze ground into a zillion tiny pieces."

"I'm sure that's not what people *hope* for," Joe counters.

"Zat is ze danger; zat is ze excitement."

"Guess so," Joe admits. "The threat of danger's all part of the thrill."

"Except when *I* want to join Papa. Zen it's all 'oh no, zis excitement we love is baaaad.'"

"Maybe when you're a bit older?"

"Papa was only five when ze circus came to town. He was so fascinated by tight rope walkers he said, 'Zis I will be.' He trains at Ecole Gymnase and performs as Boy Wonder, aged five. I am seven!"

"Over the hill, really," Elias says with a wink.

Iris eyes him suspiciously. "What 'hill' am I over?"

"Elias is just saying you've got plenty of time to be the 'Little Girl Wonder,'" explains Joe gently.

"Zat is my point! I am a girl so zey say 'non!' Him, stupid man down zere." Iris points to the balcony below where festooned lights catch the faces of dignitaries. At the end of the balcony almost directly beneath them, stands Sir Henry Majoure who took such pleasure in announcing Iris's ban and whose shove lost Joe his compass. For a second, Joe thinks Iris is going to aim a glob of spit at his head, but her next action is even more horrifying.

"Why say 'non' when I can do *zis!*"

Iris clambers up on the thin ledge. Before the lads can cry 'STOP!', she's flipped back onto her hands, legs in the air into a handstand. Frilly dress flopping over her grinning face, she walks on her hands along the ledge.

"Wow!" cries Joe.

"Wow," agrees Elias. "But please stop."

Iris bends backwards into a crab, feet landing neatly on the girder, rising upright with a curtsey.

"Ta-dah!"

Joe and Elias erupt into applause. Brock's fireworks provide a majestic eruption as if in tribute.

"Never thought nothing could top Brock's."

"You are without doubt Le Petit Wonder," adds Joe.

She claps her hands together. "I know."

The trio watch the final fireworks, sitting side by side, legs dangling.

Joe understands Iris's desire to perform alongside her papa. At her age he'd wanted nothing more than to help Dad in Paradise. Guilt grips Joe's guts at the grief he'd given Dad when he'd asked for help. Joe longed for escape and excitement and here he is, in 1888, watching Brock's fireworks on top of the Crystal Palace. Yet his mouth yearns for the comfort of Dad's lime mango milkshake, a sweet taste he'll never enjoy again unless he gets back that compass.

The fireworks reach their grand finale with a replica of an Assyrian temple lighting up the night whilst men with lit spinning Catherine Wheels strapped to their backs run across the terraces.

Joe wonders what the risk assessment looks like for that. His eyes wander down to the balcony of VIPs. The shah is on his feet applauding. Sir Henry Majoure smiles down at a girl sitting in a high-backed chair clapping excitedly. Behind the chair stands an imposing woman the height of most of the men with their top hats on.

A figure ascends the staircase, sweeping to the balcony from the terrace below. Joe recognises his weaving gait. He joins Sir Henry, leaning close to whisper in his ear.

Joe's heart leaps.

Even from this distance he can make out the man's unsettling smile.

"That's him!" cries Joe elbowing Elias and pointing. "Smiler!"

Chapter 13

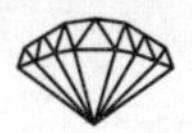

"How can you be sure that's Smiler?" Elias peers down to the balcony four levels below.

"It's him." Joe urgently rises from their make-shift seat on the iron girder, arms out so as not to lose his balance.

"Who is who?" demands Iris, rising with them.

"He's a thief and he stole my compass." Joe's eyes fix on Smiler who talks in the ear of Sir Henry Majoure.

Iris scowls. "Zis 'Smiler' knows zat stupid no brain idiot who says I cannot perform with Papa?"

"Seems like it," answers Joe.

The other member of Sir Henry's party, the imposing lady, suddenly scoops up the girl in her arms from her high-backed chair. Smiler picks up the chair which Joe realises must be a wheelchair. They descend the staircase leading from the restaurant balcony to the terraces below where crowds make their way out of the palace grounds after the fireworks.

"We need to get down there!" Joe starts running towards the spiral service staircase accessing the Grand Transept roof.

Elias grabs his shoulder. "We won't make it down in time; they'll be lost in the crowd."

"I will make it!" cries Iris hands on hips. "I will follow zem. Watch!"

Iris disappears over the edge of the palace roof.

"No!" cry the lads, running back. To their partial relief, they find Iris sliding herself down the iron frames in a masterclass of speedy free climbing. The crowd's attention is on their homeward journey recounting Brock's spectacular rather than looking up at the palace to see another spectacle unfold.

Elias whistles. "What's she like?"

"The Little Wonder!"

"What if she falls?"

"I've seen plenty of people free-climb. Just not many seven-year-olds. And definitely not in a pink hooped dress."

Joe's greater concern is how safe she'll be following Smiler.

Smiler reaches the terrace level and puts the wheelchair down. The imposing lady places the girl back in, but instead of following the crowds towards the train stations the group head in the direction of the North Transept.

"If we get ahead of Smiler up here on the roof, is there another way down?"

"Yep, we can use the stairwell at the North Transept."

Joe and Elias run along the roof, keeping eyes on their target and feet off the glass. After twenty metres, they reach the point where the roof drops down a level. They cut in towards the centre of the roof to a ladder, half climbing half sliding down to the next level, sprinting back to the edge of the roof to frantically search the terrace below.

No sign of Smiler.

Joe throws his hands to his head.

Elias points, yelling, "There he is! And there's Iris!"

Iris stands on an urn on the terrace wall waving up at them. Joe waves back, pointing urgently in the direction of their target who continues along the terrace. Iris gives a double-thumbs-up, but instead of jumping down from the urn and pushing her way through the crowd she scampers along the terrace wall, both arms out as if on a high wire.

Elias salutes. "I like her."

Joe and Elias run across the north wing of the roof, getting ahead of Smiler and company. But soon their route is blocked by the North Transept roof curving up into a giant barrel.

"How do we get over?"

"There's a ladder in the middle going up and over the other side."

"It'll take too long, and we won't be able to see them anymore. There must be another way."

Elias grimaces. "Well, a girder runs along the front of the transept, like the one we sat on back there, but the Navvies only cross it with a harness. If you fall ..."

"I can do it."

"Smiler might not even *have* your compass."

"I can't take that risk."

"Okey-dokey. I'm coming too."

"No way." He's touched, but Joe can't let Elias risk his life. "You said there's stairs down from here. Take them to the terraces, catch up with Iris and Smiler while I keep a lookout up here to see what way they go."

"Okey-dokey, but don't you go falling or it'll be yours truly having to scrape you off the terrace!"

Joe takes a deep breath and steps onto the ledge. The iron girder runs the width of the North Transept, just wide enough to attempt side-stepping across. Gripping the iron frames holding the glass in place, Joe edges along, recounting Blondin's words, 'Believe and you will achieve.'

I'm the Great Blondin. I'm Iris. I can do it. Just don't look down.

But Joe can't help risking a glance, spotting Smiler and company approaching steps leading into the grounds. The crowds have thinned out. He can just see Iris catching up.

Joe urgently picks up his pace.

I'm Blondin. I can do it. I'm ... AARGH!

His foot hits an iron rivet bolted into the girder.

He trips.

Almost plunging to the paving stones below.

Joe throws his weight flat against the palace. Heart beating against the glass, he struggles to regain his balance and nerves. With deep breaths he manages both.

There's no time to lose.

He finally reaches the other side gasping for breath.

At the end of the palace, a long single-storey building runs several hundred metres into the grounds housing the Royal Apartments built for Queen Victoria's visits.

Smiler and company are nowhere to be seen.

Nor is there any sign of Iris.

But there's Elias, gesturing down the terrace steps in a frantic game of long-distance charades.

Pointing at Joe …

Pointing at the Royal Apartments …

Making up-and-over movements with his hands. *What* the hell is he *doing*? *Why* on Earth didn't the Victorian's invent mobile phones …?

Finally it clicks. Elias saw Smiler walk *around* the Royal Apartments and wants Joe to get *onto* its flat roof and follow. Joe gives two thumbs-up.

Elias runs into the gardens to pursue on foot. Joe rushes to the end of the palace, catching sight of a ladder leading down four levels to the Royal Apartment roof. It's narrow so Joe quickly reaches the opposite side.

In his own time, this north-east area of the park accommodates Crystal Palace's caravan site which Joe knew from visits by Nan's cousin in her touring van; Joe remembers hooning around the campsite with Lauren as a BBQ grilled and adults reminisced.

There are no caravans now. Just a path in shadows leading to a gas lamp on a perimeter wall. Beyond the wall is the garden of a grand house standing in the top corner of the park. Lights from its rooms glow in the gloom.

Joe punches the air when he spots Sir Henry approaching the gas lamp, talking to the girl in her wheelchair pushed by the tall lady. They reach the garden wall. Smiler unlocks a door, holding it open to allow the others through. Smiler closes the door and they're gone.

Satisfaction stabs Joe. He knows where to find Smiler. Seconds later, a petite figure appears in the lamplight.

Iris!

Top marks for determination. She tries the door. To Joe's relief it doesn't open. He expects her to backtrack along the path where she'll bump into Elias who must be close by.

Instead, Iris begins climbing the wall.

Tailing is one thing. Breaking and entering is another.

Joe searches the dark path for Elias, praying he'll get there in time to stop her. Shouting risks alerting their quarry, placing Iris in certain danger.

Yes! There's Elias, jogging up the path. Come on, come on …

The Little Wonder stands triumphantly on the top of the wall, silhouetted against the light of the big house before disappearing over the other side.

Chapter 14

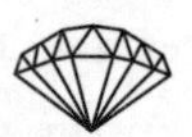

"She did *what?!"* exclaims Elias.

Joe, having eventually shimmied off the roof of the Royal Apartments via a drainpipe, explains Iris added trespass to her repertoire. Joe stares at the garden wall.

"I've gotta go after her. Anything happens, it's all my fault."

"Hey, you never told her to turn house breaker."

"She's doing this for me. Well, and to prove herself. And to get back at Sir Henry. It's just the kind of stunt my little sister would pull."

"Yeah? Look forward to meeting her."

Joe hopes the gas lamp on the garden wall doesn't illuminate his unease, knowing there's no way Elias can ever meet Lauren. He'll never see her again, either, unless he gets back the compass.

Elias gives Joe an odd look, places his palm on the brick wall.

"Well, it's no taller than New Town wall and I've been climbing that since before I can walk, so let's give it a go."

"There's no point you getting into trouble too."

"Trouble's my middle name according to Aunty Doll."

"You stay here in case Iris comes back. I'll be in and out soon as I find her."

Elias doesn't hide his unhappiness at being left playing lookout, uttering a sombre, "Okey-dokey. But I'm climbing the wall too to keep look out on top."

"Fair enough."

It takes them twice as long as Iris to get sufficient footholds and scale the wall. Eventually both stand on top, staring into the dark gardens and the house beyond.

"That's Rockhills," says Elias. "Used to belong to Joseph Paxton who built the Crystal Palace."

"Who lives here now?"

"Well, come to think of it, it's that Sir Henry's place now. Looks down his great big nose at the likes of me, if he notices us at all."

"Let's hope he doesn't notice us tonight." Joe turns himself around to drop down the other side.

"You get into trouble, shout, got it?"

"Got it."

Joe passes dark trees giving way to a large triangle of perfectly manicured lawn. The L-shaped three-storey house has a sweeping veranda hung with clematis scenting the warm night air. The Crystal Palace looms left, a proximity that will have allowed Paxton its original architect to sit out on the thrusting first-floor balcony and admire his creation.

Joe nears the house, peering through shadows in the hope of spotting Iris' pink hooped dress hiding in a bush.

Ow!

A sharp hard object strikes Joe on top of his head.

He suppresses a yelp of pain, searching tree branches above. It's too early for conkers ....

Ow!!!

Another object whacks him in the middle of the forehead.

Joe's eyes water.

Leaping out from under the tree, Joe spots the source of the missiles—Iris, legs dangling over a branch, silently giggling.

It's a perfect climbing tree. Joe clambers up, deciding it's better to get her than try signing wildly in the dark, risking drawing attention.

She whispers, "What took so long?"

"You're one helluva climber. Thanks for tailing them."

The tree stands across from the balcony. The doors are open. Heated voices carry from the study within.

"We need to get out of here before we get busted."

But as Joe speaks, Sir Henry Majoure strides onto the balcony, head shaking irritably at the night sky.

Joe doesn't move for fear of being spotted.

Four gentlemen follow Sir Henry, glancing nervously at one another. Joe remembers them being introduced to the Shah of Persia as members of the board of directors of the Crystal Palace Company. Odd time of night to have a board meeting.

Arthur Anderson, one of the directors, is nudged forward by the others. Sir Henry remains with his back to them.

"Sir Henry, please, listen to reason."

"Reason?" snaps Sir Henry. "You forget our reason and purpose here. The Crystal Palace is a place like no other."

"Indeed, and we, the Shadow Board, have tried for three decades to harness her power."

Joe's curious they're talking about the palace as if 'she's' a living thing. And 'Shadow Board' sounded decidedly shady.

"It was a worthy ambition Sir Henry but—"

"Non deficere." Sir Henry looks up at the full moon.

"Never give up," Arthur Anderson translates from Latin.

"My family motto."

"An undoubtedly admirable sentiment ..."

"Sentimentality has no place in my heart. We have yet to unlock her potential, but once the Nineveh Court is complete the gateway between the world of mortals and the world of magic stands before us. All we need is the key—"

"About that," interrupts Arthur Anderson, "and forgive me for bringing up the matter again, however, we really do need to receive your donation to pay for all the work."

Sir Henry slowly turns. His fellow director shrinks back a step. "Are you suggesting I will not honour my pledge?"

Arthur Anderson clears his throat. "Oh, no, of course, no question, the only question is ... when will *you* pay? You know the dire finances the Crystal Palace Company faces."

"You see her as a place of profit, for vulgar frivolities, not as a place of immeasurable possibilities. Make no mistake, the cost of the work will be paid for, and if I must continue the work of the Shadow Board alone, so be it. Goodnight gentlemen."

The four directors are only too glad to hastily make their farewells and leave Sir Henry Majoure gazing at the palace, lost in thoughts. Long fingers pull a glass phial from his waistcoat pocket; without looking, they pluck the cork and bring the dark liquid to Sir Henry's mouth. He drinks. His body shudders. He licks his lips and seems to grow in the moonlight.

"How much longer do we have to stay?" Iris whispers. "Zis is BORING."

"Soon as he goes in, we go." Joe's heart skips a beat. A familiar leering grin joins Sir Henry on the balcony.

Smiler. He reaches into the pocket of his long coat and pulls out a chain; a small circular object dangles at its end.

Joe's gut tells him it's the compass.

Sir Henry holds out his hand. Smiler drops the compass into his palm. Sir Henry holds it up to the moonlight, studying it closely. He snaps his fist around it, turns sharply, and walks through the French doors into the study.

Smiler lingers on the balcony a few seconds longer. For a moment, Joe fears his sneering grin is directed right at him, but Smiler follows Sir Henry into the house, closing the French doors behind him and drawing heavy curtains, sealing the study from Joe's gaze.

"Was zat your compass?"

"Yeah," whispers Joe with certainty. "And I'd never have found it without you, Little Wonder."

Iris shrugs and smirks. "It was nothing."

Now I know where it is, all I have to do is work out how to get it back.

At the foot of the tree, Joe's eyes are drawn back up to the house. From a top floor window is the silhouette of the high-backed wheelchair. Joe shudders, sensing the girl occupying the chair staring through the shadows.

Staring at him.

Yet she makes no attempt to shout or alert the rest of the house. Strange thoughts sweep Joe like a cold wind.

"What's ze matter, Strange Boy?"

"Nothing." Joe pulls his eyes from the window. "Let's go."

But he must return to Rockhills if he's ever to get back the compass and return home.

Chapter 15

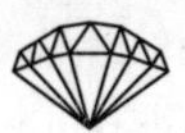

"Meeting Margaret Finch, Queen of the Gypsies, ought a take your mind off things," insists Elias as he leads Joe along a well-worn track downhill of Gipsy Hill Train Station.

Joe kicks a stone into the darkness. "Fingers crossed she'll reveal how I get my compass from Sir Henry." Dad will be climbing the walls by now. He was a total mess after Mum abandoned them. Joe can't do the same thing to him. He *has* to get home.

Smoke rises from the chimneys of brightly painted vardos, caravans parked around the clearing alongside an encampment of ladybird-shaped bender tents circling the leaping fire. Beneath a mighty old oak is the Gipsy House, a rickety wooden cottage where a girl shakes a tambourine and cries, "Queue here for your fortune!"

A crow perches on the veranda watching Joe with eyes of coal.

Joe and Elias aren't the only customers paying a visit on their way back from Brock's fireworks; a well-heeled gentlemen and two ladies discuss their audience with Margaret Finch and wait for the fourth member of their party to emerge from the Gipsy House and reveal his destiny.

"Here's Freddy!" giggle the trio like little kids.

A portly man approaches, nose in the air.

"I received a King of Clubs which apparently makes me a generous man of integrity," Freddy announces.

His gentleman friend scoffs, "Really? I thought the old girl was never wrong."

"It's all tosh if you ask me," Freddy huffs.

The thin lady takes Freddy's arm and pouts. "*I* was told to expect a disappointment."

Freddy puckers up his lips and kisses her hand. "Not with me at your side, my dear."

The quartet burst into titters.

A man approaches, peering up beneath a wide brimmed hat, smiling and shaking a tray of carved objects. "A memento to remember your visit to our Majesty?"

The quartet peer down at the tray. Joe leans behind them to see amulets ornately carved into an oak tree. He's seen one before ....

The seller declares, "An amulet carved of wood from the vicar's oak, a powerful tree of life cut down to make way for the Crystal Palace."

Freddy sniffs. "That makes the wood thirty-five-years old. I'm hardly going to pay for a rotting trinket."

The seller's eyes narrow. "The Vicar's Oak never rots. Its mystical powers still seep into the Norwood Heights. Its wood brings luck to the wearer."

Freddy chortles. "I don't see how a tree can be either mystical or lucky if it allows itself to get chopped down."

Freddy's companions roar.

Joe draws a breath as the seller straightens to his full height, suddenly seeming as tall as the surrounding trees, his flashing eyes cutting short the sniggers. "Mock the power of the Tree of Life at your peril. Many have taken a sharp blade or a sharp tongue against it and found themselves cursed by the Norwood Faeries!"

Freddy gives an audible gulp and shrinks closely to his lady friend. "Now sir, no need for talk of faerie curses, you'll, er, scare the ladies."

"I'm not scared," scoffs his companion as she takes a step away from Freddy. "I'm fascinated." She lifts one of the seller's amulets, the carved oak tree slowly spinning on leather string. "It would make a splendid gift," she says pointedly, prompting Freddy to place a trembling hand in his purse and reluctantly toss a coin to the seller who smiles smugly.

"The charm won't disappointment you, not like people will." The seller winks at Joe and Elias and strolls back to the fire.

"Come along," Freddy says weakly, "or we'll miss our train," and he hurries down the lane on his own, his three friends following on, laughing at him.

Elias snorts dismissively after Freddy and his friends. "Tourists. I'd wager a plate of Aunty Doll's gingerbread biscuits that ole Ned Righteous carved his trinkets this morning from a branch he chopped down yesterday."

But Joe shivers. He's seen those amulets before—worn by Robin Wood who'd kissed it and spoken as if it's his long lost love. Talk of the Tree of Life and mystical faerie powers reminded him of the conversation overheard between Sir Henry and members of the so-called Shadow Board referring to the Crystal Palace as if it were a living thing.

"Don't look so worried," urges Elias as he leads Joe to the front door of Gipsy House. "We ain't tourists, least not me. I'm family."

"Family?"

"Yeah, Norwood Romany blood runs through these veins on my late ma's side, so we can get our fortune told on the house, for free."

Inside the candles flicker. A smoky haze hangs in the air swirling from the long bone pipe smoked by Margaret Finch. She sits, eyes closed, on the floor, chin resting on her knees. She wears a dark purple dress trimmed with white lace and a crimson shawl wrapped around slight shoulders.

Joe jumps as a tiny terrier leaps from her lap, baring its teeth and barking at him viciously.

Elias whispers, "You must smell of cats."

"Funny." But there's nothing amusing about the dog's snarls.

Margaret Finch opens her eyes, takes in Joe and says in a voice as gnarled as her hands, "Merrilles thinks you shouldn't be here." She takes a puff of her pipe. "Perhaps he's right."

Joe's flesh marbles into goosebumps.

The dog's right. I should be a hundred and thirty years in the future.

A short sharp whistle erupts from Margaret Finch's thin lips. The terrier quits snarling and trots to his mistress, curling up at her feet but never taking his eyes off Joe.

Elias, in his element, says with a deep bow; "Your Majesty, Queen of the combined Roma nations, Guardian of the Spirits of the Great North Wood, we've come to hear our fortune, if you please. On the house on account of my ma."

"I know." Her bare arms gesture at two red satin cushions on the floor. "You young gentlemen seek something of great value."

Elias gives Joe a 'told you she could help' wink. Joe cautiously sits.

From nowhere a deck of cards appear in her hands. Her fingers are knotted as the roots of an ancient tree yet cut and shuffle the cards with the ease of a casino croupier from a James Bond movie. She places the deck on the floor, cuts the pack, holding the bottom card for Elias to see.

"Want me to tell you what card it is?"

She chuckles.

"I need no introduction to the King of Hearts." Her eyes close, face lost in thought before pronouncing ominously, "Only a star shall wake you from your dream."

Elias waits for more, but her eyes open as if that's it.

"Huh. Only a star shall wake me from my dream? That's, er, very helpful, Your Majesty, cheers. Now how's about my friend? Don't look so worried Joe, give us a smile."

"Joe knows a smile will be the death of him," says Margaret Finch gently.

Joe's frozen tongue can't ask if that's a premonition or a warning, and Margaret Finch is soon shuffling and cutting the deck. She holds the bottom card out. His eyes widen.

"Well, look at that." Elias whistles. "Snap! King of Hearts, we're like family, me and you!"

Her eyes bore into Joe's face which reddens by the second. Her eyes close. "You feel alone, child."

Her words strike Joe's yearning heart.

She inhales his sadness. "But your future happiness is rooted in your past."

Margaret Finch exhales a smoke ring spiralling above their heads. Her smile leaves Joe suspecting she knows more about their future than she's letting on.

"One last thing, Your Majesty, if you don't mind. My friend could use your magnificent wisdom to foresee how we get back something he's lost. Well, it was nicked truth be told."

Margaret Finch cocks her head to one side studying Joe. The saliva in his mouth disappears. "What you seek will find its way back to its rightful owner."

"Okey-dokey, good news. And, er, any more detail on how that might happen?"

She strokes her chin. "We stand on ancient boundaries between places, between possibilities, between the world of mortals and the world of magic. All we need to unlock them is the key."

Joe instantly recognises words spoken by Robin Wood and Sir Henry.

Elias rotates his hands urging her to elaborate. "and the key is ..."

"Truth. Always the truth."

Chapter 16

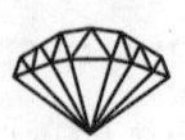

Golden rays of early morning sun catch the glass of the Crystal Palace as Joe and Elias begin their stakeout. The parade comes to life with people and carriages preparing for the day ahead. However, Joe's tired eyes never stray from across the road and the gates of Rockhills.

He'd barely slept last night. Sharing Aunty Doll's parlour with Elias and five of his cousins didn't help. One cousin spent the night babbling in his sleep about sardines, which didn't surprise Joe as they were packed tight as a tin of them. Joe's mind found no rest, imagining Dad and Nan and Uncle Tyrell and Aunty Salma and Aaliyah searching for him. When sleep finally came, his dreams were haunted by the hooded Alone Child dragging him away forever.

"Cheer up, sunshine!" says Elias. "Soon as we've got back your compass, you and me got ourselves the *Queen Marsh Mark Three* to build, and Friday night I reckon I can sneak you in to see Blondin! What's that look for? Thought you'd be up for that."

"Yeah, sounds great." But if their plan works, Joe will be long gone. Elias has everything Joe could want in a friend; funny, ballsy, generous, but out of date by a century-and-a-half.

Joe elbows Elias.

A horse-drawn carriage rides up Rockhills' drive. The pair duck behind a tree. They're a good twenty metres away but don't want to take any chances. Their caution proves wise; driving the carriage is Smiler.

Smiler leaps down from the driver's seat, swinging open the gates. He leads the horse through, closes the gate, climbs back up and cracks his whip sending the horse cantering. The passenger inside the cab has the unmistakeable hawk-like profile of Sir Henry.

"Okey-dokey, coast's clear."

"What if he's taken the compass with him?" ponders Joe.

"Won't know 'til we look. Try having a bit of faith, cos here comes our way in."

A cart piled high with coal approaches, pulled by two enormous Shire horses. Joe recognises the driver from their encounter yesterday in the belly of the palace. Elias skips across the parade as the cart stops in front of Rockhills.

"Morning Mr Grimes, and what a fine one it is!"

Grimes stares down, red-rimmed eyes adding to Joe's nervousness.

"Listen, me Aunty Doll's out of coal so might you oblige us with a small sack? Not for nothing mind, we'll help you on your rounds."

Grimes chews his tongue. Finally, he gives a big sniff. "Open up the gate then."

Elias' grin grows from ear to ear. "Okey-dokey!"

They enter Rockhills.

The cart continues past the grand house to the tradesman's entrance at the back. From here, Joe views the long lawn he'd crept around the night before. A large archery target is positioned in the centre.

Suddenly an arrow flies.

THUD.

Hitting the yellow bulls-eye.

Joe peers around the house; standing on the veranda is the imposing woman who had pushed the girl's wheelchair. With lightning speed she pulls an arrow from the quiver at her side, drawing back her bow and sending it shooting through the air, joining its predecessor in the bulls-eye.

"Come on." Elias grabs Joe's shoulder. "Time to get working."

Joe takes one final glance at the archer, hoping her sport keeps her outside while they take their chance to search inside.

Joe and Elias climb into the grimy cart, shovelling coal into sacks. Coal dust causes Joe to cough. Elias tilts his cap.

"Not used to a bit of hard labour, eh?"

Joe scowls at the truth of Elias' tease. He used to think he was hard done by compared to kids he knew because he helped out at the restaurant, but this really is tough toil. Joe just manages to carry his full sack off the cart. Grimes smokes his pipe at the kitchen door talking to the Housekeeper. She wrings her hands on her apron.

"Latest maid only lasted three days. I tell you, Mr Grimes, it's a wonder I don't pack it in myself, some of the goings on in this house, and I would as well if it weren't for all the happy memories I have serving Mr Paxton when he lived here."

Joe listens intently, a film of sweat glistening on his coal smudged brow. No maid equalled one less person inside the house to catch him hunting for the compass. He wonders what 'strange going's on' might be, but the housekeeper glances around like she's fearing someone might have overheard her words.

Joe and Elias haul their sacks into the kitchen. The aroma of baking bread rumbles Joe's stomach; it feels forever since eating one of Aunty Doll's crunchy gingerbread biscuits for breakfast. Joe just manages to reach the coal store at the back of the kitchen without dropping his sack.

Elias says, "Okey-dokey, now's your chance. I'll drop my next sack, so I have to clear it all up, buy you time to go search upstairs."

"Won't they notice I'm gone?"

"Believe me, I've helped Grimes before. People gossip at him all day, never take a second look at kids like me doing the dirty work. Now go!"

Joe bites his lip, taking the door into the main house.

"Wait!"

"What?"

"Any trouble you shout me, I'm there for you, got it?"

"Got it."

A short flight of steps leads into the main hallway. Joe gets his bearings; he'd seen Sir Henry on the balcony leading from the study on the first floor.

Coast clear, he heads to the majestic staircase. Thankfully, the stairs don't creak as he creeps up. Painted generations of Majoures hang on the wall glaring down at him. Joe approaches what he prays is the right door and listens.

Silence.

Slowly he opens the door, just wide enough to slip into a wood panelled study with walls of books and red leather furniture. A grandiose desk spread with papers sits in front of a large polar bear rug, the skinned animal's mouth in a sharp toothed snarl of justifiable wrath. The French doors onto the balcony at the other side of the study stand open. From the garden beyond arrows THWACK, embedding in the archery target.

With no time to dither, Joe goes for the desk, carefully picking through papers either headed 'South Eastern Railway Company' or 'Crystal Palace Company,' uncovering the surface of the desk. But no compass.

He tries the top drawer.

Locked.

Where would the keys be? Probably Sir Henry's pocket. This is useless. Joe's eyes are drawn to the colossal globe next to the fireplace.

There, dangling off the globe's wooden frame, is the compass!

Finally, a bit of good luck. Joe rushes across the study. Reaches for the compass, but pauses. The glass housing is no longer shattered.

Why had they repaired it?

"Are you here to play?" asks a small voice behind him.

Joe spins around.

In the balcony doorway a red-headed girl watches, her startling green eyes pinning Joe to the spot. She sits in a wheelchair with a back so high it makes her look like a princess on a throne, a thick open book resting on her lap. Joe guesses she's about his age although her body is smaller.

"I, er ..." Joe mumbles, mind racing. "I was just ..."

"Can we guess?" Her voice is as light yet cold as a chill breeze. "You were ... looking for something to steal?" There's no malice or accusation in her tone, just genuine excitement at the guessing game she's begun.

"No," says Joe quickly. "I've *lost* something and, well, this is it." He points at the dangling compass.

"Oh." She frowns like she's disappointed it's game-over.

Joe reaches to grab the compass. To his surprise, the globe spins all by itself taking the compass to the other side.

Must be a gust of wind from the open door, although Joe felt no breeze. He walks around the globe stretching out his hand ....

Again the globe spins taking the compass beyond his reach.

Startled, Joe turns to the girl. Her green eyes almost glow. A small smile spreads at the corners of her mouth.

"Do you like our new game?" she asks as if she'd spun the globe herself.

Which is impossible. Yet a shiver runs through Joe.

"Balanos likes our game, don't you?" She giggles, eyes darting to the corner of the room.

Joe spins, thinking he's missed someone else, but ... no one's there. "Umm. Who's Balanos?"

"Why, Balanos is a faerie. Balanos is my friend. She likes you."

Joe's nan would say this girl is away with the faeries, but his eye catches the shadow of a face in the swirls of the wood panelled wall.

A thankfully familiar voice cries from the study doorway, "Hey! Any luck? We need to scamper, sharpish. Look!"

Elias points at the compass dangling on the globe just beyond Joe's reach.

"Grab it, Old Grimes has finished chin wagging and ..."

Elias's voice trails off as he follows Joe's eyes, noticing the watching girl.

She looks at Elias with curious interest. Joe is struck by her strange lack of surprise at finding two boys breaking into her father's study.

Elias flashes her one of his winning grins. "Sorry to bother you, miss, just been sent to collect a compass to take it for repair, been arranged by the master of the house."

Elias's blagging abilities impress Joe as he reels off with ease the cover story they'd rehearsed. But they never expected the girl to say with genuine admiration, "You're a very good liar."

Elias splutters with indignation, unsure how to take the compliment. "Now hold on right there, miss ..."

But from her piercing stare Elias must realise there's little point continuing the charade. "Fact is that there compass belongs to my mate, alright?"

Elias strides to grab the compass. This time the whole globe spins and shifts on its wheels into the middle of the study so the compass is beyond the grasp of either boy.

"What the ..." blurts Elias, turning to Joe who is equally dumbfounded.

The girl mirrors their confused look and says to Joe, "The compass does not belong to you."

"Yes, it does," Elias retorts.

"No, it doesn't," she insists, but her eyes stay with Joe who struggles to hold her gaze.

"My mate's no liar."

"Oh," she says as if storing information for later. "He just frequents with liars."

"That's slanderous, that is!"

"But you just told us you were taking the compass away for repair.

That was a lie, no?"

"Well, just a tiny porky-pie to get back what belongs to him in the first place."

"But the compass belongs to Father," she says simply, never taking her gaze from Joe as beads of sweat pop onto his forehead.

Elias thumbs his braces. "I think you'll find your freakishly smiling manservant nicked it, gave it your old man. But it's my mate's family heirloom."

An unsettled feeling grips Joe's insides at the direction the conversation is taking; the compass isn't really a family heirloom, but he never imagined having to explain this fact.

"If so, why are Father's initials engraved on the back of the case?"

"Yeah right," scoffs Elias.

"Take a look," invites the girl.

Joe's bad feeling deepens as he slowly reaches again for the compass. This time the globe doesn't turn. Joe takes it in his palm, Elias at his shoulder. They stare at three exquisitely engraved letters. HSM.

The girl breaks the silence. "Henry Sebastian Majoure."

"Co-incidence." But doubt enters Elias's voice. He takes the compass from Joe and rubs the inscription as if hoping the letters might wipe off. "It's yours, ain't it?"

Joe swallows.

"Yeah ... well ... kind of ..." He hesitates under the weight of their stare.

"Kind of?" repeats Elias quietly.

"I found it."

Elias steps away from Joe.

"You 'found' it? So it's no family heirloom?"

"Well no, it's hard to explain ...."

A cloud falls across Elias's face. "Dunno, sounds pretty simple. Which is what you must think I am. Simple. Tricking me to help you nick it."

"I'm not 'nicking' it ...." but Joe hears the uncertainty in his voice.

Elias turns to the girl who studies their fall out with deep curiosity.

"Sincere apologies, miss. I told you my 'mate' is no liar. Turns out *that* was a lie." He angrily dangles the compass at Joe. Elias's voice rises. "And you, suggesting the master sweeps were thieves when all along you're a pickpocket."

Joe looks at the door with alarm. "I'll explain later, but right now we've got to go ...."

Joe steps forward to grab the compass, but Elias shoves his shoulder.

Caught off balance, Joe trips over the head of the polar bear skin rug. Falling backwards, he tries grabbing onto an oil lamp mounted on the wall. But the lamp proves no help at all, the fixture yanking downwards like a lever.

Joe sprawls.

His fist gripping the compass hits the parquet floor first sending shockwaves through his knuckles, the metal housing cracking under his weight and he drops it onto the polar bear rug. Wood rubs against wood as a wall panel next to the oil lamp slides aside. Pulling the oil lamp has revealed a secret compartment. Elias and Joe forget their fight, staring at a toothless human skull leering out among shelves of artefacts with strange symbols and jars filled with floating organs.

On the middle shelf, looped around a vase of entrails, hangs the shattered compass.

Elias and Joe give the compass a double take, looking to the identical compass lying face down on the floor. Elias reaches into the secret compartment, gingerly lifting the shattered compass.

They stare, amazed.

As a result, neither notice until it's too late the towering figure filling the doorway.

Elias spots her first, eyes going straight to the bow and arrow at her side.

She looks from Elias to the secret compartment. However, Joe remains hidden from view on the floor behind a leather-bound armchair. In a heavy Russian accent, she says,

"What do you want with the Cabinet of Marvels?"

Joe expects Elias to point an accusing finger down at him and tell the Russian lady he'd been tricked into robbing them, taken advantage of helping someone he thought was his friend.

Joe wouldn't blame him.

Yet Elias purposefully avoids looking down at Joe, keeping his eyes locked with hers as he moves away from Joe. He can't be certain, and heaven knows he doesn't deserves any more of Elias's aid, but he seems to be keeping her distracted so Joe can escape. How come he's still helping?

"Sorry, lady, never meant to be here, took me a wrong turn."

As he crosses the study, Elias casually lets the shattered compass drop from his hand. It lands cushioned on the furry rug next to its twin compass.

"I'll just get meself back downstairs to Mr Grimes and—"

The lady spreads her fingers in the air. "Silence!"

She's asking the wrong person, but to Joe's surprise Elias gives no quick fire retort. Instead his mouth hangs open. A quizzical look spreads across his face like he's trying to remember the punch-line to a joke.

The girl cries, "Babushka, don't!"

Her dread puts Joe on full alert.

Joe rolls a little to the left where he can see Babushka. As he rolls, he reaches out his hand and grabs his shattered compass, glancing at its broken case before stuffing it into his pocket.

Babushka's eyes burn.

Her fingers wave from side to side as if conducting the air.

Elias's eyes remain fixed on hers, head bobbing in time with her hand like he's listening to music Joe can't hear.

The girl's fear is unmistakable. "Please, don't hurt him!"

This is Joe's chance to break for it. He has the compass, Babushka's focus is on Elias, and if he runs for the door now, he can escape.

Elias's face contorts.

Joe has to help before it's too late.

Crouching against the frame of the giant globe he pushes it with all his might at Babushka. It's heavy, so he's startled when the wheels hurtle at great speed. Joe realises it's not just him moving it; the girl's glowing green eyes are fixed on the globe as it crashes into Babushka knocking her off her feet.

Elias slumps to his knees, trance broken, gripping his head in his hands.

"Leave!" orders the girl. "Now!"

Joe doesn't need telling twice.

Hooking his arm around a trembling Elias, he pulls him up towards the door. Elias shakes his head as if trying to get something out of his skull, but his feet have enough survival instinct to run. They pelt down the stairs.

The girl uses her wheelchair to block the study door, aiding their escape. There's no time to ask why or offer thanks.

They have to get out.

And very nearly make it.

Elias gets back strength in his legs, running on his own alongside Joe through the front door of Rockhills in the direction of Crystal Palace Parade.

Only to find a carriage riding up the driveway.

The driver stares right at them.

Hideous smile spreading.

Chapter 17

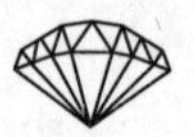

"Back through the house!"

They run for their lives. Joe stays close to Elias in case he stumbles, legs wobbly from Babushka's hypnosis. The lads burst through the back doors onto Rockhills' veranda, aiming to cross the lawn, make for the trees, and escape through the garden wall door leading into Crystal Palace grounds.

THWACK

An arrow flies right between them imbedding in the lawn.

Panicked, Joe and Elias glance back.

Babushka stands on the study balcony readying another arrow in her bow.

The first arrow had been a warning shot. Joe had seen the bulls-eye, if she wanted to hit them, she could. Yet they're only steps away from the cover of the trees. Can they make it without one of them ending up with an arrow wedged between their shoulder blades?

Joe doesn't want to be skewered.

But he can't let it happen to Elias.

So he turns, arms in the air in surrender, holding the compass aloft.

Joe steps to one side to block Babushka's aim and allow Elias to escape, shouting,

"Run!"

Thankfully Elias does what he's told. However, Babushka simply walks along the balcony to change her position, new arrow ready, aimed at Elias.

Joe moves too, hoping to block her aim, praying she won't decide to shoot him first *then* pick off Elias.

Smiler appears through the back door alongside a hulking man who almost fills the veranda, ninety-nine percent knuckles and neck and wearing a bowler hat that makes him look like a gorilla in fancy dress.

All seems lost.

Until Joe notices something Babushka hasn't; the girl wheeling her chair onto the balcony, raising her hands.

Coldness rushes over Joe, he shivers from head to toe.

Babushka stumbles. Her arrow shoots through the air impaling the lawn centimetres from Joe's left foot.

Joe takes his chance.

He charges towards the trees, expecting with each step an arrow will pierce his back. He whoops with joy as he reaches the trees, almost crashing straight into Elias.

"You waited!" Although from Elias's look, it seems he might be waiting just to watch Joe get shot. Joe's desperate to explain himself, but talk will have to wait. Smiler and his Gorilla are running across the lawn after them.

Joe and Elias reach the door in the garden wall leading into the palace grounds.

Joe tries the handle.

Locked.

Elias leans against the wall struggling to breathe and in no condition to climb. Joe tries the handle again, barging his shoulder against the door, grunting, "Open!"

To his amazement, he hears wood splintering.

On his second barge the door flies open.

Joe bundles Elias through, unsure whether to thank his lucky stars or the girl and her strange powers.

He glances at the buckled door.

A faerie's face forms in the grains of wood. The same face he'd seen in the study woodwork. She vanishes with an icy giggle.

They run best as Elias can around the Royal Apartments, passing the first palace visitors of the day.

Joe's thoughts spin. The compass really *did* belong to Sir Henry Majoure, there's every chance he lost it and it lay under the future ruins of the palace only to be discovered decades later by Joe. He wants to tell Elias he hadn't known to whom the compass really belonged, that it seemed simpler to claim it's a family heirloom because the truth was so fantastical Elias would never believe him.

In fact he'd think him crazy.

But as they catch their breath on the North Transept steps Joe decides he'd rather Elias think he's crazy than believe Joe lied and used him.

"Listen, Elias, I've not told you the truth—"

"Save it for someone who cares."

"You won't believe this, but—"

"You're right, I won't so save your stories for the next mug. You got what you wanted. Now we're safe, we're over."

Elias is right to a point. Now he has the compass, Joe can leave these dangers behind, return to his time and their friendship will be over. But he can't stand the idea of leaving with Elias hating him.

"Listen to me, will you? Thing is, I'm not from here. I'm from the ... RUN!"

Smiler and Gorilla chase towards them.

Joe and Elias burst through the North Transept doors. Ahead the Nineveh Court is roped off, awaiting workers to complete its restoration.

Elias staggers. Joe grabs his arm and they duck under the rope. Joe glimpses the inner chamber and the lion skin rug in front of the Temple altar. Hairs on the back of his neck inexplicably rise, telling him something terrible will happen here.

A painter's ladder leans against a colossal winged bull so they climb up to the backside of the Bull where they're perfectly hidden yet able to see out to the Transept below.

Smiler searches among the growing number of visitors. He may have lost the boys, but his grin doesn't falter, making it all the more hideous. The words of Margaret Finch float into Joe's consciousness,

"*Joe knows a smile will be the death of him.*"

Did she foresee Smiler killing him? That prediction seems certain if he catches Joe.

Despite his bulk Gorilla isn't out of breath from the chase. Smiler gestures they should split up and sweep south through the palace, away from the Nineveh Court.

Joe takes a deep breath.

Without looking at Elias he says, "Listen, what I was trying to tell you is ... What if I was to tell you … I'm from the future?"

"The future?"

"The future."

"I'd tell you to sod off."

"It sounds crazy but this compass brought me to the past. I never knew there was another compass, guess it must be the same compass only this compass is the future one and the other one is the past one and now I've brought them together probably mucking up the time space continuum, but that's why I need it, to get me home and that's why I couldn't tell you and that's why we haven't stolen it. Technically."

Elias stares. "You are so full of crap it's coming out your ears."

"Elias—"

"Shut up."

"But—"

"SHUT UP!" Shouting takes everything out of Elias. He swallows hard, blue eyes distant.

"You okay?"

"Don't you worry about me. Let's go."

Joe climbs down the ladder, wondering as he waits at the bottom what he can say to make things better, so they won't be saying goodbye like this.

Elias climbs down slowly as if carrying a great weight. His foot misses a rung. Elias just manages not to fall.

"You okay?"

"I'm fine!" But Elias's eyes flutter. To Joe's horror his hands slip away from the rung.

Like a nightmare everything happens in slow motion yet Joe can do nothing to help.

Elias goes limp.

Falling three meters onto a pile of dust sheets.

Despite the soft landing Elias lies there.

Still.

Silent.

Joe kneels beside him. Elias's eyelids are open just enough to see eyeballs racing in their sockets.

Joe's first-aid badge training kicks in, mind flying through steps for helping someone unconscious. But it's one thing to give CPR to a dummy, quite another doing it for real.

"Can you hear me? Elias, it's Joe, can you hear me?" Joe taps his shoulder for a reaction.

Nothing.

Thankfully he feels Elias's breath on his cheek. But placing his hands on Elias's chest, he counts his breaths at a rate of twenty per ten seconds.

Way too fast. He's hyperventilating.

Should Joe move Elias into the recovery position to help him breathe?

But he'd fallen. You shouldn't move the patient in case they've suffered a spinal injury.

Yet Elias had a soft landing on the dust sheets and whatever's wrong started before he fell off the ladder.

Joe runs his fingers down the back of Elias's head, back and legs, checking his fingers for blood, uttering reassurances he doesn't feel. "You're gonna be alright, okay? Don't worry, Elias. I'm here."

Rapid breaths become barely discernible. Joe's about to move him into the recovery position when a voice yells,

"Hey! What's going on, ducky?" Two ladies wearing overalls stare at them, carrying a box of paints and brushes to add final finishing touches to the court.

"He fell. He needs help."

One immediately runs out of the court to the Transept crying, "Help! Is there a doctor? We need a doctor!"

The other says, "You shouldn't be here."

The same words spoken by Margaret Finch. A truth that cuts Joe to the bone.

Me being here caused this ...

A doctor with a top hat and brisk manner hurries into the Court. "Step aside, boy, you've done enough."

Joe forces his legs to stand, making way for the doctor to kneel.

"Boy! Can you hear me, boy?" the doctor asks.

"His name's Elias," says Joe hotly.

The doctor waves Joe away. "I need space."

"Come on, ducky." The lady wearing a white turban and red lipstick grabs Joe's collar leading him firmly out to the rope cordon. A small crowd gathers peering around the Bulls. As more people are drawn by the commotion, a great looming bowler hat-ed figure heads Joe's way.

If Gorilla's coming, Smiler won't be far behind.

Stay and Joe falls into their hands, loses the compass, and is stuck in the past forever.

Run and he'll draw them away from Elias and escape to his own time. There's nothing else Joe can do for him now.

He allows himself one last glance at his friend lying motionless on the floor of the Nineveh Court, before running for the maze.

Chapter 18

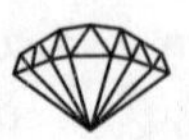

The closer Joe gets to the maze, the louder the voice in his head grows,

It won't work. You're stuck here for the rest of your life.

If Smiler and Gorilla trap him in the maze before he can make the compass work, the rest of his life won't be very long. Best bet is to hide until the coast is clear. Joe veers away from the maze, taking the left-hand path winding around the upper lake to the cricket ground at the bottom of the palace gardens.

A match is underway. Players in crisp cricket whites are watched by a hundred-strong crowd eager to see the star attraction, a big man with a big beard bowling at the stumps. Joe immediately recognises W. G. Grace who gives a hearty laugh as the opposition batsman waits apprehensively at the wicket. With movements befitting his name, Grace runs to the line, casting the ball spinning through the air, past the batsman. Stumps tumble to cheers.

Joe's heart also cheers upon recognising one of the faces sat on the boundary line.

Bertie!

With no sign of his pursuers, Joe weaves through the watching crowd, hoping to catch his breath and catch up with Bertie before doubling back to the maze. Oblivious of the game, Bertie furiously writes in his notebook, closing it protectively when he senses company.

"Joe!" Bertie cries as if greeting his oldest friend.

Joe crouches down on the grass hiding from sight. "Don't get up."

"You look terrible if you don't mind me saying." Bertie spots the compass in Joe's hand. "Ah, you found it, good show! I feared that blue-eyed fellow tricked you and swiped it. Although, I'm a little surprised you didn't see fit to come and tell a chap. I waited an age for you."

"Really sorry, something happened. Lots of things ..." Joe shudders, picturing Elias lying on the floor of the Nineveh Court.

Bertie leans in close. "You can confide in me."

Joe gives a weak smile but shakes his head. "What you don't know won't hurt you."

"Of course, no need to explain right away, old chap. Here, this might cheer you up though, been carrying it around certain we'd meet again." Bertie points at a large carpet bag next to him with a familiar object sticking out one end.

"My skateboard!"

"Skate-board." Bertie tries out the word as he hands it over. "And, er, hope you don't mind, but Father took the liberty of fixing the wheel. He's a gardener by trade and enjoys tinkering and was most impressed at the welding and this material around the wheel, said he'd never seen anything like it before."

Nobody will for a good few decades until they invent plastic. Joe spins the wheels. This definitely hadn't been how he imagined Skull Rider getting repaired. He longs for the time that had been the most important thing in his life.

"Tell him thanks."

"You can tell Father yourself when the cricket breaks for tea. Look! There!"

Joe stiffens, alert, expecting Smiler and Gorilla. Instead, Bertie points at a slim man with a round face taking up the bat.

"That's Father. Yesterday he was only two away from a century *and* caught out two London County Cricket Club players. And look! Bowling against him is the doctor.

"The 'Doctor?'" Joe repeats, thinking of his fellow time-traveller, Dr Who.

"W. G. Grace's nickname. He's a doctor you see, as is his teammate

Dr Doyle who took care of my leg."

Bertie points at a fielder in a straw boater and a long moustache waxed at the ends.

W. G. Grace tosses the ball up and down. Just as Bertie's father steels himself for the bowl, Joe spots two familiar figures stalking through the crowd focusing on the spectators rather than the game.

Joe jumps up.

"What's the matter?"

"Sorry," says Joe, eyes on Smiler and Gorilla.

"Where are you going *now*?"

At least it's only Bertie's feelings that'll get hurt. Joe can't risk anyone else harmed on his account.

Smiler sets eyes on Joe. His smile widens.

Joe cuts through the crowd to get distance between them and Bertie. He never sees W. G. Grace bowl the ball. Nor registers the WHACK as Bertie's father hits it for six. Or the 'ooos' of the crowd as the ball sails over the pitch, crossing the boundary line.

The first moment Joe's aware is when the ball strikes him on the side of the head.

Then he's aware of nothing at all.

"Hello? Can you hear me?"

Joe's head swims up from a deep long dream towards the soothing Scottish voice.

"Had yourself a nasty knock. Thought we'd lost you for a moment."

Joe tries unpeeling his eyelids. His dream felt so real; he'd been back in Victorian times and met the Queen of the Gypsies and the Great Blondin and the Shah of Persia ....

Joe finds himself on a chaise lounge in the parlour of a high-ceilinged room looking into the face of a man dressed in white with a long moustache waxed at the ends.

His dream *is* real.

Joe tries leaping up, a damp cloth falling from his head.

"Woah there, everything's alright."

No, everything's NOT alright, everything is a hundred and thirty years away from alright ....

"My name's Dr Doyle and you're quite safe." He eases Joe back down and places the cold cloth on his forehead.

Memories of Smiler and Gorilla flood back. Joe's hands urgently feel his pockets.

"The compass! I've lost it!"

Again Joe tries sitting up sending pain splitting through his head. His alarm eases on hearing a familiar voice, "Have no fear old chap, I have it!"

Bertie crosses the room with a beam on his face and the compass in his hand. "I'd never let those ruffians get their hands on your compass."

Joe wants to leap up and hug Bertie, but there's a strong chance his head will explode. Bertie places the compass in his palm.

"What happened?"

"Well!" Bertie plonks down on the arm of the chaise lounge. "Father hit a six off the doctor's bowl, which incidentally is possibly the highlight of his cricketing career, but the six hit you and you were out cold. I rushed to your aid, but a sinister pair scurried over claiming you're a thief and the compass belongs to their master. Well," Bertie angles his bowler hat, "I defended you, called them liars, and when they tried searching your pockets I bellowed, 'Stop! Help!' They wanted to take the compass and you! But Dr Doyle and Dr Grace joined me in your defence, insisting you be taken to Dr Grace's house for treatment. That's where you've been for the past two hours, two streets away from the Crystal Palace gardens, out like a light."

Dr Doyle chuckles. "You tell a good story, young Wells."

Bertie blushes. "An honour coming from you Dr Doyle. Dr Doyle is not only a doctor, Joe. He's also an author."

Dr Doyle gives a modest shrug. "Well, I'm hoping my writing

career is more successful than my medical career. Or my cricketing for that matter, I don't think I'll be missed today."

"Personally, I thought your story about the private detective, Sherlock Holmes, was first rate."

Joe's head takes another spin as he realises who's holding a cold compress to his head.

"You're Arthur Conan Doyle? Creator of *Sherlock*? I love that show."

"Show?" replies a bemused Dr Doyle. "It's only one short story at the moment."

"Don't worry, Dr Doyle," whispers Bertie. "My friend said odd things like that even before he was hit by a cricket ball."

Joe manages a laugh, glad for the cover. When driving with Nan on shopping trips to Croydon's Whitgift Centre, she'd point out a large house in South Norwood where a blue plaque announced it as Arthur Conan Doyle's former home. Nan would have a fit if Joe ever gets to tell her not only did he meet but was treated by the creator of the world's most famous fictional detective.

But first Joe has to get back to the maze. The longer he stays, the more he risks something else happening to him, the compass, or those around him.

"That compass is important to you," says Dr Doyle, noting the way Joe grips it. He gives Joe a strange look. "Those men who tried to take it from you told me who they work for. They hoped it might impress or intimidate me into handing it over, handing you over. However, I happen to know Sir Henry Majoure and his name made me trust them even less. Sir Henry is not someone to cross lightly. What's your connection?"

"It's a long story," Joe says in a voice he hopes makes clear he doesn't want to share it. Yet at the same time he wants to ask Dr Doyle what he knows about Sir Henry, his strange daughter and deadly household.

However Bertie jumps in. "You should have seen Dr Doyle tell those villains where to go! I thought that huge fellow was going to grab you and be off until W. G. Grace came over with a cricket bat, at which point I'd like to have seen them try."

"Can't abide rudeness!" a voice booms and W. G. Grace strides into the parlour, cricket bat in hand. He looks down at Joe. "How's our patient? I'm missing cheese and cucumber sandwiches and the most delectable pork pies for you, young man, so you'd better not be dead."

Dr Doyle raises an eyebrow at the champion cricketer's substantial waistline. "I think you could easily miss a few pork pies."

W. G. Grace feigns a look of outrage. "That your medical opinion, Doyle? In which case your bedside manner is as poor as your fielding, and I shall seek comfort in the pantry where I keep my own supply of pork pies. I'm sure I've enough spare to feed our young friends. Care to join me, Doyle, and I'll tell you how the morning play progressed. There won't be much play this afternoon, I'll be bound. A summer storm's brewing."

The two doctors famed for skills other than their medical abilities leave Joe and Bertie alone.

Joe takes his friends arm. "I can't stay here."

"Nonsense, you need to rest. That was a terrible knock from a fabulous hit by Father—"

"Those men will be back."

"And we'll send them packing again."

"But this compass ..." Joe hesitates, not wanting to lie to Bertie after what it had done to his friendship with Elias, but nor can he expect Bertie to understand or believe the truth.

"I need to get to the maze." Joe pulls himself upright, trying to ignore his banging head.

"Joe, you're really in no state to try and find your way through a maze ...."

"Bertie, please, I have to get to the maze."

Bertie rubs the arm of his crutch, grips it firmly and rises. "I disagree with your course of action, but I'll defend your right to take it. Furthermore, you have my aid."

CHAPTER 19

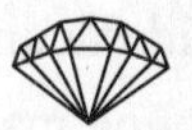

Joe stands under a tree, staring into the empty maze. The summer storm has sent visitors running for the palace's restaurants and cafes. Joe longs to go back to the palace himself and find out how Elias is, but this could be his only chance to get home. Plus, Smiler and Gorilla could still be on the hunt.

Bertie shuffles unhappily. "Keep my handkerchief, use it as a cold compress on your bump. I just wish you could see your way clear to explain what it is you're doing."

"I wish I could. Bertie ..."

"Yes?"

"There's something else I need to ask you to do for me."

"If I can, I will, old chap."

"Elias, who helped me find the compass, he got hurt pretty bad. Please can you ask Dr Doyle to see how he's doing? He lives in Norwood New Town at his Aunty Doll's house on Great Eagle Street."

Bertie places his hand on his chest. "I swear it."

"And tell him ... Joe says sorry. And tell him thanks."

"Joe, it's no good. I have to say I'm immeasurably worried about you."

"Don't be." Joe conjures up a reassuring smile and grips the compass. "If this works, I'll be fine."

Bertie's mouth opens to ask a question but closes. Joe imagines he knows he'll get no straight answer. Instead, Bertie reaches inside his pocket, pulling out a carefully rolled poster. Keeping it close to his body to avoid raindrops, he reveals Blondin's signature. "Here, old chap, for you."

"No, it's yours. Blondin signed your name on it."

"Yes, well, keep it and remember me and our little adventure together, because something tells me I'm not going to see you again."

"Thank you, Bertie. Trust me, I will never forget you or our 'adventure.' Now get going before you drown."

Bertie holds his hand out. Joe shakes it and watches him hobble into the downpour, wishing he could stuff him into a pocket too; he could do with a friend like Bertie back home. With one last look through the driving rain at the Crystal Palace looming above the trees, Joe enters the maze.

Taking its twists and turns, repeating under his breath,

"Follow—in—their—footsteps ....

Pause—here—a—while.

Listen—to—the—echoes

Past, present, future."

Joe waits for the shattered compass needle to start spinning.

Has he got the words right?

Thinking hard Joe repeats the phrases.

The shattered compass remains still. The clouds above show no sign of reversing, intent instead on teeming down on him.

"Come on! Work! Take me home!"

He shakes the compass, staring hard in the hope he might will it to work. But there's something different; the shattered glass has none of his dried blood between its cracks from where he'd cut his hand first discovering it.

Realisation drenches him like rain.

This is the wrong compass.

The screen is shattered, sure, but that must've happened when it fell to the floor in the study at Rockhills. He grabbed what he *thought* was the shattered compass, but instead he'd taken its twin, the one from *this* era, one evidently without any powers to transport him between times. *That* shattered compass must still be in the hands of Sir Henry

Majoure.

Joe staggers through the maze. Lost in every sense, getting soaked to the skin until finally he reaches the entrance. He sinks to the ground under the perimeter of trees. Their branches shield him from the downpour, but nothing can shield him from his mounting sense of doom.

Time passes. Rain falls. His thoughts get no closer to working out a way of getting back the right compass without getting himself captured and most likely killed by a member of Sir Henry's homicidal household.

Dad will be worried sick. What if he *is* sick? What if the hospital results are bad and Joe's not there for him? For Lauren? For Nan?

Weariness takes hold. He closes his eyes and slips into a restless slumber where a ghostly child with a face etched with scars haunts his sleep threatening to break through his dream and carry him away. The Alone Child whispers, *Come with me, Joe .... See what might be ....*

Joe's eyes open. He's standing at the gate of the maze.

A jogger passes plugged into headphones, a suit walks and talks into his mobile, a helicopter buzzes overhead.

Is this a dream?

Had he returned to his own time?

Only ...

Looming ahead stands the Crystal Palace. Instead of undergrowth and trees rising from where it burned to the ground, the palace remains.

Yet the more Joe stares, the more he's aware it's different to the Victorian original he'd explored from belly to rooftop. The edges of the palace are hard, glass tinted grey. It's like a Father Christmas outfit from a pound shop where the colours and design are accurate, but it's all wrong, has none of the magic of the real thing. What's more, a high concrete wall now runs in line with the Italian terrace dividing the park in two.

A sliver of fear slides deep inside Joe. There had been many plans over the years to rebuild the Crystal Palace as a cinema and shopping complex or hotel. Nan campaigned against all of them on the grounds they'd carve a huge chunk of the park into private hands and result in an ugly imitation of the original. Yet here stands a 'Crystal Palace,' one most definitely not here when Joe left.

"Excuse me!" He rushes up to a lady walking her dog, a small border terrier who growls at Joe, dropping onto its haunches ready to attack.

"Jasper, calm down."

"Sorry, can you tell me the date?"

"July thirtieth. Jasper, stop."

The same day Joe had left. But ...

"What year?"

She now eyes Joe with suspicion equal to Jasper's, tells him the date and quickly drags the barking Jasper away.

It's the same date of the same year he'd left. So what on Earth is going on?

Joe hurries along the concrete wall heading for the Triangle and the familiar comforting surroundings of Paradise. Dad will help make sense of it all.

Workers scrub red graffiti from the wall. They're flanked by two guards in peaked caps carrying big machine guns and insignias on their uniforms with the words; 'Crystal Palace Company.'

Enough graffiti remains to make out, "PRESIDENT MAJOURE SUCKS ..."

What President Majoure was sucking had already been scrubbed, but what Joe really wants to know is could 'President Majoure' be Sir Henry Majoure? Impossible, he'd be pushing two hundred years old ....

Guards glare as if Joe might be responsible for the defamation so he scurries on in search of something to explain all this. His heart performs a triple somersault when he recognises a girl walking ahead.

Aaliyah!

Joe breaks into a run calling her name. Aaliyah turns with alarm, but Joe is already wrapping his arms around her in a heartfelt hug.

Joy swiftly turns to pain as she knees him in his groin.

Joe sinks, gasping for breath. Aaliyah steps back into a karate poise. It *had* been a few years since they'd expressed their fondness for each other physically, but her reaction is beyond extreme. Joe manages to wheeze out, "What d'ya do that for?"

"Why did you hug me?"

"Sorry. I've just ... You've no idea what I've been through."

"Don't know, don't care, you little freak. Explain how you know my name?"

"Aaliyah, this isn't funny."

"No, you're damned right, you little freak."

"Stop calling me that! It's me. Joe."

Aaliyah softens a notch. "Joe who?"

"Joe Cook! Your cousin!"

"My *cousin?*" Aaliyah's nose wrinkles. "Hmm, well, let's see, firstly I don't have a cousin, secondly if I did, I can't see how he'd be white, and thirdly, I really don't have time for this stupidness."

"No, wait, we're not blood cousins but we've known each other forever. Aunty Salma, Uncle Tyrell, your mum and dad—"

"I know who my mum and dad are. Question is how do you? Are you a stalker?"

"No!" howls Joe. "I'm Joe, my dad runs the Paradise Restaurant with your parents."

"Wrong answer. My parents do not run a restaurant and come near me again you'll be eating pepper spray."

Things only get worse when Joe reaches the Triangle, transformed from a hodgepodge of independent shops and fading Victorian facades into rising glass and steel office towers reaching up to the skies, retail units on ground level as identical as the suits buzzing in and out on lunch break. It's as if the suburban outpost Joe had grown up in had become the centre of the metropolis.

Joe runs fast and hard to Paradise.

He rubs his eyes hoping it'll change what he finds.

Where the restaurant should be stands a chrome characterless coffee shop.

No. This can't be happening.

Where's my family?

Where's our restaurant?

Where's my life?

Joe runs fast and hard along Church Road towards his flat which occupies the top corner of a converted Victorian villa. Joe grips onto the bars of a high iron gate not there before, staring up at plush curtains where rickety blinds to his bedroom should be— no multiple doorbells or rows of wheelie bins, just a single bell and a Porsche watched by CCTV cameras.

Joe speeds on his skateboard down Sylvan Hill, but the estate where Nan lives is a complex of flash apartments.

Everything's changed. Everyone's gone.

Joe's numb legs take him back to the Triangle. Tears well up. He quickly wipes them away when he spots a shuffling shaggy-haired figure dragging his shopping basket of trinkets onto Haynes Lane, looking as out of place here as Joe felt.

Robin Wood!

Joe follows; unbelievably amid all the gleaming new buildings the ramshackle Collectors Market still stands.

Joe edges warily into the alleyway.

Its resident robin redbreast pops up and dances on a teacup chirping at Joe, his song making no more sense than this strange world.

The upstairs market remains filled floor to ceiling with curiosities. A vinyl record hisses from the trumpet of an old Gramophone and a singer croons above a crackling orchestra;

"For I'm dancing with tears in my eyes
Cos the girl in my arms isn't you ..."

It's the same tune playing when Joe first visited Robin Wood. There in his booth sits the man himself wearing his enormous woolly hat, whistling and swaying to the music. Without looking up he says, "You took your time."

"What the hell's going on?" splutters Joe (although 'hell' is not the word he uses). "Where's my family? Where's our restaurant?"

Robin Wood rubs a silver pot with lint.

Joe throws his skateboard clattering onto the floor to get his attention.

"Hello? Tell me where to find them!"

Robin Wood finally peers over the top of his glasses.

"You *can't* find them."

"I can. I will!"

"You can't. You won't. You don't exist. Nor do they."

"What ... but I'm *here*." Joe waves his arms in the air as proof.

"But you don't *belong* here, do you?"

"What?!'

Robin Wood twirls his nose hair in time to the music. "We stand on ancient boundaries between places, between possibilities, between the world of mortals and the world of magic. You crossed those boundaries."

"What does that even *mean*?" A thought cuts through his confusion. "*You've* done this!" shouts Joe, unsure what 'this' is but certain Robin Wood is behind it.

"Me?" Robin Wood shakes his shaggy head. "Nooooo, no, no. I did nothing, it's not true, you're mistaken, she's mistaken."

"She who?!"

Robin Wood lifts the wooden amulet worn around his neck, ornately carved into the shape of an oak tree. He kisses it gently, saying softly, "Balanos, my long lost faerie love ..."

"I've seen that amulet before …."

"Tell her it's not my fault." His watery eyes turn to Joe. "*You* did this."

"WHAT?!"

"These shadows of the future happen cos of what you did in the past. You broke your line so when you think about it, really, you could say it's all *your* fault."

"*My* fault?"

"Yes!" The notion he's not responsible prompts Robin Wood to leap up and dance a jig, waving jazz–hands at Joe.

"Stop dancing, tell me how to fix this!"

Robin Wood sticks out his bottom lip as if answers might be found there. Just as he's about to speak heavy footsteps from numerous boots stomp in the alleyway.

Robin sighs.

"Your future happiness is rooted in your past." With a small wave he says, "Time's up. Ta ta."

Joe leaps up—he doesn't need spider senses to tell him to hide.

Fortunately, Haynes Lane Market isn't short of options. As he ducks behind a suit of armour, men thunder in, wearing uniforms emblazoned with Crystal Palace Company insignias. They brandish long riot sticks and without hesitation set about smashing the place apart.

Robin Wood sits swaying, suddenly seeming very small and old as he's showered with shattered china and plastic. Sticks annihilate the gramophone, so Robin Wood quietly picks up the song.

"For I'm dancing with tears in my eyes
Coz the girl in my arms isn't you …."

Joe needs to get out before the sticks find his hiding place. He uses the chaos to dive for the door and doesn't stop running until he reaches the maze.

The Alone Child waits, scarred face hidden by his hood, whispering,

Reverse what we did or we are condemned to wander ....

Joe falls to his knees, giving in to the soft embrace of the soil.

Joe's eyes snap open. He's curled up under a tree, soaked, bones aching, alone. The original Crystal Palace looms ahead. He's woken from a nightmare where he doesn't exist to find himself back in his Victorian nightmare.

It's late in the day and the heavens have taken a break from weeping. With no idea how to get the shattered compass back, Joe resolves to concentrate on the other thing preying on his mind: Elias.

Chapter 20

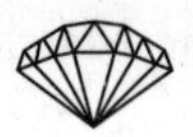

Norwood New Town looms ahead. Joe's speedy pace to reunite with Elias slows; what if Elias still hates him for not being honest about the shattered compass' origins? What if he's really badly hurt?

Kids jump puddles by the New Town wall. Joe recognises them from chasing The *Queen Marsh* on their Big Eagle Run. They spot Joe, stop and stare. He tentatively asks, "Do you know if Elias is home?"

"My ma says he's never coming home."

"What ... what do you mean?"

"I mean he's in hospital. Close to death as he can be, so my ma says."

She reveals Elias has been taken to Norwood Cottage Hospital on Hermitage Road, just the other side of Norwood New Town. It's a red-brick building built two years earlier in the style of a cottage to provide treatment to the folks of Norwood with a single ward of eight beds.

Joe's hand hovers on the doorknob, afraid of what he'll find inside. Crows caw wildly on the roof —a flock is called a 'murder of crows' and the way they look at Joe with oily eyes he understands why. Finally, he summons the will to enter.

The ward is stark and clean. Joe finds his friend in the corner bed. The low sun shines through a window giving Elias's face a faint glow, as if its rays are trying to bring life back to his deathly pale complexion.

At his bedside sits Catherine Marsh, dubbed 'Queen of New Town' by Elias. At her side stands an elegantly dressed gentleman Joe hasn't seen before.

Joe stares until a sharp voice from behind makes him jump.

"If you've come to visit the Cook boy, I've already told half of

Norwood New Town to stay in New Town and don't crowd up my ward." Matron has appeared from the back office with a tray of food for an elderly patient.

Her words attract Catherine Marsh's attention; she eyes Joe with recognition and suspicion but says, "Matron, will you kindly make an exception for this young man who *doesn't* reside in New Town."

She speaks as one who knows every local and with sufficient authority for Matron to grudgingly say, "I'll make an exception for you, Miss Marsh. Well, you going to see him or what?"

'Or what' not being an option, Joe approaches Elias's bed with legs of lead. Unable to look at his silent features any longer Joe turns to the dapper gentlemen.

"How ... how is he?"

The gentleman watches Joe with sharp eyes and gives a warm apologetic smile, replying in an American accent, "I'm no doctor, young fellow."

His voice sounds familiar, but Joe can't quite place it.

"Mr Judson heard about Elias's 'accident.'" Catherine Marsh places such a heavy emphasis on 'accident,' Joe half expects her to wave her middle fingers in mock averted commas as Aaliyah infuriatingly does.

"I'd be happy to pay for any treatment your friend needs, that much I can promise," adds the American.

"Your generosity does your country proud. A Dr Doyle has been in attendance."

"Dr Doyle?" interrupts Joe. Of course Bertie wouldn't let him down.

"You know him?" Catherine Marsh's eyebrows raise.

"Yeah, he, well he treated me, so I asked him to look on Elias."

Her steely gaze reappraises Joe while the American nods respectfully and says, "Seems Elias has three guardian angels looking over him."

Joe twists abruptly at the sound of Aunty Doll's voice. "You've got a nerve coming here."

Her face is anxious and angry in equal measure as she storms down the aisle at Joe.

"Sorry, I ... I wanted to see how Elias is."

"Now you've seen, are you happy? You satisfied with what you done? It's not enough my nephew may never wake up. If he does, I've been told he's got handcuffs to look forward to and accusations of house breaking and, heaven only knows, transportation to Australia."

"Not while I have breath in my body to vouch for his character," says Catherine Marsh firmly.

Aunty Doll shakes her head.

"I don't doubt you'd help, Miss Marsh, but life has taught me to expect the worse cos more likely than not that's what'll happen. He was always a strong-willed child, Lord knows I tried to beat that out of him, but no matter how tough times got he was never, ever, a beggar nor a thief." She wipes an angry tear. "He had a good job at the palace, but you think they'll have him back? What will my family do without the food Elias brings home? What will we do if Elias never ... if he never ..."

She swallows the emotions pouring out and adjusts her pinafore as if that might put things straight.

Joe stares at the floor, wishing it would open up, wishing he could swap places with Elias not just because he'd be away from Aunty Doll's onslaught but because he deserves to be where he lay.

"Ma'am," the American says with a formal bow. "My name is Raymond Judson from New York City. I've seen many young men like Elias go astray yet their hearts remain true."

"Amen," Catherine Marsh says quietly.

"So long as my business keeps me residing in the village of Clapham I will, with your permission, also make my business the welfare of your family and see Elias returned to work. Sir Henry Majoure happens to be an acquaintance. Any influence I have, I'll use to ask for clemency, that much I can promise. If the boy wakes up here's my card."

Joe stiffens.

It hits him where he's heard the American's voice before ...

In the under-floor ...

"Let's just say when the shah is looking up, we'll make the switch right under his nose ...."

... and behind the curtains...

"Excuse us little lady, did you happen to see two young fella's run through here ...?"

The same American he overheard plotting with Smiler to steal the Star of Nimrod, the unseen accomplice chasing Joe and Elias into the Crystal Palace School of Music. Here, masquerading as a concerned citizen. Joe's realisation must be written all over his face because Judson's eyes narrow. He gives Joe a wink.

Aunty Doll points at Joe. "As for you, I'm half minded to call the police though I'm sure Elias would never forgive me."

"I don't think the police need be bothered," soothes the American.

I bet you don't.

"You are a good man," declares Catherine Marsh.

The American shakes his head and says with a wry smile, "Oh believe me, madam, the good I do can scarcely dint the wrong. Young fellow." He addresses Joe with a twinkle, "I believe I've outstayed my welcome, and fear you are not welcome at all, so shall we?"

He gestures towards the door.

Joe looks from Aunty Doll to Catherine Marsh, desperate to tell them who this American is, what he's done, tell them he's not to be trusted.

But they'd never believe him.

Leaving with this man places Joe in certain danger, but once again he finds himself helpless. Taking one last look at his silent friend, he follows the American outside.

They stand on the steps of Cottage Hospital, Joe ready to run when the American makes his move. However, Judson simply strolls over to a chestnut horse tethered to the hospital fence.

The horse raises her head and snorts at her master who gives her a gentle rub and a treat from his pocket. As Judson untethers the horse's reins he says in casual conversation, "I am sorry about your friend. Truly. If he wakes, he'll be taken care of, that much I can promise."

Joe's rising anger overtakes any rational thought of running.

"Take care of him?" Joe's seen enough gangster movies to know when someone gets 'taken care of' it involves flowers and funerals. "Yeah, I bet, just like I bet you plan to 'take care' of me too."

The American frowns at Joe who's too angry to realise he will never have seen a gangster movie.

"Well, actually, yes, that was my plan."

Judson reaches into his coat.

Joe freezes anticipating a knife or a gun. Even if he flees, the American could easily mount his horse and run him down.

The American gives a sardonic smile.

"A man with brains has no right to carry firearms. There is always a way, a better way, by the quick exercise of the brain."

To Joe's surprise, he pulls out a heavy silk purse and fills his palm with coins.

"Here. For your troubles."

Joe stares at Judson's outstretched hand.

"I don't want your money. I want my friend back. I want my life back."

Joe is further surprised when the American gives a sad nod of seemingly genuine empathy. "You've got spirit kid. I admire that."

Joe's look tells him he wants his admiration even less than he wants his money. This has the intended impact; Judson sighs and pours the coins back into his purse.

"I am sorry about your friend. That should never have happened. Nobody should ever get hurt."

He steps closer to Joe who takes a step back, still expecting violence. The American is only a little taller than Joe and they stand for a moment, eye to eye.

Joe flinches as the American grabs his wrist and gives him his card.

"You change your mind, you need anything, this is where you can find me. I'll do what I can to keep you from harm, that much I can promise, but I'll be honest, young fella ..."

Joe gives a scathing snort at the idea this lying thief could be honest.

The American chuckles, but says in a low serious voice, "You need to watch your back. Not everyone you've crossed will be as obliging."

Judson saunters to his horse and mounts with expertise.

"Wait!" Joe takes bewildered steps towards Judson. "Why are you just letting me go?"

Judson smiles down at him.

"Why, you want me to whip you away and hand you over to Sir Henry's goons? Or silence you myself with violence rather than persuasion? Not my style. Besides, and don't take this the wrong way young fella, but you're no threat. You're just a kid. What can you possibly do?"

He winks at Joe, tips his hat, and rides up Central Hill, leaving Joe utterly lost and totally helpless.

Chapter 21

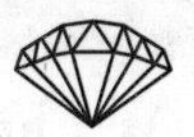

Joe huddles in the doorway of a closed Triangle grocer's shop. Carriage wheels splash him with mud.

Joe doesn't care. He's already soaked to his skeleton. He grips his skateboard. Lose this connection with his old reality, he'll lose his mind. People hurry about their end-of-day business, hats down, collars up. None pay attention to a street urchin. The only people who want Joe are the police who'll throw him in a cell and Sir Henry's goons who want him dead.

The summer downpour returned when Joe left Cottage Hospital to sneak back into the Crystal Palace grounds in the hope of locating Bertie, only to find the cricket field abandoned, rain stopped play. Joe considers walking to Bromley to search out the sports shop run by Bertie's family, but he's only ever driven to Bromley with Dad to go to the swimming pool with the water slides. He's no hope of finding his way on foot in the rain through strange country lanes.

Memories from a different life. A lost life.

Joe loses track of time. A dozen children under umbrellas parade in single file along Westow Street, tapping the ground with canes. A number of them carry instrument cases. Some wear sunglasses despite the dusk. Joe realises they're blind and notices a familiar face—Winnie, the pianist who saved them from Smiler after gate-crashing her rehearsal.

Even though they'd only spoken for a few short minutes, she'd helped him before. Would she again?

The group troop past Joe's doorway, Winnie at the rear. The leader halts opposite an impressive building on the site where Sainsbury's stands in Joe's time. Above the main entrance a sign says, The Royal Normal Academy of the Blind.

The student leading the group listens for traffic. There are no zebra crossings or lights to stop passing carts and cabs. Joe rises to help but soon realises there's no need. As a break in the traffic emerges the group leader begins crossing the road, the others following, linking hands with the person in front.

Joe darts after them, almost getting run over by a drover's cart.

As the group troop up the academy steps, Joe catches up with Winnie. But what should he say to her? In the end he's saved the bother because she stops, turns sharply and pins her cane against Joe's chest like a lunging fencer.

"Why are you following me?"

Joe doesn't move, dumbfunded.

"Well?" she asks, more curious than furious, lowering her cane. "You're wondering how I knew you were there, aren't you?" she asks with a satisfied smile.

And if they teach telepathy at your school.

"I can smell you, just as I smelt you in my rehearsal room. Only now you smell ..." Her nose twitches. "Damp."

"Try soaked," Joe says with a short laugh. Something about this odour-sensitive self-assured girl gives him something he didn't expect to feel again: hope.

"Don't you have anywhere to go?"

Don't cry, hold it together .... "No."

Winnie turns her cane towards the Academy as the last of the group file in.

"I have to go, it's suppertime." Joe's hopes fade until she adds, "Wait on the steps and I'll sneak you some out if you'd like."

"I'd like, please. I'd like very much."

Winnie hurries into the academy. Joe sits on the top step, the entrance porch providing shelter from the rain. Gas lighters walk with their tall sticks lighting streetlamps giving the rain an effervescent shimmer in the twilight.

Joe wrings out Bertie's handkerchief. The initials sewn in blue stitching read 'H. G. Wells.' The name rings a bell. Joe wishes he had Wikipedia to resort to, wondering if Bertie follows Dr Doyle's suggestion and grows up to become a writer given his love of storytelling.

What could Joe's own future possibly hold, a child, alone, trapped in the past?

Finally, Winnie appears on the steps.

"I'm here," Joe calls, "although I guess you can smell that."

Winnie smiles and sits next to him, handing over a folded napkin which he unwraps to reveal bread, a thin slice of beef and a wedge of cheddar.

"Thanks." He tucks in, realising he hasn't eaten all day.

"I didn't think soup would travel so well in the napkin. But cook knows my appetite and normally brings me extra morsels."

"Well, thanks for sharing them with me, this is lush." After devouring the offerings, he half expects Winnie to rise and leave him to it, but she shows no sign of going.

"My name is Winnie Carmichael Stopes."

"Joe Cook."

"Glad to meet you, Joe Cook."

"Really unbelievably glad to meet you." Joe wipes his mouth with the now empty napkin.

Winnie frowns. "Why are you sad?"

"Actually, I'm smiling."

"That doesn't mean you're not sad."

Joe swallows hard, her kindness overwhelming any attempt to stop tears surfacing. Winnie pats his knee, finds and takes his hand in hers. Her touch gives Joe permission to let it all out, all his fear and guilt and loneliness pouring out with the rain.

Joe has no idea how long he sobs, but when he runs out of tears, as if on cue, the Heavens also stop crying. More than anything, Joe appreciates Winnie's silent acceptance of his need to let rip. She makes no attempt to find words of comfort nor is there an embarrassed withdrawal. Just her being there means the world to Joe. Until finally he hears the inevitable words,

"I need to go in now. Recreation time will be over and soon it's lights out."

"Okay," replies Joe with a damp shudder.

"Do you have anywhere to stay?" she asks, rising but not letting go of his hand.

Joe shakes his head, realising how foolish that is.

"No."

"We shall have to fix that, shan't we?"

Joe waits by a door in the Academy perimeter wall. What will become of him if Winnie doesn't open it? But as promised, she creaks it ajar. Joe sneaks inside.

Winnie decides the outhouse is the perfect place to hide Joe, reached by a path running along the wall. Gardens sweep down a sharp slope dotted with apple trees and pear trees; this is the location of Westow Park and the Secret Garden Centre in Joe's time where he and Lauren argue every year over which Christmas Tree to buy.

"What's that you're carrying?" Winnie asks as they walk.

"It's called a skateboard."

"A skate-board?"

"You ride it. Bit like skiing, only without snow cos it's got wheels on the bottom."

"Can I touch it?"

Joe stops, takes her left hand and guides it to the skateboard. Winnie's fingers spin the wheels.

She hands Joe her cane and takes the skateboard. "I love to ski."

"Er … you ski?"

Winnie stiffens. "Why shouldn't I?"

"Well, I, no it's just …." he splutters, not wanting to ask the question on his lips but once again Winnie reads his mind.

"How can I ski when I can't see where I'm going? Allow me to demonstrate."

She puts the skateboard on the ground, asking,

"Is this the right way round?" She feels the bark of the tree next to her, reading its folds.

"Um, yeah, but you're facing down a hill. If you turn it around you can skateboard along the path …."

"Where's the fun in that?" She climbs onto the skateboard. "How do you start?"

"Er, just push off with one foot, but seriously, it's dark and—"

"It's always dark for me."

Joe internally kicks himself.

"But, I mean, there's lots of trees and you can't …"

Joe's voice trails as Winnie cries, "Watch!"

With a push from her left foot, the skateboard leaves the path. Wheels gather speed down the grassy slope. Winnie instinctively bends her legs to lower her centre of gravity. Joe's hands cover his mouth as she hurtles straight for one of the fruit trees scattered around the lawn. He's about to shout a warning, not caring if anyone else hears and he gets busted, but at the last moment Winnie leans to the left and passes the tree. To his astonishment, she seems to know what direction to go.

A pair of pear trees approach, but Winnie sails through the middle with a 'whoop,' making Joe laugh. Hurtling at breakneck speed, Winnie suddenly loses her balance, tumbling off Skull Rider.

Joe charges down the slope imagining a broken leg or worse. Why does everyone he meets end up getting hurt? He lets out a huge gasp of relief to find Winnie sitting up in no obvious pain with a toothy grin across the whole of her face.

"Now *that* was fun!"

"You hurt?"

"It takes more than a tumble to hurt me. All my life I've had falls and bumps and scrapes. I must say skate boarding is trickier than I thought. Will you teach me?" She rises up, brushing wet grass from her pinafore.

"Yeah, sure, although you've definitely got the basics. And the guts!"

Winnie shrugs. "In wintertime when it snows, Dr Campbell has us all out on the slope practising our skiing. I've come to know these grounds off by heart." She points up to the path where she began her descent. "We started by the Silver Birch Tree which is a hundred and fourteen paces from the house. I knew where I was going. Oh!" she exclaims, smile dropping. "I hope I haven't damaged your skateboard."

"Don't worry." Joe sets off to retrieve Skull Rider. "I'm sure it'll be fine, and there are more important things in life than broken skateboards."

The outhouse is filled with neat rows of gardening tools. In the dim light from the window, Joe makes out a pile of cushions.

"Sorry not to sneak you into the academy, but I don't think Dr Campbell would approve. You can use the cushions as a mattress and a pillow. They were sewn and stitched by pupils to kneel on when planting so I can't vouch for the quality of all of them, but if you find mine you'll find it's fit for purpose."

"Hey, this is amazing, thank you. I could sleep anywhere right now, but this beats being out on the street."

Since waking this morning, Joe had experienced house breaking, being shot at with arrows and hit by a cricket ball, seen his friend fall into a hypnotic coma, lost his way back to his family and became a fugitive from the Victorian police. No wonder he felt knackered.

"Would sir find breakfast at seven acceptable?"

"Hmm," ponders Joe continuing the role play. "Sir fancies a lie in.

It's been a full-on day. How about seven thirty?"

"Very good." Winnie bows. "Goodnight, and pleasant dreams."

Joe curls up on the cushions, slipping into a sleep thankfully free of alternate futures and the Alone Child who has haunted his dreams, finding himself instead back in Paradise laughing and dancing with his family.

Chapter 22

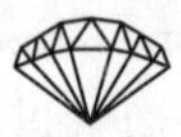

"Breakfast in bed, sir?"

Joe forces his eyes open. Winnie stands in the outhouse doorway, carrying a fabulously full napkin of food.

"Thanks," says Joe with a yawn.

Winnie taps her cane on the floor until she comes to the pile of cushions Joe fashioned for his bed, sitting down beside him.

Joe gratefully unwraps the parcel, taking out bacon and two slices of buttered bread.

"Our breakfast ended early because the dining hall is being set up for the lecture."

"Umm," munches Joe savouring every bite of his bacon butty.

"It's quite a fascinating topic actually, organised by the Upper Norwood Literary and Scientific Society. Because it's held in the academy, we all get to attend. It's open to the public too. My friend Sam is coming, the violinist you met when you crashed into our rehearsal. You could join us, if you like."

"Right." Joe licks butter from his lips. Attending a lecture wouldn't be top of his list of things to do on a summer's day (in fact it wouldn't even make the list), but it might offer a safe place to consider his next move. He can't abandon Elias when he needs him the most.

Come off it Joe. You can't help yourself, let alone anyone else. It's just like the American said, 'You're just a kid. What can you possibly do?"

"The subject is 'Elementary Detecting,' continues Winnie enthusiastically, "applying scientific approaches to solving crimes. The keynote speaker is a doctor and local author."

Joe puts these two facts together and sits up straight. "Dr Doyle! Dr

Arthur Conan Doyle?"

"Correct! Pretty impressive detecting work yourself. Do you know him?"

"Yes! And I really, really need to speak with him."

The force of his reply raises Winnie's eyebrow. She says with a touch of sarcasm, "A matter of life or death is it?"

"Yeah. Remember Elias, the boy I was with when we were being chased?"

"Who plays the spoons?"

"He's hurt, really badly hurt. Dr Doyle went to see him, and I need to find out what he thinks is wrong."

Winnie finds Joe's hand, takes it and gives a squeeze. "Of course."

The dining hall of The Royal Normal Academy for the Blind hums with the murmur of gentlemen and ladies filling seats and benches lain out between wood panelled walls. The front rows are occupied by members of the Upper Norwood Literary and Scientific Society talking earnestly, referencing their lecture notes handed out at the entrance. On the benches at the back sit pupils from the Academy and members of the public paying a one-off fee to attend.

Joe sits on the back bench next to Winnie who snuck him in through a side door.

"Keep a look out for Sam."

Joe obliges, waving at Sam as he enters the hall carrying his violin case. Sam's surprised frown eases only slightly when he sees Winnie, and his wide eyes hold Joe with a troubled look.

"Sam, you've met Joe."

"Hmmm. This is an unexpected reprise." His quiet tone is underscored with wariness. "Are you still on the run from those men?"

"Yep." Joe shudders at the thought of Smiler and changes the topic hoping a bit of friendly conversation might warm Sam up. "My cousin plays violin, how long you played?"

"Oh, er, four years. My grandpa arranged lessons for me."

"*And* he won a scholarship to attend the Crystal Palace School of Music," Winnie says with pride in her friend, prompting Sam to smile awkwardly.

"Umm, yes, although the pupils we practice with here at the academy have a far superior ear."

"And their sense of smell is also pretty sick," grins Joe.

Winnie's eyebrow shoots up. "Sick?" She lean away from Joe whilst Sam's frown deepens.

Joe kicks himself inside.

"Sick means cool."

"Cool?" asks Sam suspiciously.

"Cool means the best, so your hearing and your sense of smell is like sick, cool, awesome."

They stare at him. Just as Joe wonders if he's blown it, Sam nods.

"Mmm. You're right. Winnie's pitch-perfect and training to become a piano tuner. Some of the best were schooled right here."

Winnie shrugs. "We'll see."

"In fact," Sam adds with a flickering smile, "you could say Winnie is, umm, the 'sickest' piano tuning virtuoso."

Winnie, Sam, and Joe laugh. The tight knot inside Joe loosens just a little.

The audience hum quietens. Joe straightens as Dr Doyle steps up onto the stage and approaches the lectern. He coughs; even from the back row, Joe senses his nerves.

"Ladies and gentlemen, it's my honour to be President of the Upper Norwood Literary and Scientific Society. Therefore, it falls to me to, er, step into the breach today. This lecture on the application of science in the pursuit of solving crime was to be presented by a special guest, Mr William Pinkerton, head of Pinkerton Detective Agency in the United States of America. His agents work across the globe. However, Mr Pinkerton has been called away on urgent business, no doubt in pursuit of a dangerous criminal.

"As a consequence, I am stepping in to offer my own thoughts on the subject, having authored a private detective who employs powers of deduction, of analysis akin to a scientist, in order to uncover the perpetrator of heinous crimes. This approach contrasts tactics employed by *some* of our professional police whose predilection is to beat a confession out of their suspect, guilty or not."

Dr Doyle gives a chuckle to underline he'd told a joke to warm up his audience, but they remain decidedly silent.

"Yes, uh, well, let me begin by outlining my story, entitled *A Study in Scarlet*, and the manner in which the detective, Sherlock Holmes, goes about solving the case."

Joe seems alone in his excitement at having the future famous author describe his debut Sherlock tale until he notices another equally thrilled face near the hall entrance, crutch leaning against the wall.

Bertie!

Joe stands on tiptoes, waving, willing him to turn. Bertie spots Joe, face lighting up like one of Brock's fireworks. Grabbing his crutch, he manoeuvres himself along the back row to a chorus of tuts and a tall man lets out a curse as his foot gets impaled by Bertie who apologies profusely until reaching Joe.

"Well hello! I keep thinking I'll never see you again and you keep popping up like a pimple!"

Joe laughs at being likened to pus. Bertie however, upon noticing Joe's new companions, glares suspiciously.

"Who might these people be?"

"Oh, yeah, this is Winnie and Sam."

Winnie gives Bertie a friendly wave. Sam blinks warily.

Bertie leans into Joe, hissing accusingly. "You said you didn't know anyone here."

"No. Well, I didn't, we just met yesterday."

"When you ran off and left me?"

"Uh, I guess."

"Humph." Bertie's nose rises, and he says in a supercilious tone; "I'll introduce myself. Herbert George Wells; my friends call me Bertie."

Sam blinks rapidly and matches Bertie's disdain with a pointed reply, "Pleased to meet you, *Herbert*."

Winnie gives Sam a reproachful nudge, whispering, "Glad to meet a friend of Joe's." Her warmth sparks a gracious smile from Bertie.

"Dr Doyle saw Elias, right?" asks Joe.

"Shhhh," hisses a lady in front.

Bertie whispers, "Of course, I wouldn't let you down old chap."

"What does he think's wrong with him?"

"Afraid I can't say. I've not seen Dr Doyle since, but you and I can ask him ourselves after the lecture."

Joe gives a thumbs-up. Dr Doyle has relaxed into his subject, even enjoying himself.

"The application of reason and science, which I have afforded Sherlock Holmes, is inspired by a real man, Dr Joseph Bell, a surgeon and forensic scientist at Edinburgh Royal Infirmary where I had the good fortune to study. I worked as his clerk and witnessed first-hand how Dr Bell would investigate a crime scene or merely look at the way a person was dressed and draw large conclusions from the smallest of observations. He's able to tell from the tattoos of a sailor which seas he had sailed and can tell the profession of a patient from glancing at their hands."

The audience murmur in wonder. Joe smugly nods having seen Sherlock apply such deductive skills in numerous TV episodes and films.

At the end of the lecture, Joe and Bertie leave Winnie and Sam discussing rehearsal arrangements for Sam's latest composition and make their way through the chattering audience onto the stage where Dr Doyle beams with satisfied relief. A gentleman offers congratulations, his back turned to Joe who freezes when hearing his American accent.

"I'm a gentleman with a keen interest in the criminal mind, and your lecture was frankly fascinating."

"What's wrong?" asks Bertie as Joe backs away into the curtain on the edge of the stage. Bertie follows, sensing Joe's alarm. "Who is that?"

"Shh, I'm trying to listen, okay?" Joe snaps.

Bertie's face flushes. Joe immediately feels bad.

"I was sorry not to meet Mr Pinkerton in person," continues the American. "I've had occasion to meet associates from his detective agency from time to time."

Bet you have, probably tracking you down to arrest you.

"I hope you're not too disappointed."

"On the contrary, Dr Doyle, I will be sure to read your story."

"My lecture will have accomplished something at least!"

"Of course most professional law-breakers lack flair and brains. I wonder how Sheerluck would fair against a criminal genius?"

"Ha, it's Sherlock rather than Sheerluck, but an interesting proposition, one I must explore in a future story."

"I look forward to reading it. I'll leave you to your admirers. Good day, Dr Doyle."

"Good day Mr ..."

"Judson."

Joe watches from the wings as the American walks by. Judson pauses, turning his head almost in Joe's direction as if he can sense being watched, a small smile on his face. For a second Joe fears he'll look straight at him, but instead carries on strolling off the stage.

Joe notices he's not the only one watching Judson. At the back of the hall, a tall man doesn't take his eyes off him. It's the same man whose foot Bertie impaled with his crutch, and as the American leaves the hall he hastily follows.

"What was that all about?" Bertie's voice sounds bruised from being shut up.

"Sorry."

"No bother, old chap, but what's going on?"

Joe rubs his head, not sure where to start or if he should drag Bertie into this at all. He's saved by Winnie and Sam joining them onstage and Bertie's face brightens when Dr Doyle calls over.

"Ah, young Master Wells, and your friend who likes to header cricket balls. Here, let me see how it's healing." He moves Joe's floppy fringe aside and examines the multi-coloured bruise. "Hmm, you know you shouldn't have discharged yourself from W. G. Grace's house."

"I'm fine. It's my friend Elias I'm worried about."

Dr Doyle nods earnestly. "Yes, with just cause, I fear. I arranged for him to be taken to Cottage Hospital to make him comfortable and examined him but my medical skills, such as they are, do not extend to head trauma. Therefore, I called in a neighbour, a surgeon from Guys Hospital." Dr Doyle hesitates as if unsure whether to continue.

"What did he say?" demands Joe.

Dr Doyle glances around and gestures for Joe to follow him to the back of the stage out of earshot. Bertie, Winnie and Sam follow. Dr Doyle gives Winnie and Sam a questioning look. "Friends of yours?"

"Acquaintances," says Bertie with a sniff.

Although Sam seems likely to agree with Bertie (if it hadn't meant agreeing with Bertie), Winnie declares they're friends, sending confidence surging through Joe.

Dr Doyle gives a hesitant nod.

"Very well. I imagined your friend hit his head when he fell. However, his breathing pattern was clear and steady, his pupils responsive. To all intents and purposes, he seems to be asleep, and my surgeon friend found no sign of head trauma."

"He didn't hit his head. He landed on a pile of dust sheets. And he'd been feeling dizzy before he fell, ever since ..."

Joe stops. Dr Doyle, Bertie, Winnie and Sam wait expectantly. Joe realises if he doesn't trust them, he's truly alone. "Since he was hypnotised."

"Hypnotised?" exclaims Bertie.

Dr Doyle's face darkens.

"The symptoms Elias presented are concurrent with a hypnotic mesmeric phenomenon. When did this happen?"

"About twenty minutes before Elias collapsed."

Bertie asks, "Where?"

"Sir Henry Majoure's house. We were trying to get back the compass," Joe tells him. "That's when we got chased and Elias collapsed."

"Who hypnotised him?" interrupts Dr Doyle.

"This tall scary lady works for Sir Henry, looking after his daughter, who called her Babushka, like those Babushka Russian dolls which stack inside each other large to small. This lady could've fitted a dozen people inside her. She looked into Elias's eyes, chanted like somebody out of a fil— book."

Dr Doyle strokes his moustache. "I feared as much. Elias reminded me of someone I saw at a séance who entered a similar state."

"Umm, a séance?" echoes Sam, fingers nervously playing piano in the air.

Winnie gasps. "For communicating with spirits?"

"Correct. I've a keen interest in spiritualism and communicating with the afterlife."

"Really?" Joe's surprised someone with such a strong belief in reason would be interested in spirits.

Dr Doyle nods in earnest. "From my explorations I concluded contact with spirits is possible. They can provide knowledge and guidance to us. However, there are some who would do so for personal gain rather than for the betterment of mankind."

"Some? You mean Sir Henry, don't you?"

Dr Doyle quickly glances over their heads to make sure nobody else is listening, only to find one of the Society officials hovering impatiently.

"Dr Doyle, sorry to interrupt," the official says, although from the dismissive glance he gives the four youngsters he's not sorry at all. "Our fellow members would appreciate a little time with our esteemed president."

"Forgive me, of course." He turns to the foursome, putting on a genial smile. "This has been very informative. I will pay your sick friend a visit in the morning at eight o'clock once I've conducted my own research into how we can help him. Please do join me. In the meantime," Dr Doyle directs his last words at Joe, "my advice is to keep safe."

Joe's troubled thoughts are interrupted by Bertie. "What's going on?"

"It's dangerous. I don't want anyone else to get hurt."

"Nor do I," insists Winnie, "so you better tell us everything so we can help."

"This isn't a game!"

"Well, thank goodness for that," says Bertie. "Never really been one for games, small matter of not being able to throw, or hit, or catch. Anywho, we digress."

Sam takes a deep breath. "Umm, Winnie already risked expulsion hiding you on academy grounds. So … really, she deserves to know why."

Joe can't let them get too close in case they get hurt. And there's no way he can tell them where he's really from. But he won't get far in this Victorian world without help. The prospect of not being alone sparks a determination to show the American exactly what this 'kid' can do.

"Okay, I'll explain what I can. But not here."

"You can't go out *there*." Bertie points in the direction of the Triangle. "Not with those ruffians chasing after you."

"And, er, your distinctive style stands out like a tuba in a string orchestra," adds Sam looking Joe up and down.

"How so?" Winnie frowns.

"Well, er, his clothes ..."

Joe takes in his soot-covered skull T-shirt and his multi-pocketed shorts and trainers.

"And your hair is quite unique, old chap."

"May I?" Winnie's hand stretches out to touch Joe.

"Umm, sure."

Winnie's warm fingers touch Joe's cheeks, feeling their way around his lips, rising up his face and lightly running through his floppy fringe.

"Right. We have work to do."

Joe doesn't know what 'work' means, but he has a pretty good idea he won't like it.

And he's right.

Chapter 23

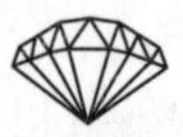

"Right, no offence, but no way am I letting a blind girl cut my hair."

"No offence taken," Winnie tells Joe sarcastically. "Would you prefer a blind boy? I'm sure I can find one."

Joe looks around the outhouse at Bertie and Sam for a little back up, but Bertie holds up his hands.

"Don't think you'd thank me if I hacked away at your head."

"Oh, don't worry." Sam smiles slyly. "They teach haircutting here, don't they Winnie?"

"They do indeed, one of the many ways they prepare us for independent life."

"Hmm, although," Sam strokes his chin, "wasn't that the only class where you came bottom?"

Joe balks. "Great. Just great."

"Don't listen to Sam and don't be a big baby. I know what I'm doing. Sit."

With a resigned groan Joe plonks down on the gardening cushions which had been last night's bed.

"Now." Winnie feels her way along the wall mounted with gardening tools. "This should do."

"What?!" Joe leaps up as Winnie takes down a pair of gardening sheers. "You have GOT to be kidding me!"

Winnie smirks. Sam sniggers. Bertie erupts into a great guffaw. Joe can't help joining their laughter.

"Of course, I'm kidding you." Winnie puts the sheers back.

Someone knocks on the outhouse door. Joe, Sam and Bertie freeze.

"It's only Harold," reassures Winnie, opening the door to her fellow student whom she'd pulled aside after the lecture to ask for help. He carries a folded pile of clothes—trousers, shirt, cap and shoes, topped with—to Joe's relief—scissors.

As Winnie sets to work, Joe tries explaining what's been going on as his blonde locks drop onto the floorboards. He can't tell them he's from the future. If he did, the only help they're likely to give him is a one-way trip to the asylum. So instead, Joe focuses on what took place in the underbelly of the palace.

"Elias took me underneath the floorboards to find the compass."

"And I was above, showing where it had fallen with a stick!"

"Yeah, thanks to you, we found it."

Bertie's chest puffs with pride.

"Hey, how much are you taking off?" Joe exclaims as a chunk of fringe flutters to the floor.

"Precisely enough. Go on, you were looking for the compass."

"But just as we got there, I overheard two men, Smiler and this American, plotting to steal the Star of Nimrod from the Shah of Persia."

"Cripes!"

"What's the Star of Nimrod?" Sam asks with wonderment.

"I've heard that name somewhere," muses Winnie.

"It's a diamond, size of a baby's fist. The shah wears it as a brooch."

"Ohh! Yes! We saw him wearing it whilst waiting for Blondin's autograph."

"You have Blondin's autograph?" asks Sam, impressed.

"Yep." Joe pats his shorts pocket smiling his thanks at Bertie for his generous gift. "And you remember how much Sir Henry Majoure was admiring the diamond?"

"You think he's the one plotting to steal it?"

"Makes sense. He's got his right-hand man, Smiler, to steal it for him."

"Smiler?" queries Winnie.

"The oily man you spoke with in the rehearsal room, carries a knife and a whip and an ugly smile you just want to wipe off his face."

"Hmm yes." Sam shudders. "I saw that smile on the man offering a reward for your whereabouts."

"Smiler was absolutely one of the ruffians who tried to nab you after Father hit you with his six," adds Bertie. "Do you think the huge fellow with Smiler was this American? He looks like he could smash his way through the shah's Royal Guard and rip the Star from his throat."

Joe shakes his head, prompting Winnie to warn, "Keep still or lose an ear."

"Sorry. No, that gorilla is one of Sir Henry's sociopathic servants, he's not American."

"I *heard* this American," says Winnie. "I'd recognise his voice again."

"Me too, I heard him talking at the end of the lecture to Dr Doyle."

"Ah," exclaims Bertie with understanding, "that's what you were doing, listening in. You recognised him?"

"I *met* him visiting Elias in hospital."

"Cripes! Close call. Lucky he didn't recognise *you*."

"But he *did* know who I was. Just didn't seem to care. Even gave me his card."

Joe fishes it from his shorts, handing it to Sam.

"'Raymond Judson Esquire, Western Lodge, Clapham Common.' About four miles from here, towards London."

"Why on earth give you his card?" asks Bertie. "Why would he not, well, try to 'silence' you too, like Smiler?"

"He told me I'm not a threat." Joe irately blows away a falling lock. "And he's right. Even if I ran around shouting what I heard to everyone I met, who'd ever believe me? Even if Elias woke up and confirmed it, who'd believe him either? We're just a couple of kids."

Sam murmurs thoughtfully, "Not anymore."

"How so?"

"Umm, we're a quartet of kids."

"Quintet," corrects Bertie earning an eye-roll from Sam. "Including Elias, not that he's much help at the moment, no offence, not his fault."

"Thanks. Seriously, it's great you all want to help. But we're still kids with no proof."

"They'll listen when the Star of Nimrod gets stolen and we can reveal who stole it," declares Bertie.

"*If* they ever realise. Smiler and the American talked about switching the diamond for a fake."

"Was there anything else you heard?" urges Winnie. "Some detail revealing their plan?"

Joe racks his brain. So much had happened it's hard to think at all let alone think straight.

"There *was* something they said about the switch. The American said he'd do it right under the shah's nose when he's looking up."

"They must plan to switch it while he's wearing it," declares Winnie.

Bertie whistles. "Audacious. I'd like to see that."

Thoughts form in Joe's nearly-shorn head. "Yes! Bertie, you're the best."

"I am?"

"He is?" frowns Sam.

"We've got to witness them do it. Catch them in the act. Expose Smiler and the American and Sir Henry Majoure and clear Elias's name so if ..." Joe swallows and corrects himself, "*When* Elias wakes up, he won't be branded a criminal."

Winnie stops snipping and runs her hand over the top of Joe's short-back-and-sides. "There, all done."

Joe rubs his crown. At least Dad will be happy he's chopped his floppy fringe, if he ever sees him again. Joe picks up the pile of clothes left by Harold and turns into a corner to change.

Winnie twirls the scissors. "To catch them in the act we need to find out everything we can about their plans."

"Hmm." Sam rhythmically taps away at a pile of plant pots. "How?"

Bertie throws his hand in the air. "I know!"

"Thought *you* might," murmurs Sam.

"I do! We need to think like Sherlock Holmes!"

Not put off by the bemused silence, Bertie continues, "The detective from Dr Doyle's story. We need to be logical and methodical, discover all we can about this American, observe this Smiler and his doings."

"Smiler's dangerous. If he catches us tailing him …"

"Tailing?" queries Winnie. "What's that?"

Joe sighs, realising they haven't been raised on a diet of CSI-random-city; Dr Doyle is the daddy of crime fiction and so far he'd only written one short story. If they're going to do this, Joe needs to give a crash course in catching criminals.

"Tailing means following a suspect, watching what they do, where they go, who they meet. But always keeping a safe distance, you can't get made."

Noting the blank expressions, Joe elaborates, "'Made' means spotted, so you've got to pretend to, say, read a newspaper or watch your target in the reflection of a shop window. And note down every detail. The smallest thing could prove critical."

"Cripes!" Bertie regards Joe with new levels of admiration. "Where did you learn all this?"

Joe shrugs. "Umm, I listened to Dr Doyle's lecture. It's elementary, my dear Bertie."

Joe smiles inwardly at his Sherlock gag that's lost on the others. He checks out his disguise; he resembles an urchin in a school production of *Oliver!* costumed by parents with a dedicated eye for period authenticity.

Bertie runs his fingers along the rim of his bowler hat. "I volunteer for 'tailing' the Smiler."

Joe frowns at Bertie's crutch. "What if you need to make a quick getaway?"

"I can move at some speed if required."

"But your crutch makes you, well, noticeable."

Bertie's face reddens.

"That is only a consideration if I get 'made,' which I have no intention of. And *you* can't follow Smiler."

"He's actually right," agrees Sam. "That is, even with your new haircut and clothes, he's seen you on more than one occasion. So ... I'll 'tail' too and ensure Herbert doesn't get 'made.'"

"I won't get made!"

"Of course, Herbert. Because I'll be there."

They give each other a good glower.

Joe dislikes the idea of sending either into danger (not least because they're liable to argue and end up busted,) but his thoughts return to Elias and he's reminded what's at stake.

"Okay, but be careful, please, don't do anything stupid."

"As if." Bertie huffs, prompting a doubtful eye-roll from Sam.

Bertie pats his satchel. "I have my notebook, and my very special opera glasses for observing from a distance, should the need arise."

"Nice one. Write down everything you see. Every detail, no matter how small, could have massive significance."

Bertie salutes.

"And just write down the facts, no elaboration."

"Elaborate? Moi?"

"We also need to find out about Raymond Judson. Who is he? Who knows him?"

"Dr Campbell," Winnie says, "our headmaster, he's from Tennessee. It's possible he's come across Judson or heard of him. Dr Campbell is incredibly lovely and I'm sure he'll help if he can. Joe and I can pay him a visit, and all meet up at The School of Music this afternoon, say four o'clock?"

Everyone nods.

"What's wrong, Joe?" asks Sam.

Joe looks at Winnie, Bertie and Sam.

I've found friends but lost my family. If I manage to find my family I'll lose my friends. Can't I have both?

What he says is,

"S'nothing. All good. It's just …" Unable to find the right words, Joe settles for a simple, "Thanks."

"Think nothing of it," insists Bertie. "That's what friends are for."

Chapter 24

The gymnasium at the Royal Normal Academy for the Blind echoes with the clang of pupils practicing their fencing skills. Joe marvels at the courageous determination of those throwing themselves into the sport.

Their spirit of adventure comes from the top; Winnie explained how their headteacher and founder Dr Campbell was the first blind person to climb Mont Blanc, the tallest mountain in Europe.

Winnie and Joe approach Dr Campbell who stands at the front of the gymnasium wearing small, tinted spectacles and stroking his bushy goatee beard, when a French woman's voice sings out, "Bonjour Dr Campbell, bonjour!"

A fashionably feathered lady approaches wearing enough bling to make a Kardashian blush.

"Madame d'Varney," greets Dr Campbell, rolling her name in a long Southern drawl. "Pleasure to see you here. Again."

"Oh, Dr Campbell, I cannot keep away!" she exclaims, eyelashes fluttering.

Winnie whispers to Joe, "It's not just the academy Madame d'Varney can't keep away from."

Joe just manages to contain a snigger.

"The academy's benefactors are always welcome to visit, although you're here so often, soon you'll be taking up residency."

"Oh, Dr Campbell, you temptress! My house, with all its empty rooms, mirrors the emptiness of a widow's heart." She throws her hand to her forehead for extra over-emphasis. "But tonight, oh, my doors will be thrown open for a soiree! I would most sincerely love some of your talented pupils to perform."

"That can be arranged."

"And of course, you would personally accompany them, Dr Campbell?" She places her hand on his chest.

"A kind invitation, but I fear Mrs Campbell would never forgive me were I to miss her mother's birthday."

Madame d'Varney removes her hand from Dr Campbell and pouts. "And I shall never forgive myself for arranging a soiree on the day your mother-in-law got born. You shall mend my broken heart by having me for lunch. I can think of many ways I'd like to help you."

Joe clears his throat. "Bet she can."

Winnie lets out a snort, her shoulders shaking as she gets the giggles.

Madame d'Varney sweeps from the gymnasium and Dr Campbell turns in their direction.

"Winnie Carmichael Stopes, I'd recognise your laugh anywhere."

Winnie swallows her snorts as she steps forward.

"Sorry, Dr Campbell."

A wry grin spreads across his face. "I'm sure you are. How may I help you and your friend, whom I don't believe I've met?"

Joe realises Dr Campbell must be responsible for training Winnie's heightened sense of smell and hearing.

"This is my second cousin," bluffs Winnie, "and we were wondering if you happened to know a man called Raymond Judson?"

"Judson," muses Dr Campbell. "Yes, I'm acquainted with him."

Joe's hand finds Winnie's, giving a small squeeze of excitement. But if Joe expects confirmation Judson is a villain, he's as disappointed as he is surprised when Dr Campbell smiles warmly at the name.

"He's an oil man, owns the *New York Times*."

"The newspaper?"

Dr Campbell rubs the gold tip of his cane. ""The very same. I met him once and experienced his charm offensive."

More like offensive charm.

"Where did you meet?"

"We were introduced by Madame d'Varney, one of our Academy's generous friends, although everyone it seems is a friend of Madame d'Varney. She's hosting one of her infamous soirees this evening and asked our pupils to demonstrate their musical talents for her guests."

A guestlist including Raymond Judson?

Before Joe can work out how to get himself in there, Winnie pipes up, "I'll do it. That is, if you feel I would adequately represent the academy."

"Adequate is not a word that comes to mind when I think of you, Winnie." Dr Campbell smiles obviously proud.

Winnie blushes.

"Perhaps my performance tonight could be accompanied by Samuel Taylor? I know he doesn't attend the academy, but we've been working on a piece together for violin and piano. It's really rather good, and if I could be excused from classes for the rest of the day we could practice."

"As you wish. Now tell me, Winnie's second cousin," Dr Campbell says in a tone suggesting he hadn't quite bought their cover story. "Do you have a particular interest in Mr Judson?"

Joe swallows, realising a man who works daily with hundreds of kids and whose hearing is more attuned to the human voice than Winnie's is capable of hearing through a lie.

"Mr Judson is offering to help a friend of mine. He's really sick, and I just want to know what kind of man he is."

"It sounds as if Mr Judson is a philanthropist using his position to aid those to whom life has not been so kind."

It may sound that way, but with Judson it's definitely a lie.

"Are you impressed I got the day off school?" Winnie asks Joe as they stand on the Academy steps. "Now I'm free to help with the investigation."

"Great." The sentiment isn't clear from Joe's tone. "Sorry, it really is great. It's just I didn't expect Raymond Judson to get a glowing character reference."

"Well, if we can return to the subject of me being quite brilliant, you should remember I also got myself and Sam invited to Madame d'Varney's party."

"That *was* quite brilliant. But how does a rich oil tycoon get employed to steal the Star of Nimrod? It doesn't make sense."

"That's it!" cries Winnie.

"That's what?"

"I've been trying to work out where I've heard the Star of Nimrod."

"And?"

"And I told you it sounded familiar."

"And?" Joe repeats with a little more force, prompting a raised eyebrow from Winnie.

"*And* . . . I heard about it from my papa."

"Your papa?"

"He's a geologist. Owns a book listing all the unearthed precious stones. It's a reference book, but I always found the descriptions of the stones and their origins fascinating. When he was home, he'd read it to me as a bedtime story, listing what they look like, where they were found, how they'd been used by great kings and queens and sultans and emperors." Winnie's head rises dreamily at happy memories. "I'm certain the book referenced the Star of Nimrod."

"If only we could get that book," muses Joe.

"We can. It's at my house. Five minutes away."

"I thought you boarded at the academy?"

"I do. It's my choice," she adds quickly and for the first time since they'd met, Winnie's face hardens. "It keeps me out of the way of my sister."

Guilt grips Joe's guts remembering his efforts to lose *his* sister. Now he'd do anything to hear Lauren roast him again.

Joe and Winnie cross the corner of the Triangle to the top of

Belvedere Road which drops steeply, either side lined with villas ranging from fancy to fantastical with jutting towers and stone lions.

Growing up, Belvedere Road and neighbouring Fox Hill had been where Joe headed every Halloween when their pavements flow with trick-or-treaters, householders joining the seasonal spirit by ghoulishly decorating their gardens. Joe remembers knocking on one flat with Lauren, Aaliyah, and the twins, ready to scare the resident with their rotting zombie make-up (courtesy of Dad) only to find the trick was on them. The door flew open and the occupier, who was disguised as a howling werewolf, sent them screaming down the garden path.

Memories forgotten like a love-worn teddy demoted to a box under the bed, the box rediscovered only to find inside it empty.

"Penny for your thoughts?" offers Winnie as they turn onto Cintra Park road snaking down and up to the Crystal Palace.

"Just thinking about my family."

"Are you close?"

"Not at the moment," he says with a short hard laugh, knowing the joke's on him; Joe pushed them away long before the shattered compass put decades of distance between them.

Winnie offers her arm. Joe gladly wraps his with hers. It's comforting to be with Winnie, to have Bertie and Sam helping him navigate this perilous past. Under different circumstances in a different time they might become true friends. But he has to remember this is all temporary. He'll be gone once he's exposed Sir Henry and got back the shattered compass. Yet will it take him back to his lost life or an alternate reality where his family doesn't exist?

Winnie stops at the gate of a three-storey white house. Joe immediately recognises the neighbouring alleyway he's used a thousand times going to the First Crystal Palace Scout troop hut tucked at the end.

The hut won't be there, it's another twenty-three years before Scouting is founded, but the white house is pretty much the same except one missing detail—in Joe's time it has a blue plaque above the front door to commemorate a famous resident.

"What's your full name?" asks Joe trying to remember the inscription on the plaque.

"Winifred Eustice Carmichael Stopes. Why do you ask?"

"I've heard your name before, that's all." Stopes is the surname on the plaque ...

"Possibly mamma? She campaigns for the advancement of women and was the first woman in Scotland to gain a Certificate of Arts."

Winnie's proud smile spreads across her face. She marches up the path to the front door where she drops down, feeling underneath a plant pot to produce a key.

Joe's memory bank races.

"Is her first name Marie?"

Winnie's smile disappears. Her voice and body stiffen.

"No. Marie is my older sister, and I can't see how you've heard of her unless her reputation for being a spiteful pig-headed bully has spread, which frankly would not surprise me."

Winnie puts the key in the door but doesn't open it.

"How *do* you know my sister's name?" She points her cane at Joe. "What aren't you telling me?"

Joe gulps. He's been made.

Chapter 25

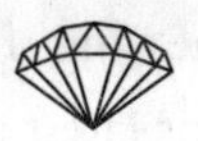

"How do you know my sister's name?" repeats Winnie, jabbing her cane at Joe.

"Lucky guess, I guess ..."

Winnie makes no move to open the door to her house.

Joe takes a breath, reaches out and holds her cane. She allows him to lower it. He takes Winnie's hand. "Do you trust me?"

Winnie doesn't nod, but nor does she pull her hand away.

"Listen, I'm not some psycho stalker following you and your family. I'm lost here with no-one, no-one to help me help Elias except you and Bertie and Sam."

"I can't help you; *we* can't help you, unless you're honest with us."

"Don't you think I want to be? I wish I could tell you everything, I want to so badly, but ..." Joe swallows, remembering what a disaster it had been when he'd tried telling Elias he's from the future, reminding himself he can't let them get too close in case they get hurt. "But I can't. Really, truly I can't. If that means you can't help me anymore, I get it. I won't blame you. You've already done loads, more than I would if I were in your shoes." Joe wipes away a stray tear with frustration.

Winnie remains motionless, her silence hurting Joe worse than a slap and a scream for him to get lost.

Finally, she lets go of Joe's hand, pushes open the door and walks inside the house. To Joe's amazement, instead of slamming the door in his face she leaves it open, walking mid-way down the hall before turning. "Are you coming then?"

Relief and gratitude sweep Joe inside the Stopes's house.

Almost every surface and floor space is littered with crates and parcels. Winnie stumbles over a half-packed box, just managing to steady herself in time with one hand against the wall.

"You okay?" Joe asks, thinking how unfair it is for Winnie's family to create an obstacle course knowing she can't see.

"Papa must be back from his latest expedition."

A woman's voice rises with passion from the dining room.

Winnie puts her finger to her lips. Joe follows her along the corridor. The dining room door is slightly ajar. Dining chairs are piled with crates forcing the assembled women to perch on top. This is made possible because they aren't wearing the enormous frilly crinoline and hooped skirts seen on the likes of Madame d'Varney, but simple and far more comfortable dress.

The women murmur their agreement at the words of the speaker, Charlotte Carmichael Stopes who stands at the head of the table.

"As women we deserve to be free from 'fashion' that deforms our figure and impedes our freedom of movement such as ridiculous tightly-fitting corsets rendering healthy exercise impossible."

"Here, here," the others concur.

"That was Mamma," whispers Winnie proudly as they sneak down the corridor.

"I guessed as much."

"Well, thank you. I'm told I have her eyebrows. Fat ugly caterpillars according to my sister."

"No," Joe says quickly. "Well, yes, you've got the same eyebrows, but they're not ugly. They're cool, like Cara Delevingne's."

"Who's she?"

"Oh, someone else who thinks you should be what you want, not what other people tell you."

"Perhaps she should join the Rational Dress Society. Come on, the book we want is in the living room. If we keep quiet, we'll be safe. They're too busy to notice us."

Joe catches a hint of sadness in her voice and wonders between her dad's travels and her mum's campaigning how much time Winnie gets with her parents.

"Let me move some of those boxes ...." Joe begins as they enter a living room littered with more crates.

"No! Please, don't touch anything."

Joe eyes up a flint axe mounted on the wall. "Your dad likes to take his work home with him."

"He's away months at a time amassing the largest collection of fossils and palaeolithic artefacts in Britain." Winnie edges towards a large bookcase along the back wall. "He was the first person to find Stone Age implements in the Thames."

"Cool."

Winnie's fingers reach the bottom shelf.

"Want me to look?"

"No," Winnie replies sharply, adding with a forgiving smile, "I know exactly what the cover feels like. Here it is."

Winnie pulls out a thick leatherbound book and holds it out to Joe, the title imprinted in faded gold lettering.

He reads, "*Precious Stones from Around the World–A Geological and Sociological Guide*, by Lord Stanley Beuford."

Winnie sits down on a packing crate waiting expectantly. As the seats are occupied by fossils, Joe leans the book on a crate and thumbs the pages to the index at the back, finding the section headed "Stones of Arabia."

"'The Star of Nimrod was so named by and after King Nimrod, founder of the Assyrian Empire approximately five hundred years before the Greek Empire which derived much of its art and religious myths from Assyria. Of all the riches of their capital city Nineveh, which rose on the banks of the Tigress, none was believed to hold such power as the Star. King Nimrod chose the diamond as his badge of supremacy. It is said to have been an instrument of the gods representing the union of wisdom, power, and the Heavens. After

Nineveh was razed to the ground, the Star of Nimrod became an heirloom of the monarchs of Persia.

"'In geological terms the Star of Nimrod is a desert diamond, a naturally occurring quartz found along the desert plains of Riyadh. It has traces of the mineral rutile, which is responsible for the star effect, known as asterism, creating a three-pointed star pattern.'"

Winnie has a wistful expression and Joe imagines she's remembering times she'd listen to these words spoken by her papa at her bedside.

The moment is broken by a harsh voice from the living room doorway, "Winnie! What do you think you're doing here?"

The girl standing in her dressing gown is little more than a year older than Joe and Winnie but has chosen to adopt the manner of someone far superior in age and worth.

Winnie leaps up, pale face growing paler. "Marie! What are *you* doing here?"

"I'm poorly," she replies tartly, blowing her nose on a handkerchief as proof. "Explain why a boy is in our house reading Father's books to you?"

Winnie replies with heavy sarcasm, "You may have forgotten, but I struggle reading."

Marie bristles.

"How could I forget my poor, pathetic, blind, little sister, no matter how hard I try. And *you*?" She turns her glare to Joe. "Who are you?"

Joe has no idea how to introduce himself or even if he should, figuring the second-cousin line isn't going to cut it.

Fortunately, Winnie intervenes. "Joe is a helper at the academy. I'm researching gemstones for a geology project and needed him to read to me."

A suggestive smile crosses Marie's face.

"What else does your little 'boyfriend' help you with?" She turns to Joe with a lurid leer. "Do you take advantage of my sister's disability? I hope not." She scrunches her nose in an exaggerated show of disgust.

"Someone of your class, and *your* defects, dear sister, breeding? It's beyond repugnant."

"It's ... it's not like that," stammers Winnie, face red with anger.

"Wow!" exclaims Joe. "I can see why you don't miss living with this first-class cow."

Winnie and Marie's mouths fall open. Giggles pour out of Winnie's, becoming a cascade of snorting guffaws. Her contagious hysterics set off Joe.

Marie's nostrils flare with outrage.

"Stop it! STOP LAUGHING! Who do you think you're laughing at you worthless little—"

"MARIE!" The force of this voice from the living room door makes all three youngsters jump.

"Mamma," says Marie defensively. "Winnie has snuck out of school with a *boy* and broken into our house and he just called me a—"

"Firstly," says Charlotte Carmichael Stopes, cutting off her eldest daughter in a no-nonsense Edinburgh accent. "Winnie can't 'break' into her own home. Secondly, I can tell the gender of her companion without your assistance. Thirdly, I suggest you reflect on your own words before complaining about those used by others in response."

Marie glowers at the rebuke, gives the still tittering Joe and Winnie looks that could massacre, and storms from the living room.

Charlotte sighs.

"Thank you, Mamma," says Winnie quietly.

"I need to return to my meeting, but would you care to take the book with you? I'm sure your papa wouldn't mind."

"Thank you. When will he be home?"

"Your guess is as good as mine." She shakes her head at the chaos. Her eyes settle on Joe. "Does your friend have a name?"

"Joe. Pleased to meet you."

"Pleased to meet you, Joe. A friend of Winnie's is always welcome, whatever gender they may be. Now I must get back. Winnie, we should arrange lunch soon."

"I'd love that," Winnie says, face brightening. "When?"

Her mamma hesitates. "Soon. I'll send a message to the academy when I'm next passing. Goodbye."

Winnie's brightness dips. "Of course, Mamma. Goodbye."

Winnie says little after leaving her house to meet Bertie and Sam and learn what they've discovered about Smiler. Having met her spiteful sister, Joe appreciates why she chose to live away from home. He manages to recall a little of the future Marie Stopes from a talk he'd attended with Nan about famous daughters of Crystal Palace, how Marie had pioneered family planning, educating women to be able to have smaller families instead of averaging half a dozen kids. It may have earned her a blue plaque, but Joe thanks his lucky stars he'd met the other Stopes sister.

Chapter 26

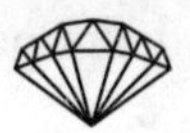

Joe and Winnie head towards the Crystal Palace School of Music, their rendezvous point with Sam and Bertie. With an hour to kill, Winnie promises to show Joe the wonders of the Egyptian Court and the recreated Tomb of Beni Hassan, sneaking the two of them through a service door connecting the school and the main palace. As they wander through crowds of visitors, Joe spots a small girl in a big dress sitting on a fountain wall kicking her feet, chin in her hands.

"Iris!" exclaims Joe, explaining to Winnie, "Blondin's daughter."

The boredom etched across Iris's face evaporates. "Strange Boy!"

"Joe," Joe reminds her.

"I remember your name. Strange Boy." She jumps onto the fountain wall so she's equal to Joe in height.

"So if you remember, maybe you could use it?"

"Non. I like to use Strange Boy."

Winnie snorts. "It does suit you."

"Thanks everybody."

"And who is zis?"

"My name's Winnie."

"Hello Wineee. Did you find your compass, Strange Boy?"

"Yeah, well, kind of I guess ...."

Their attention is drawn by a shout from above. In the rafters of the Grand Transept, the Great Blondin directs workmen busy constructing a little red house at the end of the high wire to store his props.

"That's your dad! Blondin!"

"I know who my papa is," snaps Iris. "He is up zere and I am stuck down here. It is un-fair. It is BORING."

Blondin glances down, giving Joe a smiling wave.

"Blondin waved at me!"

"So?" Iris stares at Joe as if he couldn't get more embarrassing if he stripped naked and ran around the palace. "Do you want a medal? Saying 'Blondin, he waves at me?'"

"No, I just ..."

Winnie leans in with a smile. "I'm impressed."

"Cheers, I guess it's pretty cool if your hero knows you," Joe says.

Iris pouts. "Why do you guess so much?"

"How do you mean?"

"I mean you always say, 'I guess I'll do zis,' or 'I guess zis is zat.'"

"Ha! It's just an expression. I'm not actually guessing."

"Zen why say so?"

"Dunno, just something we say where I'm from."

"Where is zat, Strange Boy?"

Joe hesitates.

"Er, not from here."

"But from where?" Iris persists. "Are we not friends? Did I not help you?"

"No, you did, we are, but ... "

Winnie regards Joe with a curious expression. "Joe likes to be a man of mystery."

"No, I don't. I'm really ordinary, trust me. Not like you, La Petit Wonder," he adds, a change of subject overdue. "Any chance the Home Office will let you up on the wire?"

Iris flaps her arms. "Non. Zey even write in ze newspapers saying I'm banned. You British are so BO-RING."

"Sorry," says Winnie, "on behalf of Britain. I know what it's like being told not to do something you know you can do, if they'd only let you try."

Iris manages a small smile. Suddenly her eyes widen.

"Wait! Winnie, Strange Boy, do you want to meet my cat?"

Joe longs to explore the Egyptian Court, but Iris's excitement reminds him of Lauren desperate to show off her latest TikTok dance, so he smiles and says, "Sure."

Iris leaps down from the wall and claps her hands together. "Her name is Tilly! You will LOVE her!" Iris scampers off and they follow her to a storeroom behind the Grand Transept.

Tilly meets them with a fierce growl.

"Is that what it sounds like?" asks Winnie in a shaky voice.

"Er, yeah," replies Joe, also with a quiver. "Tilly is a lion!"

"Please tell me he's in a cage."

"He is a she," says Iris, walking right up to the cage in the middle of the storeroom. The lioness pushes herself up to the bars, ears poking through to allow Iris to tickle them.

"Um, should you really be doing that ...?" asks Joe with alarm. "Tickling Tilly," he adds to Winnie who coughs with amazement.

"Of course! We are friends, are we not Tilly?"

The lioness purrs her apparent agreement, slumping down on her straw bed in bliss.

"Would you like to stroke Tilly?"

"Er, no ..." Joe begins, but Winnie's straight over to the cage, feeling her way with her cane.

Iris takes her hand, guiding her to sit and join her in stroking Tilly's ears.

"She's so soft," says Winnie in awe.

"I really, really don't think you should be doing that," Joe mumbles.

"Do not worry, Strange Boy. Tilly has been raised here at ze palace zoo and she is very friendly, if you are friendly to her. Zat is why she will be performing with Papa in his show."

"What's he gonna do? Get her tight rope walking?"

"Oui."

"Really?" exclaims Winnie with hushed amazement.

"It is Papa's grand finale. He cannot 'ave me, so instead he has a lioness. But I do not blame Tilly. It is not her fault she replaces me."

Iris gives the lioness' head a ruffle to show there are no hard feelings. Tilly in turn cocks her head to one side, closes her eyes, and purrs.

"How is she going to be up on a tight rope?" asks Winnie in wonder.

"Tilly will be in ze wheelbarrow. Papa will push ze wheelbarrow across ze high wire," she explains as if this were the most natural thing in the world.

"Sounds safe," says Winnie with heavy sarcasm.

"It is not safe. Zat is ze point. Although Tilly will be strapped in."

"Oh right," says Joe with a roll of his eyes, "in that case health and safety will sign off, no worries."

"What is 'health and safety?'" Iris frowns.

"My point exactly."

"Come and meet her," invites Winnie.

"Trust us," adds Iris.

Joe frowns, takes a breath, and approaches the cage. He kneels down beside them, slowly puts his hand through the bars and lets his fingers into Tilly's fur.

"She's beautiful," he exclaims, picturing how Aaliyah will react if he ever gets to tell her he'd stroked a lioness.

"Bertie and Sam should've been here half hour ago." Joe stares at the clock on the wall of the rehearsal room, fingers impatiently plonking piano keys, hating being unable to contact them. How did anyone ever cope before mobile phones? "What if they've been caught by Smiler? If anything happens to them—"

"They'll be here," says Winnie reassuring herself as much as Joe. Suddenly she rises. "They're coming!"

Joe strains his ears.

Winnie tenses. "They're running …."

The rehearsal room doors burst open. In rushes Sam followed by

Bertie, demonstrating the claim he can indeed move at speed on his crutch if required.

Joe expects Smiler to burst in after them, but this fear fades when Bertie collapses, spluttering, on the piano stool, desperate to tell them what's happened. "Cripes ... I ... we ..."

"We waited outside Rockhills for almost two hours," breaks in Sam, leaning against the piano.

"One hour and fifty minutes," pants red-faced Bertie.

"Yes, almost two hours," Sam continues with an eye-roll. "Finally Smiler came to the gate, luckily on foot, so we followed him into the Crystal Palace."

"Fortunately," cuts in Bertie, breath nearly recovered, "I have my pass on account of Father's cricketing and Sam attends the Crystal Palace School of Music so we could gain entry to the palace and continue our pursuit. Sam here is quite the genius, you know, plays piano and violin *and* composes."

Sam fidgets modestly. "Oh, just a few simple sonatas for string. Bertie is a virtuoso wordsmith."

"Oh, Sam, too kind."

"Great," interrupts Joe, pleased the pair are getting along but desperate to hear their news. "Where'd Smiler go? What did he do?"

"Oh, of course." Bertie pulls his notebook from his satchel. "May I continue?"

"The next movement is yours." Sam gestures politely.

"Great," says Joe, tapping his foot.

Bertie's finger slowly runs down the page. Joe's foot taps into overdrive. "Ah yes. We followed the target to the upper gallery."

"Upper gallery?" interrupts Joe.

"Indeed, the upper gallery of the palace, the second level, where there's hundreds of stalls and showrooms with artisans selling maps and stationary and candles and cosmetics, everything you could possibly imagine."

"Like a shopping centre," offers Joe, realising the Crystal Palace is a place people went to shop as well as be educated and entertained.

"What's a 'shopping centre?'" enquires Winnie.

"Er, where lots of people sell their stuff."

"Like a bazaar?" she suggests.

"Exactly. So, what did Smiler do next?"

"The target went shopping."

"Shopping?" Joe can't hide his disappointment Smiler hadn't been caught in a secret rendezvous with the American.

"Shopping," repeats Bertie. "However, wait until you hear where!"

Sam and Bertie exchange excited smiles

"I'm waiting ...."

"Firstly, the target stopped at Boosey and Son, purveyors of musical instruments. There he gave the attending clerk a flute to repair."

"Smiler plays flute?" Joe's surprised Smiler does anything other than skulking and scaring.

"Seems so," concurs Sam. "Boosey and Son are excellent; my grandpa purchased my violin there. But wait until you hear where he went next!"

"Still very much waiting ..."

Bertie refers to his notes. "After dropping off his flute the target went next door to ..." Bertie savours the moment with a dramatic pause, "... W. H. Gorsuch, artisan and purveyor of *precious stones*."

"Precious stones?" exclaims Winnie.

Sam conducts the air as he declares, "Gems, rubies, crystals and ... diamonds!"

"What happened?"

Bertie exchanges an anxious glance with Sam. "Unfortunately, we didn't hear much of the target's conversation with Gorsuch, on account of *someone* paying too much attention to a Stradivarius violin on display at Boosey and Sons."

"Umm, excuse me," Sam retorts defensively. "*I* noticed Smiler had gone next door to Gorsuch in the first place."

"Okay, okay," interrupts Joe before the blame game escalates. "You said you didn't hear *much*, but you did hear *something*?"

"Indubitably, however we're not sure what to make of it." Bertie consults his notes. "Smiler said ..." Bertie clears his throat and speaks in a rough nasal voice; "*'I'll bring it in the morning,'* to which Mr Gorsuch says," – swapping to a deep non-specific Eastern European accent – "*'Tell your master I'll have it ready in three days,'* to which Smiler says, '*No, you won't; you'll have it ready on Friday.*'"

Bertie is in his role-playing element, expressions swapping between sinister smile and scrunched frown.

"'*But I'll have to close my shop to finish in time,*' to which Smiler responds, '*You'll be compensated for your troubles. Refuse this offer at your peril.*'"

"Er, Bertie, I don't recall him saying 'refuse this offer at your peril?'"

Bertie flushes. "Well, no, but his smile implied it."

"So much for 'just the facts,'" murmurs Sam dryly.

"Bertie never lets the facts get in the way of a good story." Joe chuckles and adds when seeing his hurt look, "But you're making it really come alive."

"It's just like being there," adds Winnie.

"Why thank you," says Bertie, nose in the air.

"Then what happened?"

Sam takes up the story. "Smiler left the palace by the South Transept, and we 'tailed' him across the road to The Swan Hotel."

Joe can visualise The Swan Hotel on the corner of the Triangle which in his time had become Westow House pub.

Bertie reads, "The target entered this den of ruffians and met with a man."

"Was it the American we saw talking to Dr Doyle?"

"Negative. This was a one-eyed man with an eye patch. They ate a tasty looking pie, possibly beef and ale, and talked, by which time we were late to meet you, so hurried back to report."

"Good work," Winnie praises.

"Yeah, definitely."

"I make a good Holmes and you're a wonderful Watson," Bertie declares.

"Is Watson in charge?" asks Sam.

"Oh, no question."

Sam hooks his thumbs in his jacket.

"Question is, what's it all mean? What's Smiler bringing to Gorsuch in the morning?"

"The Star of Nimrod?" Winnie offers.

Bertie bangs his crutch on the floor. "Could they be stealing it tonight?"

"Guess it's possible."

"And selling it to Gorsuch!" concludes Bertie.

Joe chews his lip as a theory starts forming. "Yeah ... Sir Henry's stealing the diamond to sell cos he's broke!"

"Broke?" Sam gives his chin a sceptical stroke. "My aunty enjoys telling me musicians spend their lives broke, but if that means living at a house like Rockhills and sitting on the board of the Crystal Palace Company I won't complain."

"No, listen, I overheard Sir Henry chatting to some of the other directors of the Crystal Palace, calling themselves the 'Shadow Board.'"

"Shadow Board?" echoes Bertie. "Sounds shadowy indeed."

Joe explains, "Yeah, well, it was all a bit weird, talking about the Crystal Palace like it's a living thing with hidden powers. But one of the Shadow Board members asked when Sir Henry's gonna pay for the work on the Nineveh Court. Plus, in the under-floor I overheard the American say Smiler's boss is broke."

"You spend an awful lot of time eavesdropping, old chap," Berties says.

"So you think Sir Henry is arranging to steal and sell the Star of

Nimrod?" asks Winnie.

"And use the proceeds to pay for the restoration of the Nineveh Court," Bertie concludes.

Joe stabs a finger in the air. "Exactly!"

Sam scratches his head. "Umm, when you play back that theory, it sounds unlikely."

"No, it's starting to make sense, trust me, and this American is the key."

"Tonight might offer up some answers," reasons Winnie.

"Tonight?" chirps Bertie. "What are we doing tonight?!"

"Sam and I are performing at a soiree for Madame d'Varney and she knows this American."

A soiree Joe intends to gate crash.

Chapter 27

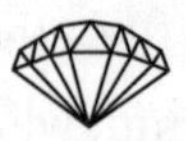

"Bonsoir! Bonsoir!" Madame d'Varney greets her guests with an extravagant manner that matches her diamond-encrusted necklace and her home, Park View Villa, an imposing mansion a few minutes stroll from the Crystal Palace. "Merci beaucoup, splendid you came, Giles show our guests to the drawing room for champagne sil vous plait."

Winnie, Sam and Joe hover by the entrance watching guests mingle under candlelit chandeliers. Joe adjusts his dark glasses borrowed from Harold along with his academy uniform which, with his new haircut, he hopes will pass him off as a pupil from The Royal Normal Academy for the Blind and ensure he isn't recognised by Raymond Judson.

Sam hasn't stopped chewing his lip with worry since being told he'd been volunteered to perform a duet. In contrast, Bertie had pleaded to join them but eventually realised he wouldn't get permission to stay out late unaccompanied and miles from Bromley. So, with sulky resignation, he'd agreed to reconvene in the morning to meet Dr Doyle at Elias's bedside. Joe was secretly relieved—he'd grown massively fond of his new friend but wasn't sure Bertie's over-the-top theatrics would enable him to carry off acting blind without his cover being blown.

Bertie's theatrics pale into insignificance next to Madame d'Varney's performance when she spots the trio. "Oh! Mes petit musiciens! Come, come, I am so 'appy, so 'onoured, so 'umbled you join us!"

"Good evening. My name is Winnifred Carmichael Stopes."

"Tres bon! What instrument will you be playing this evening?"

"The piano."

"Ah, my Steinway grand awaits you in my salon. And you, young gentleman?"

"Samuel Coleridge Taylor." Sam gives a small nervous bow. "I shall be playing the violin."

"Magnifique! And you, young sir?" Madame d'Varney beams at Joe.

"My name is Edward Sheeran. I'm the page turner."

"Oh, the ecstasy of meeting pupils of the enchanting Dr Campbell. Will he definitely not be in attendance at all this evening?"

"I'm afraid not," says Winnie.

I hope not or we're in big trouble.

Madame d'Varney throws her hand to her heart as if to stop it breaking, swiftly throws her arms open as if making an unexpected recovery.

"I shall have to pay a personal visit to show him my bottomless gratitude. Ah, listen, my piano is being played by my old friend Charley Adeleine. Go kick him off. Au revoir! Au revoir! Oh, Judge Titterington-Finch, so glad you came!" Madame d'Varney dances away to meet and greet, leaving Joe, Winnie and Sam to make their way through to the salon.

"You'll be great," Winnie reassures Sam, who blinks rapidly at all the guests.

"A duet is not the same as performing in an ensemble, and the piece really isn't ready …."

"What did you say your full name is?" asks Joe, partly to offer Sam a distraction and also because it rings big bells.

"Samuel Coleridge Taylor. You may think you've heard it before."

Joe nods, certain he has.

"My mother named me after Samuel *Taylor* Coleridge. She loves his poems. Are you alright Joe? You look a little, well, peaky."

"Me? Yeah, fine, no problem at all." Apart from the realisation it *was* Sam's name he recognised on account of his local youth club being named after the acclaimed Victorian composer and conductor. Joe had learned about the life of Samuel Coleridge Taylor at Rockmount Primary during Black History Month and Aaliyah had performed his most famous work, *Song of Hiawatha*, with Rockmount musicians playing with London Mozart Players. And here he is, 'Sam,' in the flesh, hanging out with Joe.

"You have an odd smile on your face," Sam warns.

"Right, sorry." Joe fixes up his face. "And listen, like Winnie says, you'll be amazing. Trust me."

"Thank you." Sam manages a lop-sided smile. His attention is drawn to the man sitting at the grand piano tinkling the ivories in a decidedly ragtime rhythm belonging in a Wild West drinking saloon rather than an elegant English salon. He revels in disapproving glances from nearby guests, taking a long swig of whisky, shooting them a wink and playing louder than ever. He spots Joe, Sam and Winnie, greeting them with a grin. "Ah, the professionals have arrived to commandeer the 'Joanna' as I believe you English call it, the fun ones who drink in pubs, not these stiff upper-lippers."

He speaks in a slightly slurred Southern accent which immediately alerts the trio.

"Is that the American?" whispers Sam.

"He doesn't sound like the American I overhead," replies Winnie.

"That's not him," agrees Joe and the trio relax.

Sam watches the notes with fascination. "What are you playing?"

"Music to ease an aching soul."

"I've never heard anything like it before."

"Nor I, until I bumped into an itinerant young musician from Arkansas, a fine fella by the name of Scott Joplin. Here," he says shuffling along on the piano stool. "You're welcome to freestyle on the left while I take the right."

Sam hesitates.

"Life's deadly dull without taking a little risk, kid."

Joe whispers, "Remember you tailed Smiler today, you've got this."

Sam puts his hands together in prayer and slides onto the stool. "I can try. Do you have the music?"

"You already have the music," says the man putting his hand on his heart. "In here. I'm Charley Adeleine."

Sam's shoulders tense but his eyes gleam and he begins replicating the loose rhythmic playing.

"That's it, kid. Relax."

Sam lets his fingers slide across the keys. A grinning Charley Adeleine joins the top octaves.

"Let's swap," cries Charley, jumping up from the stool, crossing over Sam's hands to the lower keys. With a laugh Sam ducks under Charley's arms, taking the top notes. As they vibe off each other, guests gather around the piano to listen. Sam tinkles away, head nodding, fingers flying across the keys until Charley takes the baseline down to a finale build mirrored by Sam. The duet ends with a flourish to applause from Joe, Winnie, and other guests. Charley and Sam shake hands.

Suddenly a second alarmingly familiar American voice cries, "Encore, encore!"

Joe dares not turn around. Winnie's hand locks into his, squeezing confirmation the American behind them is Raymond Judson.

"Raymond!" greets Charley. He slaps Sam on the back. "When I sail back to Chicago, I shall invite my new friend to join. He'd love hearing what they're starting to play."

Carried away with the moment, Sam jumps up. "Samuel Coleridge Taylor at your service and happy to stow away to Chicago!"

"Do your friends have names too?"

Joe tries alerting Sam, but even if he noticed Joe's jerking head, he wouldn't necessarily read it as code for 'BE CAREFUL THIS OTHER AMERICAN IS THE ONE!'

"This is my musical partner Winifred Carmichael Stopes, and, er, this is Edward Sheeran. He turns the pages."

Every muscle in Joe's body tenses. He's sure Raymond Judson's eyes are studying him, and Winnie also keeps her face down.

A saviour approaches in the form of Madame d'Varney. "Charley, Raymond, mon amis, stop leading our special young guests astray with your bar room melodies! They have their own divine compositions to perform."

"Forgive me Madame d'Varney." Charley Adeleine pours himself a large whisky. "I wouldn't want to spoil your *soiree*."

He knocks his drink down in one go. Madame d'Varney's dancing eyes steel for a moment before slipping back into friendly bon homie, addressing Sam, Winnie, and Joe, "Forgive my American friends. Their cities lack the elegance of London or Paris."

Joe keeps staring at his shoes, praying the adults remain too engrossed with each other to pay him any attention.

"Raymond, perhaps you can escort Charley upstairs to the gaming table? I believe the Prince of Wales is keen to be parted from some of his mother's riches."

"The Prince of Wales?" Sam's wide eyes blink overtime. "I didn't know we'd be performing for royalty."

"Don't fret kid." Charley rises from the piano stool with a sway. "No matter how gifted the musicians or beautiful the music you won't entice the prince from his mistress."

"Lilly Langtry, the most beautiful face in London?" Raymond Judson winks.

"No, his other mistress. Poker."

"Sacre bleu!" cries Madame d'Varney, hands waving in the air. "You two have much to learn about discretion."

"We'll revise on the way upstairs, that much I can promise," says Judson as he clamps his arm around Charley.

Charley says loudly to the trio and for the benefit of the older guests, "Play from the heart, kids. Don't let these old suckers drain you of life."

To Joe and Winnie's great relief, the Americans saunter away to the hall. Joe isn't the only person surreptitiously watching them go. A tall man stands alone at the back of the room, eyes locked on Judson. He follows at a discreet distance. Joe realises it's the same tall man surveilling Judson at the lecture earlier.

With a strange look, Madame d'Varney also watches the Americans exit before switching her smile back on and seemingly saying to herself, "Charley is homesick, longs for his native land. Perhaps soon we shall return."

Joe knows how Charley feels.

"Did you three meet in the United States?" asks Winnie conjuring up a casual air.

"Oui, I confess a weakness for Americans. Raymond Judson is in oil, and Charley is, well, from a family renown across the city. However, there are guests here tonight of far greater interest."

Not likely.

Madame d'Varney announces, "We are expecting the Shah of Persia!"

Looking at the shocked faces of Joe, Winnie, and Sam, she smiles benevolently. "Have no fear, my children. I hear the shah is a most gracious monarch and feel certain your music will inspire his royal ear-holes. But here I am, droning on, let me let you prepare. Au revoir!"

As she sweeps away out of earshot Joe and Winnie exclaim in unison, "That was him!"

"Umm, him who?" frowns Sam.

"The American! The jewel thief!" whispers Joe. Bubbles of excitement pop inside his belly, his plan appears to be working.

"Charley Adeleine?" From Sam's disquiet he hopes his new piano partner isn't implicated.

"No, his friend," Winnie explains. "*He's* the man I heard chase after Joe and Elias."

"And visited Elias. And if the shah is coming here tonight, I bet this is when they're planning to steal the Star of Nimrod!"

CHAPTER 28

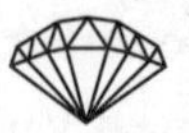

"Err, you don't look convinced either," says Sam, observing Winnie's frown.

"Come on," insists Joe, pushing his borrowed dark glasses back up his nose. "If the Shah of Persia's here, plus Raymond Judson, he could be swiping the Star of Nimrod tonight."

"His voice *does* sound like the man I heard chasing you, but Madame d'Varney confirmed Raymond Judson is a wealthy gentlemen," reasons Winnie. "Which doesn't make sense, someone in his position running around stealing diamonds. Although ..."

"What?" demands Joe.

"I heard a quality in her voice, as if something's troubling her or she's hiding something."

"Well ..." Joe's mind races. "We've only got Madame d'Varney's word to vouch for Judson. What if she's in on it too?"

"Hmm." Sam takes out his violin, replying dryly, "And perhaps she'll get the Prince of Wales to be their lookout."

"We need to keep an open mind," Joe retorts, trying to convince himself as much as Sam and Winnie of what admittedly seemed a preposterous theory. "I'm just saying people aren't always what they seem."

"Agreed." Winnie sits at the piano to begin the recital. Joe feels sure her remark is aimed at him.

As the recital approaches its climax, Madame d'Varney enters the salon in an animated conversation with the shah.

"He's wearing the Star of Nimrod!" Joe tells Winnie and Sam as they play. The gemstone's blue star sparkles in the candlelight, even putting Madame d'Varney's necklace in the shade. "Plus, he's not surrounded by his elite guard."

"But he *is* surrounded by London's elite," hisses Sam. "Turn!"

"What? Oh, right." Joe quickly turns the page of music before returning to his theorising. "Think about it, a party's perfect. The shah's relaxed. They could swipe it when he's not looking. We have to warn him."

"And say what?" whispers Winnie.

"Well, I … dunno, but it can't be when Madame d'Varney's around. We have to get her away from the shah. Trust me."

Something passes between Sam and Winnie when Joe asks them to trust him. They play to the duet's crescendo. Afterwards, they stand side by side.

"An ovation!" whispers a beaming Sam as he gives a short bow whilst Winnie curtseys to the applauding guests.

Madame d'Varney waltzes over, diamond rings clapping together. "Bravo! Bravo!"

"Umm, excuse me Madame d'Varney," says Sam with butter-wouldn't-melt-in-his-mouth politeness. "I would be grateful if you could take me to your acquaintance, Mr Charley. I'd very much like to arrange another opportunity to duet with him."

"Oh, I can never refuse a charming gentleman! Come, come."

As Sam follows Madame d'Varney from the salon, he shoots Joe a chuffed smile which Joe returns with a grateful thumbs-up.

"Now Sam's got Madame d'Varney out of the way all we need to do is work out how to get talking to the shah."

"And what to say," adds Winnie.

Part one of their mission is accomplished when the shah himself approaches.

"Ah, a fine performance, children. Madame d'Varney tells me you attend the Royal Normal Academy for the Blind, which I pass on the way to my apartment at The Queens Hotel. Tonight, you exemplify their reputation for excellence."

Winnie curtseys. "Thank you, Your Majesty."

The shah turns to leave.

Joe has to act.

He blurts, "Your brooch is awesome."

The shah stops and frowns. Joe immediately realises his mistake; complimenting something he's not supposed to be able to see.

Fortunately, Winnie leaps to the rescue;

"Our friend, Sam, was just describing it to us."

"Ah, yes. The Star of Nimrod is a special treasure. Possesses great healing powers, harnessing the life-giving energy of the Heavens and Earth. Enjoy your evening."

"Wait!" exclaim Joe and Winnie.

"Yes?"

Joe cracks his knuckles and goes for broke. "Your Majesty, there's a plot to steal the Star of Nimrod."

The shah gives a sequence of puzzled blinks as he processes the revelation.

"What makes you say that?"

Joe senses Winnie's tension but can't stop now.

"Me and my friend Elias overhead two men plotting. I think they're gonna try and steal it tonight when you don't have your guards."

A benevolent smile crosses the shah's face.

"I think my treasure is quite safe amongst these distinguished ladies and gentlemen. And although you will not be able to see them of course, two of my guards accompany me at all times." The shah glances over to the back of the room where Joe spots two men in dinner jackets watching them intently. He hadn't recognised them as members of the shah's elite guard without their grand uniforms.

"They never leave my side so you have nothing to worry about."

Joe's familiar with the shah's look, the one when adults aim for nice but land on patronising. "Believe me, they're going to try and steal the Star of Nimrod and—"

"Whatever you thought you heard," interrupts the shah, "it's quite safe. I never let it out of my sight. Nevertheless, I promise to be additionally vigilant. Now excuse me, and congratulations once again on your performance."

"That went as well as could be expected," Winnie says once the shah had moved on to greet other guests. "You did everything you could."

"Yeah, and it wasn't enough." Joe resists adding 'as usual,' not wanting to throw himself another pity party. But he spots a familiar face through the cigar smoke across the other side of the salon. "Sir Henry Majoure!"

Joe studies Sir Henry. Something about him doesn't seem right as he leans heavily on his ivory tipped cane.

"What's he doing?"

"He's just spotted the shah, can't take his eyes off him. Now the shah's leaving the room, talking to another guest. Sir Henry's following. Quick, come on!" Joe grabs Winnie's hand.

"Coming, but remember you're not supposed to be able to see."

They make haste to the hall, thick with laughter and gossip.

"What's happening now?" Winnie asks.

"The shah's going upstairs. Sir Henry's hanging around at the bottom. Wait!"

"What?"

"Madame d'Varney's coming downstairs. She's with Sam. She's stopped, now she's talking to the shah. She's looking right at the Star of Nimrod. *She's touching it.* They're laughing, now she's coming down the stairs right for us."

"Merci for making my humble soiree so special!" Madame d'Varney opens a diamond encrusted handbag. "Please accept a teeny-tiny token of my appreciation." She brings out two small purple velvet bags, handing one to Sam, taking Winnie's hands and giving her the other.

Sam excitedly pulls out a silver clip in the shape of a treble clef.

Winnie's fingers feel around her silver clip. A beaming Madame d'Varney hands Joe a round box.

"For my petit page-turner, Turkish delights from my personal collection."

"Thank you," they chorus.

However, behind his dark glasses Joe's eyes are fixed on Sir Henry hovering at the bottom of the stairs waiting for someone or something.

Madame d'Varney also notices Sir Henry and waves at him. He responds with a curt nod. He seems older. Skin thinner.

"Ah, excuse me, children. I have one more present to give, so farewell, I will have Giles arrange carriages to carry you to your beds. Au revoir!" Madame d'Varney bends down and kisses all three on the cheek before hurrying to join Sir Henry.

"What a lovely lady," says Sam, admiring his pin.

Joe hisses. "That lovely lady is talking to Sir Henry Majoure, and did you hear what she told us? She's *giving him a present.*"

"Riiiight," Sam replies. "So she likes giving presents, is that a crime?"

"Yeah, if it's a stolen diamond!"

"Wasn't the shah still wearing his brooch a few moments ago?" asks Winnie.

"But they could've switched it already for a fake, or switched it on the stairs."

"Er, when you say 'they,' do you mean Madame d'Varney?" asks an incredulous Sam.

"Shhh, she's talking now to Sir Henry."

"Tell me what's going on."

"Sir Henry's kissing her hand, but from the look on his face he thinks he might catch something. Now he's whispering in her ear. She's looking in her handbag and she's bringing something out ....

What the ...?"

Two talking guests suddenly move and block Joe's view. Sam can still see from his position so immediately takes up the baton describing what's happening;

"Madame d'Varney's handing Sir Henry a small velvet bag like ours. He's taking it. He's looking around to see if anyone's watching. He's opening the bag."

"Can you see what's in it?" Joe moves around to where Sam stands, straining to see whilst at the same time trying to look like he's not looking.

"Has he opened it?" Winnie asks.

"Yes," Joe and Sam reply.

"And?"

Neither say a word.

Finally, Sam speaks, "It's something really very sparkly."

"A diamond," adds Joe, catching a glint of blue as Sir Henry closes the bag and puts it in his pocket, giving Madame d'Varney a small bow.

"Sir Henry's leaving," says Sam.

"Yeah, and he's leaving with the Star of Nimrod!"

Chapter 29

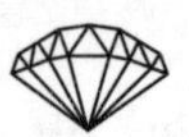

"No visitors outside visiting hours, and eight o'clock in the morning's NOT visiting hours," declares Matron standing firmly in the door of Cottage Hospital in case Joe, Winnie, Sam and Bertie try sneaking past. "Besides, Elias is with the doctor."

"Dr Doyle?" asks Joe.

Matron's eyes narrow. "Yes."

"Dr Doyle is expecting us," Winnie explains with an appealing smile.

"We're meeting him right this minute," adds Bertie in case Matron had missed the point.

She huffs her disapproval at such irregularities, closing the door in their faces. The crows on top of the building caw with laughter.

"Umm, what now?" asks Sam.

Joe rubs his cheeks in frustration, desperate to see Elias.

"We don't have much time if we're gonna get back and stake out Rockhills *and* Gorsuch's showroom. Smiler said he's delivering at eleven, right?"

"Correct," Bertie concurs.

"And he *has* to be delivering the Star of Nimrod."

"Can't believe I missed it being stolen," complains Bertie for the umpteenth time.

"Er, none of us actually *witnessed* it being stolen," corrects Sam, the doubt in his voice continuing to irk Joe.

"Is that or is that not a diamond we saw Madame d'Varney hand Sir Henry? A diamond that looked pretty much like the Star of Nimrod, complete with a blue star. They must be taking it to Gorsuch to remove the diamond from the brooch and sell. Trust me"

The three of them glance at each other. Joe senses them wondering if his judgement could be trusted. He can't blame them. After all he hasn't trusted them enough to tell the truth about who he is.

Sam's elegant fingers scratch his chin. "Your theory suggests Madame d'Varney is a jewel thief in league with Raymond Judson and Charley Adeleine which is, well, a little improbable?"

Joe takes a breath and quotes the Sherlock Holmes mug Dad got him last Christmas, "Once you've ruled out the impossible, whatever remains, no matter how improbable, must be the truth."

The four youngsters spin around as Dr Doyle says, "What a marvellous saying, young Joe. Where did you hear it?"

Joe stares at Dr Doyle standing in the now open doorway. "Umm, er ... I think *you* said it in your lecture yesterday?"

"I did?" he muses with surprise. "Much of what I said was off the cuff, must note that for a future story. It's precisely the sort of thing Sherlock would say. Now apologies, my friends. Please come in."

Dr Doyle leads the quartet inside. "It's alright, Matron. They're with me."

"Undeniably, we're with him!" chimes Bertie, sending Matron's displeasure to boiling point.

In the ward Elias remains still, electric blue eyes closed. Joe wants to take his hand, his own life to reignite Elias's. Instead, he stands lamely at the bedstead, guilt sloshing around his gut.

Dr Doyle puts his hand on Joe's shoulder. "Elias is comfortable."

"Did you discover anything that might help him?" Bertie asks.

Dr Doyle glances around the small ward. The elderly patients in two of the seven other beds are asleep, and Matron has huffed to her office. Even so, Dr Doyle fears the walls have ears because he beckons the foursome to come close around Elias's bed.

"I have conducted enquiries of my own. This 'Babushka' you said who works for Sir Henry and put Elias in a trance goes by the name of Blatovsky. She's a spiritualist of some infamy, able to use her powers of hypnosis to control minds and summon spirits. She was involved in the Breigstock incident when a séance went badly wrong."

"How?" asks Winnie.

"In séances a medium communicates with the Spirit World, either directly or through another. However, in Breigstock, Blatovsky placed a gentleman in a trance from which he never awoke."

Everyone immediately turns to Elias.

"What happened to him?" Joe demands but realises the answer from Dr Doyle's grim face.

"Doctors and healers tried their best, but nothing could be done."

Dr Doyle doesn't want to say the words, so Joe does. "He died?"

Dr Doyle nods. "Blatovsky fled West, her whereabouts unknown."

"Into the pay of Sir Henry Majoure," Joe says through gritted teeth. "Tell us what you know about him."

Dr Doyle's face flickers with surprise at the forcefulness of Joe's demand. Joe is just as surprised but that doesn't stop him holding the doctor's eye, waiting for answers.

"He is a man not to be trifled with, in business or his personal affairs. I can't tell you as much as I'd like."

"You need to tell us everything," says Joe flatly. "We can't help my friend if we don't know the truth."

Dr Doyle looks at their four grave faces and the silent Elias. "Very well. As I said yesterday, I'm an avid member of the spiritualist movement. We believe spirits exist and have both the ability and desire to communicate with the living and share their infinite intelligence with us."

"Infinite intelligence?" Bertie repeats.

"We believe everything around us, nature both physical and spiritual, is the expression of infinite intelligence. Our modern times with our scientific enquiries place us close to unlocking their secrets, secrets lost when ancient civilisations fell such as Egypt, Greece and

Nineveh."

"Civilisations re-created in the Crystal Palace," Winnie observes.

"Indeed. There are many in this period of enlightenment who would wish to learn from the past, a time when communicating with the afterlife was commonplace."

"Not me." Sam's fingers nervously play the bedpost. "I'm happy for the afterlife to remain after."

"Understandable," Dr Doyle replies with a small smile. "And perhaps wise, but you cannot halt mankind's thirst for knowledge. It was such a thirst that led me to join a club."

Joe guesses he isn't talking cricket.

Dr Doyle touches a signet ring on his index finger. "The Ghost Club."

"The Ghost Club?" echo all four, causing Dr Doyle to urgently look around as if expecting the sleeping pensioners to sit up and repeat it too.

"It was formed as a paranormal investigation organisation, a research group if you will, looking into spiritual phenomenon, ghosts and hauntings, to verify and learn from them or expose them as hoaxes."

"Ghostbusters," murmurs Joe.

"The Club examined phenomenon which for hundreds of years the hysterical and uninformed in Western civilisation decried as witchcraft, before our current age of learning and enquiry. The Ghost Club had a distinguished membership. Charles Dickens was a founding member, as was ..." Dr Doyle hesitates.

So Joe finishes, "Sir Henry Majoure."

"Correct. When Dickens departed for the other side which so fascinated him, Sir Henry took over as Chair of the Ghost Club. But it became increasingly clear he was seeking infinite knowledge not for the benefit of mankind, but for the benefit of himself. The Club was dissolved after an acrimonious meeting when Sir Henry was forced to resign having brought the Club into disrepute, conversing with the likes of 'Babushka Blatovsky.'"

Dr Doyle's words confirm all Joe's worst suspicions about Sir Henry.

"Now he's stolen the Star of Nimrod from the Shah of Persia."

Dr Doyle's eyes widen.

Joe goes on, "Me and Elias overheard his henchman planning the theft. That's why they were chasing us. Why they want us silenced."

Bertie straightens to attention and declares, "He must be stopped. And we must stop him!"

"Brave sentiments to be lauded, young Wells. However, I cannot over emphasise the dangerous nature of Sir Henry and his acolytes. I don't want any more beds in this ward filled with his victims."

"But we want to help," Winnie says.

"As do I, therefore I'm leaving London at once."

Dr Doyle sees the disappointment on their faces. Joe planned to enlist his help catching Smiler taking the Star of Nimrod to Gorsuch at 11 o'clock, knowing they needed back up from respected adults if they're to be believed.

"I'm consulting somebody who may be able to aid Elias, or at least suggest a course of action to reverse his trance, somebody well versed in the spiritual world."

Joe nods. "Then you have to try. When will you be back?"

"By tonight, God willing. In the meantime, promise you won't put yourselves in danger, you'll keep away from Sir Henry and his people."

The four friends glance at each other, their showdown with Sir Henry less than three hours away.

Joe takes Elias's hand and crosses the fingers of his other hand behind his back.

"We promise."

Chapter 30

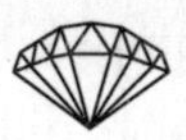

A delivery cart spills at the top of Crystal Palace Park Road sending apples rolling down the hill to be plucked up by laughing passers-by. The morning traffic becomes chaos when all the horses stop pulling their carriages, ignore the cries of their drivers, and start munching on the unexpected treats.

Bertie chortles at the spectacle. Joe wishes he could, instead he feels for the drivers helplessly steering through chaos. But at least Joe finally has things under control, his friends where he wants them, his eyes locked on the gates of Rockhills.

At eleven o'clock, in fifteen minutes, Smiler is due at Gorsuch's showroom. He might leave Rockhills via the garden entrance directly into the palace grounds, but if he does, Sam and Winnie are already on stake-out in the Upper Gallery. If by five-to-eleven Joe and Bertie haven't seen Smiler leave, they'll sprint as fast as they can to join them and catch Smiler with the stolen Star of Nimrod.

Joe's mind and body aches, running on the adrenaline of helping Elias, exposing Sir Henry and getting a shot at retrieving the compass that will bring him back to his family. Yet success will wrench him away from his new friends. Try as he might not to let them get too close, knowing this is all temporary, it's proving near impossible not to feel more attached every second spent with them.

"Juicy!" declares Bertie, crunching on an escaped apple before adopting a more serious expression to match Joe's. "Do you think Catherine Marsh will come?"

"Here's hoping."

Joe knows they need adult back up when confronting Smiler to ensure they're believed. With Dr Doyle off on his mission to find Elias a cure, Catherine Marsh is the perfect person of good standing to protect his friends.

Earlier the foursome had bumped into her walking to visit Elias, so Joe tentatively asked, "Miss Marsh, did you really believe it when they said Elias was a thief?"

"The Elias I've watched grow up is generous of deed and spirit. He is also trusting and perhaps placed his trust in the wrong person."

The lady dubbed by Elias 'Queen of New Town' looked pointedly at Joe, seeming to share Aunty Doll's conviction he'd led Elias to his ruin.

Bertie, Winnie, and Sam who had been waiting a few paces away stepped forward.

"I can vouch for my friend," declared Bertie.

"He's doing everything he can to help Elias," added Winnie, "from getting him medical help to trying to clear his name."

Catherine Marsh studied them carefully.

Spurred by their support, Joe made his pitch. "What if I told you there's a way to prove the man who chased us and accused Elias and me is the real thief? Then if … *when* Elias wakes up everyone will know he's innocent."

Catherine Marsh frowned in thought. "This is really a matter for the police."

"If I go to the police, I'll be arrested and no-one's gonna believe our word against theirs. But the police will *have* to believe us if someone like you is a witness. My Nan told me how you stopped a riot single-handed when the Navvies were about to go off to fight in a war."

"The Crimean War," she replied, a glint in her eye.

"Right. Some of the Navvies got drunk before they left and had a brawl and police tried arresting them and next thing it's a massive riot, police verses Navvies. It was nearly a blood bath until you come riding your carriage smack bang in the middle asking the Navvies to stop. They listened to you, hundreds of them, because you've stuck up for them and they respect you. Everyone does. Stick up for Elias now."

"You too are a powerful speaker, young man. Perhaps your persuasive tongue placed poor Elias in trouble."

Joe's shoulders sagged, the partial truth of her words not lost on him.

"Nevertheless, a man is innocent until proven guilty. If by helping you, I may help Elias and his family, I know where my duty lies."

"So, you'll come?" cried Joe.

"Tell me where I need to be and when."

The second adult they enlist to help is Winnie's father. Joe and Winnie ambush him unloading crates containing his latest geological finds, his thin glum face listening with surprised silence as she explains how the stolen Star of Nimrod is about to be taken to Gorsuch. When Winnie speaks to him, Joe notices her usual confidence replaced with self-doubt.

"You can help us, Papa," she pleads. "You can verify the diamond is in fact the Star of Nimrod and catch the culprits."

Mr Stopes picks up a fossil from an open packing case, staring as if it might come back to life and suggest what he should do.

"Serious matter," he murmurs, "very serious indeed." He rotates the fossil, lost in its million-year-old curves.

"Please, Papa, help me and I promise I won't get into any more disagreements with Marie. If she goads me, I'll turn the other cheek. I won't say anything to upset her, and you and Mama can go about your work in peace."

From Joe's brief encounter with Marie Stopes, he knows the sacrifice Winnie would be making and is unsure he could do the same faced with her malicious taunts. However, the prospect of a peaceful home seems to prompt Mr Stopes to tell his fossil, "Mmm. Yes. Gorsuch. Eleven O'Clock. I'll be there."

That hour fast approaches.

"You've definitely got both tickets?" asks Joe.

"Have no fear," replies Bertie, demonstrating his trick. "I'll hold last week's expired ticket behind my valid ticket, and if I smile and act politely the guard will simply glance at the top ticket and usher us through without even looking at the other."

"You think that'll work?" Joe is unconvinced good manners are all they need to guarantee sneaking him in.

"Joe, you're always telling us 'Trust me', but that goes both ways you know."

Joe backs up a step. "Yeah, I know, and I do."

"I sometimes wonder. I can't claim to be an expert on friendship, but at some point one has to have faith in one's friends, much as I respect your secretive 'man of mystery' demeanor."

"Winnie called me that, but it's your kind of phrase."

"Why thank you."

"Good to know you're chatting about me behind my back."

"Do you blame us?" Bertie takes an indignant bite of his apple.

Joe rubs his head. "No. It's just … there are some things, about me, you wouldn't understand."

"How can we when you won't confide in us? It sometimes feels you're deliberately trying to keep us at a distance, as if one day 'poof!' like a magician's rabbit you'll disappear."

Joe puts his hand on Bertie's shoulder. "I just want to protect you, that's all."

"Are you certain it's us you're protecting?"

"How do you—"

Suddenly Bertie splutters his apple, pointing urgently.

Smiler walks up Rockhills driveway looking like the cat that got the cream and the mouse and the canary.

Right behind is Sir Henry himself, putting on gloves as if annoyed they didn't do so themselves. Once on, he holds his gloved hand out to Smiler who passes a small velvet bag.

Joe knows what's inside and where it's heading.

Game on.

Hearts beating at high-speed, Joe and Bertie cross Crystal Palace Parade walking ten paces behind Sir Henry and Smiler as they enter the North Transept. Sir Henry has a youthful spring in his step, his weary gait from last night gone, his skin glowing.

Queues of visitors line the foyer to pay their half a shilling and pass the turnstiles, but Sir Henry and Smiler walk straight up to the ticket booth. The guard stands to attention, doffing his cap.

"Morning, sir."

Sir Henry marches past without even looking at him, Smiler in tow.

Joe and Bertie cut to the front of the queue. Bertie addresses the guard, "Good morning, fine sir. If you could let us through, we'd be most grateful. My father's playing cricket with W. G. Grace and they'll be starting soon, thanks awfully."

"We're in a hurry," adds Joe, immediately realising his error as the guard scowls.

"Let me see those tickets."

Bertie hesitates before handing them over. Joe's heart sinks. The guard studies them.

"This ticket's valid but the other ticket's for last week."

Joe groans as he watches Sir Henry and Smiler disappearing into the palace.

"Ah," Bertie exclaims perplexed. "Uncle must've picked up the wrong ticket. Uncle! Uncle Henry!" shouts Bertie after Sir Henry.

Joe's mouth drops open. Does Bertie really expect Sir Henry to pretend to be his uncle and sneak them in?

Fortunately, Sir Henry is too far away to hear, which Joe realises Bertie is counting on.

"Oh dear." Bertie wrings his hands. "Uncle Henry will be *most* upset."

Bertie's words are deliberately vague enough to suggest the guard might be the subject of Sir Henry's displeasure. He stands aside.

"Don't worry, young sir, none of us want to upset Sir Henry, do we?"

"No," whispers Joe as they hurry through the gate. "Least not for another three minutes."

The palace fills with visitors. The hour nears, although the hands of Dent's giant clock remain mysteriously still since Joe's arrival in the past. Joe and Bertie rush past the Nineveh Court where workmen add finishing touches to the colossal winged bulls. Joe senses the bulls staring down on him with expectation to save Nineveh's ancient artefact from the hands of Sir Henry, who by now has reached the Upper Gallery steps.

Bertie struggles to keep up with Joe, so he shouts, "Go on, I'll catch up."

The humid palace air makes sweat prick Joe's skin as he climbs the steps two at a time.

The Upper Gallery buzzes with artisans, craftsmen and traders enticing the public into stalls and showrooms. Sam and Bertie had explained Gorsuch's showroom is in-between the North and Grand Transepts. Joe picks up pace scanning stall signs—

Stanford Maps ...

Letts Stationery ...

Rimmel Cosmetics ...

Twenty meters ahead, he spots a sign in the shape of a violin. Joe remembers Gorsuch's showroom is next door to Boosey and Son's musical instrument emporium.

Sure enough, Sir Henry and Smiler turn into the neighbouring showroom.

Watching them enter near the Upper Gallery railings stand Sam,

Winnie, Mr Stopes, and Catherine Marsh.

The plan's coming together! Joe runs to meet them. "Great! We're all here, except Bertie, but he's on his way."

Adrenalin pumping, Joe takes a moment to notice Winnie and Sam's uncomfortable faces. Mr Stopes wears a puzzled frown and Catherine Marsh appears deeply unimpressed.

"When you came to me, you failed to mention your so-called 'thief' is Sir Henry Majoure."

Joe hadn't expected Sir Henry to be here either, anticipating Smiler would continue doing his dirty work, but this is even better, a chance to catch him red-handed if only he can get them all into Gorsuch's showroom ....

"Sir Henry may have a particular manner to him," Catherine Marsh continues in a voice suggesting it's a manner she doesn't particularly care for, "but he's a generous philanthropist donating to the Navvies Relief Fund and," she says to Winnie, "the Royal Normal Academy for the Blind."

Joe flushes. "Just because he's wealthy and powerful doesn't mean he's above the law."

Catherine Marsh rises up to her full height. Expecting the full force of her admonishment, Joe is caught off guard when she says, "You truly believe he is responsible, don't you?"

"Yes."

"And you two agree?"

"I trust Joe," Winnie says.

Sam looks at Joe, and to his relief and gratitude says, "I take my cue from Joe, too."

"Me three!" cries Bertie as he hobbles over panting.

Had time allowed, Joe would've hugged them all.

All clocks in the Vieyes and Repingdon showroom chime eleven.

Catherine Marsh turns to Mr Stopes. "You, sir, you believe your daughter has sound judgement?"

"Hmmm."

Joe just about manages not to cry, "Come on!"

Finally Mr Stopes says, "I believe so."

Winnie takes her papa's hand.

Catherine Marsh hesitates as if considering asking the opinion of someone else—in which case Joe's prepared to charge in alone—but to his great relief she says, "I hope so too. Very well. Shall we?"

Chapter 31

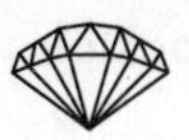

The blinds in Gorsuch's showroom remain down and a handwritten sign says, CLOSED TODAY.

Joe grips the door handle, exchanging glances with his three friends, friends he could never have got here without even though they look like they're about to undertake a group parachute jump without knowing if the parachute works. Winnie feels for Joe's hand and squeezes it. Sam and Bertie nod.

They burst in.

"The sign says we're closed!"

A flustered Gorsuch is at his lapidary table used to cut, grind and polish gemstones.

Smiler, leaning against the showroom wall, pushes himself forward, poised to intervene.

Sir Henry stands quite still, empty velvet bag in his hand, its contents on the felt table.

All eyes focus on the gemstone.

It must already have been removed from its ornamental brooch, but the greyish blue diamond has a distinctive milky star which Joe points at triumphantly.

"The Star of Nimrod! You had it stolen from the Shah of Persia. Look, there's even an illustration on the table." Joe points at a detailed hand drawing of the brooch.

All eyes are now on Sir Henry. His eyebrows rise a little higher but otherwise the accusation has no impact whatsoever.

Cool as a snake, but still going down ...

Gorsuch, however, is indignant enough for both of them.

"Stolen?" He gasps. "I do not deal in stolen gems! A preposterous allegation, how dare you burst into my showroom when the sign clearly says *we are closed!*"

But Joe's on a roll. "Sam, book please."

With great ceremony Sam lays the *Encyclopaedia of Gemstones* on the counter, opens the cover, licks his fingers, and turns to the page.

"Look at the illustration," Joe says to Catherine Marsh and Mr Stopes who still stand in the showroom doorway as if unsure whether to step in or run away. "And look at *this* diamond."

This draws Catherine Marsh across to the table to examine the evidence. Sir Henry gives her a small smile.

"Miss Marsh, an unexpected pleasure," he purrs.

"Sir Henry. Forgive my intrusion, however I have promised to listen to these children's allegations, no matter how unlikely they may seem."

"You have always dedicated yourself to lost causes." He smiles.

Catherine Marsh bristles.

Sam reads, "'The Star of Nimrod has traces of the mineral rutile, which is responsible for the star effect, known as asterism, creating a three-pointed star pattern.'"

Catherine Marsh looks from the illustration to the diamond on the table, her mouth opening and closing with realisation. "Can you explain this, Sir Henry?"

In a voice of icy reasonableness, he replies, "I believe there has been a mistake."

"Yes, there has!" cries Bertie before Joe has a chance to get out his own retort. "Your mistake was stealing the diamond, attacking my friend," putting his hand on Joe's shoulder, "injuring our other friend and thinking you can get away with it! That is to say, you jolly well can't!"

A small smile flickers in the corner of Sir Henry's lips. "This is not the Star of Nimrod," he says with the calm authority of someone who always expects others to agree with him.

But not Joe.

"Oh right, they just happen to look the same do they?" he mocks, desperate for Sir Henry to crack under the weight of their evidence and fess up.

He's overjoyed when Winnie steps forward to deliver the coup de grace. "Papa, please can you verify this is the Star of Nimrod?"

Mr Stopes has been examining illustrations of gemstones on the showroom wall.

"Papa?"

"Hmm?" he murmurs. "Ah." He crosses to the lapidary table, seemingly oblivious to the suspense filling the room. He points at the diamond, saying to Gorsuch, "May I?"

Gorsuch mops sweat from his brow. He glances at Sir Henry who says, "Be my guest."

Joe can't believe how unruffled Sir Henry remains but is about to discover why.

Mr Stopes gently holds up the diamond, the milky star catching the light.

"Remarkable asterism," he says with near-enthusiasm. "An almost flawless diamond."

"So it is the Star of Nimrod?" asks Catherine Marsh.

Mr Stopes takes a breath while everyone holds theirs, finally delivering his verdict.

"No. It is not."

Suddenly the stuffy showroom feels like its closing in on Joe. "But ... it must be."

"It has an asterism just like the Star of Nimrod. However," Mr Stopes continues, warming to his subject, "this is a *real* diamond, one of significant quality and value, whereas the Star of Nimrod is a desert diamond, a crystallised semi-precious quartz harvested in the deserts of Arabia. They are often used as diamond substitutes for costume jewellery. However, they've little financial value."

As his words slowly sink in Bertie finds the use of his mouth again. "You mean to tell us the Star of Nimrod is worthless?"

"Oh, no, well, yes, well yes and no."

"Which is it, Papa?"

"In historical terms and as an heirloom of the Kings of Assyria the Star of Nimrod has great value, not that you'd be able to sell it of course, too distinctive. However, if the exact same desert diamond was discovered today it would fetch no more than a few pounds. Whereas this," he holds the diamond up to the light, "is a real diamond of rare natural beauty. Given its size I imagine its worth, oh, thousands of pounds."

"Three thousand," says Sir Henry. "However, my daughter is worth every penny."

"Your daughter?" asks Catherine Marsh in a thin voice.

"Indeed," replies Sir Henry in a conversational manner as if he'd invited them all here for the purpose of sharing his surprise. "Ada was quite smitten with the Star of Nimrod when she saw the shah wearing it. Therefore, I decided to have a replica brooch made for her birthday. Madame d'Varney is a considerable collector of gemstones. She had one in her possession that struck a remarkable similarity. She agreed to let me purchase the diamond. I collected it from her last night and brought it here today along with a picture of the brooch so Mr Gorsuch can work his magic and create a unique birthday gift for her."

Gorsuch finally manages a smile. "Thank you, too kind."

Joe can only stand there with a look as stupid as he feels. However, Bertie isn't done yet, gesturing at Smiler. "If that's the case, why did *he* tell Mr Gorsuch to keep silent?"

Sir Henry raises both eyebrows.

"Have you children been following us?" He chuckles. "You really have let your imaginations run riot, haven't you? Children will be children," he says, spreading his hands out magnanimously. "Although

Miss Marsh, I'm surprised somebody with your solid reputation would allow themselves to get caught up in such nonsense."

Catherine Marsh looks as if she couldn't agree more but doesn't appreciate hearing it from Sir Henry. Nevertheless, she swallows her pride. "Sir Henry, I owe you my deepest apologies."

"Hmmm." Mr Stopes nods agreement. "As do I. I assure you my daughter was not raised to make up stories."

"Papa," Winnie begins, "I didn't—"

"Winifred, please." Mr Stopes closes his eyes as if that might make his embarrassment go away. "I fear the company you keep has led you astray." Opening his eyes, he looks from Joe to Bertie to Sam.

"Papa, my friends and I, we thought—"

"If these are your 'friends,' I question the judgement you've learned at the academy. Perhaps it's best you come home where we can keep a closer eye."

"Home?" She gasps, face contorting with the prospect of no longer attending her beloved Academy.

"Your mother can tutor alongside Marie."

"But you don't understand what it's like at home, you're away so much and—"

"I'm home now," Mr Stopes voice rises, "and will be for the foreseeable future. As will you be. Sir Henry, excuse us please. I wish my daughter was as deserving of a such a fine gift."

Sir Henry smiles graciously. "No harm done sir, really."

But the harm done is written all over Winnie's face and reflected in Sam's distraught expression as Mr Stopes takes her firmly by the shoulders and marches her out of the showroom, slamming the door behind them.

"Sir Henry, please also accept my sincere apologies," says Catherine Marsh.

"Your apology is received with the good grace it is given."

"And I'm certain these young gentlemen will offer you the apology you deserve."

Joe, Bertie and Sam glance at each other. Sam begins with a sheepish bow. "Sorry sir."

Bertie follows with a cough. "My apologies."

All eyes turn to Joe. He's no idea how the tables have been turned so completely, or how he can have got everything so very wrong. He *does* know he desperately wants to wipe the smile off Smiler's face and take down Sir Henry's patronising raised eyebrow. But he knows when he's been beaten and says in a low voice, "Sorry."

"Sorry ..." echoes Sir Henry leaning forward, "I didn't catch what you said."

Joe chews his lip at Sir Henry's childish game.

"Well?" says Catherine Marsh with stern impatience.

"*Sorry.*"

Sir Henry throws his arms open. "Apology accepted! All forgiven, all forgotten. To show there are no hard feelings, why don't you boys join me for lemonade at the Grand Salon Restaurant? It has the best views in the palace."

Joe, Bertie and Sam exchange urgent glances.

"And of course Miss Marsh you are also most welcome."

"A kind offer, one none of us deserves. I regret I've an appointment in Beckenham visiting an ailing women with the pox, but I'm certain these boys will want to demonstrate their remorse and gratitude for your kindness."

Joe would personally prefer to visit a thousand pox-ridden people than go with Smiler and Sir Henry. From Bertie and Sam's faces they feel exactly the same, but have little choice.

"Very well." Sir Henry smiles at each in turn, his gaze lingering on Joe. "Gentlemen. Shall we?"

Chapter 32

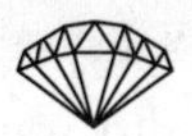

The Grand Salon Restaurant is the jewel in the palace's dining experience; marble floors, tables with the best Egyptian linen and views across the palace grounds to the Surrey hills beyond. White-jacketed staff prepare for lunchtime guests laying silverware in a well rehearsed dance, working as silently as Joe, Bertie and Sam who sit at a round table watched by Sir Henry like endangered species at the zoo.

"Just what you need," says Sir Henry as the waiter pours a jug of lemonade. "A little pick me up. Well, go ahead. Drink!"

The trio oblige. Ice cold bubbles and bitter fresh lemons help jolt Joe out of his shock.

What went wrong? Why were they here? Where had Smiler disappeared to?

"Tell me," says Sir Henry making a church with his fingers. "Who is the leader of your little pack?"

"I am, it's me," says Bertie quickly.

"I think not."

Bertie blushes.

"You spoke too eagerly as one trying to cover for another. You're loyal, an admirable quality."

Bertie blinks, unsure how to take the praise as Sir Henry turns his stare to Sam and Joe.

"The young lady had a strong independent streak to be sure, but I sense one of you pulls the strings."

Sir Henry waves his finger at Sam.

"You, young man. I sense the quiet determination of somebody with great potential."

Sam shuffles uneasily in his seat, fingers playing his legs. But Joe isn't about to let the others take the fall for the mess he's led them into.

"They're here because of me."

Sir Henry feigns surprise. "You?"

"It was all my idea; they didn't want to get involved, but I made them."

"I am a reader of men and I can sense you are a leader of men. Just as I sense you are a conundrum."

Joe chews his lip.

"An enigma, a riddle if you will. Do you like riddles? I do, and it's a mystery to me how you came to believe I'd stolen the Star of Nimrod from the Shah of Persia."

His tone is light; his words make Joe's past suspicions feel fanciful. Yet Joe cannot forget what happened to Elias, nor Dr Doyle's warnings, or his premonition of 'President Majoure.' Joe was wrong about the diamond, but was he wrong not to trust Sir Henry?

"Come, come. I'm owed an explanation, surely?" A debt he expects to be paid as he turns his focus to Bertie. "Tell me your story, I suspect it's fascinating."

"Well, it's rather silly when you think about it. It all began when Joe here lost his compass and ... OW!"

Bertie is silenced by a kick under the table from Joe who mistakenly kicks his bad leg. Eyes filling with tears, Bertie's face screws up with pain and anger. "Why'd you do that?"

Before Joe can apologise Sir Henry offers his answer;

"Because he doesn't trust you. Either of you." He shakes his head sadly at Sam who is also glowering at Joe.

"Sorry, I didn't mean to hurt your leg, but don't tell him ..."

"Why not?" cries Bertie. "We got it all wrong. Why can't you admit it?"

"Don't you see what he's doing? He's manipulating us."

Bertie scoffs. "Oh, *he* is? What about *you*? Ever since we met you've been keeping secrets. We're not friends, we're pawns on your chess board."

"That's not fair—"

"Isn't it?" says Sam quietly. "Winnie told me you were hiding things from us. Where are you from? Where's your family? Who *are* you?"

Joe scrambles for words, finding none.

"Simple questions," Sam continues in sad measured tones cutting deep as Bertie's fury. "But you won't tell us. We tried to be an ensemble, but you always play solo. Winnie trusted you. I told her to follow her instincts. Now she has to leave the academy she loves, and we'll never play again."

Joe sinks in his seat, unable to look at either of them, staring instead at the bubbles in his lemonade glass which pop and disappear like his friendships.

Sir Henry sighs. "Perhaps, gentlemen, it's best to call time on our elevenses."

Sir Henry rises. Bertie follows, his leg still in pain so he grips the back of his chair. Sam wraps his arm around Bertie to support him.

"Thank you for the lemonade," says Sam, "umm, and apologies again."

"Profusely," murmurs Bertie.

Sam and Bertie walk away without even looking at Joe. Joe rises but waits, knowing when he's not wanted. Knowing the distance he'd kept between them had eventually pushed them away.

"A minute more of your time, Joseph, if I may? Please, sit, you look peaky."

Joe sinks into his seat, all his fight gone.

"Alone at last." Sir Henry spreads his hands on the table, stroking the Ghost Club signet ring on his index finger. "You intrigue me, Joseph. And I'm fascinated as to how you have a compass identical to mine in every way."

"I found it."

"Where?"

"Here, in the grounds of the palace."

Sir Henry searches Joe's face, eventually nodding, seemingly satisfied Joe isn't lying.

"A curious matter," he muses as he reaches inside the breast pocket of his jacket, pulling out the shattered compass.

Joe's body tightens. The key to his return home dangles in front of him.

"The makers, Vieyes and Repingdon, have a showroom here at the palace. They swear they never made a replica. Indeed, what would the purpose be? They couldn't sell it unless somebody happened to share my initials. Do you still have the other one?"

Joe shakes his head. He'd taken the precaution of keeping it hidden under a plant pot at the Royal Normal Academy for the Blind.

"I take it you've sold it?"

Joe nods, figuring it's better Sir Henry thinks it's gone.

"To whom? Where is it now?"

Joe swallows.

"Some guy in a pub, The White Hart."

"Hmmm. I hope you got a decent price given the trouble it brought you." He puts the shattered compass in his breast pocket and rises. "I'll pay double what you sold it for if you tell me, truthfully, what led you to believe I wanted to steal the Star of Nimrod? Satisfy my curiosity. You see, Joseph, when you have power and wealth, curiosity is all that's left to keep the world interesting."

"What about friends? Family?" challenges Joe, a flicker of defiance reigniting.

Sir Henry chuckles behind Joe's chair. "It strikes me, Joseph, you have neither. Your 'friends' turned their back on you."

"That's not their fault."

It's mine.

His friends risked everything for him. A gift he'd never returned. Never risking opening up to them, telling himself don't let them get too close in case they get hurt. In truth, he's afraid *he'll* get hurt.

"Joseph, you don't need them. Who wants to be a sheep lost in the herd when you can be an eagle, alone but soaring above, touching the heavens?"

Joe's mind conjures up pictures like an old lost photo album of Bertie, Sam, Winnie and Elias.

A thought strikes.

"I'll tell you what you want to know, for a price."

He senses Sir Henry smiling. "How much?"

"I don't want your money." Joe gets a stab of satisfaction catching Sir Henry by surprise.

His face leans in; Joe smells oiled skin. "What *do* you want?"

"Two things. Give me the compass. And I want that woman who works for you, Babushka Blatovsky, to undo whatever she did and bring Elias back. Do that, I'll tell you what you want."

Sir Henry slides into the seat next to him. "Very well."

Joe finally feels a glimmer of hope at the prospect of reviving Elias and going home.

But Sir Henry's eyes sparkle with amusement and secret knowledge. "You may have *one* of your wishes."

The saliva in Joe's mouth disappears.

"Which will you choose?"

Which indeed? Without the shattered compass, he'll never see his family again. But he can't abandon Elias to slip away into death.

Sir Henry watches as if seeing and enjoying the turmoil inside Joe's head.

Finally Joe says, "Help Elias."

Sir Henry leans back in his chair.

"You would rather use your bargaining power to benefit your friend, rather than yourself?" He studies Joe closely. "I can see why others follow you. You are a young man of strong character."

"I don't care what you think of me. Deal?"

Sir Henry laughs and holds out his hand. "Deal. Babushka

Blatovsky will do all within her power to aid your friend."

Joe shakes Sir Henry's hand. His skin feels strangely cold.

"So, tell me all."

"First you help Elias," counters Joe.

"You seem not to trust me, yet we are gentlemen and have shaken hands. I will be true to my word. Now it is time to be true to yours. Then we can attend to your friend."

Joe sighs, not wanting to lose the chance of helping Elias.

"I overheard the man who works for you, the one who smiles all the time."

"Mr Smyle."

Joe gives a short laugh. "Perfect name."

"Indeed." Sir Henry chuckles.

"Elias and me heard Mr Smyle talking to an American about the Star of Nimrod. We followed him, then we followed you, and I thought I'd got it all worked out. Thought you were planning to steal it, not planning a birthday present for your daughter."

"That explains things. Except one. How do you know the name Blatovsky?"

Joe bites his lip, realising his mistake. He'd first heard her name from Dr Doyle and didn't want to get him into trouble as he had so many others.

"Must've heard your daughter say her name when we tried to get the compass back."

Sir Henry's smile cools.

"Joseph. We were doing so well. Why lie to me now?"

"I'm not lying," Joe lies.

And from the look on his face Sir Henry knows it.

"Who's behind all this, Joseph? There's one way to find out," he declares, looking over Joe's shoulder. "Ada, my dear, please join us."

Joe turns to find two people approaching their table. Sir Henry's daughter, and pushing her wheelchair is Babushka Blatovsky.

CHAPTER 33

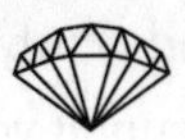

"Joseph, I believe you already met my daughter, Ada, and her governess?" introduces Sir Henry as they approach the table.

Ada lays eyes on Joe. Her brightness fades.

Sir Henry soothes, "You and I shall enjoy your birthday lunch as promised. Joseph will be gone soon."

Ada's wheelchair is pushed up to the dining table by the looming Babushka Blatovsky whose dark eyes stare at Joe. He tries avoiding them.

"How do you feel, my dear?" Sir Henry gives his daughter a kiss on the forehead, an act of affection that surprises Joe.

"A little calmer, Father." Ada doesn't look at Joe. It's as if he isn't there. She hands Sir Henry a glass phial.

"Ah, my dear, what would I do without you?" The dark liquid appears blood red in the sunlight as Sir Henry brings it to his lips and drinks. He shudders, smiles, and pats his daughter's shoulder before taking the seat between her and Joe. "You remember our friend, Joseph, don't you? When he broke into our home?"

Ada stares silently at the jug of lemonade.

"Come now. Look at him. You won't hurt him, I'm sure."

Joe wonders what Sir Henry could possibly mean, but Ada's focus remains on the jug of lemonade.

Suddenly the jug explodes.

Joe stares in amazement as glass, ice, and lemonade spread over the white tablecloth.

Ada's face crumples in shame and fear.

Babushka Blatovsky places a hand on Ada's shoulder and incants,

"El quito de quirum."

Ada's panicked breathing slows.

Sir Henry sighs, seemingly unsurprised by his daughter's apparent gift for exploding glassware, and gently takes her hand.

"Forgive me. I don't wish to upset you on your birthday. All I need, my dear, is for you to ask Joseph where he heard the name of your Governess. Do you know her name?"

Ada frowns. "Babushka," she replies in a small voice.

"An affectionate nickname you have for her, but what's her actual name?"

Joe's heart sinks as he realises his error.

"We don't know."

"Of course you don't. I've no reason to tell you. Which is why I'm curious Joseph knows. Aren't you curious, Ada? Could you ask him for me please? And in return I promise to bring you to Blondin's performance tonight. As a special birthday treat."

Ada stares at the lemonade stain spreading over the tablecloth and turns her intense green eyes to Joe with an apologetic look. Those eyes wash through Joe's head as she speaks, "Where did you hear Babushka's name?"

Joe feels overwhelming comfort as he finds himself saying,

"Dr Doyle."

Joe slams his mouth shut, as if that might draw the words back in. Ada's eyes lower. Sir Henry claps his hands together.

"Doyle, that second-rate physician and third-rate writer. This explains things. Thank you, Ada. Joseph, I believe our business is concluded."

Joe may not know what just happened, but their business isn't over yet.

"What about Elias?" he demands, pointing at Babushka Blatovsky. "Is she going to help him?"

"Ah yes," declares Sir Henry brightly. "Babushka, I promised Joseph you would do all within your power to help his friend recover. Do you have that power?"

Babushka Blatovsky's lips purse resentfully.

"No. His fate is with the Heavens now."

Sir Henry gives a pained expression. "I'm afraid that's all we can do."

"What?" cries Joe, rising up so hard his chair crashes to the floor. He turns to Sir Henry, their eyes lock like sabres. "You lying, cheating sack of—"

"Enough!"

"You promised you'd help him!"

"Please help him, Father. For us?"

Sir Henry hesitates, thrown off guard by his daughter's appeal. Into the silent surprise Ada presses on, "Can't the Star of Nimrod heal Elias just as you hope it can help us?"

Joe runs her words through his head trying to work out what she means. How can the Star of Nimrod help to heal? And ...

"Hold up! You saying he really *is* trying to get his hands on the Star of Nimrod?"

Before she can reply, Sir Henry says quietly, "Ada, my dear, you have been listening to thoughts that do not concern you."

"Forgive us, Father. It's just—"

"The Star of Nimrod is an object of great power. Power we will unlock, I promise." Sir Henry looks around as if making the promise to the Crystal Palace itself. "When we do, your health will be the first of many marvels to unfold. The Shadow Board will regret their lack of faith."

"Can we not then help his friend?" pleads Ada.

Sir Henry bends down by her wheelchair.

"I gave you life, and you give me life. However, a time must come when a child realises their parents cannot magic away every problem. Joseph and his friend broke into our home and must pay the price for their actions. Ah, and here they are now."

Sir Henry gestures like a ringmaster introducing the grand finale—Smiler sauntering towards them accompanied by two policemen.

Joe looks around the restaurant. He's scaled the roof of the palace, raced through the belly of the building, but there's no escape for him this time.

"Please, Father, don't ..." begs Ada as the policemen yanks Joe up from his seat.

Sir Henry gives Joe a sad smile, like a vet about to put down a cherished pet for its own good.

"Goodbye Joseph. It really has been fascinating to meet you."

The police station stands near the top of Gipsy Hill, a rising mass of sandstone brick. In Joe's time it had long been converted into 'luxury flats,' but there's nothing luxurious about it now.

The desk Sergeant in the station reception looks Joe up and down as he reads the arresting officer the charge sheet.

"Thief. Nicked from a gentleman's house." His eyes widen. "Sir Henry Majoure, no less! The gent what sends us that Christmas hamper."

"What?" his colleague exclaims with outrage. "With the bottle of brandy in it?"

WHACK.

Joe's head explodes with pain as the policeman gives him a violent smack around the back of the head. His knees hit the stone floor.

"That'll teach you, little toe rag."

The sergeant rolls his eyes. "You looking for a bottle of brandy all to yourself, Constable Ned?"

"Won't say no."

"Alright lad," says the sergeant, getting down to business. "Up you get. Name?"

Struggling up from the floor he manages, "Joe. Joseph Cook."

"Know when you was born?"

How does he answer that?

"Come on," snarls Constable Ned. "When did your scurvy mother squeeze you out?"

"Know where you live then?"

Saying he lives in one of the grand villas on Church Road will earn Joe another smash around the head, so he stays silent. The sergeant fills in the blanks.

"Vagrant."

"Excuse me, sir," says Joe in a voice he hopes is sufficiently respectful to get a reply rather than a whack. "How long will I be here?"

"Why, got somewhere else to be?"

No. I've got nowhere.

After taking a moment to laugh at his joke, the sergeant replies, "Hmm, Judge Titterington-Finch sits on a Thursday, so that's six days 'til your case gets heard."

If I last six days in here.

The shared cell in the cellar stinks from the sweat and stench of drunk and disorderlies left to sober up. Joe avoids eye contact. He can't forget Smiler's words on the police station steps,

"Best watch your back in there, boy. Never know who might want to use a blade to play xylophone on yer ribs."

Imagining every one of his dozen cell mates might try, Joe sits small and still in the corner. His life is in ruins, but he doesn't want it to end.

Not now.

Not here.

Heat rises as the day draws on. Joe huddles near the window but no breeze blows through the basement bars. There's no way of escaping this time, and no-one to help. He's as alone as the scarred child haunting his dreams.

"*Don't push everyone away,*" Nan had warned him, "*Life's too short to live it alone, kid.*"

Lesson learned too late. Now his life is going to be very short and very much alone.

Lunchtime comes and goes minus lunch, not that Joe fancies eating anything prepared here. His stomach disagrees, rumbling so loudly he's afraid it'll draw attention.

But Joe already has the attention of a new arrival, a man with long lank mousy-brown hair and broken nose with a leather eye patch over his right eye. He's brought in by Constable Ned, the child-whacker, who says a little too loudly, "Here you go, 'til you sober up."

Just before leaving, Constable Ned whispers something to the new arrival, both darting a glance at Joe.

Joe had seen his fair share of Paradise punters on the tipsy-to-drunk scale. This man seems stone cold sober.

No swaying, no singing, no shouting.

Just plenty of staring.

Staring at Joe with a single sapphire blue eye, the only colour against his grey skin and dusty hooded cloak.

Joe forces himself to keep focused on the feet of people passing up and down Gipsy Hill, yet feels that worryingly familiar eye on him.

Smiler's words return. *"Best watch your back in there, boy. Never know who might want to use a blade to play xylophone on yer ribs."*

Joe remembers the description of the man Sam and Bertie witnessed meeting Smiler in the White Swan.

A one-eyed man with an eye patch

Unable to help himself, Joe looks at the one-eyed man. He holds a blade, using it to stroke his stubble.

Joe won't be down here for six days after all. Smiler and his staring friend will make sure of that, just as Margaret Finch predicted.

"Joe knows a smile will be the death of him."

Joe squeezes into the corner, hoping when the one-eyed man strikes, a passer-by might hear his cries and actually do something before he bleeds to death. He certainly can't rely on any help from Constable

Ned when it's evident he's in on the scheme to silence Joe forever.

The one-eyed man slowly pushes himself up from the bench, stretching like a runner preparing for the big race.

Joe's hands grip the bars, ready to scream.

The one-eyed man bears down on him, blade rotating between long fingers.

"Help!" cries Joe. "Somebody help me!"

Chapter 34

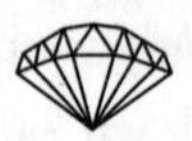

"Help!" cries Joe.

The one-eyed man closes in, blade ready.

Suddenly a voice shouts from the cell entrance, "Alright, alright, enough of your racket! You best not make noise all the way to Millbank Prison."

The one-eyed man spins around.

Joe pauses mid-scream.

Speaking on the other side of the bars is a small man wearing a prison guard uniform and the most enormous beard. This prison guard is accompanied by the one-eyed man's co-conspirator, Constable Ned, who unhappily swings open the cell door.

"Most irregular," grumbles Constable Ned, glancing at the one-eyed man whose blade has disappeared into his cloak, both men evidently thrown by the arrival of the prison guard. "Never heard of a little scum bag getting transported to Millbank before his trial."

"'Ours is not to question why,'" replies the prison guard sagely, "just to follow bloomin' orders. And mine's to transport this here young fella without delay."

Joe considers running up and hugging the prison guard.

Ned scoffs. "How's this toe-rag a 'high security risk'? He just needs to be taught what's for."

Joe's head explodes again. Ned follows up his smack by shoving Joe towards the prison guard who just manages to catch him.

The prison guard steps protectively in front of Joe, giving Ned a strange look. "Seems the only one here needs teaching, Constable, is *you.*"

Confusion spreads across Ned's face. "How'dya mean?"

"I mean," says the guard expanding his words the way a teacher might deal with a dim pupil, "he's *my* prisoner now. A responsibility I happens to take seriously, including delivery minus bruises or breaks or bleedings. Unless of course he does a runner, in which case I catches 'im and *I* give 'im what he deserves. So, constable. Keep. Your. Bullying. Mitts. To. Your-Self."

It takes a moment for Ned to move from shock to outrage, snarling, "Or *what*?!"

The prison guard is a head smaller than Ned, but steps right up to him, replying pleasantly, "Or *you* will have to deal with *me*; that much I can promise."

He smiles up at Ned, but his fists clench as beads of sweat pop onto Ned's forehead. "What's the problem?" asks the prison guard. "I'm not much bigger than the lad. Dont'cha wanna try getting handy with me?"

Ned quickly glances at the one-eyed man for backup but doesn't find it; he's sat himself back on the bench, arms folded, watching with a small smile.

Ned forces out a hollow laugh. "Look, you want him, he's yours, no skin off my nose."

"Glad to hear it," declares the prison guard as if they've just agreed to meet later for a swift pint at the Albert. He winks at Joe. "Come on lad, let's be having you."

Joe doesn't need a written invitation to get the hell out. Nor does he need to look back to know the one-eyed man is still watching him.

Parked outside the police station is a closed black wagon used to transport prisoners.

"Alright lad. You promise me no trouble you can ride up top with me," says the guard.

"Promise."

"But one peep you're in the back of the Black Maria with a whack around your head that'll make that scumbag's smack seem like a tickle."

Joe climbs up next to the drivers' seat, inhaling the fresh air.

"Thanks."

"Thanks? First time I've ever been thanked for taking someone to Millbank. It's the most notorious, hardest penitentiary in London. Prisoners counted themselves lucky when they got shipped from there to Australia."

"Least I'll be alive," Joe replies quietly.

The guard strokes his big beard. "Course you will be. So long as I'm around, no harm will come to you, that much I can promise."

Joe manages a small smile. But how long will it take Smiler to pay off someone else and get the one-eyed man inside his cell so his blade can finish its job? Still, that's a future worry. Right now, he's alive, breathing open air, something he no longer takes for granted.

The Black Maria rides down Central Hill past Norwood New Town. Joe watches Cottage Hospital pass by, looking up at the murder of crows circling the building cawing.

"Friends of yours?" jokes the guard.

Joe resists replying he has no friends, that he'd failed them all, especially Elias. He just hopes Dr Doyle returns with a way to awaken him, although Joe realises he's no way of ever finding out his fate. Just as there's no way he'll see his family again.

They pass sheep grazing on the open plains of Streatham Common. After an hour passing road signs pointing to London Joe recognises Clapham Common. The open land is thick with brambles and bushes that would've put paid to the weekend football games in Joe's time. The Black Maria crosses the west side of the common lined with grand mansions to rival those built around the Crystal Palace. Joe thought Millbank Prison was by the Thames and wonders why they're here.

As if reading his curiosity, the guard says, "Got one more pick-up before Millbank. A notorious villain of ill repute."

"Hope I get to stay up here and not in the back of the wagon with him."

The guard guffaws. "Keep up your good behaviour, we'll see."

Joe imagined they'd be picking up the prisoner from a police station. Instead the Black Maria drives through the double gates of a grand Georgian mansion. The sign on the high wall outside reads 'Western Lodge.' The guard stops the horses and climbs down.

"Well, you don't want to go in the back of the wagon, and I can't leave you out here on your lonesome, no offence, so best come with me."

"Thanks." Joe leaps down, following the guard up to the double front doors. Instead of knocking, the guard tries the doorknob. It swings open and the guard steps inside. Joe pauses in the porch, uncertain whether to follow as this seems pretty much like breaking and entering, only without the breaking.

"You waiting for a written invitation?"

Joe follows, finding himself in a vast hall. The guard listens intently. Billiard balls strike each other upstairs. The guard gestures Joe to follow and they make their way up black marble stairs to a hallway lined with impressive paintings and pedestals of antique urns.

Joe follows the guard to the open door of a room at the front of the house. Inside at the billiard table, cue in hand, a man lines up his next shot. Joe recognises him at once.

Charley Adeleine, the piano-playing gambling American they'd met at Madame d'Varney's soiree.

What's he doing here?

The guard cries, "Mr Charles Bullard?"

Charley doesn't take his eye off the ball.

"Also known," the guard continues as he takes out handcuffs, "as Piano Charley?"

Charley strikes the white ball down the table. It ricochets a red ball off two cushions into a corner pocket. Smiling at his success he appears oblivious to the guard who continues, "Notorious safe cracker who robbed the vault of the Boston National Bank?"

Charley swigs a glass of whisky on the edge of the pool table, "What of it?"

Joe can't believe Charley hasn't even blinked, let alone deny it, let alone do a runner. Yet the guard seems neither surprised nor concerned at 'Piano Charley's' nonchalance. Instead, the guard picks a pool cue from the rack on the wall. Joe wonders if he's about to use it to apprehend Piano Charley. Instead, to Joe's astonishment, the guard walks up to the table and lines the cue up with the white ball.

"A wager for you," says the guard peering down the cue.

"I'm listening." Piano Charley leans on his cue, taking another swig.

"If I get the black into the top corner pocket on a rebound off the far cushion, you'll come quietly and spend the rest of your days in Sing Sing."

Piano Charley grins. "A damn safe bet."

"Oh really?" The guard takes aim and shoots the white. The ball strikes the black which rebounds and pings to and fro in front of the corner pocket before falling in with a plop.

Charley sighs, drinks, and holds his hands out for cuffs. Joe has no idea what to think. This certainly wasn't the way criminals got arrested in his time.

The guard blows chalk off the tip of his cue and walks up to Charley.

Suddenly, in bursts Madame d'Varney, all glittering diamonds and dramatic exclamations.

"Oh! Monsieur! Non! Please do not take my Charley away!"

Madame d'Varney runs into Piano Charley's arms, kissing him passionately.

"Careful," warns Charley. "You'll spill my drink."

"Oh!" cries Madame d'Varney, the back of her hand against her forehead in dramatic distress. "This drunk callous criminal will be my ruin! You sir!" She turns to the guard. "Take him and you'll have to take me too!"

"I have every intention of taking you too," replies the guard with a wicked wink that shocks Joe. "Madame d'Varney, or should I say ... Sophie Lyons!"

Madame d'Varney replies in a thick Liverpudlian accent, "Yer wha, fella?" She immediately throws her hands over her mouth as if only just realising her mistake.

"What the ..." gasps a baffled Joe.

"This here, lad," says the guard, "is Sophie Lyons, notorious international pickpocket and confidence trickster."

"Oh 'eck, I'm blown!" she tells Joe before dropping to her knees, hands clenched for mercy. "I had no choice, officer. Me granddad was a safe cracker, me ma a shoplifter and keeper of a disorderly house. She got me out on the street stealing from age three."

"Save your sob story for the beak," the guard replies.

"Come on." Charley rolls his eyes at her hysterics and holds his wrists out to be cuffed. "Put us out of my misery but have mercy and don't stick me in a cell with *her.*"

"Oy!" cries Madame d'Varney/Sophie Lyons giving Charley a back-hander in the stomach.

As the guard tries putting the cuffs on, Charley grabs his great beard and gives it a hard yank.

"Ouch!" cries the guard as his beard comes off in Charley's hands. "What did you do that for?" he demands, only ... now his voice has a distinct and familiar American accent.

Charley and Sophie Lyons burst out laughing, although Joe realises the joke is very much on him.

"That was the dumbest beard I ever saw. It really fooled them?" asks Charley.

"Poor lamb, come here pet," says Sophie Lyons, smattering the 'guard's' smarting cheeks with tender kisses.

"What can I tell you? The Napoleon of Crime is a master of disguise. That right, young fella?"

Joe finally manages, "You! Raymond Judson!"

Chapter 35

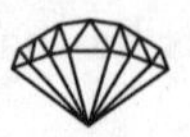

The American gives a bow.

"Of course!" Joe cries. "We're in Clapham Common, this is your house."

"My out-of-town pad," Raymond Judson replies taking off his Prison Guard hat and tossing it onto one of the cues on the rack. "I have a Mayfair apartment."

"Show-off," snorts Piano Charley.

"But ..." exclaims Joe trying to make sense of it all and failing spectacularly. "But why are you dressing up as a prison guard and helping me escape jail?"

"Good question," yells Piano Charley taking his glass to the decanter for a refill.

"Charley, the bigger question is why I bothered digging a whole goddamn tunnel to break *you* out of jail when all you do is drink and whinge."

"Boys, boys, boys." Sophie Lyons chides in her thick Liverpudlian accent, all signs of Madame d'Varney vanished. "Here, Charley, get the ale in, I'm dying for a bevvie."

Judson smiles at Joe with sympathy.

"I sprung you for three reasons. Number one, my golden rule—nobody gets hurt. If a job can't be done without harming someone, it doesn't get done."

"Amen!" cries Charley, throwing his hands in the air like a gospel preacher.

"Earlier, I had business with Mr Smyle, who boasted you were at the police station awaiting a visit from one of his associates. So, I had to act fast. You realise you were about to come to harm?"

Joe nods, picturing the one-eyed man and his blade.

"Course you did! Which brings me to point number two. You are a perceptive young fella of character. Smart. The kind of talent I could use in my organisation. Qualities that, to be honest," he leans in conspiratorially, "are in short supply among my current associates."

"Cheers to that!" Sophie Lyons clinks glasses with Piano Charley and takes a most un-Victorian-Lady-like gulp.

"Hold on …" Joe goes to run his hands through his floppy fringe but realises it's gone, so instead rubs his short crop. "Are you telling me you broke me out of jail to offer me a *job*?"

"I told you the lad's got smarts."

"Doing what?!"

"Burglaries. Jewel thefts. Heists."

Joe steps back, pointing at all three of them.

"I was right!"

Judson's grin widens. "Yep, which brings me onto point number three. You *were* right Joe. About all of it. As I said, you could have a bright future."

"As a thief? Because that's what you are. Thieves."

Piano Charley scratches his chin. "I'm pretty sure we just told you that. Adam, this kid ain't as sharp as you think."

"Give him a chance; it's a lot to take in."

"Who the hell is 'Adam?'" Joe demands.

"Adam Worth." Raymond Judson steps forward to take Joe's hand as if being introduced for the first time, but Joe just glares at it and leaves 'Adam' hanging, though this doesn't appear to bother him.

"Born in Germany, grew up and educated in the ways of the world in Boston and New York cities to become the Napoleon of Crime."

"They only call you that cos you're short," mocks Sophie Lyons.

"So you *were* planning to steal the Star of Nimrod for Sir Henry?"

Worth rolls a billiard ball. "That was the plan. Still is, in fact. Sir

Henry hired our services. You had most of the pieces of the puzzle right, just a few in the wrong place."

"Here pet, you look like you could do with a drink," says Sophie Lyons, bringing Joe a generous glass of whisky.

Joe sips, the taste blazing the inside of his mouth but also scorching through his confusion.

"You haven't actually stolen it yet," Joe declares.

Sophie Lyons's eyes sparkle. "Looks like you've got your smarts back as well as your eyesight."

"My eyesight ..." Joe remembers his disguise at the soiree as a pupil of The Royal Normal Academy for the Blind. Realisation dawns. "You knew!"

Sophie Lyons winks. "Very clever, pretending to be blind so you can watch unnoticed. I'll be taking a leaf out of your book. But you misunderstood what you saw. The diamond I sold to Sir Henry—"

"One of the diamonds we stole from the Grand Duke of Cassel-Felstien," Piano Charley interrupts.

"Now that was a heist," Worth adds wistfully.

"Alright, alright, boys, am I telling this story or what?"

"Sorry," both reply.

"Sir Henry bought that diamond off me because it's a dead ringer for the Star of Nimrod."

"Which is why he took it to Gorsuch," Joe exclaims as it starts making sense.

Sophie Lyons rolls her eyes. "Wonderful, now our kid is finishing off me story." She follows up with an affectionate brush of Joe's cheek.

"That's why Sir Henry took it to Gorsuch, to make a copy, which you'll use to switch with the *real* Star of Nimrod."

"Told you he was sharp." Worth unbuttons his guard's uniform.

"As a nail," says Charley. "A nail in our coffin now he knows our business."

"Why *are* you telling me all this?"

"Why not? What can you do with this information?"

"Well," Joe begins defiantly, "I could ..." His voice trails off.

"Go to the police?" Worth offers. "It's your word against ours. Who do you think they'd believe? A kid accused of stealing, one who's just escaped from jail?"

"You're the one who broke me out!"

"That's gratitude for you," grumbles Piano Charley. "We could arrange for your return if you'd prefer."

Joe begins pacing, mind racing.

"I could ... I mean, if I ... you can't just get away with it!"

"Joe, lad, look around you." Worth walks in a wide circle, gesturing at the expensive paintings and the best furniture. "Getting away with it is what we do." He walks up to Joe and puts his hands on his shoulders. "And I can teach you how."

For a moment, Joe imagines becoming the apprentice of this trio of international thieves. If he's going to be stuck in this era, why not live in luxury, swiping jewels, springing accomplices from jail? Until Joe remembers, steps back out of Worth's reach and says quietly, "Do you think your crimes don't have victims?"

Charley scoffs. "Sorry if I don't lose sleep for the filthy rich socialites and big banks we steal from, who make *their* money stealing from poor working men in the first place."

"Ha!" Sophie Lyons exclaims. "Since when were *you* a working man, eh?"

"And you're sure not poor anymore," adds Worth.

The three thieves laugh.

Joe's blood boils.

"What about Elias? Do you lose any sleep for him?"

Their laughter falters.

"That," says Worth seriously, "was not supposed to happen."

"And it wasn't us," adds Piano Charley.

"Wasn't it?" Joe looks accusingly at each of them. "He's where he is because we overheard your plan. He's there thanks to the people you're working for."

Worth nods gravely. "When you and I spoke at the hospital, I meant every word I said. I will look out for him, make sure he gets the best medical help money can buy, and when he wakes up, no harm will come to him. Just as I've made sure no harm comes to you."

"No harm?" splutters Joe. "You're kidding me, right? I've lost my compass, my friends, my home, everything. Can you steal that back for me? Can you bring back Elias?"

Despite their silver tongues the trio stand in uncomfortable silence.

"You think you get it, but you don't. Sir Henry, he's dangerous," Joe says.

"So are we, if we need to be," says Sophie Lyons. "Listen our kid, we know what we're doing."

"Sir Henry's a monster."

"The kids' right there," says Piano Charley. "Can't stand the man, or his snivelling smirking sidekick."

Worth responds slowly, evidently not for the first time, "We don't need to like our clients."

"Clients just need to pay," adds Sophie Lyons sitting herself on the window seat.

Joe shakes his head with disgust. "It's all about money."

"No," says Worth sharply. "Not anymore. It's about the challenge. Imagine, stealing the Star of Nimrod right under the nose of the Shah of Persia!" Worth's eyes glisten like a child anticipating the biggest present under the Christmas tree, but this does nothing to impress Joe.

"You get your kicks and everyone else pays. Nice."

Worth bristles.

Piano Charley laughs. "The kid's got your number. Gotta say he's growing on me. Maybe there *is* a place for you here, my friend."

"Why you acting like you're my friends? You're not."

Worth puts on a hurt pout. "Beggars can't be choosers and last I checked your friends abandoned you."

Joe rubs his face. "That was my fault, not theirs. I thought I could have friends without being honest about who I am."

Piano Charley snorts. "Listen kid, honesty is for suckers and trust leaves you open to danger."

"Yeah? It also leaves you open to love, support, surprise."

"True, our kid, I get that and more from this pair." Sophie Lyons winks.

"For better or for worse," says Worth raising a glass.

"For richer, or richer," grins Piano Charley.

"In sickness and in wealth," declares Sophie Lyons, but her glass halts at her lips. She points out of the window.

Worth strides over.

A carriage speeds across Clapham Common. Smiler cracks the whip, Gorilla squeezed next to him.

For the first time Joe sees worry cross Worth's face as their apparently unexpected visitors approach.

Piano Charley raises his glass. "This oughta be fun!"

Chapter 36

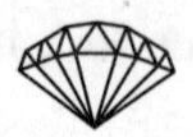

"Sir Henry!" greets Worth having thrown an elegant silk bath robe over his undergarments.

Sir Henry stands in the centre of the hall, spinning his gold eagle-tipped cane, taking in the mansion as if deciding whether to buy it or burn it down.

He's flanked by Smiler, whose hand remains in his jacket in readiness to pull out whatever weapon lay hidden, Gorilla looming with his huge fists clenched. On the other side, stands Babushka Blatovsky exuding an imperious air.

"May I get you a drink?" Worth offers.

Piano Charley leans casually on the banister of the grand staircase and pipes up, "Mine's a treble," as he tops up his glass from a bottle of whisky.

"I shan't be staying long." Sir Henry smiles pleasantly.

"Bon soir, bon soir!" exclaims Sophie Lyons, slipping back into her Madame d'Varney routine and waltzing up to Sir Henry. He goes through the motions of giving her hand a light kiss with a brittle smile.

Joe watches hidden behind the banister at the top of the stairs—Worth told him to remain in the billiard room, but if he's sold out Joe wants the chance to hear and attempt to get away. Despite Worth's 'code of honour,' Joe trusts none of them.

"Madame d'Varney, I have something for you."

Sir Henry reaches inside the breast of his jacket.

Worth and Piano Charley stiffen, but instead of a weapon Sir Henry pulls out a compass.

From his hiding place Joe recognises it at once.

Sir Henry frowns, continues searching and finally pulls out a brooch; a copy of the Star of Nimrod ready to be switched with the original. Sir Henry pops the compass safely back in his pocket and hands the imitation brooch to Sophie Lyons, who holds it up to admire the handiwork.

"Monsieur, what a beautiful creation."

"Exceptional craftsmanship," adds Worth, edging a step closer to Sophie Lyons.

"The very best," agrees Sir Henry. As if addressing naughty children discovered stealing the whole sweet jar, he says, "Now I believe *you* have something for *me*?"

Sophie Lyons, Worth, and Piano Charley feign bemusement.

"What might that be?" Worth imitates Sir Henry's playful tone.

Sir Henry tuts and wags his finger.

"I think you know."

"I fear we don't," replies Worth, hands in the air in mock-surrender.

Sir Henry sighs at the effort of having to say it.

"The boy, if you please. Hand him over and we can be on our way."

Joe freezes.

Worth scratches his head.

Sir Henry let out a mirthless laugh. "The boy you took from jail today in the Black Maria parked outside your house. The very same boy currently peering down at us from the staircase."

Without even looking, Sir Henry points his cane right at Joe.

"Oh!" Worth turns to Joe with surprise. "*That* boy!"

Sophie Lyons clasps her hands together with astonishment and Piano Charley gives Joe a double-take.

Sir Henry finally turns his gaze to Joe and says, "Come down, Joseph, and join the grown-ups."

Joe rises, looking to Worth to see what he should do. Worth beckons him down. Could he manage to get through one of the windows and escape before Sir Henry's minions catch him? Maybe, but his gut tells him he has to trust Worth.

"I promise I won't let anything happen to you."

He'd saved him once. Time to see if a thief can really be good as his word.

Joe holds his head high and descends the stairs. All eyes are on him, although Joe tries not to look at Babushka Blatovsky's deadly gaze. Smiler rubs his hands together. Joe reaches the bottom step where Piano Charley lounges. He stops, unsure what to do next.

Sir Henry has no such doubts, holding out his hand in invitation. "Come, Joseph."

Joe doesn't move.

Piano Charley shrugs. "Looks like the kid wants to stay."

Sir Henry's eyes flash. "Come, come. We aren't letting a child interfere with our business arrangements, are we?"

Worth waggles his finger. "No, Sir Henry, because the kid's not part of our arrangement."

"And yet," Sir Henry's eyes do not leave Joe's, "he seems to insist on getting himself entangled in my affairs."

Sophie Lyons places one hand on her heart and the other on Sir Henry's breast. "You will have no more trouble from le boy, you have our word."

Sir Henry's eyes widen.

"Oh, I have your word?" He looks at her hand, lifts it from his breast and says with contempt, "The word of common thieves?" He drops her hand suddenly as if realising thieving is a disease that might be catching.

Piano Charley pushes himself upright and grips the whisky bottle so tightly his knuckles go white. Worth tenses but his friendly tone remains.

"Thieves we may be. Common? I don't think so."

Sir Henry smiles around the grand hallway.

"Oh, I make no judgement. I admire what the three of you have achieved. Mixing with royalty, the trappings of a high society equally packed with charlatans and hypocrites. However," he says, twirling his cane, "in your case, a word with the home secretary, an old chum of mine from Eton, and your charade would crumble rather quickly."

Worth smirks. "Were that to happen, awkward questions would be asked of you too, Sir Henry."

Sir Henry laughs. "Do you really think the authorities would believe your word against mine?"

Worth bristles. Those are the same manipulating words he'd said to Joe earlier.

"You, however, don't get your hands on the Star of Nimrod."

"Come, come. Are you prepared to risk everything, throw all this away, and renege on our deal, for him?"

Worth gives Joe a serious look, followed by an apologetic shrug. "Sir Henry, I ask the same question right back 'atcha."

"I believe your answer is 'no,' whereas mine is empathetically 'yes.' Mr Smyle, if you please."

Smiler launches into action. He pulls a pistol and strides towards Joe. Gorilla closes in from the other side, knuckle dusters catching the light.

Smashing glass echoes as Piano Charley breaks the whisky bottle on the banister and steps in front of Joe.

Gorilla stops in his tracks when he finds Sophie Lyons whisking a long sharp hair pin from her head and pressing it against his thick neck.

In a flash Sir Henry unveils a blade from his cane, pressing it against Worth's heart.

Smiler aims his pistol at Charley.

Only Babushka Blatovsky doesn't move. Slowly she glides behind Gorilla, her eyes taking on the burning quality Joe witnessed in the study at Rockhills.

"Don't look at her!" Joe warns, pulling his own eyes away from her deadly gaze.

"Ladies and gentlemen," cries Worth, "a moment, if you will!"

Sir Henry raises his hand for his people to pause, although his blade remains against Worth's chest. "Pray continue."

"This kid's no threat to any of us and you know it. He's under my protection now. But as a gesture of goodwill, I will waive my fee for tonight's work."

"Really?" frowns Sir Henry.

"Really?" exclaims Piano Charley, seemingly aghast.

"Consider it compensation," says Worth in a reasonable tone belying the fact he has a blade at his heart. "A gift, if you will. One I'm sure will be welcome given your financial situation, Sir Henry."

Sir Henry flushes, but his anger passes as he realises the truth of Worth's barbed words.

"Very well." In one swift motion, Sir Henry sheaths his blade back into the cane.

Babushka Blatovsky glowers with disappointment.

Sophie Lyons takes a step back from Gorilla and her hair pin disappears back inside her locks.

Smiler nearly loses his trademark expression as he reluctantly puts his pistol away while Charley holds the remaining half of his whisky bottle over his mouth to catch the final drops.

"Do come again." Worth smiles with a small bow.

"Yes," declares Sir Henry turning to leave, "you can be certain."

"Can't wait." Piano Charley salutes.

Sophie Lyons waves. "Au reviour, until later."

Sir Henry pauses and turns to Joe. "Farewell, Joseph. I mean you no ill will when I say this, yet somehow I feel certain we shall meet again."

Sir Henry, Smiler, Gorilla, and Babushka Blatovsky sweep out of the house, Gorilla pulling together the double doors with a heavy bang.

"That was fun," says Piano Charley.

Joe massages his temples. "Thanks for not giving me up."

"Give you up?" exclaims Sophie Lyons slipping out of her Madame d'Varney routine. "As if. In fact I've got a pressie for ya."

Joe frowns as she reaches up her sleeve.

"From Sir Henry," she adds with a sly grin.

"What?" Joe's mouth falls open as she executes her reveal like a magician, slowly pulling a chain from her sleeve at the end of which dangles ...

"The compass!" cries Joe. "How did you ...?" but his voice tails off realising she's employed on Sir Henry the same pick-pocketing skills she intends to use on the shah.

"You can't help yourself, can you my love?" Piano Charley laughs.

"Ey, he was asking for it."

Joe rushes over and Sophie Lyons lowers the compass into the palm of his hand.

"See?" says Worth. "Stick with us, young fella, we look after our own."

Joe stares at the compass, studying its shattered glass. Sure enough, there in the edges he spots his dried blood.

Finally, Joe has his key to get home.

Chapter 37

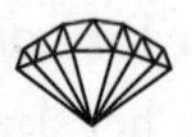

"It's hardly a *cell,*" insists Worth in a hurt voice.

Joe folds his arms. "You're locking me up in here, so how's it not a cell?"

Worth runs his fingers over an elegant armchair in his private inner sanctum, a windowless room hidden in the heart of the mansion and accessed through a false bookshelf in the library.

"Do you think you'd find an armchair from the palace of the Sun King in Wormwood Scrubs? Or this?" He gestures to a painting hung in prime position. "The Duchess of Devonshire, painted by Thomas Gainsborough." Worth sighs with loving pride as if he'd painted the duchess himself rather than stealing her. She looks down, arms folded like Joe's wearing a flirtatious expression beneath her grand black hat. "What do you think?"

Joe screws his face. "S'Okay, if you like that sort of thing."

"Okay?" Worth splutters. "I fell for her charms and stole her personally from the gallery of Thomas Agnew and Son. Not to sell," he adds hastily, "but to admire. Young fella, we need to educate you in the finer things in life."

"I told you already, if you want me to join your gang, take me with you tonight. Tell me how you're gonna steal the Star of Nimrod."

Worth claps.

"Nice try. No really, quite convincing, but I know how much you've sacrificed to stop the Star being stolen so, no offence, you can't be trusted not to try and foil us."

"I won't! I promise," Joe lies, figuring lying to professional liars is okay.

"If Sir Henry and his goons get within grabbing distance of you, I won't be able to save you a third time, no matter what our arrangement."

"Arrangement? You don't think they're not coming for me anyway? You're getting paid by killers."

"Er, correction, we're *not* getting paid, Charley will probably never forgive me …."

"Listen to me! They're more dangerous than you realise."

"I pretty much realised when they tried killing us half an hour ago …."

"So why do it?"

"We shook hands," Worth says simply. "I'm a man of my word."

"Do you understand *why* they're stealing the Star of Nimrod?"

"Does that matter?"

"'Course it matters. It's an object of power, real power, you can't just hand it over."

Worth winces. "We *shook hands*. I'm sure I just explained that bit. You're really going to have to start paying more attention if we're gonna work together …"

"All because of a stupid deal?"

Worth puts his hand on Joe's shoulder. "A man's gotta have a code. We'll be back tonight; this'll all be over, and we can look to the future."

Worth leaves the hideaway and locks the secret panel from the library beyond.

Joe shouts after him, "I'm not joining you!"

"Enjoy the duchess!"

Joe paces his prison of priceless stolen loot. He feels around the secret door; there's no means of opening it from inside. He glowers at the duchess.

"I *will* get out of here. And I *will* stop them. You watch."

Positive thinking Joe, positive thinking …

He opens a walnut cabinet of silverware and golden goblets searching for something to pry open the door or beat a hole through it. Five bent silver knives and a busted gold ladle later and Joe sinks onto the chaise longue. He feels the compass in his pocket, pulls it out and stares at its shattered face.

Could he use it now to get back to his own time?

Does it have to be in the maze to work?

If he *did* get back to his own time, would he even *exist*?

"Any ideas?" Joe asks the duchess.

"*Joe ...*" comes a faint reply.

He sits up straight. Talking sphinxes, now talking paintings ...

"*Joe!*" the voice repeats. But it isn't the duchess. The sound comes from the library beyond.

Joe beats his fists against the secret panel.

"Help! Help! I'm in here!"

As he shouts, Joe wonders who exactly *is* out there, realising it might be someone he doesn't want finding him ....

"*Joe!*" A girl's voice.

"*Joe!*" chorus two more voices, both boys.

A volcano of joy erupts inside Joe. "Winnie! Bertie! Sam! I'm in here!"

"*He's on the other side of this bookshelf.*" Bless Winnie's astute hearing!

Joe beats the panel so they can work out the location of the hidden door.

"*A secret chamber! Splendid!*"

Joe laughs at Bertie's ability to find exhilaration in any situation.

"The mechanism is a book," Joe cries, remembering Worth pulling it back to reveal his hideaway.

"*Which one?*" Sam shouts.

"Um, my height, end of the bookcase."

"Try that book about Napoleon."

"Yes, Sam! That'll be the one!"

Joe hears books scraping on shelves. CLICK. With a push the secret door swings open. Joe rushes out into the arms of Winnie, Sam, and Bertie, grabbing them for a hug which they happily return.

"What are you all doing here?"

"That's gratitude for you." Bertie grins.

"We wouldn't abandon a damsel in distress," says Winnie with a raised eyebrow.

"Thought you'd given up on me, after everything."

"Friends," Sam says solemnly, "don't give up on friends."

"Well," corrects Bertie, "we did at first. We were pretty darn angry after all that business at the palace. But as Sam and I were saying our farewells, we saw you being marched away by the police. Once upon a time, not so long ago, I would've simply gone on imagining all the things I wish I could have done to help you. Now, since we met, I'm jolly well doing them!"

"Me too!" says Sam blinking excitedly. "I'd never dreamed I'd be chasing prison vans across Streatham Common, yet here we are! First we followed you to the police station and saw that officer strike you."

Joe's hand instinctively goes to the lump.

Bertie tilts his bowler. "Nobody does that to *our* friend, no matter how much he'd lied and kept secrets and got us all into serious trouble."

Sam gives Bertie a dig in the ribs.

"What? I'm saying it doesn't matter is all."

Joe smiles. "Thanks Bertie."

"They needed a bit of leadership so paid me a visit," says Winnie twirling her cane.

"I thought you were grounded for life?"

"Grounded? You mean told I can't leave the house until I die?"

"Exactly."

"Mamma raised me to think for myself, and since meeting you reprobates I can't stop no matter the consequence. Besides, if I'm not going back to the academy or seeing you all, I don't have anything left to lose. So when I heard pebbles thrown at my window, and Sam shouted up what had happened to you, I waited until my parents went out and shimmied down the drainpipe to avoid Marie, who thinks all her Christmases have come at once because of the grief I'm getting. By the time we got to the police station, you were being taken away in the Black Maria."

"We had no idea where they were taking you," adds Sam.

"So, I hailed a cab," Bertie says proudly, "and told the driver 'follow that Black Maria and don't spare the horses!'"

"That's an adlib, you didn't mention horses," Sam corrects.

"Of course not, I'd never actually say that, I love horses, just getting a little carried away with the story."

Joe laughs. "Then what?"

"We followed you," explains Winnie.

"Just like Sherlock Holmes," Bertie adds.

"We waited outside trying to decide our next move," Sam continues, "wondering why you were here and not in prison."

"I deduced that," says Winnie smugly. "I remembered Raymond Judson lived at Western Lodge in Clapham Common. But who should arrive, galloping across the common?"

"Sir Henry," the trio chime in unison.

"Looking angrier than an angry man winning a 'who can look the angriest' contest," Bertie observes. "We hid behind a tree and saw you in some sort of commotion in the hall."

"Sir Henry left," says Winnie.

"Looking even angrier than an angry man who *didn't* win a 'who can look the angriest' contest."

"Judson, Madame d'Varney, and Charley left," Winnie continues. "We waited until the house was empty, apart from you as you hadn't come out."

"We feared the worst," admits Sam.

"But we snuck in through a cellar window and here we are!"

"Here you are." Joe grins. "I dunno what to say."

"I do." Winnie playfully points her cane at Joe. "Starting with telling us what's going on?"

Joe explains all that happened since the restaurant at the Crystal Palace. How Judson is in fact Adam Worth, international criminal, and Madame d'Varney, a Liverpudlian confidence trickster, called Sophie Lyons and 'Piano' Charley, a robber, all conspiring to steal the Star of Nimrod for Sir Henry.

Bertie whistles. "You were right all along."

"And we ended up disbelieving you," says Sam quietly.

"Hey, don't beat yourselves up. For a while they fooled me too. And I don't blame you for not trusting me."

The trio glance at each other.

"About that," says Winnie slowly.

"No need to apologise."

Winnie raises an eyebrow. "We're not."

"Oh?"

"The reason we struggled to trust you is because *you* don't trust *us.*"

Bertie nods vigorously and Sam joins in with a sympathetic smile.

"Oh." Joe's hands fidget, gripping and ungripping. "Yeah."

"Be honest with us," Winnie implores, feeling for Joe's hand and taking it. "Who are you? Where are you really from? What's really going on with you?"

Joe takes in the faces of his three friends. They'd done all he asked of them and more. They had without doubt earned his trust and deserved the truth. He just didn't know what they'd make of it. "You'll think I've lost the plot."

"Umm, we already do," Sam replies kindly. "We just don't understand why."

"Okay. But you best sit down."

The foursome each take a perch on the library's finely upholstered furniture.

Joe takes a breath.

Closes his eyes.

And takes a leap …

"I'm from Crystal Palace, Upper Norwood. Lived here all my life. Only ... Only I'm not from this time. I'm from the future."

He watches and waits.

"The future," Sam repeats finally. "Huh."

Bertie whistles. "Gosh. How far into the future exactly?"

From Bertie's earnest expression he isn't humouring Joe. "Hundred and thirty years."

Silence follows, but they don't burst out laughing or run or try to bundle him back into his luxurious cell. To Joe's amazement they actually seem to be taking him seriously. Winnie eventually speaks.

"That's why you have nowhere to go." She nods as if all makes sense now.

"A time traveller!" Bertie's fingers waggle. "How marvellous! How do you travel, old chap? Have you built a time machine?"
"What's the future like?" gasps Sam.

"Can you travel to any time you want?" demands Winnie.

Joe replies to their bombardment with laughter, such is his relief at finally opening up to them. "Okay, well, no I don't have a time machine; the compass somehow opens up a gateway in the maze."

"Ah, that's what you were up to, old chap!"

"Only I had the wrong compass, but I've got the right one back now."

"What's the future like?" repeats Sam, eyes wide.

"It's, well, it's different in so many ways, like cars and aeroplanes and phones you can carry in your pocket."

"What's a phone?" frowns Sam.

"A telephone," says Joe, putting his fingers to his ears to demonstrate a handset.

The others look blankly.

"Sure, no phones at all yet ... A phone lets you talk to someone else over a distance, and I really can't wait for them to arrive."

"Can we travel with you?" asks Winnie, face alive with excitement at the possibilities.

"No. I mean I don't know if you can or if it's safe or how much we should mess with the space-time continuum."

"The space-time continuum? Do tell old chap!"

"I could be fundamentally altering what happens in the future, your future; it's possible I've already mucked up my existence just by being here. That's why I couldn't tell you, plus ... I never expected any of you to believe any of it, thought you'd be weirded out and I'd lose you."

Bertie beams. "Lose us? Now that *is* implausible!"

The murky puddle of Joe's worst fears evaporate under the warm glow of his friends, leaving his mind and limbs feeling light and fresh and ready to take on whatever gets thrown at him in this world or his own.

"Hmm, now you've got the correct compass you can get home," muses Sam.

"If we go to the maze, I think so. I hope so. No offence."

"None taken," says Bertie doing his best. "After all, you have your family to get back to."

"So, let's go now." Winnie rises. "To the maze. Let's get you somewhere where Sir Henry and the others can't hurt you, where you'll be safe."

Joe sits in silence. "I can't go. Not yet."

"Umm, but if Sir Henry or Smiler or the others find you again, they'll kill you," argues Sam.

"Yeah, but I can't leave without helping Elias. What happened to him was because of me. If the Star of Nimrod can help him, I have to stop it getting stolen. Stop Sir Henry getting his hands on its power. Which is why I've got to stop Worth and Sophie Lyons and Piano

Charley tonight."

"There was a lot of 'I' in there," says Winnie quietly, "which needs replacing with 'we.'"

"She's right, old chap. We're a team. We do this together."

"In harmonious unison," adds Sam.

"Winnie, what will your parents say if you don't go home?"

"Nothing they haven't already so I might as well make the most of our final adventure."

"Ditto," says Bertie. "There's more at stake than a thrashing."

Joe gives his three friends a grateful laugh. "You lot are the best."

Sam gives a lop-sided grin. "Can't argue there. However, how do we halt them when we don't know their plans?"

"Did you hear them say anything?" asks Winnie. "Anything giving us a clue?"

Joe shakes his head ruefully. "When I first heard Smiler talking to Worth he said, 'We'll take it when everyone's looking up.'"

Sam scratches his chin. "What did he mean?"

"Ooo! Ooo!" Bertie shoots his arm in the air. "I know! I know!"

"So, go on," urges Winnie, "before you explode."

"Brock's fireworks! They must be watching the display."

"Is there a display tonight?" asks Sam.

"Ah, no," says Bertie deflating. "Not tonight."

"Besides, fireworks are impressive, but they're not guaranteed to have everyone looking up," observes Sam.

"Ooo! Ooo! I know!" Bertie's arm shoots up again.

"Don't let us stop you," says Joe.

"Tonight! At the Crystal Palace! A performance that will have *everyone* looking up, guaranteed!"

"Blondin!" they cry.

"Yes! Bertie, you're brilliant."

"If you insist!"

"So, what's our next move?" ponders Sam.

"We know they'll make the switch at the most dramatic moment in the show, the moment when even the shah's Royal Guard will be distracted."

"I understand," says Sam, "but how do we get close enough to the shah to warn him?"

"We're not going to warn the shah." A determined smile crosses Joe's face. "We're going to catch them in the act!"

Chapter 38

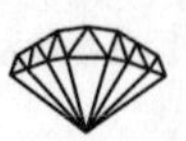

It's standing room only in the packed palace. People have flocked from across London and beyond in their thousands clasping the hottest ticket of the year: seeing the Mighty Blondin perform his daredevil feats.

"The entrance between the School of Music and the palace is closed during ticketed events," Sam explains on the cab journey from Clapham Common.

"You can still get us into the front of the School of Music, right?" enquires Joe as the cab bumps over rough road at speed, the driver encouraged by a tip in the form of a pricy looking silver spoon liberated from Worth's inner sanctum. Joe reasoned it isn't stealing to steal from a thief.

Winnie nods. "The porter on the front desk doesn't mind Sam and I practicing at odd hours, and we'll pass you two off as our playing partners."

"Nice one. We go to the practice room where me and Elias first met you, take the service door leading underneath the palace, make our way under the floorboards and up into the Grand Transept, find Blondin and Iris."

"Won't Blondin be a bit busy performing in front of thousands?" asks Sam.

"His show starts soon," Bertie adds.

Joe thinks hard. "There has to be an interval. We find him then."

"Umm, if he won't help us?" Sam sees Bertie's eyes roll. "No discord intended. We just need to consider all possibilities and what we do should they arise."

"You're right," says Joe. "But we only get one chance to catch the Star of Nimrod getting stolen. We *have* to make this work."

Joe put his hands in the middle of the quartet, taking Winnie's hand and placing it on top of his.

"You too," he tells Sam and Bertie, each laying their hands on top.

Their fingers entwine and four become one.

As predicted, the porter waves them into the Crystal Palace School of Music without question. Through the rehearsal room, they take the service stairs beneath the palace, Joe leading them into the under-floor, Sam guiding Winnie to ensure she doesn't hit her head.

From the 'oohs' and 'ahhhs' of the crowds above, it's clear Blondin is in full flow.

Joe tries recalling the route taken with Elias. "Does this seem right to you?"

Sam peers up through the floorboards. "I can see chair legs so we must be near the seating sections, they're always arranged around the Grand Transept for Saturday Concerts. They'll have the same layout for Blondin."

They clamber through a hatch, climbing down a ladder into Paxton's Corridor. Fortunately, it's mostly empty, staff squeezing above to watch Blondin. They take the spiral staircase up to the main level of the palace.

The four friends warily step out just as the entire palace bursts into rapturous applause. Above them, Blondin takes a bow wearing a magnificent bejewelled suit.

"End of the first half," assesses Bertie.

"We've not got much time. Winnie, Bertie, find Iris. Winnie, I'm sure you can make her listen."

"I'll try."

"What if she's not up there?" asks Sam, peering up towards the rafters.

"She's never missed one of her dad's performances, and if she's not in it, she'll at least want to be close as she can. Me and Bertie will go to the Nineveh Court, get the rug, work out where the shah's sitting and meet back here."

They split off into their pairs, Joe and Bertie squeezing their way through the crowd to reach the North Transept as punters buy interval snacks from the long line of temporary refreshment stalls erected alongside the courts.

"... Unbelievable ..."

"... How does he do that ...?"

"... Bet I could do that. ..!"

Joe and Bertie duck under the rope surrounding the Nineveh Court. The colossal winged bulls at the entrance stare down at Joe. Something about this place scrambles his senses and he has an urge to get in and out as soon as possible.

Bertie points. "There it is."

Joe hurries into the inner chamber, grabbing the rug. It's a dead weight, and he wrinkles his nose at the musty stench.

"I'll grab the head, old chap."

"Great, now let's go find the shah."

Back in the Grand Transept, they scan the bank of seats rising in semicircles around the Handel Organ.

Joe spots a familiar face, her high-backed wheelchair at the end of a row of dignitaries. Ada has a wide smile, eyes fixed upwards at the tight rope, determined not to miss a moment when the second act begins. Joe's glad she got her birthday treat, but shudders at Babushka Blatovsy sitting at Ada's side. Fortunately, her deadly eyes are engrossed in the programme.

Suddenly Ada's eyes lower and stare straight at Joe.

Once again, seeing Ada sends strange thoughts sweeping through Joe's mind like a cold wind, yet this time there's the promise of a thaw to come as she smiles.

Something passes between them, the moment broken by Bertie crying, "Sir Henry's daughter's seen us! She'll warn him and the others."

"No," replies Joe flatly. "She won't."

"How do you know?"

"Just do."

Ada's eyes turn along the row. Joe follows their gaze.

"There!"

In the centre of the first row, the Royal Guard stand in formation behind the shah in a specially constructed royal enclosure.

"And look who he's with!" cries Bertie, pulling out his very special opera glasses.

Deep in conversation with the shah is Sir Henry Majoure, his status as director of the Crystal Palace Company earning him prime position next to the royal guest. Joe looks back to Ada, but she's gazing once again at the high wire above.

"And there." Joe points. A dozen guests along, there's no mistaking the outrageous hat and dramatic gesticulations of Sophie Lyons aka Madame d'Varney.

"How's she going to steal the Star of Nimrod if she's sitting so far from the shah?"

"I don't know," admits Joe.

Their plan had been predicated on Sophie Lyons making the switch at the climax of the show when everyone's looking up.

What if I'm wrong? Wouldn't be the first time. What if the switch is being made after the show, or had already happened?

As Joe pushes these doubts from his mind he cries, "Look!"

Sophie Lyons stands and makes her way along the front row, other guests rising politely as she passes. She reaches Sir Henry and the shah and curtsies. Joe nudges Bertie as Sir Henry steps aside from his seat so she can take his place whilst they chat.

"I bet when the second half starts, Sir Henry lets her have his seat," predicts Joe, their plan unfolding as he'd hoped.

"Splendid!"

"She's waving at someone in the stalls below."

"Oh, wait ... yes! The other American!

Sure enough, lounging with his legs crossed just below the royal enclosure sits Piano Charley.

"Keep an eye out for Worth; he'll be here somewhere too."

"Now we just have to work out how on earth *we* get past the ushers on either side, not to mention his guards and actually get to the shah."

"Same way we snuck in here. Under the floor. Remember the grates at regular intervals? We find the grate nearest the shah, remove it and crawl up. But first let's get this rug to Iris before the second half begins."

Joe and Bertie head to the service stairwell, unaware they've been spotted by a familiar face whose leering smile broadens as he follows them to their rendezvous.

"You are all crazy," Iris tells Joe, Winnie, Sam, and Bertie who gather in a backroom corridor.

"But you said you'd do it," reminds Winnie in a strained voice as Sam taps away at the wall.

Iris pouts at the rug. "It stinks like a wet dog. A dead wet dog."

"I know, sorry," says Joe. "If there was another way ..."

"Don't worry, Strange Boy. You are all crazy and I like crazy."

"So, you'll do it?" Joe's desperate to be a hundred percent sure.

In Joe's time Iris would've let out a massive 'Duh!,' but instead scornfully exclaims, "I said I will, I will!"

"Yes! Thanks Iris, our petit wonder."

Iris can't resist a satisfied smirk.

"Did Blondin agree too?"

Sam glances at Winnie and Iris. "We, er, haven't asked. Yet."

Joe's fists clench. "What?"

"By the time we'd found Iris and got her on board he was preparing to begin the second half," Winnie explains defensively.

"Without his help none of this'll work."

"Leave Papa to me. When he comes off ze wire to prepare for ze grand finale, when aerial clowns fill in, I ask."

"That's cutting it a bit fine." Bertie notes. "What if he says no, after the home secretary's decree?"

"Poo poo to the British government," Iris declares. "Zey are BORING. Papa will do as I ask. Trust me."

Joe manages a smile, knowing there's a lot of hope and trust spread thinly tonight. "Okay. Winnie and Bertie, go with Iris in case she needs help convincing Blondin. He's met you Bertie and you know how to tell a story, and Winnie you could persuade Eskimos to buy snow. Me and Sam will get as near as we can to the shah so when the moment comes, bang, we're there to catch them in the act. Questions?"

"Got it," replies Winnie.

"On it," salutes Bertie.

"Comprendere," says Sam.

"Good luck," declares Joe.

"We need it." Iris giggles.

Suddenly Winnie stiffens, sniffing the air.

"What's wrong?"

"I can smell hair oil," says Winnie in a low voice, raising her cane like a rapier. "And grease. I can smell ..."

"SMILER!" cries Bertie.

The five youngsters spin around. Looming in the spiral stairwell stands Smiler, his grin the widest they'd ever seen it. In one hand he holds his whip, in the other a knife, and filling all the space behind him is Gorilla.

"Run!" yells Sam, taking Winnie's hand and fleeing down the corridor. Iris, however, stands her ground, hands on hips glowering up at Smiler. Joe doubles back, drags her after the others. Smiler sniggers and follows.

Joe kicks himself, realising Smiler spotted and followed Joe where nobody will see him finish his job.

"You guys split off. It's me he wants."

"We're not abandoning you," insists Sam.

"All for one," adds Bertie as the corridor turns and they hit a dead end.

The quintet are trapped.

Iris points at the only door. "In here."

Joe unbolts the door. As they rush inside, he immediately recognises the storeroom. In the middle sits a cage where Tilly paces, eyes moving from the box of sausages in the corner to the kids.

"A lion!" declares Bertie.

"A lioness," corrects Winnie.

"Tilly," insists Iris.

"The only door out of here is the one we came through," cries Sam.

Winnie orders, "Bolt it."

"We can't," Joe replies. "there's only a bolt on the outside."

Sam slaps his forehead.

"Bravo, a dead-end room with two killers on one side and a lion on the other."

"Her name is *Tilly!*" yells Iris, earning an eye-roll from Sam.

The door has a rectangular viewing hole in the middle. Joe can see Smiler and Gorilla approaching fast.

"Quick, lean against the door!"

Joe, Bertie, Sam, Winnie, and Iris gather against the door. Tilly watches, intrigued.

The doorknob turns. The door pushes.

The quintet lean in to hold it shut.

Suddenly THUD, Gorilla slams the door. Wood buckles and they're knocked back. Luckily Joe and Bertie manage to throw their weight back against the door, swiftly joined by the others.

Smiler's grin appears in the viewing hole, reminding Joe of the poster of Dad's favourite film, *The Shining*, when the murderous Jack Torrance leers through the broken door with an axe. Smiler disappears and another *thud* shakes the door. They just manage to hold their position, but Sam says, "We can't hold them off forever."

"You're right," says Joe. "Iris, open up the cage."

"Let out the lion?!" exclaims Sam.

"HER NAME IS TILLY!" cries Iris who doesn't need asking twice, sliding the bolt and swinging the cage door open.

"Here Tilly, Tilly! Here Tilly!"

Tilly also doesn't need asking twice, stalking out of the cage, eyes fixed on sausages.

Joe peeks through the viewing hole. Gorilla prepares to make another charge like a bull ready to finish off the Matador.

"On the count of three," whispers Joe, "open the door. They come in, we rush out and trap them."

"That plan is ..." begins Sam, but they never find out his verdict because Gorilla charges and Joe cries, "Three!"

Winnie, Bertie, Sam, and Joe yank the door open. Gorilla charges through with such speed he crashes into the cage bars, the force sending him onto his back with a winded thud.

Smiler enters, eyes fixed on the friends and sneering at Winnie who's assumed an en garde position with her cane aimed at him. He doesn't notice Tilly behind him in the corner munching her way through her third batch of sausages, Iris gleefully at her side.

Smiler's grin widens until Joe says, "Look behind you!"

Smiler scoffs at what he assumes to be a trick, but nevertheless turns his leer over his shoulder and freezes at the sight. Smiler spins, attention now firmly on the big beast. In unison, Joe, Sam and Bertie rush forward, shoving Smiler as hard as they can, sending him tumbling to the floor.

With an acrobatic leap, Iris bounds over the prone Smiler and is first out the door, swiftly followed by Bertie and Sam leading Winnie.

Joe's last to run out of the storeroom. But as he does, Smiler reaches and grabs his ankle, sending Joe tumbling over in the doorway.

The others can only stare in horror.

Smiler tightens his clamped grip. His knife hand intent on slicing. There's no way Joe'll be able to run with his Achilles tendon severed.

Smiler raises his knife.

Joe feels a coldness rush over him.

He shivers from head to toe. It's the same sensation he felt under Ada's gaze.

Without explanation the door takes on a life of its own. Scratches in the timber form a face. An icy giggle sounds. With a great unseen force the door slams into Smiler's outstretched arm.

Bones crack. Smiler screams, releasing Joe's ankle.

Bertie and Winnie drag Joe through the doorway.

Sam pulls the door shut.

Iris slams across the bolt.

Joe staggers to his feet. The face in the door has disappeared. He joins Sam peering through the viewing hatch.

"What's happening?" demands Iris who's too small to look, so for her benefit and Winnie's, Joe describes the scene.

"Gorilla's crawling to hide behind a box in the corner away from Tilly!"

"Tres bon! Has Tilly eaten ze smiling one?" asks Iris with macabre excitement.

"No, but he's not smiling now," Joe says triumphantly. "Tilly's circling him. He's backing into a corner with his whip out."

Smiler cracks his whip in Tilly's face. This only serves to shift her mood from curious to furious. She lets out a low dangerous growl, teeth snarling. Smiler's face collapses in terror, eyes darting to the open door of Tilly's cage.

With a burst of speed, Smiler leaps into the cage, slams the door behind him, and slides the lock. He does this with his good arm, the other sticking out at an unpleasant angle from when the door slammed on it, which Joe feels certain was the doing of Ada and her faerie friend ...

"What's happening?" demands Iris.

"Smiler's shut himself in the cage, Gorilla's squeezed on top of a pile of crates up near the ceiling, and Tilly's lost interest in them, she's happily helping herself to another box of sausages."

"Tip-top! That should keep them out of our way!" declares Bertie. "Sir Henry's daughter must've warned them when she saw us."

"No." Joe touches the door. "In fact, I think she was the one who saved me by slamming the door on Smiler's arm."

Everyone stares at the door as if it might perform another mystical feat.

"How—" begins Sam.

"Later. We're running out of time." Joe's satisfaction at turning the tables on Smiler evaporates as he realises the delay it's caused. "The second act will be well underway by now. We're gonna miss the Star of Nimrod being stolen!"

CHAPTER 39

Blondin wears a chef's hat and apron. He's wheeled a portable stove to the centre of the high wire and busily cooks an omelette, making a big show of flipping and catching it in the frying pan. Placing the omelette on a tray, he lowers it down from the high wire for the shah to taste.

The shah claps away like a small child as the tray nears. 'Madame d'Varney' makes a big show of exclaiming her wonder in the shah's ear. He happily takes the knife and fork, tastes the omelette and cries, "Bravo! Bravo!"

Meanwhile Joe and Sam try finding the fastest way to get to the royal enclosure. Two young lads hang near the refreshment stalls, sweeps in hand to tidy up from the interval. Joe recognises Dick, the master sweep, gesturing Sam to follow.

It's slow work squeezing through the standing crowds. Joe has to grudgingly respect Worth's plan—everyone is looking up. Joe glances across to where Ada had been seated and finds her and Babushka Blatovsky gone. What had the effort of helping him escape Smiler done to Ada? Sir Henry, however, remains seated with a glacial smile.

The orchestra music changes. Blondin bows, dancing off the high wire to be replaced by three aerialists dressed as clowns. Winnie, Bertie, and Iris should be waiting for him to enlist his help. The grand finale is fast approaching as Joe and Sam finally reach the master sweeps.

"Hi, it's me, Joe, Elias's friend. I really need your help."

Their faces switch to angry scowls.

"You got a bloody nerve," says Dick. "You're no friend of Elias. Friends don't get you good as dead."

"And called a thief to boot," adds the other.

Joe clasps his hands together. "Listen—"

"Why? We don't know you, now get, before I break this over your head." Dick brandishes his broom. It's clear he'd happily oblige.

Time's running out. Joe has no idea what to say. Until Sam steps forward and speaks with calm confidence.

"Whatever you've heard about Joe and Elias is a lie. They're not thieves. They're friends. Joe's doing everything to clear Elias's name. Are you going to help?"

The master sweeps glance at each other, Sam's sincerity circling in their heads. Joe holds his breath. Finally Dick says, "What d'you need?"

Joe slaps Sam's back. He gives a shy shrug. Pointing over to the royal enclosure, Joe declares, "Get us to the shah."

Joe and Sam follow Dick through the under-floor. They clamber below the orchestra who play comical music to accompany the aerial clowns. The audience burst into applause.

"The brass section has reached its crescendo," cries Sam.

"The finale's about to start!" shouts Joe above the claps.

"Nearly there," cries Dick, pausing to get his bearings. Above them the orchestra strikes up foreboding music building anticipation for Blondin's final act of daredevilry.

"This way."

The hems of the dresses and the shine of the shoes become more expensive as they advance below rows of VIPs.

A huge gasp erupts from above. Exclamations can be heard.

"*Is it real?*"

"*A lion!*"

"*In a wheelbarrow!*"

"We're too late!" shouts Sam.

"No, he's got to wheel the barrow to the middle of the wire first."

The light between the floorboards disappears plunging them into near darkness.

"Carpet!" exclaims Joe. "They've put red carpet down for the shah's royal enclosure. We need to get behind it and come up into the scaffolding, where the rows of seats start rising."

"Gotcha." Dick darts sideways.

Joe and Sam are right behind. Neither can make out a grate but fortunately their guide finds one and pushes. It doesn't budge.

The crowd cheer.

"Let's do it together," Joe tells Dick.

All three squeeze shoulder to shoulder. They push up with all their might.

"Open!" shouts Joe. As if the palace hears his command, the grate gives way with a clatter lost among the audience roar. Joe and Sam scramble up. Joe shouts down to Dick, "Cheers, we've got it from here."

He doesn't want Dick in the level of trouble they're about to land in.

"We're right behind the royal enclosure," assesses Sam.

The wall along the back of the royal enclosure had been constructed with red fabric panels. Joe takes out the silver bread knife he'd tried using to open the secret door to Worth's hideaway. He presses the blade against the fabric, pushing it through to the other side, tearing a rip to reveal the backs of dignitaries seated a metre ahead.

Adrenaline pumping, Joe's hand grips Sam's shoulder. Sam's usually cautious eyes have a wild glint.

To their left, behind the shah, stand his Royal Guard, their eyes fixed to the rafters.

The shah himself leaps up, one hand over his mouth the other pointing up in amazement. This isn't surprising–Blondin balances at the centre of the tight rope, lioness strapped in the wheelbarrow, its two wheels no wider than the wire.

As if this isn't enough of a spectacle, Blondin has a stricken expression on his face. His right arm begins flailing.

He's losing his balance.

Thousands of spectators gasp as one.

All except one.

'Madame d'Varney' doesn't look up. Instead, her focus is on the Star of Nimrod pinned to the breast of the shah's uniform. The imitation brooch glitters as she slips it from her sleeve and prepares to make the switch right under the shah's nose.

"Ready?"

"PRESTISSIMO!" cries Sam.

They burst through the tear in the fabric.

Blondin above loses his battle to regain his balance.

A gasp rips through the palace.

'Madame d'Varney's' hand slips with professional ease to the shah's breast.

Joe and Sam charge forward, glimpsing Sir Henry a few seats away, watching them in shock horror, but it all happens too quickly for him to intervene.

Blondin tumbles.

The wheelbarrow has nothing holding it and begins to sway.

As he falls, Blondin's hand grabs the zip wire. He spins himself full circle, back up the other side, landing neatly with both feet on the wire. With a wide grin, he catches the wheelbarrow before it topples.

The crowd roar.

Madame d'Varney's fingers unclip the Star of Nimrod. Her other hand moves to clip the imitation in place.

Right at that moment the 'lioness' leaps up. Its head and fur fall away, and the lion-skin rug Joe and Bertie liberated from the Nineveh Court tumbles to the floor far below.

Standing in its place, hands on hips, is Le Petit Wonder, a triumphant smile on her face. In that moment of stunned audience silence, Iris points dramatically with both hands at the royal enclosure where the shah looks up enthralled.

At that same moment, Joe and Sam reach the back of the shah's seat and cry, "Look!"

They point at a wide-eyed 'Madame d'Varney,' who now has the Star of Nimrod in one hand and the imitation in the other.

The startled shah looks at her as the rest of the audience erupt into applause for the Great Blondin and Le Petit Wonder.

The Royal Guards whose attention had been skywards snap back on duty, giving bewildered looks from 'Madame d'Varney' to the shah.

She looks at Joe and Sam, a tiny smile of respect flickering across her face before her instincts kick in. In a single action, she throws the Star of Nimrod over her shoulder. It sails into the stalls below to be caught one handed by Piano Charley. The action is so smooth and swift they may even have got away with it if Joe and Sam hadn't seen and shouted above the now cheering crowd, "He's got the Star of Nimrod!"

Piano Charley downs his drink, rises and with cool casualness walks along the front row of the aisle to make his getaway.

Chapter 40

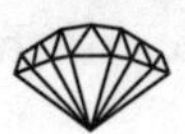

The shah grabs 'Madame d'Varney's' hand which still holds the imitation Star of Nimrod. With feigned innocence and gumption that can't help earning Joe's admiration, she cries, "Your Majesty, your brooch fell off."

For a second, the shah seems to believe her silky performance and quickly lets go of her arm, until Joe cries, "That's a fake! And *he's* escaping with the real one!"

He points after Piano Charley briskly strolling down the aisle.

The Elite guard don't quite know what to do, their training not covering kids popping up out of nowhere. One seizes Sam's shoulder. Another makes a grab for Joe, but he slips out of reach.

Employing his parkour skills Joe leaps onto the barrier along the front of the royal enclosure. Balancing in a move that'd make the Blondins proud, Joe runs along the barrier in pursuit of Piano Charley below, past frowning and confused VIPs giving Blondin a standing ovation.

Joe passes Sir Henry.

He reaches out to grab his legs.

Joe jumps.

Sir Henry is left grasping at thin air.

Piano Charley nears the end of the stalls—if he makes it to the standing section, he'll easily disappear into the crowd. Joe speeds up but realises he'll never make it.

"Stop him!" Joe shouts to the usher at the end of the aisle, but his voice is lost in the continuing applause.

Piano Charley glances back at Joe, giving him a salute as he passes the usher into the crowd.

What Piano Charley fails to see is the crutch sticking out at shin level held on one side by Bertie and Winnie on the other.

Piano Charley trips over the crutch landing in an unceremonious heap on the floor.

The impact also sends Bertie and Winnie over, all three ending in a tangle.

Joe punches the air. He catches a familiar face on the first level balcony.

Adam Worth.

Watching his plan fall apart.

Yet instead of anger, Worth gives Joe a grudging grin. Or perhaps his smile says, 'this ain't over yet ...' because Piano Charley is back on his feet before Winnie and Bertie pick themselves up. However, he staggers (and not from the amount he's drunk), pain etched across his face.

Worth holds up his hands inviting Piano Charley to throw him their prize.

Joe runs even though he'll never reach the balcony in time to intercept.

Piano Charley's arm pulls back and he catapults the Star of Nimrod.

The Star catches the light as it spins through the air.

Worth reaches out to grab it.

But another figure jumps into its path, arm outstretched, hand open in readiness.

Joe gasps.

Dr Doyle!

In a stunning display of agility, Dr Doyle plucks the flying Star from the air, landing on a group of disgruntled guests. Ushers rush over to deal with the commotion.

Joe reaches the end of the enclosure and looks up. Worth slowly claps. Unlike the rest of the audience he isn't admiring Blondin and

Iris who continue to take their bows. Worth's applause is for Joe. Stepping back, he melts into the crowd.

"Great catch!" Joe tells Dr Doyle as they join Bertie and Winnie standing over Piano Charley who sits gripping a heavily swollen ankle.

"Thank you." Dr Doyle grins, holding up the Star of Nimrod. "Sometimes it helps to have been goalkeeper for Portsmouth FC." He looks down at Piano Charley. "But with my doctor's hat on, I'd say you've fractured your ankle."

"Cheers, Doc," Piano Charley replies ruefully pulling a hip flask from his jacket. "Medicinal," he adds. "Cheers, kids."

"You two were amazing!" says Joe.

"Indubitably!" agrees Bertie.

Winnie pushes her dark glasses up her nose. "We weren't going to let you and Sam have all the fun."

"Sam!" Joe looks at the uproar in the royal enclosure. Two Elite guards hold Sam whilst Sophie Lyons gesticulates like a windmill, no doubt conjuring up a cover story for an angry shah.

Another member of the Elite guard rushes down the aisle, sword aimed at Joe.

"Wait!" appeals Dr Doyle holding up the Star of Nimrod. "This is what you're looking for and we're returning it to the shah."

"This chap on the floor is one of the thieves," interjects Bertie. "So point your sword at him and ensure he doesn't escape."

The Elite guard's sword swings uncertainly between Joe and Piano Charley until a tall man steps from the crowd and says with authority, "They're telling the truth. William Pinkerton, head of Pinkerton Detective Agency. I've been tracking these notorious thieves."

"Pleasure to meet you properly, Mr Pinkerton!" exclaims Dr Doyle. "I was told you missed your lecture because you were tracking down a criminal but had no idea these thieves were your target."

Joe recognises the tall man. "You were following Worth at Dr

Doyle's lecture and at Madame d'Varney's party."

Pinkerton frowns, surprised. "Correct. I've tracked Adam Worth and his associates across Europe."

Piano Charley laughs. "Seems like the kid could give you a few lessons in subtlety."

"So it seems. You youngsters succeeded where many skilled lawman failed, myself included. Congratulations."

The Elite guard finally directs his sword at Piano Charley who holds his hands up in mock surrender. "Don't worry, I'm not running away any time soon."

Sophie Lyons is in full flow as Joe, Winnie, Bertie and Dr Doyle reach the royal enclosure where a flustered George Grove, the secretary of the Crystal Palace Company, stands accompanied by two policemen.

"So you see it was all a silly wager, a bet among bored but ultimately harmless society folk to while away the day," claims 'Madame d'Varney's.'

"You expect us to believe that?" scoffs the shah, waving the imitation Star of Nimrod in her face. "Where is the real Star?"

"Here," Joe cries from the aisle below.

Joe reaches up and places it in the shah's palm.

"Identical to the eye," he muses with wonder, holding it against the imitation, before turning to Joe. "And this boy is one of the thieves?"

"No, Your Majesty," says Dr Doyle quickly. "Forgive me, but Joe here saved it, as did these two." He points at Winnie and Bertie. "And the lad over there." Sam responds with a relieved wave at having his name cleared.

"Do not forget Le Petit Wonder!" cries Iris indignantly as she rushes down the aisle holding Blondin's hand. "I too saved ze Star, didn't I, Papa?"

"This is true?" asks the shah, obviously suspecting this might be part of some elaborate encore. Blondin gives a small bow.

"My daughter speaks true. These young folk came to us, told me what was planned during my grand finale and enlisted our aid to foil these thieves."

"Monsieur Blondin!" exclaims Madame d'Varney. "How could you accuse one of your fellow citizens?"

Blondin blushes. "Forgive me, Madame. Where is your hometown?"

"Why Dijon, Monsieur."

"Ah." Blondin smiles wistfully. "The rolling orange groves."

"Oui, how I miss them."

"Although," says Blondin with a sly smile, "Dijon has no orange groves. Too far north, but it does make exquisite pinot noir."

Sophie Lyons's shoulders slump and she exclaims in her real accent, "I know, mate, I love a swig of pinot."

The shah solemnly tells Joe, "I am in your debt."

"No problem. Would your guards mind letting Sam go?"

One nod from the shah and Sam's towering captors release him. He hastily moves to the edge of the barrier to be closer to Joe, Bertie, Winnie, and Iris. The guards take hold of Sophie Lyons.

"Gerrof, not so hard."

Joe glances along to an empty seat. "Where's Sir Henry? He's the one behind all this."

"Sir Henry Majoure?" exclaims Secretary Grove. "Preposterous."

"Please, Miss Lyons, can you tell them?" urges Joe.

"Tell them what, our kid?"

"That Sir Henry hired you to steal the star."

Sophie Lyons smiles. "Can't help you there. Like I said, we just took it for sport."

From her resolute smile it's clear she shares Worth's dubious code and has no intention of implicating others. Joe feels sure Piano Charley will be the same no matter how much he loathes Sir Henry and his goons. Winnie touches his arm.

"At least he hasn't got his hands on the Star of Nimrod," she says softly.

"Yeah, that's something."

"And zanks to you, Strange Boy, le Petit Wonder performs at ze Crystal Palace! Nobody dare object when I catch criminals red handed."

Joe laughs. "True."

"With a little help from us," adds Bertie.

"A little," concedes Iris, magnanimously putting her thumb and index finger a few centimetres apart to illustrate just how little.

"And your actions today may still aid Elias," muses Dr Doyle.

"Really?"

"My contact gave me a healing incantation to be used with an object of ancient mystical power."

"Like the Star of Nimrod," declares Joe, remembering Ada's words.

"It can help bring Elias back?" asks Sam.

Dr Doyle hesitates.

Joe says, "It can. It has to. Like the Queen of the Gypsies told Elias—'Only a star can awake you from your dream.'" Joe addresses the shah, "Your Majesty? About that debt. I've got a way to repay it …"

Chapter 41

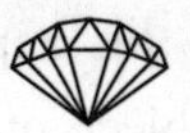

Outside Cottage Hospital, in glorious sunshine, Joe stands side by side with Bertie, Winnie, Sam and a growing crowd of Norwood New Towners for a morning of surprising royal visits.

Firstly, the full force of the Elite guard ride on horseback down Central Hill surrounding the Shah of Persia in his royal carriage.

Bertie whistles. "He knows how to make an entrance."

"Indeed," agrees Winnie. "Last night his royal escort was even enough to impress and mollify my parents, especially when the shah personally explained what happened and begged their forgiveness on my behalf. I can just picture the look on Marie's face!"

Sam links arms with Winnie. "Just as well you're returning to the academy. I've a new piece developing in my head, a fantastical adventure about a mystical amulet …."

Bertie peers through his very special opera glasses. "His Elite guard look justifiably alert what with Adam Worth still at large."

Joe smiles reassuringly. "Worth won't be trying to steal the Star of Nimrod. He's got other things to worry about, like keeping one step ahead of Pinkerton and working out a way to break Sophie Lyons and Piano Charley out of jail. But I doubt Sir Henry's given up getting his hands on the Star."

Bertie juts out his jowls. "Shame there's no proof against Sir Henry."

"Interesting timing," observes Sam with sarcasm at factor-fifty, "Sir Henry and his entire household leaving suddenly on 'holiday' right after Blondin's show."

Winnie snorts. "I imagine Smiler and Gorilla certainly needed a holiday when they finally escaped their encounter with Tilly."

Joe's thoughts return once more to Ada Majoure and her strange powers. She'd helped him escape the clutches of Smiler and Babushka Blatovsky even though it meant going against her father and denying herself a cure for her ailments. Joe hopes Ada can be helped without letting Sir Henry possess any objects of mystical power. He's certain he hasn't seen the last of Ada. Or her father.

"Sir Henry will be back, trust me."

"Who needs Margaret Finch," declares Bertie, "when we have our very own fortune teller right here?"

Sam taps his chin. "Hmm, easy to tell the future when you can travel to see it happen."

"True, I ever get the hang of controlling this compass, I could *make* a fortune." Joe smiles. The crows on top of Cottage Hospital erupt into cackling caws.

Right on cue, New Towners point excitedly up Central Hill where three brightly painted horse drawn vardos slowly and ceremoniously approach.

"She's here!" cries a New Towner. "The Queen of the Gypsies is coming!"

And with her comes Joe's hopes for awakening Elias.

"Most irregular, not even visiting hours," mutters the matron, turning back and forth on the spot like a stuck wind-up toy.

Not that there's much space left in the small ward filled with the shah accompanied by two Elite guards, Joe, Winnie, Sam, and Bertie and, carried on either side by two of her clan, the tiny figure of Margaret Finch. The shah bows respectfully.

"I believe my forebearer, Shah Bahram Gur, welcomed your ancestors from India, bringing music and pleasure to his people."

"Your memories do us great honour," smiles Margaret Finch, "may they bring you *baxt.*"

"'Luck' in Persian."

"And Romany the language of my people. May we both bring *baxt* to this sleeping boy."

Aunty Doll stands at Elias's bedside holding her nephew's hand, her face as uneasy as the matron's. However, the reassuring presence of Catherine Marsh and Dr Doyle persuaded her to allow this extraordinary scene to unfold.

Catherine Marsh closes the curtains behind Elias's bed to shut out faces pressed against the window, leaving the ward dimly lit. Margaret Finch is gently set down next to Elias.

Aunty Doll clears her throat. "We've not always seen eye to eye but thank you for coming. If you can help Elias, please ..." she swallows hard, "please do."

Margaret Finch runs a wrinkled hand over Elias's pale forehead.

With ceremony, Dr Doyle hands a thick scroll of parchment to Margaret Finch which she unfolds, placing it right up to her nose to read. Finally, she holds out her other hand expectantly.

Joe realises what she's waiting for.

"The Star of Nimrod please, Your Majesty."

The shah unclasps the brooch from his breast. He grips it as if unsure whether to let it leave his grasp after all that's happened, but hands it to Joe.

"Thank you."

"For you, it is the least I can do."

Joe brings the jewel to Elias' bedside. He places it carefully in the palm of Margaret Finch. Her fingers wrap around Joe's, her tight grip startling him at first. Her dark eyes look into his blue and green. She releases him with a satisfied nod. Turning to Elias, she places the brooch on his chest and without a further glance at the parchment begins chanting the words. Everyone leans forward to catch her barely audible voice, "From this world to the next,

"Step back from the bridge,

"My blood is your blood,

"May the Tree of Life carry you home."

Joe searches Elias's face for a flicker of life, a sign the rite is working. After repeating the incantation three times, Margaret Finch falls silent, removing her hand from his chest.

Nobody in the room speaks.

Finally, unable to wait any longer, Aunty Doll asks, "Has it worked?"

But from the pale still look on Elias's face, Joe knows the answer.

Margaret Finch slowly shakes her head.

Aunty Doll closes her eyes. Catherine Marsh puts her arm around her.

"I'm sorry," says Dr Doyle gently. "My contact hoped this was a way, but ..."

Disappointment spreads around the room like a melancholy Mexican wave. Winnie squeezes Joe's hand.

Suddenly Margaret Finch says in her cracked voice, "*This is* the way. But I am not the one."

"Then who is?" demands Joe, sick of riddles and wanting a straight answer for once.

Turning slowly to Joe she says with a toothless grin, "You."

"Me? Why me?"

"Is that what's important?"

Joe frowns, knowing the most important thing in the world right now is helping his friend, although it'd be nice to know how he could possibly make the rite work when Margaret Finch had failed.

Aunty Doll gives Joe an imploring look. He steps up to the bedside. Margaret Finch passes the parchment, takes his hand and places it over the Star of Nimrod. She whispers in Joe's ear,

"You are the King of Hearts. He is the King of Hearts."

Joe gives his lip a chew, takes a deep breath and reads; "From this world to the next,

"Step back from the bridge,

"My blood is your blood,

"May the Tree of Life carry you home."

Joe studies Elias's face.

It remains lifeless.

Behind him Bertie says, "Perhaps worth doing the chant again?"

Joe's about to tell him it's no use, that this is all a load of stupidness, and nothing will bring Elias back, when a sudden breeze springs through the still room. The closed curtains wave and whip as the breeze builds into a wind. Margaret Finch raises her hands and cackles, her voice echoed by a cacophony of crows outside.

"What's happening?" asks Winnie.

"I … I don't know," admits Sam, who alongside everyone can feel energy pulse through the ward.

"Life!" cries Margaret Finch as if that explains it all.

Suddenly Aunty Doll gasps, hands going to her mouth.

"Heavens be praised …" cries Catherine Marsh.

"What is it?" asks Winnie.

"It's …" Joe begins, struggling to find the words to tell her what he sees. "Elias is waking up!"

Sure enough, Elias's long dark eyelashes flicker, half open, half closed, like butterfly wings taking flight, until finally Elias's electric blue eyes look around at a room of silent stunned expressions.

"Okey-dokey," he croaks. "This still a dream?"

"No, you daft apeth!" Aunty Doll bursts into tears. "It's real." She leans down, planting kisses all over his face where colour already returns.

"Gerroff." Elias laughs, surprised at his auntie's uncharacteristic explosion of affection. "What've I missed? And when did I get so popular?"

He pushes himself up onto his elbows looking from the Shah of Persia and his Elite guard to Margaret Finch and her companions.

"Take it slowly," advises Dr Doyle, but now he's awake, Elias has lots of talking time to make up for.

"I was having the oddest dream you've ever had, until you," he points at Joe, "you come along, take my hand, and lead me out."

Joe, swinging from joy at Elias's awakening and bewilderment at his part in it, says, "That's what friends do."

Elias's old grin beams back, any resentment from their last encounter gone.

"I felt I'd never wake up at all, let alone find myself in the company of three lots of royalty."

"Three?" Dr Doyle smiles, checking Elias's pulse.

"Queen of the Gypsies, the Shah of Persia–that's you, ain't it?"

"A pleasure to make your conscious acquaintance."

"Pleasure's all mine. And last but no means least, *Queen Marsh*," says Elias, beaming up at Catherine Marsh, who laughs.

"I'm glad your role as Sleeping Beauty hasn't changed you, your friends would be disappointed."

Elias looks at Winnie, Sam, Bertie, and Joe. "I've got a feeling I owe you lot."

"It's quite a tale," declares Bertie.

"Great. Let's hear it over breakfast. I'm bloomin' starving."

By the time Joe leaves Cottage Hospital, most of Norwood New Town has gathered outside as word spreads Elias had returned. Margaret Finch's entourage strike up music on an accordion and a party breaks out on Central Hill, with Sam borrowing a fiddle. Elias is even able for a short time to demonstrate his skills on the spoons.

Eventually Matron recovers her domain, insisting the celebration be taken outside leaving her patients in peace, but not before Bertie gives Elias the edited highlights of how they'd stopped the theft of the Star of Nimrod with the aid of the Great Blondin and Le Petit Wonder.

Amidst the celebrations, Joe plucks up the courage to approach Margaret Finch on her vardo steps.

"Your Majesty … how did I manage to wake Elias?"

She takes a puff of her bone pipe. "How do you think?"

"Well … The words said, 'My blood is your blood.'"

"They did."

"Back when you dealt cards to me and Elias, we both got the King of Hearts …."

"You did."

"And Elias said, 'Snap! We're like family, me and you.'"

"He did."

Joe steadies himself against the painted caravan.

"But we're not *like* family …. We *are* family!"

"You are."

"That's why I dreamt I didn't exist. If Elias had died, I'd never be born. But now he's saved, my family will exist, right? Everything's worked out. Right?"

Margaret Finch silently blows a swirling smoke ring.

"Okay, you're not gonna tell me. But can I tell him? Elias? Or will it mess with the future?"

"The future is already a mess. Question is, can you fix it?"

"Me? How?"

The murder of crows launch from the Cottage Hospital roof cawing into the sky. Margaret Finch smiles.

"Ask the faeries."

"Huh. Right. Thanks."

Everyone waves off the shah and his entourage. Joe feels relief the Star of Nimrod will soon be far away from the Crystal Palace. He'd felt the power it holds.

"What was it like?" asks Bertie.

Joe considers how best to describe it. "Like all my senses were alert, like I could smell, taste, feel everything for the first time. Scary, but amazing."

Bertie slaps Joe's back. "Time traveller, detective, healer, is there no end to your talents?"

Joe laughs as he blushes.

"A word if I may," interrupts Catherine Marsh. The appearance of his nan's heroine prompts Joe and his friends to straighten up, even though she smiles down at them.

"I owe you an apology. You were correct about the theft of the Star of Nimrod."

"S'okay. I doubted myself in the end."

Dr Doyle joins them. "This thief Adam Worth is worthy of a case for Sherlock Holmes."

"Shame Sherlock isn't around to catch the Napoleon of Crime." Winnie sighs.

"The Napoleon of Crime," mulls Dr Doyle. "An appropriate moniker."

Bertie pipes up, "Don't forget Joe was also right about Sir Henry Majoure being behind it all."

Catherine Marsh nods gravely. "Dr Doyle and I won't forget and we can assure you we will be keeping a very close eye on Sir Henry in the event he shows his face again."

"Good show, it'd be most unfair if that villain gets away scot free."

He won't if Joe has anything to do with it. And although he desperately wants to return home now Elias is healed, Joe needs to speak with Worth and doesn't need Sherlock's help to guess where to find him ….

Chapter 42

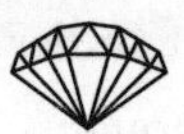

A row of police wagons stand in the driveway of Western Lodge, a far cry from the exclusive carriages that once brought the Prince of Wales and London's high society to visit Adam Worth.

Joe surveys the scene, having snuck away from the celebrations and nabbed a lift to Clapham Common with one of Margaret Finch's companions. William Pinkerton draws on his pipe as he studies a long list.

"We'll be comparing this inventory of luxury items against Scotland Yard's list of stolen goods, and I'll be speaking to my detectives in Paris too. Your friends Worth, Sophie Lyons, and Piano Charley were quite prolific."

"They're not friends," says Joe quickly. "Although I do owe them my life."

"Hey! Where's that going?" Pinkerton calls after two men in overalls carrying a painting to a waiting carriage engraved with *The Gallery of Thomas Agnew & Son.*

A gap in the wrapping gives Joe a glimpse of the Duchess of Devonshire painting. The shorter delivery man sports a grandiose moustache and waggles a receipt in his free hand. Pinkerton takes the paperwork as the man explains in a heavy Welsh accent,

"This painting is the property of Mr Thomas Agnew, stolen from his gallery. Mr Agnew is the brother in law of Chief Inspector Marlow of Scotland Yard, who's personally given permission for its immediate return."

Pinkerton rolls his eyes, thrusting the paperwork back at the removal man. "Don't want to upset Chief Inspector Marlow's brother-in-law now, do we? Go on, be quick about it."

"That much I can promise, sir."

As the men load Worth's prize possession into the back of the carriage, Joe senses something familiar about the Welshman ....

Pinkerton interrupts Joe's thoughts. "My organisation could always use someone like you as an apprentice."

Joe smiles to himself; his Victorian job offers just keep coming.

The Welsh removal man carefully secures the Duchess of Devonshire painting in the back of the carriage. He steps away to admire her smile more intently than might be expected of a removal man. Finally, he turns to find Joe leaning against the open carriage doors shaking his head.

"You enjoyed that a little too much, didn't you? Walking your pride and joy right under Pinkerton's nose with a false document and a false moustache?"

Worth puts his hand to his heart in mock innocence.

"There's nothing false about this letter. It's genuinely signed by Chief Inspector Marlow of Scotland Yard. Course, he didn't realise *I'd* be the one doing the collecting. But you knew, didn't you, young fella? You expected to find me here."

Joe can't stop his chest pumping up at the pride in Worth's voice.

"I thought you might be busy plotting to break out Sophie Lyons and Piano Charley."

Worth shrugs.

"Been there, done that. This time I was thinking of leaving them to it. Forming a new partnership." He winks. "If you're interested."

"Still not."

Worth gives a sad sigh that actually sounds genuine, although with a fraudster like him Joe could never be sure. "Shame. Suppose I'll just have to break those reprobates out after all."

"Better hurry before they start talking."

"They know better."

"Well, I was thinking how about you get Piano Charley and Sophie a message, tell them to tell the police Sir Henry hired you all, and *then* break them out?"

"You never give up kid; I'll give you that."

"If you do it, I won't call Pinkerton over right now."

Worth grins. "I'm willing to bet the fact I saved your life earns me a little credit."

"Don't bet on that."

Worth's grin widens. "Even if I did ask them to implicate Sir Henry and even if they agreed, once we got out of prison the case against Sir Henry goes with us. Face it, he'd snake his way out of this even if I stood in the dock next to him. Life doesn't work like that for people like him."

"Yeah?" Joe simmers. "Well one day, he will pay, believe me."

Worth gives a grim smile. "Kid, I do. But be careful."

"You almost sound like you give a damn."

Worth looks genuinely puzzled. "Do I? Must be getting old. Definitely need a holiday. I hear Reichenbach Falls in Switzerland is lovely this time of year."

Worth takes each of the carriage doors in his hands. "See you around, kid."

With a wink, Worth closes the doors and bangs the roof. The driver cracks his whip and the horses speed off across Clapham Common.

"Yeah, see you around," says Joe and has an overwhelming urge to see his dad.

"Are you sure we can't come too?" asks Bertie for the umpteenth time as they stand outside the maze.

Fortunately, before Joe has a chance, Sam repeats Joe's previous replies word for word. "You might be blown to pieces along with Joe if two people try crossing at the same time."

"I understand, but …"

"Umm, if you understand," laughs Sam, "why keep asking?"

"I'm only asking what you're all thinking." Bertie huffs. "You're not telling me you don't all want to time travel too?"

Winnie and Sam look a little sheepish but neither can argue.

"Listen," says Joe, "there's someone in my time I reckon can tell me what this compass is and how it works." Joe pictures the puzzling Robin Wood and his talk of keys unlocking ancient boundaries. "And if it's safe to travel more than one at a time, sure. We will. Trust me."

Three faces brighten.

Winnie declares, "Since when did being safe or not stop us doing anything?"

They laugh their agreement. Bertie quickly wipes away the start of a tear.

"You will return, won't you?"

"*I'll be back,*" Joe jokes, doing his best impression of Arnold Schwarzenegger playing the time-travelling Terminator. They don't get the reference but laugh anyway. Joe has found the kind of friends he never imagined he'd have again after Zahid moved away, and found them in a way he never imagined possible. And in Elias he'd found friendship *and* family. Joe would most definitely be back; so long as he has the compass, he has family and friends. "Look in on Elias, won't you?"

"Indubitably," Bertie replies, thrusting his chin in the air.

"We await your encore." Sam smiles.

"Stay out of trouble. As much as you're able." Winnie squeezes Joe's hand before letting it go.

Joe takes one final look at his friends, grips Skull Rider and moves into the twists and turns of the maze, shattered compass in hand, repeating the phrase,

"Follow—in—their—footsteps ….

"Pause—here—a—while,

"Listen—to—the—echoes ....

"Past, present, future ..."

Deep inside the palace, the hands of Dent's gigantic clock jolt and the timepiece ticks once more.

Joe stands at the gate of the maze and stares.

A jogger passes, plugged into his headphones, a suit walks and talks into his mobile, a helicopter buzzes overhead, all confirming everything Joe experienced in the maze – gale-force wind, clouds rushing in reverse ....

Joe's back. In his own time.

The palace has gone, nature reclaiming where it once stood, wild bushes and roots of mighty trees clinging to its foundations far beneath the soil.

But the dream where he no longer exists still haunts Joe.

"Excuse me," he says, rushing up to a lady walking her dog, a small border terrier. Joe hesitates, remembering, ready for the dog to bare its teeth and growl ....

Instead, it barks up at Joe, rubbing up against his leg and acting as excited and overjoyed as Joe.

"Jasper, calm down."

"Sorry, can you tell me the date?"

"July twenty-seventh. Jasper, stop."

The same day Joe had left. But ...

He whispers the year he left.

She nods, now eying Joe as if he's as barking mad as Jasper who rolls around at Joe's feet before his owner finally manages to drag him away.

Joe leaps onto his skateboard and speeds along the path towards the Triangle. He passes the crumbling walls of the Italian terrace and waves up at the sphinxes, not caring how dumb he looks, his elation only increasing when they don't respond with a wink or a cryptic sarky remark. They simply stare out like guardians of the past.

Joe almost tumbles off Skull Rider when he spots a familiar figure walking up the path towards the Triangle proudly wearing her green Capel Manor Farm volunteer sweatshirt.

He's afraid of shouting her name, not knowing what he'll do if she doesn't recognise him. Joe takes a breath and finally cries, "Aaliyah!"

She spins around, watching Joe approach with confusion.

He slows.

His stomach lurches.

"Who …" she begins, but her words falter along with Joe's hopes.

"It's me! Joe! Joe Cook!" he cries, keeping enough distance to avoid a knee in his groin.

Aaliyah looks him up and down with a face screwed up with bafflement.

"Who …" she repeats slowly, "cut your *hair*?!"

Joe instinctively strokes his cropped head. "My hair!"

His manic laughter prompts Aaliyah's head to drop to one side. "Yes, your hair. Did you lose your brains too?"

"Yes!" Joe punches the air, fists so tight with glee his fingernails dig into his palms but he doesn't care any more than he cares about his cousin's put-down or her supercilious expression.

"Have you snuck a bottle of rum out of the restaurant?"

"The restaurant! It's still there?"

"Umm, duh, where else would Paradise be? What's with all the stupidness? Why are you *crying* …?!"

Joe tries wiping his tears of joy but they come too quickly and he gives up, no longer caring.

"Joe, what is it? What's wrong?" Aaliyah reaches out a worried hand, placing it on his arm.

Joe puts his hand on hers. "Nothing's wrong. Everything's right."

"I think we best get you to your dad."

"I'd like that." Joe smiles. "I'd like that very much."

Face in the sunshine, Joe doesn't see the shadow of the Alone Child watching him, watching a child who no longer feels alone. The Alone Child reaches back for memories of joy, knowing such feelings are fleeting as the sands of time.

As Joe will discover soon enough.

Real life characters from Victorian Crystal Palace

Growing up in the Norwoods I was aware the area is named after the Great North Wood that once spread across London's hinterland. My granddad sold programmes at the Crystal Palace and I love the mystical feel of Crystal Palace Park, the crumbling terraces of the 'People's Palace,' the dinosaurs and sphinxes like phantoms from the past.

What I didn't know until I began my own adventure making this tale a reality, is the area's incredible history and the extraordinary people drawn to live in the palace's shadow. So I wanted to share some of their biographies with you–it's best to read them after finishing *Star of Nimrod* as there are a few spoilers ....

In order for Joe to meet these people, I've been elastic with some of their actual timelines. For example, 'Sam' Samuel Coleridge Taylor would've been thirteen in 1888 and 'Bertie' H. G. Wells twenty-one, whereas I've made them both thirteen. Most of the historical characters can be found on Wikipedia, but if you want to find out more you can visit The Crystal Palace Museum (**www.crystalpalacemuseum.org.uk**) and the local history section in Upper Norwood Library Hub is excellent (**www.uppernorwoodlibraryhub.org**). Also The Norwood Society (**www.thenorwoodsociety.co.uk**) and The Crystal Palace Foundation (**www.crystalpalacefoundation.org**) have a great online library of information about local people and places.

Some of the characters in the book I've invented, like Sir Henry Majoure. And if you ever travel back in time through the maze to 1888, you won't find the North Transept standing because it burnt down in a fire in 1866. The fire destroyed the Ninevah Court, which was never rebuilt due to a lack of funds, leaving the palace oddly lopsided. Finally, contrary to popular myth, the ancient Vicar's Oak which marked the boundaries of four Parishes was cut down in 1780 before the palace was constructed. However, the faerie curse suffered by those who did the deed is said to be real …

Otherwise, I've tried to stay true to the facts and weave them into a tale about the extraordinary history of this area and its people.

'Bertie' H. G. Wells (born 1866, died 1946)
Described as 'The Shakespeare of Science Fiction,' Herbert 'Bertie' George Wells was born in Bromley High Street where Lakeland stands today (there's a blue plaque outside the shop). He was the fourth child of Sarah, a former domestic servant, and Joseph, a former domestic gardener and professional cricketer, who was the first bowler to take four wickets in four balls.

Bertie's parents used an inheritance to acquire a shop selling sporting goods and china, although it provided unsteady income as the stock was old and the location wasn't great. Back then, Bromley was a village, long before The Glades shopping centre. Bertie had a lung condition and broke his leg at seven; bedridden, he passed the time reading books which inspired his desire to become a writer and creator of other worlds.

A fractured leg ended Bertie's father's cricketing career and his mother had to return to work as a lady's maid in a country house away from her children and husband. At fourteen, Bertie unhappily worked thirteen-hour days far from home as an apprentice draper. These experiences shaped his strong belief in the fair distribution of wealth, and he grew up to be a campaigner for social justice. These themes can be found in H. G. Wells's books, which continue to be adapted for TV and film and include *War of the Worlds, The Invisible Man, The Time Machine* and *The Island of Doctor Moreau.*

'Sam' Samuel Coleridge Taylor (born 1875, died 1912)
The composer and conductor became renown in the music world of Britain and the United States. 'Sam' was the son of Dr Daniel Taylor from Sierra Leone who returned to Africa unaware Alice, a seventeen-year-old English girl, was carrying his child. She named her son after the poet Samuel Taylor Coleridge and brought him up with Sam's granddad who shoed horses. They lived at 30 Dagnall Park in Selhurst close to Crystal Palace FC today. A blue memorial plaque was erected on the house.

Sam's granddad played violin and began teaching Sam; he showed talent, so when he turned fifteen, his extended family arranged for him to study at The Royal College of Music where he learned composition. Although Sam didn't study at The Crystal Palace School of Music, when he graduated, he was appointed a professor there and he conducted the orchestra at the Croydon Conservatoire.

Sam married fellow musician, Jessie, and named their son Hiawatha after the Native American immortalised in poetry. Sam's acclaimed composition *Hiawatha's Wedding Feast* presented at The Royal Albert Hall and became one of the most popular pieces in the world. He toured the United States and was received by President Theodore Roosevelt at the White House, a rare event in those days for a man of African descent.

Keenly proud of his heritage, his later compositions drew from his Sierra Leonean ancestry and the music of the African continent and he participated as the youngest delegate at the 1900 First Pan-African Conference. Sam died of pneumonia when he was only thirty-seven and his widow was granted an annual pension by King George V.

The Stopes Family
The Stopes Family lived in Upper Norwood for twelve years beginning in 1880.

Charlotte Carmichael Stopes was the first woman in Scotland to gain a Certificate of Arts and became a scholar of Shakespeare and refuted speculation he wasn't the real author of his plays. A campaigner for women's rights, her 1894 book, *British Freewomen–Their Historical Privilege,* influenced and inspired the women's emancipation movement. Later in life, she was elected an honorary member of the Royal Society of Literature.

Charlotte married Henry Stopes, a palaeontologist who was the first person to find stone-age implements in the Thames. He amassed the largest collection of fossils in Britain, which today can be found at the National Museum of Wales. He tried his hand in the brewing business, but it ended in bankruptcy and they had to sell their family home in Upper Norwood. They moved to the coast where he continued hunting for evidence of early man. Today, the Geologists Association awards the Henry Stopes Memorial Medal for work on the Prehistory of Man.

Marie Stopes was born in 1880 and grew up to pioneer family planning advice. A campaigner for women's rights and birth control, her work earned her a blue memorial plaque on their family home at 28 Cintra Park. However, she also admired Hitler and both shared views on eugenics which seeks to 'improve genetic purity' and Marie advocated the forced sterilisation of poorer women she considered 'unfit for parenthood.'

Marie disowned her son for marrying somebody with an eye disorder, arguing any grandchildren might inherit this condition. This led me to create the character of Winnie, a fictionalised version of Marie's younger sister. The real Winifred was born in 1884 and by imagining she was blind, I was able to link in the inspiring Royal Normal Academy for the Blind.

Dr Joseph Campbell (born 1832, died 1914) **& The Royal Normal College and Academy for the Blind**

Joseph Campbell grew up in Nashville in the United States and became blind aged five after an accident. He benefited from attending the Tennessee School for the Blind and at sixteen was appointed master of music at the Wisconsin School for the Blind. He became known for his strong anti-slavery views; a group of men gave him twenty-four hours to renounce them or face being hanged, but he refused and was spared death because of public sympathy for his blindness.

In 1872, Campbell founded The Royal Normal College and Academy for the Blind. At the time, most blind people in Britain lived in poverty and depended upon charity, but Campbell's aim was to give students the highest possible education so they might achieve independence and 'meet their sighted fellow-beings on equal terms.' The Upper Norwood site was chosen because of its proximity to the Crystal Palace and its reputation for music. Pupils were invited to attend concerts for free and rehearsals.

Campbell believed blind students needed to greatly improve their physical strength and abilities to reach their true overall potential. Students learned to dance, swim, and perform gymnastics, whilst the choir and instrumentalists toured Europe. It built a reputation as the most progressive school for the blind in the world. Fortuitously, it moved from Upper Norwood at the start of World War II as the building was bombed during the Blitz, but its work continues at its location in Hereford known as The Royal National College for the Blind.

Charles 'The Great' Blondin (born 1824, died 1897)
Blondin was a household name in the nineteenth century, thanks to his daredevil acrobatics. At five, he enrolled at the Ecole de Gymnase in Lyon, France, and toured as 'The Little Wonder.'

Fifty-thousand thrill-seekers watched Blondin cross the Niagara Falls on a tight rope. Halfway across, he called on a tourist boat to anchor beneath him so he could cast down a line, haul up a bottle of wine and have a drink. Blondin crossed and somersaulted his way over

Niagara Falls three-hundred times, including with a sack over his head and on another occasion with his manager on his back.

Blondin performed feats throughout the world, his daredevilry becoming associated with the Crystal Palace when he first performed there in 1861. He was joined by his five-year-old daughter who whilst sitting in a wheelbarrow, threw rose petals onto the sell-out crowd below. The press and some audiences were horrified, and the Home Secretary ordered Blondin to stop placing his daughter in danger. So, in Liverpool he pushed a lion across the tightrope in a wheelbarrow instead.

Blondin presented many times at the Crystal Palace, performing into his seventies and his family moved to Ealing in London where Blondin Park is named in his honour.

Catherine Marsh (born 1818, died 1912).

The daughter of the vicar at St George's Church in Beckenham, Catherine Marsh became concerned for the welfare of the thousands of labourers known as Navvies who gathered from across the country to work on the nearby re-erection of the Crystal Palace. On Christmas Eve 1851, when heavy snow stopped work, Catherine discovered the Navvies had not been paid and therefore had no food. She immediately organised soup-making on a grand scale with coffee and bread and butter served on the grounds.

This began a lifetime of looking out for their physical and spiritual welfare. This was long before employment laws protected the safety of workers, so Catherine intervened when she felt the Crystal Palace Company misused their labourers. She praised their 'noble strength and character' in her book, *English Hearts and English Hands,* and she credited Navvies with having a positive influence on local lads.

In 1854 a contingent of Navvies were assembled to build roads for troops in the Crimean War. On the eve of embarking for the war, police intervened in a brawl between two Navvies. This escalated into a riot between police and Navvies at the Penge entrance to the Crystal Palace until Catherine rode her carriage into the middle of the fighting and appealed to the Navvies to stop. Such was their respect for her that they stopped at once.

Catherine saw the Navvies off on their ship and looked after their army wages to ensure their families were provided for if they didn't return. She struck up lifelong friendships with the men and their families, hosting famous tea parties in the garden of her father's rectory. She lived to the grand age of ninety-four.

Arthur Conan Doyle (born 1859, died 1930)
Doyle grew up in squalid Edinburgh tenement flats. He studied medicine at The University of Edinburgh, but his attempts to set up a doctor's practice in Portsmouth (where he played as goalkeeper for Portsmouth FC) and in London failed.

Doyle eventually quit medicine to concentrate on his real passion— writing. Following the success of two short stories featuring the detective Sherlock Holmes, Doyle moved in 1891 to a house at 12 Tennison Road in South Norwood. During the three years he lived there, he wrote the majority of his Sherlock stories including *The Norwood Builder* with a sequence set in The Anerley Arms pub.

Doyle got involved in local life; he loved cricket (once taking a wicket against W. G. Grace) and regularly played for Norwood Cricket Club at South Norwood Lake. He was elected president of the Upper Norwood Literary and Scientific Society which met in the hall at The Royal Normal College and Academy for the Blind and their regular lectures included 'Recent Evidences as to Man's Survival of Death.'

This topic reflects Doyle's own fascination with spiritualism, a major movement in Victorian times. He joined The Ghost Club formed earlier by Charles Dickens to explore the paranormal, and whilst living in South Norwood, he joined the Society for Psychical Research. Doyle believed the existence of faeries was proven by 'The

Cottingley Fairies' photos in 1922, later revealed to be a hoax.

Before he left Norwood, Doyle wanted to end Sherlock and concentrate on other writing. He invented an arch-nemesis, Professor Moriarty, who fought Sherlock on the Reichenbach Falls before both plunged to their deaths (Sherlock was resurrected seven years later by popular demand). The inspiration for Moriarty is said to be international criminal Adam Worth, dubbed 'The Napoleon of Crime.'

Adam Worth, 'Piano Charley' Bullard, and Sophie Lyons

Born in Germany and raised in New York, Worth was an army deserter in the American Civil War and moved from pickpocketing to organising robberies and heists. Never letting jail get in the way of his criminal career, Worth escaped Sing Sing prison and later broke out the safecracker 'Piano Charley' Bullard by digging a tunnel. The pair teamed up to rob the vault of the National Bank in Boston through a tunnel in the neighbouring shop (an idea used by Arthur Conon Doyle in the Sherlock story *The Red-Headed League*) before moving to Europe to evade Pinkerton Agency detectives on their tail.

The pair both became romantically involved with a barmaid named Kitty Flynn (for the purposes of my book I've swapped Kitty with real-life criminal Sophie Lyons). The trio ran a gambling den in Paris but Worth was recognised by William Pinkerton and after police raids, they moved their criminal enterprises to London. Worth masqueraded as an oilman, joining high society and taking up residence in Western Lodge on Clapham Common (which today is a homeless shelter).

From here, Worth and company formed a criminal network organising major robberies of uncut diamonds and personally stealing Thomas Gainsborough's painting *The Duchess of Devonshire*. Dubbed 'The Napoleon of Crime' by Scotland Yard (a title Conan Doyle borrowed for Sherlock's nemesis Professor Moriarty) Worth prided himself in never committing a robbery where force or firearms had to be resorted to. However, the heavy-drinking Charley Bullard became increasingly violent and they parted company. Charley was arrested in Belgium and died before Worth could visit his old friend, and later Worth himself spent four years in a Belgium jail when a heist went wrong

Worth returned to New York to retire. He met with William Pinkerton who recorded Worth's exploits and organised the return of *The Duchess of Devonshire* for a payment of $25,000 to Worth. As part of their agreement, Worth arranged for his son to become a Pinkerton detective.

Sophie Lyons was a notorious pickpocket and confidence trickster born into a family of Liverpudlian criminals. Sent to steal from the age of three, Sophie became a talented actress. She moved to New York and married Ned Lyons 'King of the Bank Robbers.' When Sophie was jailed, Ned used a disguise to break into Sing Sing prison and broke through the walls of her cell. Sophie escaped to Paris, continuing her criminal exploits under the guise of 'Madame d'Varney.'

When her fourteen-year-old son, George, kept getting kicked out of boarding schools and embarked on his own criminal career, Sophie had him arrested and requested he be put in a juvenile correctional facility. George told the judge his mum was guilty of theft and child neglect.

Sophie eventually retired and wrote her autobiography, *Why Crime Doesn't Pay*. She became a philanthropist and prison reformer, owning forty homes and offering them rent-free to rehabilitated criminals and their families. Sophie established a home for juvenile delinquents on the condition: 'The home is devoted to the work of convincing children who have begun to be criminals that they have chosen the wrong path and also to training them so they will have the strength to go alright.'

Margaret Finch, Queen of the Gypsies (born 1632, died 1748)
The most famous fortune teller of her era, people throughout society

travelled far and wide to visit Margaret Finch to ask her advice. Those people included the wife of diarist Samuel Pepys in 1668. To be elected queen of the combined Roma nations, Margaret would have been hugely important and respected in the community settling disputes, choosing elder leaders and having her wisdom sought on any important issues.

Margaret settled in Norwood amidst the Great North Wood, the heart of Roma London leading to local road names such as Romany Road, Gipsy Road and Gipsy Hill where Margaret lived in the 'Gipsy House.' She sat with her chin resting on her knees and her muscles became so set in that position that when she died at age 109 she was buried in a box-shaped coffin at St George's Church in Beckenham. Large crowds gathered for the funeral, which was paid for by local publicans as a mark of respect and thanks for the tourists she attracted to their pubs.

Her fame, and that of the Norwood Roma, continued after her death (a popular pantomime called 'The Norwood Gypsies' performed at the Theatre Royal in Covent Garden), and her role of queen passed on within Finch's family to her niece and great-niece. By the nineteenth century, the introduction of laws against vagrancy led to authorities scapegoating and persecuting the Roma community who were forced to leave Norwood.

Owen Jones and George Grove

Owen Jones (born 1809, died 1874) was a pioneering Welsh architect and designer. Responsible for the interior decoration and layout of the Great Exhibition and its relocated site in Sydenham, Jones aimed to faithfully interpret the past. He wanted the palace to educate and inspire by showing the best of previous civilisations to generate a new wave of art, design and appreciation. Jones looked towards the Islamic world for design inspiration and pioneered modern colour theory involving the visual effects of combining different colours. His book, *The Grammar of Ornament* is still used today.

George Grove (born 1820, died 1900) trained as a civil engineer and loved music, writing the definitive dictionary of music and musicians. Appointed the first secretary of the Crystal Palace, Grove was responsible for programming and operations helping it become a dynamic force in Victorian culture, education, innovation and entertainment. Grove appointed August Manns as the palace's musical director and their concerts transformed popular music tastes providing the public with classical music for only a shilling. Their epic Handel Festivals in the palace involved four thousand singers and four hundred instrumentals. Grove went on to become the first director of the Royal College of Music.

Naser al-Din Shah Qajar, The Shah of Persia (born 1831, died 1896)
Naser ruled Persia for almost fifty years, his early reign including reforms in education and infrastructure. A patron of the arts, Naser was passionate about photography and was a talented painter and avid poet.

In 1873, he became the first shah to formally visit Europe and kept and published a diary of his tour. When Naser visited Britain, he became one in a long line of monarchs and leaders to visit the Crystal Palace, watching Japanese acrobats in the Grand Transept and staying at the Queens Hotel. He attended Brock's firework display in his honour and was reputedly so impressed that he postponed his departure from London so that he could see another display, arriving on the second occasion as an ordinary paying customer so he could mix with the crowds.

Naser visited the palace again in 1889. Later in his reign, he resisted growing pressures for new reforms and was assassinated in 1896.

W. G. Grace (born 1848, died 1915)
William Gilbert Grace is considered one of cricket's greatest ever all-round players. Credited with inventing modern batting Grace played for forty-four seasons in which he took nearly three thousand wickets, scored over fifty thousand runs and usually captained the many teams he played for including England.

Although a trained doctor and amateur cricketer, he made more money from the sport than any professional cricketer and had a reputation for treating poorer patients without charge. This was before Britain had free healthcare. A big man with a reputation for being noisy and boisterous on the field, Grace believed that cricketers are not born but must be nurtured to develop their skills through coaching and practice.

In 1899, Grace moved to 7 Lawrie Park Road, a stroll from the Crystal Palace where he regularly played at its cricket ground which was used for matches between England and the touring Australians and by Kent County Cricket Club (whose players included Joseph Wells, father of H. G. Wells). In 1900, the London County Cricket Club was formed by the Crystal Palace Company who invited Grace to become manager, captain, and an attraction at the palace until 1904.

They played at a new ground next to the site of one of the two largest fountains which were grassed over in 1894; for twenty years the site also hosted the first FA Cup finals. The site was demolished in 1960 to make way for the Crystal Palace National Sports Centre.

Acknowledgements

This book was finished during lockdown but its journey began when I was a toddler wandering around the mystical world of Crystal Palace Park. It was, and remains, a place that inspires the imagination and I'd like to thank the following people for helping bring my own imaginings to life. My family; the wordsmith Maia who created on-the-spot the book's strap-line, 'What if the past became your future?', Dan whose screwball imagination conjured up the whirling shattered compass, and Mel for her continuous support, her eagle-eye for grammar and for putting up with me treading on every floorboard at 5:30am. Thank you to my insightful test-readers Abdur-rehman Hassan, Spike Townend, Ely Roberts, Darcey Bradler, Mark Jones and Rona Glynn for their invaluable feedback. I really appreciate the historical fact-checking by Ken Kiss the curator of the Crystal Palace Museum (**www.crystalpalacemuseum.org.uk**), Stephen Oxford Secretary of the Norwood Society (**www.thenorwoodsociety.co.uk**) and Melvyn Harrison president of The Crystal Palace Foundation (**www.crystalpalacefoundation.org**). Thanks to Carrie Jones for all her intuition and encouragement during the editing process, Florian Mefisheye Garbay for the most awesome cover design I could've imagined, Libby Hamilton for her expert advice on blurbs and layout, Myfie Mountford for the video and Wayne Roberts for the music. I'm thankful for the time given by Emma Nuttall at Friends, Families and Travellers (**www.gypsy-traveller.org**). Getting my head around the world of self-publishing was hugely assisted by the authors N S Blackman from Dinosaur Books (**www.dinosaurbooks.co.uk**) and Judy Skidmore from Parakeet Books (**www.parakeetbooks.com**). Special mentions for Susan Milford and Judy Harris for our meet-ups to discuss our work, and to Malaika Rose Stanley who brought us together for her inspirational writing for children course and whose generosity and influence lives on.

Finally, thanks to everyone who supported my crowd-funding campaign. Special shout-outs to the following backers for their generosity which helped make this book possible:

Wayne Roberts
Louise Machin and Richard Steele
Sandra and John Whitlock
Steve Potts
Hilary Scanlon
John Hyatt
Simon Ryder
Anne-Marie Reid
Pete and Julia Ainsworth

COMING SOON…

PALACE OF SHADOWS
THE CHRYSTAL PALACE CHRONICLES
BOOK II

Sign up to my newsletter to keep up to date with the next instalment and be the first to get exclusive stories from the series, plus giveaways, treasure hunts and more ….

Go to **www.grahamwhitlock.com**

Here's a taster of what's to come for Joe.

"Table six want two more Paradise peach and pineapple milkshakes. And the toddler on table three's re-laying the floor with mac and cheese." Joe grins as he puts the tray of empty plates onto the bamboo-fronted bar.

"Just like you at that age, a messy little apeth." Dad laughs as he opens a new pack of cocktail umbrellas and tosses each one with well-rehearsed skill into waiting glasses. "I'll get the dustpan and brush."

"No worries, I'll sort it. I know it's not easy for you bending down these days."

"Cheeky! I'm thirty-nine, not dead. Hospital says I've got the body of a twenty-one-year-old."

"And the mind of a five-year-old!" Uncle Tyrell shouts from the kitchen, voice rising above the sound of sea bass fillets searing in the pan.

"That's why you've been friends since primary school, two peas in a pod," Aunty Salma tells her husband as she shimmies to the counter to collect two plates piled high with roti flatbread.

"Aaaa! You got tooold!" mocks Dad, waggling his cocktail shaker at Uncle Tyrell who sticks out his bottom lip like a sulky reception kid. Dad places a hand on Joe's shoulder. "I could get used to you helping out 'round here. Just like old times."

"Cheers to old times."

It has only been a day since Joe returned from his adventures in Victorian Crystal Palace, but he's spent every second with his senses on overdrive, savouring the sights, sounds and smells of a life he'd taken for granted. Joe gorges on the sweet aromas of caramelised sugar and coconut milk, the comforting smells of Paradise Bar and Restaurant filling him with delight that had faded in his teenage years.

What a difference twenty-four hours can make. Albeit during those hours, Joe had time-travelled, been chased over the roof and through the belly of the Crystal Palace, foiled international jewel thieves and murderous smiling sociopaths, witnessed Blondin's high-wire daredevilry, almost died in a dank Victorian prison cell, met amazing people like the Shah of Persia, the Queen of the Gypsies and the creator of Sherlock Holmes, and found four friends who had put their lives on the line for Joe; friends who make Joe grin as he pictures a cheeky 'Okey-dokey' from Elias, Winnie's arched eyebrow, Bertie's bubbling enthusiasm, or Sam's soft strength. Friends Joe can't wait to travel back and see again once he's discovered how the shattered compass in his hand works.

"What's that?" demands Lauren, chewing on a bubble gum like it deserves to be taught a lesson.

Joe's fingers snap around the compass, stuffing it in his pocket. No way is he letting his little sister discover his secret.

"S'nothing. Cool unicorn T-shirt."

Lauren inspects her top as if a compliment from Joe is grounds to go home and change. She scowls suspiciously at her brother who shrugs in genuine confusion and asks, "What?"

"Why you acting all weird."

"Weird how?"

"Weird nice."

"Nice is weird?"

"It is when you do it. What are you trying to get with all this 'ooo, Dad, I'll help' and 'Ooo, Dad let me do this,' and 'Ooo, sis, cool unicorn T-shirt?"

Joe can't help laughing. Lauren angrily juts her chin at him.

"I'm not trying to 'get' anything, honest. Well, apart from ..." Joe struggles to find words that capture all the feelings circling inside. Lauren's eyes glint, she clearly thinks she's got her brother nailed, so her mouth drops open with disbelief when he finally says,
"Being happy."

"Are you on drugs?!"

"Call it a newfound love of life."

"I call it lame. You might fool Dad, but not me. I know you're up to something."

Just to make sure Joe knows she's watching him, Lauren pokes two fingers at her eyeballs then jabs one accusing finger at her brother before flouncing over to Dad at the bar.

Joe smiles after Lauren, reminded of Iris Blondin and her sassy retorts to anyone regardless of age or status. She'd been fearless, just like Lauren, a quality Joe once envied in his sister. Now he just feels proud. But it'll evidently take time to show Lauren he's changed. Fair enough, given the past few years he only spoke to her to roast her.

"Our best lunchtime takings in ages," declares Dad with a shake of the credit card reader.

Joe sits on a bar stool, slurping the last of his complimentary lime and chocolate milkshake. Lauren had gone off on a playdate with Molly, this month's best buddy.

Aunty Salma wraps a warm arm around Joe and gives him a squeeze. "And no way could we have kept atop of everything without you, Joe."

"I know." He leans his head onto Aunty Salma's shoulder, her soft skin cooling his hot sweaty cheek. Although not related to Joe by blood, Aunty Salma, Uncle Tyrell, Aaliyah and even the terrible twins Brendon and Kendon are family in every other way that really matters.

"So, this is fair dues," Dad declares, pulling a crisp twenty-pound-note from the cash till and waving it at Joe, a frown crossing his face when Joe makes no move to nab it.

"S'okay, you need it, for the business."

"But you've earned it," insists Dad. "And you need to get your skateboard wheel fixed, don't you?"

"Oh, no, that's sorted."

"Sorted how?" Dad frowns, clearly wondering how Joe had repaired the busted wheel of Skull Rider for gratis.

Joe tenses; he doesn't want to lie but can't exactly explain it had been fixed a hundred and thirty years ago by the dad of the famous science fiction writer H. G. Wells—aka Bertie. So Joe settles with saying, "A mate's dad fixed it."

"Oh."

Before Dad has the chance to ask the identity of the dad with superior DIY skills, Joe changes the subject by grabbing the twenty out of his hand. "Tell you what, this can pay for my work this afternoon *and* tonight."

"Tonight?" Dad's face lights up. "You thinking of doing another shift?"

"Sure," Joe exclaims as if that should be obvious.

"Then you best go make the most of this sunny afternoon. Got any plans?"

"Nah, not really, just hanging out, go to the park, might have a mooch around Haynes Lane Market ..."

... and see a man about a magical compass.

The alleyway leading into the upper floor of Haynes Lane indoor market is cluttered with collectables and cast-offs. The alley feels a dozen degrees cooler than the rest of the sun-baked Triangle. At the entrance into the ramshackle building, a robin red-breast dances on top of a teacup chirping at Joe.

"Good to see you too." However, there's something different about the usually chipper chirp of the robin, an anxious urgency to his song.

"What's up with you?" enquires Joe before noticing the heavy padlock on the door. Weird. It's well into the afternoon when the top floor occupied by Robin Wood would usually open.

"Where's the old beardy oddball?"

The way the robin chirps in reply the answer isn't good.

The lower floor of Haynes Lane Market is an Aladdin's cave lined with booths some selling antique Art Deco furniture, others crates of discarded vinyl records, all as quirky and curious as their stall holders. Two chatter away while Joe hovers attempting to catch their attention.

"I told Barb, I did. I told her, 'You shoulda checked they're chickens before you bought 'em." Instead, we've got a dozen cockerels having a crowing competition every sunrise," complains a lady with a billowing patchwork gown that made her look like an enormous teapot wearing a gigantic tea-cosy.

"Dear oh dear," declares a man small enough to have jumped down from the shelves of his booth crammed with toys from childhood's past. He twirls his prim waxed moustache. "So no eggs then?"

"No, but a lovely cockerel pot roast to look forward to once I've wrung their necks."

"And a pot roasted Barb once you've wrung her neck," chortles the toy man.

"Er, excuse me?" interjects Joe.

"Can I help you?" teapot lady and toy man reply in unison.

"Do you know what time Robin Wood opens?"

"I do know," replies teapot lady as if such information wasn't for the likes of Joe.

"Um, can you tell me?"

"Ten o'clock, just like the rest of us."

It's well past three.

"Most peculiar," chimes in toy man. "Never known him not open in all the years I've been here, and he's been here longer than me."

"Longer than any of us," adds teapot lady.

"Right. He's not called or anything?"

"Called?" Teapot lady shakes with laughter. "Robin Wood don't do phones!"

"More likely to use carrier pigeons," chortles toy man.

Teapot lady reads Joe's worried expression and gestures enticingly into her booth. "Fretting cos you forgot your mum's birthday? Hoping to pick up a special trinket for her?"

Joe shakes his head. Mum moved to the other side of the world more than a decade ago to raise donkeys rather than her own kids.

"Oh." The teapot lady sulks until her eyes fix on the shattered compass Joe grips in his hand. "Ooo, you looking to sell that, are you?"

Teapot lady leans towards Joe. He takes a quick step back, instinctively hiding the shattered compass behind his back. After everything he'd gone through he isn't going to let it go again and certainly not until he's learned its secrets . . . .

"We stand on ancient boundaries between places, between possibilities, between the world of mortals and the world of magic. All we need to unlock them is the key."

Joe's desperate to discover what Robin Wood meant, what he knows, and whilst Joe clearly won't find answers here, he's got an idea where to try next.

"Sorry, I just need to see Robin Wood."

"Suit yourself." Teapot lady sniffs, her eyes lingering after the shattered compass.

"He'll be back, no doubt about that," pronounces the toy man. "Robin Wood and Crystal Palace is like the ravens and the Tower of London. Anything happens to him the place will fall down! He'll turn up."

As he skateboards through the Triangle, Joe counts all the buildings he'd seen back in its 1888 heyday, thinking how little had actually changed as shopkeepers and restaurateurs and grand old pubs still tempt in trade coming 'up the palace.' Above the old bank on Westow Street, now a café and flower shop, stone faces of Nymphs stare down at Joe, their eyes seeming to follow him.

Joe turns onto Crystal Palace Parade where the glittering glass People's Palace once stood until burning to the ground in the mysterious fire of 1936. Nature had reclaimed the Eighth Wonder of the World, visitors in their millions and a legion of porters and master sweeps and cooks and bottle washers and musicians and engineers replaced over time with wild brambles and tall trees.

Only the sphinxes that stood at the entrance steps to the old North and South Transepts remain intact, staring out like guardians of the past. Joe waves; the sphinxes are old friends, he'd practiced parkour leaping off their lion backs and they'd spoken to him in his dreams prophesising his journey to the past.

Lounging over the back of the farthest sphinx is Lauren and two of her little friends, Carly and Simone. A third friend Joe doesn't recognise desperately tries joining them but keeps slipping down the sphinx's smooth red concrete. They've not seen Joe, which is good, no distractions from his mission. Yet he finds himself unable to walk past as Lauren mocks the struggling girl, her laughs echoed by Carly and Simone. Joe cuts to the sphinx and says to the girl,

"Want a push up?"

She blinks at Joe with wet eyes as he interlinks his fingers and lowers his hands. He allows himself a glance at Lauren whose freckles flush red.

Good.

Joe pushes the girl up onto the sphinx's back, her face torn between being pleased and uncertain whether Lauren will allow it.

"Check you out, my brother the big hero."

"Just big enough to know you help your friends."

"I don't take lessons on friendship from Billy No Mates."

Lauren's more agile lackies giggle.

"I have friends, thanks."

Lauren makes a big deal of putting her hand to her forehead, searching the horizon.

"Where?"

"You don't know 'em."

"Invisible friends don't count." The girls all cackle, including the one Joe just helped. His blood boils.

"Funny, I wouldn't call what you've got 'friendship,' surrounding yourself with mini-Laurens kissing your butt as you boss them about. They're not friends. They're pets."

The offence on her friends faces cause Joe a pang of regret, he'd meant to get at his sister who merely declares,

"It's not my fault *I'm* a born leader and *you're* a born loser."

Lauren's cuss meets with howls of mocking approval.

"Yeah, well I can't wait to see how you get on at secondary school when you stop being a big fish in a little pond." Joe flips down Skull Rider to leave with the last word but can't quite push off in time.

"*I* can't wait to tell everyone what a sad loser you are, so even your imaginary friends dump you. Looos-eer!"

A cacophony of cackles follow and they all join in the taunt, "Looos-eer! Looos-eer!"

Joe just manages to bite his tongue and not retort. It's beneath him. They're beneath him. This whole thing is beneath him. He's got bigger more important things to do, like finding Robin Wood.

Crystal Palace Caravan and Camping Site occupies the top north corner of the park where Rockhills once stood, a grand house built right next to the palace by its ground-breaking architect Joseph Paxton so he could admire his creation. After Paxton died, Rockhills had been purchased by a director of the Crystal Palace Company, Sir Henry Majoure, a gentleman with a deadly thirst for mystical powers whose lackeys had tried murdering Joe and his Victorian friends. He'd been saved more than once by the strange powers of Sir Henry's mysterious daughter Ada, physically weak and wheelchair-bound yet able to move objects with her mind, read thoughts and conjure a shadowy faerie that sent shivers through Joe.

All that seems a world away as the sun beats down. Only Rockhills gate posts remain, each top shaped like the curved palace transepts. Joe rides into the caravan park nipping around the barrier pole and ignoring the sign saying;

PRIVATE, campers only beyond this point. All visitors and new arrivals report to reception.

No-one seems to notice Joe so he swiftly skateboards behind a trimmed hedge into the caravan park. Joe knows the layout; Nan's cigar-chomping cousin Vera used to stay here on visits from Norwich in her touring caravan. Joe recalls happy memories hooning around the site while Nan and Vera barbequed and polished off bottles of Rosé reminiscing about their own early years hooning around the beaches of Norfolk.

Long-term-stay caravans have their territory marked by low white plastic picket fences surrounding clipped lawns and bright flowerpots.

All except one.

This caravan is tucked tightly into the corner of the caravan park near where the boundary wall to the palace gardens would once have stood. An aging caravan like a leftover from the set of one of those old *Carry on Camping* films Nan loves to watch. Climbers rise from long grass clinging to the caravan as if trying to pull it down into the earth.

It's just how Joe remembered from Vera's final visit before cancer claimed her. Joe recalled the caravan creeping out him and his sister, how Nan told them it belonged to Robin Wood and quadrupled its eeriness by warning them with a wicked glint behind her thick glasses: *"Beware, Robin Wood is really a woodland sprite who'll carry you away if you get too close to his door ...."*

That had inevitably prompted Lauren and Joe into a game of double-dare to see who could get the closest. Only for Joe to end the game in a huff when Lauren won, going right up to its door and knocking, the pair of them charging away to hide behind bushes and watch from a safe distance. Nobody came out.

That had been five years ago but the caravan's lost none of its creepiness. Once again Joe's sense of deep unease rises like a snake in his throat as he approaches the door.

Knock, knock.

Silence

"Hello? Mr Wood? Are you there?"

The only sound is the cawing of a murder of crows in the trees.

Joe puts his ear close to the door.

No noise inside.

Joe knocks a little harder, confidence growing with the realisation no-one's home.

"Hi, Mr Wood, you there? You okay?"

Having come this far he might as well sneak a peek through the window. Joe edges along the van and tiptoes up, but his view is blocked by chintzy net curtains.

Okay, he's done all he can.

Joe takes a step away from the van.

Out of the corner of his eye, he sees something move.

Joe jumps.

Finds his hand on his pumping heart before blowing in relief to see a robin red breast dancing from one passionflower to another.

"You! You're from Haynes Lane Market, right? Or you got a dancing twin?"

The robin chirps furiously at him.

"Sorry, don't speak bird."

The robin flutters off around the side of the caravan.

Off to catch a worm. Joe's own stomach gives a rumble. He fishes out a Snickers bar, rips off the wrapper, and is about to walk when suddenly the robin flies around the corner flapping right in his face.

Joe yelps, dropping his chocolate bar in the long grass.

"Great, thanks a lot," Joe complains to the bird. It continues fluttering near his face before disappearing around the corner again.

"Okay, you want me to follow? Fine."

Joe walks around to the back of the caravan.

Anxiety sneaks back up his throat.

Joe sighs with relief to find nothing except a bunch of crows pecking at the grass. They all quit pecking as one and turn their oily eyes to Joe.

Meanwhile the robin sits on a caravan window ledge and starts pecking at the glass.

"Okay, okay, I'm coming, don't break your beak."

The window is just like the others, covered with lace net curtains. However, Joe notices a tiny crack between the window and the frame. He hesitantly slides the window open. Moves the net curtain aside.

"Hello?" Joe shouts into the darkness. "Anyone there?"

He waits for a moment. Turns to the robin perched on the windowsill.

"See? No-one home."

Suddenly the robin flies right inside.

A bird indoors is Nan's worst nightmare. The only time he'd ever seen her afraid was when a pigeon found his way into the Crystal Palace Museum and Dad had to be called to shoo it out, but not before it'd pooped on the display cases exhibiting photos and relics from the old palace. Joe doesn't share Nan's avian aversion. But he is most definitely afraid of following his feathered friend inside which seems exactly what the robin expects of him.

"I'm not coming in," Joe calls after it, determined not to be bossed about by a bird.

But what if Robin Wood is in there?

What if he's hurt?

Unconscious?

He'd seen YouTube films about animals who'd saved the lives of humans by leading others to their rescue when they'd fallen down a ravine or broken a leg deep in a forest.

If this robin is the same bird from Haynes Lane alleyway (Is that possible? Weren't robin's supposed to have their own territory?), it must know Robin Wood and it might be trying to help him.

Joe rubs the top of his cropped hair. With a flash of enlightened self-interest, he realises that if anything *did* happen to Robin Wood he'd lose his only chance to find out what lay behind the power of the shattered compass.

So, with a sigh, Joe moves a wild-flower-filled plant pot beneath the window.

"Fine, I'm coming in."

Get a grip, Joe.

After everything he'd faced in Victorian times, how dangerous can taking a look inside an old caravan be?

To be continued ...

GET YOUR FREE CRYSTAL PALACE CHRONICLES SHORT STORY!

Find out what happened the first time Elias attempts Big Eagle Run, and how his dad and fellow Navie's came close to starving to death whilst building the Crystal Palace...

Just sign up to my newsletter and you'll also get exclusive give-aways, stories, treasure hunts and more....

Got to www.grahamwhitlock.com